Life in London

BrambleHill Press
Interesting books for Interesting people.

A likeness of Pierce Egan,
in his upper story, asking himself a few questions.
Drawn by George Sharples.

TOM & JERRY
LIFE IN LONDON.

OR
THE DAY AND NIGHT SCENES

OF
JERRY HAWTHORN, ESQ.

AND HIS ELEGANT FRIEND
CORINTHIAN TOM

IN THEIR
Rambles and Sprees Through the Metropolis

BY
PIERCE EGAN

WITH NUMEROUS COLOURED ILLUSTRATIONS
FROM REAL LIFE DESIGNED BY
I.R. & G. CRUIKSHANK

DEDICATION

TO HIS MOST EXCELLENT MAJESTY
KING GEORGE THE FOURTH.

Most Gracious Sovereign,

I AM ENCOURAGED humbly to entreat permission to dedicate the following Work to your MAJESTY by that love and patronage which your Majesty has at all times evinced for the protection of LITERATURE and the encouragement of the FINE ARTS; so eminently characteristic of the accomplished Gentleman, the profound and elegant Scholar, and the liberal and enlightened Prince.

And I am further emboldened by the numerous opportunities which your Majesty has had of witnessing LIFE IN LONDON, as well in the humblest of dwellings as in the most splendid of palaces. In the words of our immortal Shakespeare—

> The prince but studies his companions,
> Like a strange tongue: wherein, to gain the language,
> 'Tis needful that the most immodest word
> Be look'd upon and learn'd; which, once attain'd,
> Comes to no further use
> But to be known and hated. So, like gross terms,
> The Prince will, in the perfection of time,
> Cast off his followers; and their memory
> Shall, as a PATTERN, or a MEASURE, live;

> By which his grace must mete the lives of others,
> Turning past evils to advantages.

"Born and bred amongst you, I glory in the name of an Englishman," were the words of your late most revered, venerable, and august Father; and it is well known that they have been repeated by your MAJESTY with redoubled energy, pathos, and admiration.

Permit me, then, most gracious SIRE, to observe, that an accurate knowledge of the manners, habits, and feelings of a brave and free people is not to be acquired in the CLOSET, nor is it to be derived from the formal routine precepts of tutors. It is only by means of a free and unrestrained intercourse with society, most gracious SIRE, that an intimate acquaintance is to be obtained with Englishmen: for this purpose it is necessary to view their pastimes, to hear their remarks, and, from such sources, to be enabled to study their *character*.

Your MAJESTY's *education*, habits, early introduction to life, and connexions with the most eminent persons in the state, distinguished for their superior talents and experience, have enabled your MAJESTY to accomplish this most important point, so essential to the mind of a BRITISH MONARCH, and so congenial with that constitution under which we live, and which may bid defiance to the whole world, for solidity and permanence.

Indeed, the whole chapter of Life in London has been so repeatedly perused by your Majesty, in such a variety of shapes, from the *elegant* A. the *refined* B. the *polite* C. the *lively* D. the *eloquent* E. the *honest* F. the *stately* G. the *peep-o-day* H. the *tasteful* I. the *manly* J. the *good* K. the *noble* L. the *stylish* M. the *brave* N. the *liberal* O. the *proud* P. the *long-headed* Q. the *animated* R. the *witty* S. the *flash* T. the *knowing* U. the *honourable* V. the *consummate* W. the *funny* X. the *musical* Y. and the *poetical* Z., that it would only be a waste of your Majesty's valuable time to expatiate further upon this subject.

Pardon me, most gracious SIRE, in remarking, that the exalted Personage whom we all look up to has been, without adulation, enabled, by such opportunities, to have, as it were, the PULSE of the people in his hands, to feel how it beats, and to prescribe accordingly. That your MAJESTY's people may never be insensible to your MAJESTY's care and exertion for their welfare; that the heart of the KING may be always directed towards the happiness of his subjects, and his ears open to a "bit of good truth,"

 Is the most sincere
   and honest wish of
      Your Majesty's
         Very humble, loyal, and
            obedient subject,

              PIERCE EGAN.

July 19, 1821.

CONTENTS.

INTRODUCTION

XVIII

CHAPTER I.

1

Or, rather, "an invocation;" scarcely important enough to be denominated a Chapter, yet, nevertheless, thought expedient.

CHAPTER II.

14

A Camera Obscura View of the Metropolis, with the Light and Shade attached to "seeing Life."

CHAPTER III.

31

A Short Sketch of the Author's Talents in taking a Likeness; or, in other words (and, perhaps, far more appropriate), a Pen-and-Ink Drawing of Corinthian TOM.

CHAPTER IV.

41

The great Advantages resulting from a Man's Father being "born" before him, illustrated with some curious Facts; and also pointing out, that a true Knowledge of the World is gained only by Conversation, and that the Manners of every Rank must be seen in order to be known.

CHAPTER V.

56

Corinthian Tom's unceasing Anxiety to mix with the World uncontrolled. His Acquaintance with Young Logic, an Oxonian. Character of the latter. Death of Tom's Parents.

CHAPTER VI.

65

A Word or two respecting "Architects of their own Fortunes." Tom out of his Leading-Strings. Poetic Invocation to the Pleasures of Life. His hurried Entrance into all Classes of Society. A few additional Touches of the Author towards finishing Tom's Likeness. The Impression Tom made upon the Town. Acquirement of his Title. A slight Glance at Tom's Choice of a Female—Corinthian Kate.

CHAPTER VII.

Corinthian Tom's Excesses render Rustication necessary. A Visit to Hawthorn-Hall. Jerry Hawthorn's Introduction to Tom. Character of the latter. A Day's Sporting. A Jollification at Hawthorn-Hall. Tom's descriptive Song of the Metropolis. Jerry's Arrival in London.

CHAPTER VIII.

Jerry an Inmate of *Corinthian House*—Its Taste and Elegance described—Useful Hints from *Tom* to *Jerry*—The latter in training to become a *Swell*—His Introduction to BOB LOGIC—A Ride in Rotten Row.

CHAPTER IX.

Tom and Jerry visit the Playhouses. A Stroll through the Saloon of Covent Garden Theatre. Taking "Blue Ruin" at the "Sluicery" after the "Spell is broke up" A Peep into a Coffee-Shop at Midnight. Tom and Jerry in "Trouble" after a "Spree." A Night-Charge at Bow Street Office; with other matters worth knowing, respecting the unfortunate Cyprian, the feeling Coachman, and, the generous Magistrate.

CHAPTER X.

Tom and *Jerry* at a Masquerade Supper at the Opera House. An Assignation. A Lounge in Bond Street. A Visit to Mr *Jackson's* Rooms. *Tom, Logic,* and *Jerry* call upon the *Champion of England*, to view his Parlour and the Silver Cup. A Turn into the Westminster Pit, to sport their Blunt ON the Phenomenon Monkey. Finishing the Evening, and "getting the best of a *Charley*."

CHAPTER XI.

The Contrast—*Country* and *Town*: Evil Communication corrupts good Manners. A "Look-in" at *Tattersall's*. Gay Moments; or, an Introduction of *Jerry* and *Logic* by *Tom* to *Corinthian Kate*. *Tom* exhibits his knowledge of Fencing in an "Assault" with Mr *O'Shaunessy*. *Kate* and *Sue* caught upon the Sly, on their visit to the Old Fortune-Teller, by *Hawthorn* and the *Corinthian*. The "Ne plus ultra of *Life in London*." A visit to Carlton Palace by *Kate, Sue, Tom, Jerry,* and *Logic*.

CHAPTER XII. 250

A short Digression in the Shape of an *Apology*, but not intended by way of an *Excuse*, for Persons witnessing "*Life in London.*" Peep-o'-Day-Boys. A Street-Row. The *Author* losing his "Reader." *Tom* and *Jerry* "showing Fight," and *Logic* floored. Honour among Thieves. The Pocket Book—a rich Anecdote. The *Trio* visit the Condemned Yard in Newgate. Symptoms of the "*Finish of some sorts* of Life" in London. A Glance at the Royal Exchange. *Tom, Jerry,* and *Logic* entering into the *Spirit* of the *Lark,* at *ALL-MAX,* in the East. Invocation to *Politeness*—a Touch of the *Sublime!* The Contrast. *Climax* of "*Life in London*" in the *West. Tom* and *Jerry* on their *P's* and *Q's* at *ALMACK'S*; or, a Fat Sorrow better than a Lean One.

CHAPTER XIII. 285

Logic's Descriptive crambo Chaunt of the Traits of the Trio. Tempus Fugit in the Metropolis. Varieties of Life in London. Tom, Jerry, and Logic sporting their Blunt at the Royal Cockpit. What is termed, "A friendly Game of Whist." The Trio "larking" at the Grand Carnival. A Peep *en passant* at the Green-Room at Drury Lane Theatre. A Stroll to the London Docks. The Effects of tasting Wine in the Wood. The Italian Opera.

CHAPTER XIV. 307

The Trio making the most of an Evening at Vauxhall. Tom and Jerry visiting the Exhibition of Pictures at the Royal Academy. Hawthorn, Tom, and Logic "Masquerading it" among the Cadgers in the "Back Slums" in the Holy Land. The Corinthian and his Coz taking the Hint at Logic's being' "Blown up" at Point Non-Plus, or long wanted by John Doe and Richard Roe, and must come. Symptoms of Jerry being rather out of Condition.

CHAPTER XV. 325

The Oxonian's Card. Tom and Jerry visiting Logic on "board the Fleet!" The Humours of a Whistling-Shop. Logic's Horse. Jerry "beat to a standstill!" Dr Please'em's Prescription. The Oxonian and Tom's Condolence. A Man cannot have his Cake and eat it. Pleasure versus Pain. The Manuscript. White Horse Cellar, Piccadilly. Tom and Logic bidding Jerry "goodbye" on his Return to Hawthorn Hall.

ILLUSTRATIONS.

THE FRONTISPIECE REPRESENTS an architectural column, in order to afford a sufficient space to delineate the varieties of LIFE IN LONDON, the top of which is:

THE CORINTHIAN CAPITAL:

The KING on his throne, giving an audience to his subjects, and which, for derivation, the UNIVERSITIES must admit is "*the top of the tree!*" (The ROSES, PINKS, and TULIPS: the *flowers* of SOCIETY.)

The CIRCLE portrays TOM, LOGIC, and JERRY, "*all happiness,*" and who do not care a *fig* for the *Blue Devils;* the CORINTHIAN singing a verse from BURNS:—

> Here are we met, THREE *merry boys*,
> Three merry boys I trow are we;
> And mony a night we've merry been,
> And mony mae we hope to be!

LOGIC (who is nearly done over) *hiccoughing* 'LIFE'S a bumper!" and JERRY roaring out part of TOM'S *chaunt* of

> "Dancing, singing, full of glee,
> O, London, London town for me!"

At the FOUR corners of the *Circle* are depicted the INS (a gaol;

a *covey* peeping through the bars); the OUTS (the finest view of a prison is the outside; and it is enough to make any lad dance without music when he obtains that much-wished-for spot): the UPS (that is, to be *up* to "push along," and to "keep moving," while a *chance* remains, to sport a *natty* gig, a prime *fast* one, and to have a pretty *"piece of goods"* by your side, just to show the world what a gay fellow you are): and the DOWNS of LIFE IN LONDON. (When a man is DOWN, *down* with him: he is then of no *use* to anybody; and who would *lose* his time to give him any help? therefore, he must get upon his *pins* how he can. He had no business to get into such a *sitivation!)*

The other FOUR ANGLES represent the different classes of society in the *Metropolis.* The NOBLE (high birth; on such good terms with himself that if a *commoner* accidentally touch him in crossing his path, he looks down, with a sort of contempt, muttering, "*Damn you, who are you?)* the RESPECTABLE (the merchant, &c., their *stilted* place in life acquired by talent, or from lucky circumstances, with more *upstart* pride than the former character, and fastidiously squeamish in mixing with any but *upper* customers): the MECHANICAL (honest, industrious, merry, and happy, if not more so in London, perhaps, than the other two classes put together, and so independent in mind as to *chaff* "win gold and wear it"): and the TAG-RAG and BOB-TAIL *squad* (who do not care how the *blunt* comes or how it goes. *Togs* or no *togs!* but, nevertheless, who must live at any price, and see a "*bit of life?* let the world jog on how it will; yet who can drop a *tear* upon a sorrowful event—*laugh* heartily at fun—*shake* with cold—*perspire* with heat—and go to *roost* much sounder upon a dust-hill than many of the *swells* can *snooze* upon their *dabs;* likewise, in comparing *notes,* feel happy in the presumption that there are hundreds worse off in society than themselves.

THE BASE,

or *groundwork,* of the design, is a sort of *sweeping* clause to the whole of the picture, and serves to show, from the HIGHEST to the LOWEST member of society, that the *ramifications* would not have been complete if a *shade* only had been forgotten in the portraiture of LIFE IN LONDON. The *Vegetables*—*Bunches* of *Turn*-ups; and *Strings* of *Ingens.*

INTRODUCTION

EIGHT-AND-FORTY YEARS AGO the most popular work in British literature bore this title

> "LIFE IN LONDON; or, THE DAY AND NIGHT SCENES OF JERRY HAWTHORN, ESQ., and his elegant friend CORINTHIAN TOM, accompanied by BOB LOGIC, the OXONIAN, in their Rambles and Sprees through the Metropolis. By PIERCE EGAN (author of 'Walks through Bath,' "Sporting Anecdotes" 'Picture of the Fancy,' 'Boxiana.' &c.), dedicated to His Most Gracious Majesty King George the Fourth. Embellished, with 36 Scenes from Real Life, designed and etched by I. R. & G. Cruikshank; and enriched with numerous original Designs on Wood, by the same Artists. 1821."

This was *the* book—*the* literature—of that period, the one work which many elderly gentlemen still remember far away in the distance of their youth.

A tedious—and by some will be considered an absurd—composition, when judged by similarly descriptive works of the present day, it has just this claim to our attention, that it is, perhaps, the best picture of "Society"—or as they of the period defined it, of *"Life, Fashion, and Frolic"*—in the days when George IV. was king, that has been bequeathed to us.

Just ten years before this, another popular picture of English life had appeared under the title of "Doctor Syntax," also illustrated with coloured pictures; but Combe's rhymed story of the Quixotic clergyman is altogether of a milder character than that brilliant picture of "fun and spree"—those astounding "Day and Night Scenes" of the glorious heroes, Tom, Jerry, and Logic—which Mr Egan has chronicled for our instruction and amusement.

How delightful the book was to the youths of England, and how eagerly all its promised feasts of pleasure were devoured by them, Thackeray has told us in his Roundabout Paper, "*De Juventute.*" Thackeray pictures himself with a coin in his hand, the crown-piece of 1823,—the very period of our book's success,—and after reading the inscription, "GEORGIUS IV. BRITANNIARUM REX. FID. DEF.," he conjures back his past life.

"What is that I see? A boy,—a boy in a jacket. He is at a desk; he has great books before him, Latin and Greek books and dictionaries. Yes; but behind the great books, which he pretends to read, is a little one with pictures, which he is really reading. It is—yes, I can read now—it is the 'Heart of Mid-Lothian,' by the author *of* 'Waverley'—or, no, it is '*Life in London, or the Adventures of Corinthian Tom, Jeremiah Hawthorn, and their friend Bob Logic,*' by Pierce Egan; and it has pictures—oh! such funny pictures! As he reads, there comes behind the boy a man, a dervish, in a black gown, like a woman, and a black square cap, and he has a book in each hand; and he seizes the boy who is reading the picture-book, and lays his head upon one of his books, and smacks it with the other. The boy makes faces, and so that picture disappears."

Long, however, before this recollection of "Tom and Jerry" was penned, Thackeray had told his readers of a partiality— a lingering fondness—which he had for the old book. In an article on George Cruikshank, which appeared in the *Westminster Review*, he says:—

"'Tom and Jerry' must have a word of notice here; for although by no means Mr Cruikshank's best work, his reputation was extraordinarily raised by it. Tom and Jerry were as popular twenty years since as Mr Pickwick and Sam Weller now are; and often have we wished, while reading the biographies of the latter celebrated personages, that they had been described as well by Mr Cruikshank's pencil as by Mr Dickens's pen.

"As for Tom and Jerry, to show the mutability of human affairs, and the evanescent nature of reputation, we have been to the British Museum, and no less than five circulating libraries, in quest of the book, and 'Life in London,' alas! is not to be found at any one of them. We can only, therefore, speak of the work from recollection, but have still a very clear remembrance of the leather gaiters of Jerry Hawthorn, the green spectacles of Logic, and the hooked nose of Corinthian Tom. They were the schoolboy's delight; and in the days when the work appeared, we firmly believed the three heroes above named to be types of the most elegant, fashionable young fellows the town afforded, and thought their occupations and amusements were those of all high-bred English gentlemen. Tom knocking down the watchman at Temple Bar; Tom and Jerry dancing at Almack's; or flirting in the saloon at the theatre; at the night-houses after the play; at Tom Cribb's, examining the silver-cup then in the possession of that champion; at Bob Logic's chambers, where, if we mistake not, 'Corinthian Kate' was at a cabinet piano, singing a song; ambling gallantly in Rotten Row; or examining the poor fellow at Newgate who was having his chains knocked off before hanging; all these scenes remain indelibly engraved upon the mind, and so far we are independent of all the circulating libraries in London.

"As to the literary contents of the book, they have passed sheer away .... But it must have had some merit of its own, that is clear; it must have given striking descriptions of life in some part or other of London, for all London read it, and went to see it in its dramatic shape. The artist, it is said, wished to close the career of the three heroes by bringing them all to ruin; but the writer, or publishers, would not allow any such melancholy subjects to dash the merriment of the public, and we believe Tom, Jerry, and Logic were married off at the end of the tale, as if they had been the most moral personages in the world. There is some goodness in this pity, which authors and the public are disposed to show towards certain agreeable, disreputable characters of romance. And in regard of Jerry Hawthorn, and that hero without a surname, Corinthian Tom, Mr Cruikshank, we make little doubt, was glad in his heart that he was not allowed to have his own way."

Exactly twenty years afterwards, Thackeray paid another visit to the great National Library, and this time was successful in finding his old favourite; and it is curious to observe how, even with the book before him, he writes upon it[1] in almost the same words as when he described it from memory:—

"As for Thomas and Jeremiah (it is only my witty way of calling Tom and Jerry), I went to the British Museum the other day on purpose to get it; but somehow, if you will press the question so closely, on reperusal, Tom and Jerry is not so brilliant as I had supposed it to be. The pictures are just as fine as ever; and I shook hands with broad-backed Jerry Hawthorn and Corinthian Tom with delight, after many years' absence. But the style of the writing, I own, was not pleasing to me; I even thought it a little vulgar—well! well! other writers have been considered vulgar—and as a description of the sports and amusements of London in the ancient times, more curious than amusing.

"But the pictures!—oh! the pictures are noble still! First, there is Jerry arriving from the country, in a green coat and leather gaiters, and being measured for a fashionable suit at Corinthian House, by Corinthian Tom's tailor. Then away for the career of pleasure and fashion. The park! delicious excitement! The theatre! the saloon!! the green-room!!! Rapturous bliss — the opera itself! and then, perhaps, to Temple Bar, to *knock down a Charley there!* There are Jerry and Tom, with their tights and little cocked hats, coming from the opera—very much as gentlemen in waiting on royalty are habited now. There they are at Almack's itself, amidst a crowd of high-bred personages, with the Duke of Clarence himself looking at them dancing. Now, strange change—they are in Tom Cribb's parlour, where they don't seem to be a whit less at home than in fashion's gilded halls; and now they are at Newgate, seeing the irons knocked off the malefactor's legs previous to execution. What hardened ferocity in the countenance of the desperado in yellow breeches! What compunction in the face of the gentleman

---

1 Roundabout Papers, Oct. 1860.

in black (who, I suppose, has been forging), and who clasps his hands, and listens "to the chaplain! Now we haste away to merrier scenes: to Tattersall's (ah! gracious powers! what a funny fellow that actor was who performed Dicky Green in that scene at the play!); and now we are at a private party, at which Corinthian Tom is waltzing (and very gracefully too, as you must confess) with Corinthian Kate, whilst Bob Logic, the Oxonian, is playing on the piano!

"After," the text says, "*the Oxonian* had played several pieces of lively music, he requested as a favour that Kate and his friend Tom would perform a waltz. Kate without any hesitation immediately stood up. Tom offered his hand to his fascinating partner, and the dance took place. The plate conveys a correct representation of the 'gay scene' at that precise moment. The anxiety of *the Oxonian* to witness the attitudes of the elegant pair had nearly put a stop to their movements.[2]

---

2   Above is given a reduced facsimile of Mr Thackeray's sketch.

On turning round from the pianoforte and presenting his comical *mug*, Kate could scarcely suppress a laugh."

And no wonder; just look at it now (as I have copied it to the best of my humble ability), and compare Master Logic's countenance and attitude with the splendid elegance of Tom! Now every London man is weary and *blasé.* There is an enjoyment of life in these young bucks of 1823 which contrasts strangely with our feelings of 1869. Here, for instance, is a specimen of their talk and walk. "'If,' says LOGIC — 'if *enjoyment* is your *motto*, you may make the most of an evening at Vauxhall, more than at any other place in the metropolis. It is all free-and-easy. Stay as long as you like, and depart when you think proper.'—'Your description is so flattering,' replied JERRY, 'that I do not care how soon the time arrives for us to start.' LOGIC proposed a '*bit of a stroll,*' in order to get rid of an hour or two, which was immediately accepted by Tom and Jerry A *turn* or two in Bond Street, a *stroll* through Piccadilly, a *look in* at TATTERSALL's, a *ramble* through Pall Mall, and a *strut* on the Corinthian path, fully occupied the time of our heroes until the hour for dinner arrived, when a few glasses of TOM's rich wines soon put them on the *qui vive.* VAUXHALL was then the object in view, and the TRIO started, bent upon enjoying the pleasures which this place so amply affords."

How nobly those inverted commas, those italics, those capitals, bring out the writer's wit and relieve the eye! They are as good as jokes, though you may not quite perceive the point. Mark the varieties of lounge in which the young men indulge—now *a stroll,* then *a look in,* then *a ramble,* and presently *a strut.* When George, Prince of Wales, was twenty, I have read in an old magazine, "the Prince's lounge" was a peculiar manner of walking which the young bucks imitated. At Windsor George III. had *a cat's path*—a sly early walk which the good old king took in the gray morning before his household was astir. What was the Corinthian path here recorded? Does any antiquary know? And what were the rich wines which our friends took, and which enabled them to enjoy Vauxhall? Vauxhall is gone, but the wines which could occasion such a delightful perversion of the intellect as to enable it to enjoy ample pleasures there, what were they?

So the game of life proceeds, until Jerry Hawthorn, the rustic, is fairly knocked up by all this excitement, and is forced to go home, and the last picture represents him getting into the coach at the "White Horse Cellar," he being one of six inside; whilst his friends shake him by the hand; whilst the sailor mounts, on the roof; whilst the Jews hang round with oranges, knives, and sealing-wax; whilst the guard is closing the door. Where are they now, those sealing-wax Vendors? where are the guards? where are the jolly teams? where are the coaches? and where the youth that climbed inside and out of them; that heard the merry horn which sounds no more; that saw the sun rise over Stonehenge; that rubbed away the bitter tears at night after parting, as the coach sped on the journey to school and London; that looked out with beating heart as the milestones flew by, for the welcome corner where began home and holidays?

No better criticism of the book could be given than that conveyed in the preceding sentences; the style of writing is not pleasing, according to our notions of descriptive writing,[3] but the pictures! oh I the pictures are noble still! The age was the age of excesses—of vulgar refinement, and unreal politeness. Even the laughs and smiles of the "*Bon Ton*," noisy and grotesque as we are bound to believe them, were very hollow affairs—something like its wit, now discovered only by the printer's italics. These were the last days of coarse caricatures, of duelling, and of the glorious three-bottle system after dinner. There is no deception about the present book; it very well reflects all these peculiarities—the literature of the time included—and therefore its value as a true picture of life fifty years ago.

And now for a few words about the "Tom and Jerry" literature generally, and of the furor which accompanied the publication of the original work.

---

[3] *The European Magazine*, November 1821, had its own opinion of fine writing, and declared the present book to be "one of the most amusing books ever published. For our part, we prefer it to many of the sketches of mankind which have appeared since the days of the *Spectator!*"

Introduction

Some time previous to its appearance a great taste had exhibited itself amongst fashionable bloods for sporting works— books upon the chase, upon racing, upon boxing, and "sport" generally. The demand soon brought an excellent supply, and *Boxiana*, in its own peculiar department, at once became a great favourite. Artists, too, arose, who devoted all their powers to hunting subjects, to racing favourites, and to pugilistic encounters. Amongst these the names of Aiken, Dighton, and Brooke became very popular. One day it occurred to the editor of *Boxiana* that if Londoners were so anxious for books about country and out-of-door sports, why should not provincials and even the Cockneys themselves be equally anxious to know something of "Life in London"? The editor of *Boxiana* was Mr Pierce Egan, who, as the literary representative of sport and high life, had already been introduced to George IV. The character of the proposed work was mentioned to the King, and His Gracious Majesty seems to have heartily approved of it, for he at once gave permission for it to be dedicated to himself. The services of Messrs I.R. and George Cruikshank were secured as illustrators, and on the 15th of July 1821, the first number, price one shilling, was published by Messrs Sherwood, Neely, *&* Jones, of Paternoster Row. This sample, or first instalment, of the entire work was quite enough for society to judge by. It took both town and country by storm. It was found to be the exact thing in literature that the readers of those days wanted. Edition after edition was called for—and supplied, as fast as the illustrations could be got away from the small army of women and children who were colouring them. With the appearance of Numbers II. and III. the demand only increased, and a revolution in our literature, in one drama, and even in our nomenclature, began to develop itself. All the announcements from Paternoster Row were of books, great and small, depicting life in London; dramatists at once turned their attention to the same subject; and tailors, bootmakers, and hatters recommended nothing but Corinthian shapes and Tom and Jerry patterns. Immediately Messrs Sherwood & Co. issued the first shilling number of Mr Egan's work, out came Jones &

Co.[4] with the following in sixpenny numbers:—

> "*REAL LIFE IN LONDON;* or, The Rambles and Adventures of BOB TALLYHO, Esq., and his cousin, the Hon. TOM DASHALL, &c., through the Metropolis. Exhibiting a Living Picture of Fashionable Characters, Manners, and Amusements in High and Low Life. By an Amateur. Embellished and Illustrated with a Series of Coloured Prints, Designed and Engraved by Messrs Heath, Aiken, Dighton, Brooke, Rowlandson, &c."

The author of Jones and Company's speculation is said to have been John Badcock,[5] who some years previously had compiled what was then termed a "Flash Dictionary"—that is, a dictionary of vulgar or slang words. In the immense demand which had arisen for "Life in London" books, this rival to Egan's great original obtained a fair share of popularity, and a second volume was soon issued under the title of "*Further* Rambles and Adventures." In some respects the text of the counterfeit is more amusing reading than the original. It contains a trifle less of those charming words of the ring, and the stable, which characterise the conversation of Pierce Egan's "bloods" and "pinks," and therefore we are very thankful; but the living "pinks" and "bloods"— the *Bon Ton*—who subscribed to "Tom and Jerry," thought otherwise. They relished the "flash," the "St Giles Greek," with a gusto which we cannot now enjoy, and therefore the meed of praise was given to the original.

Immediately a translation of Pierce Egan's work was published

---

4   Jones & Co., of Finsbury Square, the successors of the famous Lackington, who would have been shocked at the very idea of such a work.

5   Badcock wrote under various names, but his favourite pseudonym was "Jonathan Bee." It is this name that is affixed to "*The Dictionary* of the Turf, the Ring, the Chase, the Pit, the Bon Ton, and the Varieties of Life, forming the completest and most authentic Balatronicum hitherto offered to the notice of *the Sporting World*", by Jon. Bee:" *1823. "A Living Picture of London* for *1828,* and Strangers' Guide through the Streets *Of* the Metropolis; showing the Frauds, the Arts, Snares, and Wiles of all description of Rogues that everywhere abound, *by Jon. Bee:*" *1828.* This same author published books on stable economy, under the name of "Hinds." As the editor of "The Fancy," "Fancy Gazette," "Picture of London, *&c.,* he was the sporting rival of Pierce Egan. Professor Wilson, in an amusing article in Blackwood, reviewed "*The Dictionary.*"

in Paris, under the title of THE ENGLISH DIORAMA, or Picturesque Rambles in London; containing *the most faithful notices of the character, manners, and customs of the English nation,* in the various classes of society." By M. S.

On this work a French critic of the time made, with all seriousness, the following amusing observations:—

"It is an Englishman, and an Englishman already known by *several esteemed descriptive publications,* who has here painted his countrymen. Pierce Egan, the author of *The Picture of London,* and who may be called the Mercier of England, has, like him, carefully studied the manners of all classes of the community. He conducts his reader from the royal palace to the most miserable pot-house, the resort of beggars and the dregs of the people. Such, indeed, in these latter scenes is the scrupulous fidelity of his pencil, that the enlightened taste of his translator has frequently induced him to soften the features of the picture. These suppressions are dictated by a sound discretion and considerable tact, and include several long digressions, and some circumstances which would wound delicacy and French taste at the same time."[6]

What renders the work one of the most valuable which have appeared on England and London, are the twenty-four *(sic)* engravings, which represent almost all the incidents described in the book. They are from the arch pencil of Mr Cruikshank. He, like the author, may congratulate himself on having caused us to see "Life in London;" and on having, as was said of Charles Vernet, composed "Epigrams of design."

As may be readily conceived, the Stage soon claimed Tom and Jerry. The first drama founded upon the book was from the pen of Mr Barrymore; the second was written for the Olympic Theatre by Charles Dibdin; the third, and by far the most successful, version was Moncrieff's. It came out upon the Adelphi boards on Monday, November 26, 1821, and created a furor amongst play-goers, the like of which never occurred before, and has never occurred since. It ran for upwards of three hundred nights, and only gave over

---

6   This seems straining at a gnat and swallowing a camel for a nation that can devour Paul de Kock's novels.

because the actors were tired out; the audience were as mad for it as ever. It made the fortune of the house, and everybody connected with it—except the author. But why should I spoil the story, when the dramatist himself has told it in his own earnest words,[7] written long, long before he was a blind old man, living on the bounty of the Charter House:—

"It is scarcely necessary to observe that this drama is founded on the Life in London of my friends, Pierce Egan, and the inimitable Cruikshank. Aided by Pierce's clever illustrations to the matchless series of plates in that work, I have in this piece endeavoured to put them into dramatic motion; running a connecting story through the whole.

"From the popularity of the subject, the novelty and acknowledged truth of the various scenes comprised in it, the inimitable manner in which it was originally acted, and the beauty of the music I fortunately selected, this piece obtained a popularity and excited a sensation totally unprecedented in theatrical history: from the highest to the lowest, all classes were alike anxious to witness its representation. Dukes and dustmen were equally interested in its performance, and peers might be seen mobbing it with apprentices to obtain an admission. Seats were sold for weeks before they could be occupied; every theatre in the United Kingdom, and even in the United States, enriched its coffers by performing it; and the smallest tithe-portion of its profits would for ever have rendered it unnecessary for its author to have troubled the public with any further productions of his Muse. It established the fortunes of most of the actors engaged in its representation, and gave birth to several newspapers. The success of the Beggars' Opera, the Castle Spectre, and Pizarro, sunk into the shade before it. In the furor of its popularity, persons have been known to travel post from the farthest parts of the kingdom to see it; and five guineas have been offered in an evening for a single seat. Its language became the language of the day; drawing-rooms were turned into *chaffing*

---

7   Preface to "Tom and Jerry, or *Life in London;* an Operatic Extravaganza, in Three Acts; first performed at the Adelphi Theatre, Monday, November 26, 1821." By W. T. Moncrieff.

cribs, and rank and beauty learned to *patter slang*.

"With respect to the cry of immorality, so loudly raised by those inimical to the success and plain speaking of this piece, it is soon answered. To say nothing of the envy of rival theatres feeling its attraction most sensibly in their Saturday treasuries, those notorious pests, the watchmen, dexterously joined in the war-howl of detraction raised against it, and by converting every trifling street broil into a '*Tom and Jerry row*' endeavoured to revenge themselves for the *exposé* its scenes afforded of their villainy and extortion—but all in vain. In vain, too, it was that the actors' old rivals, the Methodists, took the alarm,—in vain they distributed the whole of the stock of the Religious Tract Society at the doors of the theatre,—in vain they denounced *Tom and Jerry* from the pulpit,—in vain the puritanical portion of the press prated of its immorality: they but increased the number of its followers, and added to its popularity. Vainly, too, was the Lord Chamberlain called upon to suppress, it. His Grace came one night to see it, and brought his Duchess the next. It was nearly the same with the chief magistrate of Bow Street. His experience rendered him perfectly sensible that long before the appearance of *Tom and Jerry*, young men and country gentlemen would, in moments of hilarity, sometimes exceed in their potations, be provoked into quarrels by designing watchmen, and consigned for purposes of extortion, on the following morning, to the custody of His Honour, the Night Constable; but according to the Saints' Accounts, to believe their tales, it must be held as a point of faith that no one previous to the appearance of 'Tom and Jerry' ever got into a row. Oh, no! drinking and all its train of follies were unknown to youth, till inculcated into their minds by the example of 'Tom and Jerry.' How many an unsuspecting country cousin has been converted, in the public prints, through an hour of harmless frolic, into a JERRY, while his equally unconscious town relation figured as a TOM; and any honest plodder they might have with them was transformed into a LOGIC—his first appearance in that character!

"The thing speaks for itself. So far from being immoral, if the piece be fairly examined, it will be found to be of as correct tendency as any production ever brought on the stage. The obnoxious scenes of life are only shown that they may be avoided; the danger of mixing in them is strikingly exemplified, and every incident tends to prove that happiness is only to be found in the domestic circle.

"To those venerable noodles who complain that I and my prototype, Pierce, have made this the age of *flash*, I answer, Any age is better than *The age of Cant.*"

Besides the authors already mentioned, Tom Dibdin, Farrell, and Douglas Jerrold each produced dramas upon the popular theme; and in the summer of 1822 "Life in London" was being performed at no less than *ten* theatres in and around London. Mr Egan, in his *"Finish* to the Adventures of Tom and Jerry," states that he reckoned no less than sixty-five separate publications all derived from his own work.

Even the Juvenile Library was found to be deficient without an appropriate edition of "Tom and Jerry," and Mr Hodgson, the popular caterer for the young in those days, at once set to work to supply the want. Forthwith there appeared:—

> 'Hodgson's Juvenile Drama, *Life in London*[8] *A Play*, in Three Acts; depicting the Day and Night Scenes of Tom, Jerry, Logic, & Co., adapted to London, by and for Hodgson & Co., price 6d."

The rage actually extended to Bartholomew Fair, where Mister Richardson, in his large dramatic booth, lighted with paper lanterns, issued the following bill of the performance:—

---

[8] At the end it says:—"A key to the Cant Terms made use of in this play will be found in the 'Modern Flash Dictionary' published by Hodgson & Co., price 6d."

> 1823.
> *RICHARDSON'S THEATRE.*
> This Day will be Presented, an entire New Melo-Drama, Called, The
> VIRGIN BRIDE!
> OR THE
> SPECTRE OF THE TOMB.
> ───
> To conclude with an entire New Extravaganza Harlequinade, Called
> TOM,
> LOGIC AND JERRY,
> OR
> LIFE IN LONDON.
> Old Hawthorn, *afterwards Pantaloon*, Mr ODEY.
> Corinthian Tom, *afterwards Harlequin*, Mr SULTER.
> Jerry Hawthorn, *afterwards Clown*, Mr WEBB.
> Logic, Mr REID.   Genii of London, Mr BROWN.
> Finished Dandy, Mr LEE.
> Dusty Bob, Mr GILLETT.   Billy Waters, Mr GREEN.
> Huntsmen, Messrs CLARKE and BENNET.
> Watchmen, Messrs GRAY, ATWOOD, PERRY, &c.
> Columbine, Miss SMITH.   Black Sall, Mr JENKINS.
> Coffee-shop Woman, Mrs BROWN.
> The Scenery entirely New, and by the First Artists.
> To finish with a Splendid Panorama View of the
> CITY OF LONDON.
> Boxes, 2s.   Pit, 1s.   Gal., 6d.

But Mr Egan was beginning to tire of the successes of the playwrights in using his book,—even in the face of their high compliments as to his abilities and talents,—and resolved to try his own hand at a dramatic version, and this was the result:—

> "The Songs, Parodies, &c., introduced in the New Pedestrian, Equestrian Extravaganza, in Three Acts of Gaiety, Frisk, Fun, and Patter, called 'TOM and JERRY,' or, Life IN London: written by Pierce Egan, with a highly-finished Picture of the Pony Races, by Mr Geo. Cruikshank: 1822."

The Author commences by saying, that "he trusts it will not be deemed unfair that he should take a leaf or two out of his own book, several other persons having made very free with the work." The "Extravaganza" was performed at Astley's, but, with the exception of a pony-race around the theatre, on a raised boarding, it does not seem to have caught the public taste. It was to the Adelphi that the crowds flocked.

It is not generally known that George Cruikshank painted

a public-house sign to celebrate the success of *Dusty Bob* in Tom and Jerry. Walbourn, the comedian, who personated this character with extraordinary success, kept the "Maidenhead" public-house at Battle Bridge, and the artist painted a whole-length portrait of him in character, which was hung out as his signboard. Moncrieff used to say that the three characters, Tom, Jerry, and Logic, stood for George Cruikshank, Robert Cruikshank, and Pierce Egan; that many of the adventures in the book were in part autobiographical, and that the portraits of the heroes in the pictures bore a striking resemblance to the portraits of the three artists in actual life.

The biographical dictionaries are silent upon the subject of Mr Egan's literary and social career. A few particulars, however, are remembered of him.[9] He came of a respectable family, and received a better education than he was usually credited with. He followed many avocations—compositor, bookseller, sporting writer, and reporter to the newspapers. In his particular line, he was the greatest man in England. In the event of opposition to his views and opinions, he and those who looked up to him had a mode of enforcing authority which had the efficacy without the tediousness of discussion, and "though," says one who knew him, "in personal strength far from a match for any sturdy opponent, he had a courage and a vivacity in action which were very highly estimated both by his friends and foes."

Mr Egan was employed by the proprietor of the *Weekly Despatch* to record the "doings of the ring;" in which employment his peculiar phraseology, and his superior knowledge of his business, soon rendered him eminent beyond all rivalry and competition. He was flattered and petted by pugilists and peers: his patronage and countenance were sought for by all who considered the road to a prize-fight the road to reputation and honour. Sixty years ago, his presence was understood to confer respectability on any meeting convened for the furtherance of bull-baiting, cock-fighting, cudgelling, wrestling, boxing, and all

---

9 I am indebted to the Rev. Dr Richardson for some personal anecdotes.

B

that comes within the category of "manly sports." If he "took the chair," success was hailed as certain in the object in question. On the occasions of his presence he was accompanied by a "tail," if not as numerous, perhaps as respectable as that by which another great man was attended, and certainly, in its way, quite as influential.

Few persons now remember anything of the origin of *Bell's Life in London*. It appears that the success which had befallen Tom; and Jerry made the conductors of the *Despatch* very jealous, and they forthwith resolved upon excluding Mr Egan's contributions from their paper. One evening, upon reaching home, he found a note from the printer to this effect

> Dear Sir,—I am most unpleasantly situated, as I have received orders not to insert one line of your own communications this week. I wish you would come down and put all to rights. —Your humble servant,   *E. YOUNG.*
>
> *⁎⁎⁎* I received this order early this morning, but I did not like to say so to you. It has since been repeated

Pierce Egan at once made up his mind how to act. He would start a new Sunday-paper of his own, and the title should be taken from his successful book—*Pierce Egan's Life in London, and Sporting Guide.* The first number appeared Feb. 1, 1824; and after a leader of congratulations to friends, and promises to all sporting patrons, the editor gave the above printer's letter, with the following note from his own pen:—

> N.B.—The printer acted according to his order; not a line of my communications was inserted. Pierce Egan is too *GAME* yet to be made a dummy of; therefore he is determined to have a shy for himself, and a new Sunday-paper is the result.

The Editor was, at this time, the popular ready-writer of the hour. In the very first number there are advertisements of the thirteenth edition(!) of "Mr Pierce Egan's Account of the Trial of John Thurtell and Joseph Hunt." "The Life of an Actor. By Pierce Egan."

It was the editor of this new sporting-paper who first introduced that charming familiarity of style and address in literary composition which distinguishes journals of the same class at the present day, and seems to make all the readers members of one family, over which the friendly and accommodating editor presides, asking now for half a crown, and then for five pounds, in the same slangy, good-natured manner. Before half a dozen numbers had appeared, we find these "benefit" advertisements in Mr Egan's new journal:—

> "A Likeness of Pierce Egan, *in his upper story—asking himself a few questions.* The above portrait was exhibited in the Royal Academy in 1821. Drawn by George Sharples, Esq., and is now engraved by Charles Turner, Esq., mezzotinto-engraver in ordinary to His Majesty. P. E. will be much obliged to those gentlemen who intend to honour him with their commands, to give their orders as soon as possible, as but very few proof-plates will be struck off. Proofs, £1, 1s. Prints, 10s. 6d."

TO THE SPORTING WORLD.

> "THE FRIENDS OF PIERCE EGAN are solicited to purchase the following work, to place by the side of his celebrated 'Life in London,' 'LIFE IN PARIS;' comprising the Rambles, Sprees, and Amours of Dick Wildfire, of Corinthian Celebrity, and his bang-up companions, Squire Jenkins and Captain O'Shuffleton, with twenty-one coloured plates, by Mr George Cruikshank. In 1 vol., £1, 1s.; or in 21 Nos., 1s. each."

It was of the artist who designed the plates to this work that Thackeray once remarked, that though he had never been in Paris, his pictures had "a great deal of life in them, and would pass muster very well. A villainous race of shoulder-shrugging mortals are his Frenchmen indeed. And the heroes of the tale, a certain Mr Dick Wildfire, Squire Jenkins, and Captain O'Shuffleton, are made to show the true British superiority on every occasion when Britons and French are brought together."

Pierce Egan's Sporting Journal was published at the high price of 8|d. per copy. Upon reaching its ninety-fourth number, January 4, 1824, a new series was commenced, and the price was lowered to 7d. It continued to October 28, 1827, when it announced itself for sale in the following advertisement:—

> To Newspaper Proprietors, News-Agents, Booksellers, &c.

TO BE SOLD BY AUCTION, on Friday, November 2, that well-known, long-established, and highly-esteemed Sunday-newspaper, entitled,

"PIERCE EGANS LIFE IN LONDON, AND SPORTING GUIDE,"
Connected with the events of the Turf, the Chase, and the Ring.

It was purchased by a Mr Bell, and henceforth the sporting world was enlightened by BELL'S LIFE IN LONDON.

When the literature of the prize ring began to decline, Mr Egan directed his attention to the literature of the theatre, and his tact in the delineation of a certain side of life is exemplified in the farces which he has written. He often went to Oxford and Cambridge, where he was a great favourite, and "glorious nights" with him in the Colleges there are yet remembered. As *the* representative of "Life and Sport" in the great metropolis, it is not to be wondered at that his company should be sought after in the provinces.

Mr Egan had assisted at a banquet in Newgate, in the days when the Rev. Mr Cotton (the great book and curiosity collector) had the pastoral charge of the black sheep there. Matters are changed now, and the gay parties and drinking bouts of Newgate are no more. He had also assisted at the *Noctes Ambrosianae* at Edinburgh, to which he had been invited by a hoaxing letter from Professor Wilson, or some gentleman of equal eminence, and at which, to the dismay of the Professor and his learned associates, he actually made his appearance.

At one time he was treasurer or secretary to Mr Calcraft, the lessee of a theatre in Dublin. During his engagement, the then popular piece of *Monsieur Jacques* was being performed in London, in which a popular actor achieved a very remarkable success. About the same time, another gentleman acquired in his profession an eminence unattainable by imitators in another line. The last-mentioned actor took his niche in the temple of fame as "Jacko,"[10] his personation of a monkey being so true to nature that

---

10   Jacco Macacco, the famous fighting monkey of the Westminster Pit, was then attracting the attention of the sporting world.

many persons thought nature had made a mistake in conferring any instinct or attributes upon him beyond those enjoyed by the tribe "Simia." Mr Calcraft being anxious to enlighten, instruct, and amuse his audiences, secured the services of him who represented Monsieur Jacques, and also of him who represented "Jacko." Their names were announced in the bills in the usual manner, and the house was crowded to the ceiling.

Whether or not the majority, more especially in the gallery, had read the announcement, or whether or not whisky, the nectar of the Milesian "gods," had washed away the knowledge which the play-bills contained from their memories, is uncertain; certain it is that when "Monsieur Jacques" appeared, a universal shout from Olympus demanded "Jacko," and, as in Dublin such demonstrations are significant of something more vigorous "to follow," the affair was becoming alarming. Unfortunately "Jacko" had not arrived at the theatre; a crisis seemed inevitable, when the presence of mind of Mr Egan came to the rescue. He rushed upon the stage, took "Monsieur Jacques" by the hand, and advancing to the foot-lights, demanded a hearing. For a moment the clamour subsided; he took advantage of it, and addressed the clamourers. "Ladies and gentlemen, the manager is aware that you have paid your money, and honoured the house with your attendance, to witness the extraordinary performance of the man-monkey,

'Jacko.' That gentleman is unavoidably absent from the theatre this evening, but he will be here to-morrow. In the meantime, here is a gentleman about to appear as 'Monsieur Jacques/ The mistake in the names might be readily made. 'Jacques' and 'Jacko' are two different individuals, both eminent in their respective lines. We cannot produce the monkey to-night. Ladies and gentlemen, allow me to introduce for your approval the best substitute we can find in his absence."

Whether the eloquence of the speaker, or the prepossessing appearance of the substitute, operated to allay the indignation of the audience, is immaterial. There were no dissentients; "Monsieur Jacques" reconciled everybody, and when the man-monkey did make his appearance, he met with none the less hearty reception.

After a time Mr Egan returned to London. From his youth he had been fond of masquerades and private theatricals, and frequently appeared in those characters which he could personate with the greatest success. As he advanced in years he declined in the energies required for sustaining an assumed character, and latterly made his appearance "as *himself*" It one evening happened that he had partaken too freely of the good things provided at the supper-table at one of these entertainments. A temporary state of collapse ensued, and in that condition he was consigned to a cab-driver, into whose vehicle he was with some difficulty lifted by his associates. Eighteen pence was placed in his waistcoat pocket, and his address given to his consignee, with a particular injunction to be careful in the delivery of his load, as he was no less a personage than a foreign nobleman recently arrived in London. The cabman, true to his duty, trundled him to a street near Soho Square, and discovered the house set forth in the document. On one of the door-posts of the house there was a row of bell-handles, some eight or ten in number, communicating with the rooms of some eight or ten tenants of the premises. The cabman, without loss of time, set all the bell-wires in motion, and, without much delay, the heads of eight or ten people appeared at the windows above, inquiring the cause of such interruption of their rest at four o'clock in the morning.

"I have a foreign nobleman in the cab," replied the man, "and I am to set him down here."

"No nobleman, foreign or domestic, lodges here," answered the best-informed occupant: "and the sooner you move off the better."

The cabman was not so easily satisfied as to the fact.

"I'm positive he's a foreign nobleman," he returned. "I've brought him from the masquerade, and he's got money in his pocket."

The last clause in the sentence produced an immediate sensation; the heads withdrew from the windows, and the rapid descent of feet was heard on the staircase. At the same moment, a policeman made his appearance, whose presence was probably less Welcome than useful. The door was opened, and a perfect colony surrounded the cab.

Poor Mr Egan, still insensible to everything around him, was extricated from his recumbent position at the bottom of the vehicle, rolled up after the manner of a hedgehog at the approach of winter, owned by the affectionate partner of his sorrows and his joys, conveyed up-stairs with some difficulty, put to bed, and tended with conjugal solicitude. He arose next morning like a "giant refreshed with wine," and made his appearance at his usual haunts unscathed by the effects of his nocturnal indulgence, and ready to commence *de novo*. He was accustomed to relate the story with great good humour.

Mr Egan was one of the principal members of the famous club known as THE OWLS—a society held at the "Sheridan Knowles" Tavern, in Bridge Street, Covent Garden, opposite to the box entrance of Drury Lane Theatre. One who remembers the *Owls*[11] says, that the session was what the French call *en permanence*—continuous, without intermission, day or night. Something of the same kind was attempted two years ago, under the title of THE ONE O'CLOCK CLUB; but it came to nothing. Night drinking is not so fashionable as formerly. Night, indeed, was the season of glory for the "Owls;" the *elite* of the members, of whom there were about two hundred, either from their occupations or their habits, were not able, or not inclined, to congregate for the purpose of pleasure till after midnight. They then assembled for social merriment, and that sharp conflict of wit which formed, or was intended to form, the principal staple of their meeting. Sheridan Knowles, the best dramatist of his day, was the patron, or, to use the correct term, the "Chancellor" of the society. His presence at the club was a guarantee that those assembled there would hear something worth being remembered, and that noisy or equivocal jocularity, and everything approaching to indecorum, would be restrained. As a "vice-chair," he was the best manager of such an assembly in England.

---

11 The Rev. Dr Richardson.

The honorary "chairman," or president of the club, was Augustine Wade, a most odd character, and a fine specimen of the Bohemian class. He had a vigorous intellect, was always in difficulties, perpetually planning grand schemes and performing nothing. He was a first-rate classical scholar, a splendid musician, and composed admirably. "Meet me by Moonlight alone" is one of his many pieces.

Some very droll stories are told of this eccentric and M. Anati, whose daughter Wade was engaged to teach music. The tutor, in a jovial moment, proposed to marry the lady, when the father, in true Italian fashion, forced a pistol into the trembling hand of Wade, and bade him get into the further corner of the room, that they might exchange shots. Wade, who before was somewhat intoxicated, became suddenly sober, bolted from M. Anati's house at Winchester, and—it is said—never stopped until he was met in New Street, Covent Garden, covered in dust, and utterly exhausted.

Another member of the "Owls" was Mr Leman Rede, well known as a popular writer of farces and melodramas. Rede was in the club what they termed the "translator." Before any new member could be admitted, he had to attend and make a short speech, showing in what way he was capable of contributing to the amusement or edification of the club. As not unfrequently happens, the proposed member was "unaccustomed to public speaking," when it was "the Translator's" place to speak, or "translate," for the neophyte. In doing this, he of course took such liberties with the gentleman's meaning and diction as he thought proper; and in the process of "translating," made plenty of amusement for his brother "Owls." It required no little wit and no little tact to do this properly. Rede eminently possessed all the necessary qualifications.

But we are straying from our subject. The club stories of Old Covent Garden must have a book to themselves.

JOHN CAMDEN HOTTEN.
74 PICCADILLY, *27th Nov.* 1869.

LIFE IN LONDON.

CHAPTER I.

Or, rather, "an invocation;" scarcely important enough to be denominated a Chapter, yet, nevertheless, thought expedient.

IT WILL, PERHAPS, scarcely be denied, that few, if any, writers, out of the great mass of living scribblers, whether of Grub Street[12] *fabrication*, or of University *passport*, who possess "souls above buttons," can be so insensibly *frigid* as to be careless *about* the pleasing, grateful, inspiring, nay, golden advantages resulting from the smiles of that supreme Goddess of the gods, FAME! It is the " flattering unction" that all authors sigh

---

12   This phrase, respecting the *residence* of authors, is nearly obsolete; and, in point of fact, it is altogether erroneous. If it might not be deemed trespassing rather too *feelingly* upon so delicate a subject, in consulting the best authorities, both living and dead, it will be found that *hungry* authors, in the best of times, have had very little to do with GRUB STREET! the *smell* of the joint being more within their province than the actual possession of the substance, the latter being left to grace the table of the bookseller. But, to return to the phrase in question, an *original* author might likewise be averred to be as nearly *obsolete*. That *intense* study formerly required to make up the *character* of an author, is, at the present period (1820), greatly relieved, as it should seem that literature has kept pace with the new buildings in the Metropolis; and new streets and new books have been produced, as it were, by magic. This rapid improvement made in the literary world is owing to those extensive manufacturers of new works, Messrs Scissors and Paste. These heroes of steam-engine velocity have not only produced *huge* quartos without being at the expense of a pennyworth of ink, but have also had the *knack* of procuring high prices too: so say the shopmen westward; and these behind-the-counter gentry will sometimes let the *cat out of the bag!* But then, after all, where is the surprise? Is it *new* in London?

to be anointed with. The bookseller's *hack*, of Rosinante quality, even mends his *pace* upon it; the *spare* Poet, too, having once obtained only a small ray of this sunshine of public favour, spurs his Pegasus into a hurried trot to bring forth another production; and the once characterised *faithful* historian, and equally animated biographer, pushes forward at full *gallop* to the winning-post, that not only again promulgates their rapidity of action and correctness of feature, but erects a sort of *standard* whereby their future interesting and noble qualities may be anticipated. It is, therefore, a *stimulus* to exertion; it must also be admitted that it is laudable to exercise the MIND, if improvement be the object in view, and it is equally so to excel: nay more, it is the secret gratifying reward, whether in public or in private,[13] of all writers.

---

13   It may be proper here to state, that one instance offers itself directly in opposition to the former part of this sentence. Nothing, it seems, could draw JUNIUS from his *hiding-place* to receive the crown of laurel which an admiring public would have bestowed upon him, as a reward due to his great and powerful talents. What were the amount of his feelings upon this occasion, in *private*, it is impossible to make any remarks; but if there is any scale attached to self-gratification, we imagine they must have been *felicitous* in the extreme. At all events, the above self-denial is a proof of an enlarged mind. Silence, however, it is well known, is not without its advantages; and Junius may, in a great degree, have preserved his vast eminence, from this quality; for, such is the caprice of fleeting popularity, that while excellence and admiration are acknowledged when the author is anonymous, yet, no sooner is a signature attached to the performance, than the work becomes unheeded, unsought after, and ultimately sinks into oblivion. Numerous instances might be cited to prove the truth of this assertion in the records of literature; one of which is a fact so demonstrative, that, as a guide to writers in general, it ought not to be passed over. In the year 1811, an obscure individual projected a weekly newspaper, the profits arising from which were to be applied for the benefit of a large body of subscribers, all of whom were connected with works of literature. The prospectuses, &c., were well received by the public, and in a short time the newspaper in question was produced, much to the satisfaction of the subscribers, by the individual alone alluded to. Yet, rather strange to remark (but it should have been previously mentioned, this literary concern was *managed* by a Committee), that, at the expiration of five weeks, a public meeting of the subscribers was summoned, and among the subjects submitted to their consideration was the *incapacity* of the Editor. This circumstance brought on a long debate, when one of the subscribers, (Mr Wooler) then unknown to the *obscure* Editor, urged, with much eloquence, the capability already displayed by the person conducting the five newspapers published, and a majority of seventy was obtained out of one hundred that voted in his favour.

CHAPTER I.

Ah I who can tell how hard it is to climb
The steep where Fame's proud temple shines afar!

Then, thou bewitching, all-captivating goddess, make me a ladder higher than the architects can use, that I may reach thy *presence*, invoke thy cheering smiles, and at thy dazzling shrine humbly prostrate myself; and, although I solicit not GLENDOWER'S art, to call forth "spirits from the vasty deep," yet, fair goddess, stretch forth thy *"knighthood"* hand, and render me thy assistance to catch some portion of that real departed talent, if possible, which once animated a FIELDING, a GOLDSMITH, a SMOLLETT, and a STERNE, in their portraitures of "Life." Also, thou matchless deity, let me crave it as a boon, that, under thy flowery mantle, I may imbibe a *little* of that *"excellence,* NOVELTY, and *naiveté,"* which still hover about the heads of the MODERN WRITERS, who *"sit in the whirlwind of* LITERATURE, *and direct the* STORM" in the Metropolis. But, above all, as my last request, if it please thee to shower down thy favours on my humble efforts, let not thy powerful rays render me insensible nor unmindful of the triumphant beauties of imperishable TRUTH. Let ARGUS keep his hundred eyes always open, and be my sentinel towards preventing the appearance of FALSEHOOD in any shape: and, before I say farewell, also give CERBERUS an appointment to watch over my desk, that no horrifying imaginary

---

The Editor, in consequence, continued his labours for a few more weeks; but still the Committee were so far from being satisfied with his efforts, that they came to a resolution of offering a liberal remuneration to any person who should send them the best written Political Essays. This intimation was made public by an advertisement in their own journal. The Editor was advised by a friend to take advantage of this opportunity, and he actually sent two essays, under different signatures, which were approved of, and inserted in the newspaper. A deliberation soon afterwards took place among the Committee, in what manner these Essays should be paid for, when they generously determined the value they placed upon them should "be deducted from the Editor's salary. But when the latter convinced them the essays which had been the theme of discussion were his own productions, it would be needless to describe the confusion and shame which occurred. However, the obscure Editor derived one important satisfaction to his feelings, that the Committee had been caught in their own trap, and could not retreat from the praises they had bestowed upon his talents. The Editor, of course, after such treatment, retired in disgust. The above fact clearly points out the advantages derived from writing anonymously.

spectres may introduce themselves into this work, and none but real portraits illuminate "Life in London."

Come, then, thou shades of departed talent, enrich my judgment, guide my pen, and inspire me with confidence to commence my arduous undertaking. It is to thee, STERNE, I first humbly bend my knee, and solicit thy most powerful aid. If thou didst not *use up* all thy stock of SENSIBILITY before thou wert called away to enjoy the reward of thy exertions in the bowers of Elysium, pray tell me where thou didst deposit that most precious bottle, that I may with an eagerness unexampled, uncork its treasures, and apply every drop after thy rich felicity: I have great need of it. And FIELDING, too, thou true delineator of HUMAN NATURE, if only a small *remnant* of thy MANTLE has been left behind, let me but know it, that I may ransack every piece-broker's house in the kingdom, till I become the master of such an invaluable stimulus to exertion. And, although another SOPHIA WESTERN, perhaps, is not to be met with in the walks of the present day, if it were my precise object, yet, let me but produce some similarity towards the *double* of a TOM JONES or a BOOTH, and the highest pinnacle of my ambition is attained. SMOLLETT, thy touching heartfelt qualities break in upon me so penetratingly, that I must also invoke thy friendly shrine! And if a RORY RANDOM or a Lieutenant BOWLING should ever cross my path, instruct me to portray their noble traits with all that richness of colouring, and peculiar happiness of style, that once embellished thy truly characteristic pen.

Advance, also, thou Metropolitan Heroes of Literary Renown, whether of GENIUS great, either of *romantic* style, or POETRY exquisite, of Don Juan or Lalla Rookh quality, it matters not, if *generosity* lie within thine inkstands, and ye put forth your good wishes for my success; show me your *pass-ports* to excellence, and put me in the right road, that I may ultimately obtain your proud signatures and arrive safe at the end of my journey.

REVIEWS, those terrific Censors of the timid writer, and arbiters of the press, whether QUARTERLY, or at EDINBURGH, you apply the *knife,* bear it in mind that VAN BUTCHELL *advertises* to perform *cures* without *cutting;* and that ABERNETHY is himself, alone! and also remember, thou *sages* of the quill, that many an unfortunate *homo* who has been "damned to everlasting Fame," and disposed of in a *Jef,* in thy most omnipotent pages; yet has, from the *resuscitating* glossy aid of Messrs DAY and MARTIN, become a *shining* Literary Character in Paternoster Row, and formed one of the real Portraits of LIFE IN LONDON!

Come forth, my M*ag.* of BLACKWOOD; thee, too, I must invoke! thou *chiel* of SATIRE, whose lively sallies and "laughing-in-the-sleeve greatness," that would have paralysed the pencil of a HOGARTH, or struck dumb the *piquant* ridicule of a CHURCHILL, if the grim King of Terrors had not deprived us of their talents; I challenge thee to the *scratch*! Tis ONE OF THE FANCY calls! But, from thy *lamb-like* qualities and *playful* artillery, it must only be a private *set-to* with the *gloves*. My hand grapples with you in friendship—it possesses not *weight* enough to combat with thee, although the *pluck,* perhaps, attached to it may be always *gay*. Be it remembered, that BLACKWOOD is always in *training* he *hits* so very hard—and his backers[14] are likewise so numerous amongst the Greeks, Latins, Hebrews, and Classics, that it would be two to one against an open contest: therefore, good Mr Blackwood, be just, nay, be more, "be merciful. It is doubly bless'd;" and you know, *Blacky*[15] "it blesseth him that *gives*[16] and him that *takes.*" Then *floor* me not; but, instead,—

> Shoot thine arrow o'er thy house,—
> And do not wound thy brother;

but whisper to the PACK, and particularly to the *whipper-in*, Old

---

14 "*Pon Honour* there is not the slightest allusion intended to the *back shop!*
15 A friendly term, rest assured, although it has a singular sound: and however I may feel, nay, almost perceive, the late Colossus of Literature's frown upon me in regard to *punning*, it is but gentlemanly conduct to state, there is nothing *opaque* about the *Mag.* of this Literary Purveyor, and that *fairness* floats, like a triumphant car, proudly on the surface of all his pages.
16 However synonymous, in this instance they do not belong to the Prize Ring; therefore, to be parliamentary upon the subject (and I am sure, Blacky, you will not quarrel with me for imitating my betters), this must be taken as a sort of whisper of explanation across the table, which, perhaps, if otherwise noticed by the Speaker, he might be induced to cry out, Order, order!

Christopher North, that "'TIS I" — (your *flash-y* friend of the South). But let me entreat of you, Mr Blackwood, to *bottle-off* a few of thy little mastery touches (as full of fire as thy famed whisky), and send them to me with all the speed of the mail, lest my stock of *spirits* should be exhausted, and that LIFE IN LONDON may be enriched with the fine colouring of a *Meg Merrilees*, if it be only in perspective.

And, Mr COLBURN (thou indefatigable promoter of literature thy assistance I most humbly crave! indeed, I feel assured that thy spirited and liberal disposition will not permit thee to omit informing those dashing belles and beaux, whose morning lounge gives thy repository of the mind an air of fashion, that LIFE IN. LONDON is worthy of their perusal.

HUMPHREYS, too, thou plentiful caterer for the sons of Momus, only one little pane of glass in thy attractive shop-front I entreat for the display of CORINTHIAN TOM, that he may be viewed quite "at home" in St James's Street. Thou know'st me, and I already anticipate 'tis done.

But thou, O MURRAY! whose classic front defies, with terrific awe, ill-starred, pale, wan, and *shabbily-clad* GENIUS from approaching thy splendid threshold, retreat a little from thy rigid reserve, and for once open thy doors, and take the unsophisticated JERRY HAWTHORN by the hand; and although not a CHILDE HAROLD in birth, a CORSAIR bold, or a HARDY VAUX, *wretched* exile; yet let me solicit thee to introduce him to thy numerous acquaintance, that, having once obtained thy *smiling* sanction, JERRY may not only have the honour of being allowed to call again, but to offer his services throughout thy extended circle. Grant me but this, and whether in simple quires, in humble boards, or in Russia, triumphantly gilt, so that thou promote my fame, my gratitude attends thee, and values not the mode of thy favours.

PROFESSORS of the Royal Academy, let me entreat you not to avert your microscopic eyes from my palpitating efforts; but second my elevated wishes, if it seem good to your taste, that CORINTHIAN TOM may prove so "fine a subject" as to occupy one of the interesting lectures of a CARLYLE; and also that his "beauty of form" may be found worthy of a page of the unassuming, enlightened, and communicative FLAXMAN. And FUSELI, thou great master of the pencil, let me solicit thy aid to prevent JERRY HAWTHORN's portrait from being *out of drawing;* and let the *perspective* of my tale be as accurate as a TURNER could wish or accomplish: and, as the *desideratum* of the whole, may the *architecture* of LIFE IN LONDON merit the elegant and liberal criticism of a SOANE.

Accum, be thou kind enough to furnish me with a gentle hint, that I may not only enjoy all thy *nicety* of palate and taste, but reject every *poisonous* ingredient to the mind,[17] and be enabled to *dish-up* a most sumptuous repast for all my readers.

CHRISTIE, I am sure thy goodness will not refuse me the loan of thy *erudite* hammer, if not to *knock down,* yet to dispose of every coarse and offensive article; nay more, let them not be numbered in the *catalogue* of my offences.

O'SHAUGHNESSY, fashion me into thy fine attitudes and guard, to protect me from assaults in all the hair-breadth escapes I may have to encounter in my day and midnight rambles. And thou, O mighty and powerful champion, CRIBB, admired hero of the stage, teach me to make a *hit* of so KEAN a quality, that it may not only *tell,* but be long remembered in the Metropolis, and Paternoster-Row trumpet forth its praise and excellence throughout the most distant provinces.

ACKERMAN, if ever thou didst *value* the Tour of Dr SYNTAX, I call upon thee now to lend thy friendly assistance and protection to CORINTHIAN TOM and his rustic *protégé* poor JERRY. Present a copy of their SPREES and RAMBLES to the learned Doctor, and his "Picturesque" brain will be all on fire for another tour, from the new scenes it will develop to his unbounded thirst for enterprise and knowledge.

And thou, too, HONE, thou king of parodists! turn not a deaf ear to my request, but condescendingly grant the petition of your

---

17   Second Edition, Jan. 8, 1821.—Recent circumstances, disclosed to the Subscribers of Life in London, imperatively compel me to state, that the MIND of this *Chemist* will not bear *analysing,* as I had previously anticipated. "Out, damned spot!"

most humble suitor. In my diversity of research, teach me "how to tell my story," that I may not only woo the public with success and fame, but produce that fine edge in *sharpening* up my ideas, yet, withal so smooth and *oily*, that instead of *wounding* characters, I may merely *tickle* them and create a smile!

Tremblingly alive! nay, heavily oppressed with agitation and fear, I now intrude myself into thy presence, thou renowned hero of the police, TOWNSHEND. Do not frown upon me, but stretch out thine hand to my assistance, thou bashaw of the *pigs*[18] and all-but *beak!*[19] The satellite of kings and princes, protector of the nobility, and one of the *safeguards* of the Metropolis. Listen to my application, I entreat of thee, "my knowing one," and for once let me take a *peep* into thy hidden invaluable secrets. It is only a *glance* at thy *reader*[20] that I request:

> Wherein, of hundreds *topp'd*,[21] thousands *lagg'd*;[22]
> And of the innumerable *teazings*[23] thou has book'd;

thy "Life in London," alone, is a history of such magnitude, that, if once developed, the "Adventures of Robinson Crusoe" must be forgotten. O teach me, TOWNSY, to be as *down* in my portraits as thou art in giving all the light and shade of criminality to the nightly mysteries of the wary FENCE,[24] when pressing for a conviction; and, likewise, to keep as sharp a look-out after *Characters* in the ball-room of the CORINTHIANS as thy penetrating eyes scour the abodes of the great when "at home"[25] to make all right. I ask

---

18 Thief-takers.
19 Magistrate
20 Pocket-book. Townshend's first introduction to the police, it seems, was owing to his knowledge of the numerous persons hanged, transported, &c.; he having kept a regular journal to that effect. This calendar of offences gave him a great superiority over his fellows.
21 Hanged
22 Transported
23 Floggings
24 A receiver of stolen goods.
25 To the Provincials, this phrase may operate rather as a sort of paradox—as houses and persons, in general, are robbed not "at home," but when the parties are abroad. But more of this anon, as it most certainly forms a very prominent feature

no more than

> Sit mihi fas audita loqui: sit numine vestro
> Paudere res altâ terra et caligine mersas.

In all the varied portraiture of the interesting scenes of Life, let me invoke thy superior talents, BOB and GEORGE CRUIKSIANK (thou *Gillray* of the day, and of *Don Saltero* greatness), to my anxious aid. Indeed, I have need of all thy illustrative touches; and may we be hand-and-glove together in depicting the richness of nature, which so wantonly, at times, plays off her freaks upon the half-famished bone-rakers and cinder-sifters round the dust-hill, that we may be found, *en passant*, so identified with the scene in question, as almost to form a part of the group. May thou also, BOB and GEORGE, *grapple* with *Hogarthian* energy in displaying *tout a la mode* the sublime and *finished* part of the creation, whether *screwed* up to a *semi-tone* of ART, or in nobly delineating what must always be a welcome visitor at every residence, and likewise an admired portrait over all the chimney-pieces in the kingdom, a PERFECT GENTLEMAN. But, before I dismiss thee to thy studies, bear it in remembrance, "nothing to extenuate or set down aught in malice yet be tremblingly alive to the *shrug* of the fastidious critic, who might, in his sneer, remark, that CARICATURE would be as much out of time and place in holding up to ridicule the interior of the religious good man's closet as it is animatedly required in giving all the rusticity and fun incident to the humours of a country fair.

And, thou, O BOXIANA! my dearest friend and well-wisher, thou beloved companion of all my hours, thou "note-book" of my MIND, and "pen and ink remembrancer" of my passing scenes, whether in splendid palaces, lost in admiration over the fascinating works of art, or in *diving* into the humble cellar, passing an hour with some of mankind's worthiest children, poor, but contented and happy,—be thou my guide and assistant! Do not desert me, neither at *peep o' day*, when drowsy watchmen quit their posts, and coffee-shops *vomit* forth their *snoozing* customers—those outcasts

---

of Life in London.

of society to whom a table is a luxury to rest their thoughtless heads upon, and whose

> Dry desert of a leathern pocket does not contain
> A solitary farthing!

Be also at my elbow, upon the *strut* in Hyde-park, on Sunday's stare, when Sol's BRIGHT rays over *Fashion's* splendid scene gives such a brilliancy of appearance. And be thou near to me, should midnight Covent-Garden rows claim my attention, when *noisy rattles* collect together the dissipated ramblers *touched* with the potent juice of Bacchus, and entangled with *hoarse* Cyprians in the last stage of existence, till dragged to the watch-house, where the black hole gives a *limit* to their depravity of exclamation. In this respect, BOXIANA, let thine ear be as nice as SPAGNIOLETTI's; anxious, like this great master of the Cremona, to give all the force and beauty of composition, but carefully to avoid a note being out of tune.[26] Then, for once, let me entreat of you, in soliciting your assistance, that you will take off the *gloves*, quit the prize ring, put down thy *steamer*,[27] and for awhile dispense with thy DAFFY,[28] but, above all, steer clear from the *slang*, [29] except, indeed, where the instances decidedly call it forth, in order to produce an effect, and *emphasis* of character. Then, fare thee well!

Yet, if to the *shrine* of one unrivalled genius more than another I lastly pay my court, having felt so great an awe when first admitted into thy presence,[30] it is from the recollection, SHERIDAN, of

---

26   It is said of this admired leader of the band at the Opera-House, that, during his private rehearsals at his own residence, lest any of the itinerant street musicians should arrest his attention for a single instant with their music in passing his door, he immediately puts aside his violin, in order to avoid any incorrect sound operating upon his ear, so scrupulously does Mr Spagniolletti adhere to a highly cultivated, as well as a most finished taste.

27   Pipe.

28   By the vulgar called *gin*.

29   This is certainly good and correct advice, but, perhaps the metaphor might have proved rather more *illustrative,* if the old adage had been quoted, that, "*when* at Rome *do as* Rome *does?*"

30   It cannot be a matter of surprise that an obscure individual like myself should have felt an awe upon such an occasion, when it may be recollected that

those great talents which once not only *"set the table in a roar"* from the splendid pavilion to the thatched cot, in both of which thou hadst no equal in relating an anecdote, for lively sallies of wit, *bonnes bouches*, and quickness of repartee; but also from the remembrance that thy ELOQUENCE has even astounded the *eloquent* with thy matchless inexhaustible powers in that great House, where such another body of comprehensive and active intellect is not to be met with in the whole range of Europe. If PATHOS was thy *forte*, not a dry eye ever listened to thee, but the tears of sensibility trickled down the cheeks of all that enrapturedly heard thy penetrating tale. Human Nature could not resist thy most powerful appeals; and even the haughty, callous, and phlegmatic, only found relief in these involuntary sympathies. SATIRE, too, in thy hands was of so piercing a description, that the most cold-hearted and high-born subjects instantly became warm and angry at the keenness of its application, independent of the laughter, ridicule, and contempt it never failed to produce. But when the services of thy country roused thee into action, thou wert great indeed. Every thing else was forgotten. Thine oratory was like a mighty flood that swept all kind of masses in opposition to it, big and little, into one vortex; thyself outliving the storm like a real senator and a true patriot. But, respecting "Life in London," O SHERIDAN,[31] nationally, much

---

Monsieur Tallien, who had rendered himself so conspicuous in the National Convention, by flourishing a dagger (similar to the conduct of the Sublime and Beautiful in the House of Commons) when he denounced Robespierre, upon his being introduced to the late Mr Sheridan, was so embarrassed, nay, he felt so much confused, that for a short time his powers of articulation seemed almost suspended. Upon his recovery, Monsieur Tallien declared, it was under the impression of Sheridan's great talents that he was quite overwhelmed. This circumstance must be viewed as a fine compliment to the English orator, when it is well known that Tallien was looked up to as being one of the most accomplished gentlemen and scholars in Paris.

31   When to stand a fourth bottle no longer I'm able
(Excuse a fond tear, for the thought makes me sad),
May jolly dogs point to me under the table,
And say, with a sigh, "That's *Tom Sheridan's* dad."

When in life's latest scene, from theatrical duties,
Unequal to Green-room cabals, I retire,
All the notice I crave, from wits, critics, and beauties,
Is, "He's gone, poor old fellow, *Tom Sheridans* sire."

lamented shade, thou wert a painter indeed! either in the efforts of thy eloquence, or the exertions of thy pen, thy productions evinced the hands of a master. Who could depict the light and shade of the company of princes and their *bon vivant* companions like thee? And alike, whom portray the poorest Irish hay-maker in the Metropolis that sought his twopenny resting-place from the fatigues of his sun-burnt occupation; and also the wretched outcast, compelled to pass his nights upon the step of a door; both being objects not unworthy of thy inquiry. Thy feeling heart was accessible to all mankind—thy mind was as enlarged and as capacious as the boundless ocean; and be it engraven upon the memories of all thy admirers, that neither pride nor arrogance ever for a single instant disgraced thy manly composition. Thou wert a man at all times, whether viewed at dashing routes, surrounded by the most accomplished beauties, or *caught* upon the *sly*, peeping at midnight revels in the precincts[32] of Covent-Garden. Thy refinement and gallantry was as conspicuous at the one as thy knowledge of life and appropriate behaviour was admired at the other. The *green-room* looked up to thee for original characters; and the great and little world, with acclamations, united with the energies of the grateful press, in loudly promulgating thy inimitable portraiture of fashionable life. Splendour and distress have both been allied to thy name: thou hast not been elevated by the dazzling rays of the former, nor sunk in despair when oppressed by the latter;

> When reason no more shall be answer'd with raillery,
> No "laugh" sprinkled speeches by Quid-nuncs be read;
> After some long debate, may they say in the Gallery,
> "Ah! what would *Tom Sheridan's* Father have said?"
>
> When no more I shall try, with vexation tho' bursting,
> To carry the day with a forced ha! ha! ha!
> May the green-coated Orator gaze at the hustings,
> And smile when he thinks of *Tom Sherry's* Papa.

32   Mrs (but familiarly termed Mother) Butler's. Ask any of the gentlemen connected with the public press to describe, "if it live in their memories," only a few of the frequenters of that back-parlour so often *crammed* full of talent, scholars, and *choice* spirits.

although cruel, unfeeling Fortune jilted thee in thy last moments. Thy talents were never bartered,[33] neither did they ever desert thee; and thy love of independence never ceased to animate thy frame while one vital spark of life remained in thy great soul. Thy pen has often procured thee a dinner, when no other source offered itself; and might, if only attended to, have produced a splendid fortune. But Fame, in handing down her records of great men to posterity, will never slumber over the merits of the patriot, uniting the man of genius with the gentleman and the scholar. To thee, departed great genius, if it be possible, let me, however far behind I may be placed in distance, yet most humbly endeavour to aim at treading in thy steps, when crossing those paths where another Lady Teazle and a Charles Surface animate the *Beau Monde;* but to avoid the buz of surrounding *scandal;* and also to shun such an associate as a *Snake!*

The metropolis is now before me: POUSSIN never had a more luxuriant, variegated, and interesting subject for a landscape; nor had SIR JOSHUA REYNOLDS finer characters for his canvas than what have already had a sitting for their likenesses to embellish LIFE IN LONDON.

To thee, FAME, my finger-post towards the right road, I once more look up, and if I cannot command success, at least, it shall not be averred that I did not exert myself to deserve it.

---

33   Can such things be, and overcome us
                Like a summer's cloud, without our special wonder?
Yet such was the fact, that the last act of feeling and kindness administered to this great character was from the hands of a sheriff's officer; and to his honour be it spoken, although it was intimated to him that he would be fixed with the debt and costs, this humane officer refused to remove Mr Sheridan from his residence to, the security of a lock up house, when he was informed that such removal might be the immediate cause of that great man's death.

CHAPTER II.

A Camera Obscura View of the Metropolis, with the Light and
Shade attached to "seeing Life."

> The youth comes up to town to learn all modern foppery,
> For London Town, no better place to teach those from the country!
> He soon finds what is wanting, and like him not sees one in ten,
> But *rolls* into a barber's shop to get a *"knowing cut,"* and then—
> He becomes a prime *rolling* kiddy O!
> The girls all admire him, and swear he is quite a tippy O!
> Old Ballad.

PREVENTION, EITHER IN days of yore or at the present enlightened period, has always been considered much better than cure; and, therefore, safety, at all times, should be the primary object of the traveller. The curious, likewise, in their anxiety to behold delightful prospects or interesting views, ought to be equally careful to prevent the recurrence of accidents. The author, in consequence, has chosen for his readers a *Camera Obscura* View of London, not only from its safety, but because it is so *snug*, and also possessing the invaluable advantages of seeing and not being *seen*. The author of the *Devil upon two Sticks*, it appears, preferred taking a *flight* over the houses for his remarks and views of society; but if I had adopted that mode of travelling, and perchance had fallen to the ground, an hospital might have been the reward of my presumption, and have also become a *cripple* during the remainder of my existence. Such a misfortune, it is true, might have been deplored, and even pitied, by the lovers of "*hairbreadth 'scape adventures;*" yet, with all their compassion, it would have been a great chance, perhaps, if it had not sooner or later have escaped from their lips, that the worst of *bores* and the most tiresome of all other companions is that of A LITERARY CRIPPLE! Therefore, from this extreme caution, I hope to be enabled to proceed on my journey without *stilts,* and also to prove so strong on my legs as to walk over the ground without *limping*, or to require the need and assistance of anything in the shape of a *Crutch*. This will be thought enough. The *Camera Obscura* is now at work; the table is covered with objects for the amusement of my readers; and whenever it is necessary to change the scene it is only requisite to pull the string, *i.e.,* to turn over leaf after leaf, and LIFE IN LONDON will be seen without any fear or apprehension of danger either from *fire* or *water;* avoiding also breaking a limb, receiving a *black* eye, losing a pocket-book, and getting into a watch-house; picking up a *Cyprian,* and being exposed the next morning before a magistrate for being found *disorderly*. Likewise in steering clear of all those innumerable rows and troubles incident or allied to "keeping it up, and loving of fun." It would have been fortunate indeed for poor JERRY and CORINTHIAN TOM if they had possessed such advantages. But "experience makes fools wise," and as good-natured HAWTHORN and laughing TOM are now about to relate their *adventures,* for the benefit of *fire-side* heroes and sprightly maidens who may feel a wish to "see Life" without receiving a *scratch,* it must be considered that the Metropolis is now before them.

> LONDON! thou comprehensive word,
> What joy thy streets and squares afford I
> And think not thy admirer rallies
> If he should add thy *lanes* and *alleys*.
> Thy INDEPENDENCE let me share
> Though clogged with smoke and foggy air;
> Though I'm obliged my doors to make fast;
> Though I can get no cream for breakfast;
> Though knaves, within thee, cheat and plunder.
> And fires can scarcely be kept under;
> And many a rook finds many a pigeon
> In LAW, and *physic,* and *religion,*
> Eager to help a thriving trade on,

> And proud and happy to be preyed on;
> What signify such paltry blots?
> The glorious sun himself has spots.

Then it seems ONLY in London are the finishing touches of *character* to be obtained. To acquire "excellence" in the Metropolis is a circumstance so "devoutly to be wished," that it is the genuine passport throughout all the provinces in England; nay more, it is wafted across the briny deep, and this sort of "greatness" is acknowledged, admired, and sought after in all parts of the world.

LONDON is the looking-glass for TALENT—it is the faithful emporium of the enterprising, the bold, the timid, and the bashful individual, and where all can view themselves at full length, affording innumerable opportunities either to push forward, to retreat, to improve, or to decide. In no other place can FORTUNE be so successfully wooed as in London; and in no other place does she distribute her favours with so liberal a hand.

It is in LONDON too, that, almost at every step, TALENT will be found jostling against TALENT—and greatness continually meeting with greatness—where ABILITY stares ABILITY full in the face—and where *learning*, however extensive and refined, is opposed by *learning* equally erudite and classical. *Intellect* also meets with a formidable opponent in *intellect*. *Independence* likewise challenges *independence* to its post. And where *superiority* on the one side always operates as a check upon *superiority* on the other, that *self-importance* may be humbled, and *egotism* pulled down and exposed.

> Here I endure no throbs, no twitches
> Of envy at a neighbour's riches,
> But, smiling, from my window, see
> A dozen quite as rich as he:
> Or if I stroll, am sure to meet
> A dozen more in every street,
> Who like tall ships at home appear.
> *But* dwindle *into* cock-boats *here*.
> None are distinguished, none are rare
> From wealth which hundreds round them share,
> But (*neutralised* by one another Whene'er they think to raise a pother)
> Be they kind-hearted or capricious,

CHAPTER II.

> Vain, prodigal, or avaricious,
> Proud, popular, or what they will,
> Are *elbowed* by their RIVALS still.
> In LONDON, blest with competence,
> With temper, health, and common sense,
> None need repine or murmur,—nay,
> ALL MAY BE HAPPY IN THEIR WAY.
> E'en the lone dwelling of the poor
> And suffering are at least obscure;
> And in obscurity exempt
> From poverty's worst scourge, *contempt.*
> Unmark'd the poor man seeks his den,
> Unheeded issues forth again.
> Wherefore appears he none inquires,
> Nor why, nor whether he retires;
> All that his pride would fain conceal,
> All that shame blushes to reveal,
> The petty shifts, the grovelling cares,
> To which the sons of want are heirs.
> Those evils which, grievous to be borne.
> Call forth—not sympathy, but scorn,
> Here hidd'n, elude the searching eye
> Of *callous* CURIOSITY!

In order to give weight to these remarks, let us state, that it was the opinion of Dr Johnson, "that in London a man stored his mind better than anywhere else; and that in remote situations a *man's body* might be *feasted,* but his mind was *starved* and his FACULTIES *apt to degenerate from want of exercise and competition.*" "No place," he said, "cured a man's vanity or arrogance so well as London; for as no man was either great or good *per se,* but as compared with others not so good or great, he was sure to find in the Metropolis many his equals and some his superiors."

> Such London *is,* by taste and wealth proclaim'd
> The fairest CAPITAL of all the world,
> By riot and incontinence the worst.

The EXTREMES, in every point of view, are daily to be met with in the Metropolis; from the most rigid, persevering, never-tiring industry, down to laziness, which, in its consequences, frequently operates far worse than idleness. The greatest love of and contempt for money are equally conspicuous; and in no place are pleasure and business so much united as in London. The highest veneration for and practice of religion distinguishes the Metropolis, contrasted with the most horrid commission of crimes: and the *experience* of the oldest inhabitant scarcely renders him safe against the specious plans and artifices continually laid to entrap the most vigilant. The next-door neighbour of a man in London is generally as great a stranger to him, as if he lived at the distance of York. And it is in the Metropolis that *prostitution* is so profitable a business, and conducted so openly, that hundreds of persons keep houses of ill-fame, for the reception of girls not more than *twelve* and *thirteen* years of age, without a blush upon their cheeks, and mix with society heedless of stigma or reproach; yet honour, integrity, and independence of soul, that nothing can remove from its basis, are to be found in every street in London. Hundreds of persons are always going to bed in the morning, besotted with dissipation and gaming, while thousands of his Majesty's liege subjects are quitting their pillows to pursue their useful occupations. The most bare-faced villains, swindlers, and thieves, walk about the streets in the day-time, committing their various depredations, with as much confidence as men of unblemished reputation and honesty. In short, the most vicious and abandoned wretches, who are lost to every friendly tie that binds man to man, are to be found in swarms in the Metropolis; and so depraved are they in principle, as to be considered, from their uncalled-for outrages upon the inhabitants, a *waste of wickedness*, operating as a complete terror, in spite of the *activity* of the police. Yet, notwithstanding this dark and melancholy part of the picture, there are some of the worthiest, most tender-hearted, liberal minds, and charitable dispositions, which ornament London, and render it the delight and happiness of society.

Indeed, the Metropolis is a complete CYCLOPÆDIA, where every man of the most religious or moral habits, attached to any sect, may find something to please his palate, regulate his taste, suit his pocket, enlarge his mind, and make him happy and comfortable. If places of worship give any sort of character to the *goodness* of the Metropolis, between four and five hundred are opened for religious purposes on Sundays. In fact, every SQUARE in the Metropolis is a sort of *map* well worthy of exploring, if riches and titles operate as a source of curiosity to the visitor. There is not a *street* also in London; but what may be compared to a large or small volume of intelligence, abounding with anecdote, incident, and peculiarities. A *court* or *alley* must be obscure indeed, if it does not afford some remarks; and even the *poorest* cellar contains some *trait* or other, in unison with the manners and feelings of this great city, that may be put down in the note-book, and reviewed, at an after period, with much pleasure and satisfaction.

Then, the grand object of this work is an attempt to portray what is termed "SEEING LIFE" in all its various bearings upon society, from the *high-mettled* CORINTHIAN of St James's, *swaddled* in luxury, down to the *needy* FLUE-FAKER of Wapping, *born without a shirt*, and not a *bit of scran*[34] in his cup to allay his piteous cravings.

"LIFE IN LONDON" is the sport in view, and provided the *chase* is turned to a good account, "*seeing Life*" will be found to have its advantages; and, upon this calculation, whether an evening is spent over a bottle of champagne at *Long's*, or in taking a "*third of a daffy*"[35] at *Tom Belcher's*, if the MIND does not decide it *barren*, then the purposes are gained. Equally so, in *waltzing* with the *angelics* at my *Lady* FUBB's assembly, at Almack's, or *sporting a toe* at Mrs SNOOKS's *hop* at St Kit's, among the pretty *straw* damsels and *dashing* chippers, if a *knowledge* of "Life," an acquaintance with *character*, and the importance of *comparison*, are the ultimate results.

> If once to *Almack's* you belong,
> Like Monarchs you can *do no wrong;*
> But banished thence, on Wednesday night,
> By Jove, you can do nothing right.
> I hear (perhaps the story false is),
> From *Almack's,* that he never *waltzes*
> With Lady Anne, or Lady Biddy,
> *Twirling* till he's in love, or giddy,
> The girl a pigmy, he a giant,
> *His* cravat stiff, *her* corset pliant.
> There, while some *jaded* couple stops,
> The rest go round like humming-tops,
> Each in the circle with its neighbour,

---

34   Food
35   Third part of a quartern of gin.

Sharing alternate rest and labour:
While many a gentle *chaperon*
(As the fair Dervises spin on)
Sighs with regret, that *she* was courted
Ere this new fashion was imported,
Ere the dull minuet-step had vanished,
With jigs and country-capers banished.
But Charles, whose energy relaxes,
No more revolves upon his axis,
At sounds of cymbal and of drum
Deep clanging, from th' orchestra come,
And round him moves, in radiance bright,
Some beauteous beaming satellite;
Nor ventures, as the night advances,
On a new partner in French dances;
Nor, his high destiny fulfilling
Through all the mazes of *quadrilling,*
Holds, lest the figure should be hard,
Close to his nose a printed card,
Which, for their *special use* invented,
To Beaux, on entrance, is presented;
A strange device, one must allow,
But useful—as it tells them how[36]
To foot it in the proper places
Much better than their partners' faces.
Mark, how the married and the single
In yon gay groups delighted mingle!
'Midst diamonds blazing, tapers beaming,
'Midst Georges, stars, and crosses gleaming,
We gaze on beauty, catch the sound
Of music, and of mirth around;
And Discord feels her empire ended

---

36   Who would not be a *gentleman* for the comforts attendant upon such a situation? If a rich man is not a sensible, interesting, and polite character, with whom does the fault rest? Himself! Every thing to render him *complete* in life is within his reach. *Dress*, to give him the *cut* of an Adonis, is not only made for him, but he has a valet to decorate his exterior; and an address, *a la Chesterfield*, is also *chalked* out for him, to leave the *canaille* at an immeasurable distance. Indeed, that anything like *trouble* might not be too much for him, the choice of a *wife* even is left to some obliging friend. All his business transactions are done by attorney. Thelwall, for a *trifle,* can teach him to pronounce hard words without difficulty; and his duties as a Member of Parliament are summed up in those decisive little words Aye and No, which operate in importance a thousand times more than the eloquent volume speeches of Phillips on Crim. Con. For an opinion, long or short, upon any subject, not the slightest *study* is requisite,—thanks to upwards of sixty Newspapers published weekly, eighty-four Magazines, Reviews, &c., monthly, besides myriads of minor publications in London; so that a gentleman has only to name a particular work, and the thing is disposed of *instanter.* Therefore, in the Metropolis, *a monied man* has nothing else left to wish for, except—a never-ceasing existence! to avoid the fatality of the *Strudulburghs,* and to realise, at all periods, the bloom and vigour of health of twenty-seven years of age.

Chapter II.

At Almack's—or at least *suspended*.

A *blow out* may likewise be found as *savory* and as *high scented* at Mother O'Shaughncssy's, in the *back settlements* of the *Holy Land*, by the hungry *cut-away* Paddy Mulroony, as the *Mulligatawny soup* may be swallowed with peculiar *goût* by one of the fastidious, squeamish, screwed-up descendants of the Ogelby train at Grillion's hotel. A morning at Tattersal's, among the *top-of-the-tree* heroes in society, *legs* and *levanters;* or an hour *en passant* at Smithfield, on a Friday afternoon, among "I's Yorkshire" and the *copers*, may also have its effect.

Rubbing against the Corinthians in the circle of Hyde Park on Sundays, and breathing the air of nobility, contrasted with the aping, behind-the-counter, *soi-disant* gentry, supported by their *helegant* tender creatures, decked out in all the made-up paraphernalia of Cranbourne Alley; and carrying the contrast still further, of the various modes of disposing of time, practised by the rude unsophisticated residents in the purlieus of St Giles's, down to the vulgar inmates of St Catherine's, Wapping,—if, duly appreciated, the *tout ensemble* is one of the finest pictures of "Life in London!"

> *Avast!* Achilles, Grecian famed,
> And fiery Hector, Trojan named;
> Avast! your Philips, Alexanders,
> Your Cæsars too, war's Salamanders;
> And eke gave way, Imperial Nap,
> *For thou alike didst doff the cap*
> To Neptune's darling son of war,
> I mean Jack Junk, the British tar.
> Woman! the sailor's darling care,
> For Jack would die to serve the fair;
> And though he yields to Cyprian bands,
> A girl *distressed* no less commands
> The sailor's purse, his maxim true,
> That Love keeps Pity's shrine in view,
> And thus the matter *argufies*—
> "I've rhino plenty, bless my eyes!
> "But *vat's* the good of this here cash?
> "On board I cannot make a splash;
> "Give me the girls ashore, and prog,
> "The elbow-scraper, flip, and grog;
> "'Tis then I shows I've got some spunk,
> "I' faith it's true—for I'm Jack Junk."
> Onward he goes, with rolling stride,
> In hopes he may not be denied

The liberty on shore to go,
A welcome—*yes*—wakes Pleasure's glow;
Then rubbing hands, cries—"Here's sea-room,
"Now safe ashore I'll top my boom."
The cruize commences, off they veer,
For fiddlers, prog, and girls they steer.
Bet Stride her ruby colour shows;
Sail Walker shows her bowsprit nose;
Nan Brag her bulky breeching rears,
Poll Sherwin shows the bottle's tears;
And last, far famed for *fisty* prize,
Moll Chauntress view, with bung'd up eyes.
No ceremonies here can nip
The pastimes found in Pleasure's ship;
A dance becomes the gen'ral cry.
All hands agreed, for no one's shy;
The call is bitters now and gin,
"While fiddlers twain increase the din.
The dance begins, they foot it neat,
And JACK believes 'tis heav'n's own seat.
Of JUNK the choice you fain would know,
Who makes these lines heroic flow?
Yes, she that could some *ruby* boast,
Of every tar the standing toast:
'Twas sterling *Moll,* who with each *glim*
Bung'd up excited Jack Junk's whim;
Long known to brave all stormy weather,
Her tail ne'er showing *one white feather.*
Such was the choice of fighting Jack,
Who loved no sniv'lers at his back,
But bred to warfare, lived for fight,
And spent YEARS' EARNINGS IN A NIGHT!
They dance till limbs no more can move,
Then, *half-seas over,* talk of love;
Aloud they chaunt, "God save the King,"
And "Rule Britannia" boisterous sing;
Of "Cease rude Boreas" verses try,
Recalling scenes that raise the sigh;
For tars, though thoughtless now and then,
Can *think* and *feel* like polish'd men.
Here ends the scene—the sand is run—
Of JACK is spent a prime day's fun.

Paying a visit to the *Fives Court*, to view the NONPAREIL and Turner exhibit, or in taking a turn in the evening, to listen to Coleridge, Fuseli, Flaxman, and Soane, if the MIND make a *hit*, and some *striking* impressions are implanted upon the memory, then the advantages resulting from the *varieties* of "LIFE" must here again be acknowledged.

The ITALIAN OPERA (this luxurious wardrobe of the great,

this jeweller's shop of the nation, this *scent* and *perfume* repository of the world, and Arabian Nights' spectacle of Fortunatus's cap) is one of the most *brilliant* collection of portraits of LIFE IN LONDON. It possesses such fascinations, and the *spell* is so powerful, that to be "*seen there*" is quite enough, the performances being mere *dumb show* to most of its visitors; and however the languishing "die away" strains of Ambroghetti's *Don Giovanni* may almost cause an earthquake in the ear of the tasteful critic, and call forth "Bravo!"

>Vivan le femine,
>Viva il buon vino,
>Sostegno e gloria,
>D'umanità.
>ATTO II. SCENA 14.

yet, how strange it is that the *Italian Opera*, to the great majority of JOHN BULL's descendants, is positively worse than *physic*, and who prefer being almost squeezed to suffocation, amidst clouds of tobacco, the fumes of porter, and the strong smell of *Deady's Fluid*, at a Free and Easy Club, to hear TOM OWEN's "*Rum Ould Mog*," and, from the richness of its slang pronounce it "fine!" Such is the diversity of Life in London.

> RUM OULD MOG was a *Ieary flash* MOT,[37] and she was round and fat,
> With *twangs* in her shoes, a wheel-barrow too, and an oil-skin round her hat,
> A blue bird's-eye deck'd her *dairy*[38] fine, as she *mizzled* through Temple-bar,
> Of vhich side of the vay, I cannot tell, but she *bon'd*[39] it from a Tar!
> Singing—Fol-lol-lol, de rol-lol-lol, de rol-lol-lol de lido!

Again, while many prefer attending to hear the elevated judgments delivered by the LORD CHANCELLOR; others listening to the wit and eloquence of CANNING, and to the solid oratory and comprehensive mind of BROUGHAM; thousands in the Metropolis are to be seen setting at defiance wind, weather, and even property, enjoying beyond description the humour and antics of CALEB

---

37   A knowing Cyprian.
38   Bosom
39   Stole

BALDWIN's *bull* upon Tothil Downs.

It should seem, then, that TASTE is everything in "this *here* LIFE!" but it is also observed to be of so meretricious a nature to its admirers, that it is as perplexing to fix a decisive hold upon "good taste," as to take into custody the "will-o'-the-wisp," that plays such whimsical tricks with the benighted traveller: and, perhaps, after all our researches and anxiety to obtain this desideratum of character, it matters but little to the mass of society in London, whether the *relish* for this chameleon sort of article is obtained over a quartern of *three outs* of Hodge's *full proof* to complete a bargain of "lively soles" at Billingsgate, before peep of day, by *Poll Fry*, so that happiness is the result; or, whether it is realised with all qualities of a barometer by Mr HAZLITT, in the evening lolling at his ease upon one of *Ben Medley's*[40] elegant couches, enjoying the reviving comforts of a good *tinney*,[41] smacking his *chaffer*[42] over a glass of old hock, and topping his *glim*[43] to a *classic* nicety, in order to throw a *new light* upon the elegant leaves of ROSCOE's "Life of Lorenzo de Medici," as a *composition* for a NEW LECTURE at the Surrey Institution. This is also LIFE IN LONDON.

A *peep* at Bow Street Office—a *stroll* through Westminster Abbey—a *lounge* at the Royal Academy—an hour passed with the Eccentrics—a *strut* through the lobbies of the Theatres, and a *trot* on Sundays in Rotten Row, in calculation, have all turned to good account. Even, if out of wind, and compelled to make a *stand still*[44] over the Elgin marbles at the British Museum, it will

---

40 A well-known hero in the Sporting World, from his determined contest with the late pugilistic phenomenon, *Dutch Sam*. Distinguished also as a *good judge* in trotting matches, and, at one period of his life, for having one of the *fastest* trotting horses in the kingdom; likewise in making *stylish couches* for the *easy* moments of the Fancy: this part of society always making it a decided point, when any opportunity offers in trade, to give each other a *turn*,—*i.e.,* anxious to promote the interest of each other. However, if Mr Hazlitt is not viewed as an admirer of "The Fancy," it will not be denied that few gentlemen have had more to do with the *"imagination"* than Mr H.
41 Fire.
42 The tongue.
43 A candle.
44 Poor Jerry's rustic simplicity must be excused in making a stand still

be found the time has not been misapplied.

Washing the *ivory* with a prime *screw*[45] under the *spikes* [46] in Saint George's Fields, or in tossing off, on the sly, some *tape*[47] with a *pal* undergoing a *three months' preparation*[48] to come out as a new member of society, is a scene that develops a great deal of the human heart.

> O Thou! whatever title is most dear,
> Among the many that salute thine ear,
> Join with thy brothers, Jack, with the dear friends,
> Whose fed applause thy wit and wine commends,
> My dearest Jack, with that same mawkish wench,
> *Jacko* at Longs, and *Captain* in the bench!
>
> Now let us analyse, but not too loud,
> If wise—the composition of this crowd,
> Made up from native soil and foreign clime,
> Of waste, of folly, accident, and crime,
> Here join the speculator and the fool,
> Gray-beards and youngsters rather fit for school
> (At least, for any school but this alone,
> Where college vices in the shade are thrown),
> Of pugilists, of haberdashers, jugglers,
> Horse-jockeys, swindlers, Bond-street beaux, and smugglers;
> By hollow friendship some in prison thrown,
> By others' follies *some*, MORE by their own.
> Here struts another, who his tradesmen's dues
> Disburses to the inmates of the stews;
> That lavishes a decent household's cost
> In wassail' mid his low retainers lost,
> 'Mid slaves, whose fawning pays him for his meat,
> Who mock the vanity that lets them eat,
> Here ruin'd lawyers ruin'd clients meet;
> Here doctors their consumptive patients greet,
> Sick of one malady that mocks all skill,
> Without the true specific golden pill.
> Here *finish'd* tailors, never to be paid,

---

over those hieroglyphics, when it is well known that several distinguished scholars of university pedigree have been dead beat as to giving anything like an accurate explanation of those precious relics of antiquity. The pious, liberal, and enlightened Dr Adam Clarke, of the Wesleyan connexion of Methodists, it is said, has displayed the greatest talents towards illuminating this hard subject.

45   A turnkey.

46   Belonging to the King's Bench, formerly called ELLENBOROUGH's *teeth;* but now ABBOTT's.

47   Gin. But spirituous liquors not being admitted into any prison, they are disguised under various appellations.

48   *Whitewashing;* but this old phrase is now nearly obsolete.

> Turn eyes on many a coat themselves have made;
> And bailiffs, caught by their own arts at last,
> Meet those their *capias* yesterday made fast.
> There walks a youth, whose father, for reform.
> Has shut him up where *countless* vices swarm:
> But little is that parent skill'd to trace
> The springs of action,—little knows the place,
> Who sends an ailing mind to where disease
> Its inmost citadel of health may seize.
> Faint are the calls of decency, when broad
> And naked Vice can show her front unawed;
> Where bold and bad examples lead the way,
> And every hour facilities betray:
> Oh, never yet was youth's unstrengthen'd mind
> *Made pure by herding with the baser kind!*

Again, hundreds of individuals in the Metropolis think *it* no loss of time, and feel as much interest in matching their *tykes* at JEM ROLFE's amphitheatre for a *quid* or two, or in drawing the badger at HARLEQUIN BILLY's menagerie, and boasting of the goodness and breed of their dogs, as my Lord CARE-FOR-NOTHING does in relating the pedigree of his high-mettled cattle, and talking with the *louters* and jockeys at Newmarket;

> In Black-boy Alley I've a *ken*,
> A *tyke* and a fighting-cock,
> A saucy, tip-slang, *moon-eyed* hen,
> Who oft mills *Doll* at block.

While the entire happiness of others, it should seem, consists in diving night after night into the *Cellar*[49] to hear a good chaunt; although emitting volumes of smoke like a furnace, and crowded together like the Black Hole in Calcutta, yet no inconvenience appears to be felt (and who, like their betters at routes, prefer rooms crowded to suffocation, than to experience what is termed *ennui*, arising from ease and comfort); and many of the singers, who from their "*good fellow*" traits have brought themselves into the last stage of a consumption, acting up to an old saying—"a short life and a merry one!" and throwing off, with the utmost *sang-froid*, that

---

[49] Spring Gardens.

CHAPTER II.

> Bright glory's a trifle, and so is ambition,
> I hate a proud heart and a lofty condition:
> Let princes reign over us with insolent disdain;
> Oh, give to me, or send to me, my bottle and my friend,
> In a little snug room, so neat and so trim,
> Oh, there will I enjoy my bottle and my friend.

There are also numbers of individuals in London who feel as much (indeed more) interest in the *election* of a *Most Noble Grand* to the chair, than a return of a member to Parliament; and whose whole evenings are continually occupied in *toddling*, as it is termed, from one lodge to another, in paying a *wisit,* and drinking the health of brother *Wice* at the ODD FELLOWS.

It may also be witnessed, that if the ODD FELLOWS in higher life are not *toddling* from one house to another, exactly upon the same sort of pursuit, it might be said, their *precious* time is equally disposed of to as *good* an account in driving from rout to rout, putting in "an appearance," giving a *nod*, and then rapidly making their *exit*.

> We see in splendid drawing-rooms the GREAT
> *Squeeze in* and then *squeeze out* again in state!
> As far removed from comfort as from mirth,
> The *dullest*, HOTTEST, COLDEST beings on earth.

LIFE IN LONDON affords such a great variety of examples, and *how* to get a "bit of bread" *honestly*, that whatever wonder it may excite in the provinces, it is quite a *routine* matter-of-fact in the Metropolis, that numerous persons, who are *obscured* in their beds the whole of the day, actually get their *living* in "Hell"[50] in the course of the night:—

> From Autumn to Winter, from Winter to June,
> The flat and the *sharp* must still play the same tune.
> What confusion of titles and persons we see
> Amongst gamesters, who spring out of ev'ry degree;
> From the PRINCE to the *pauper* all panting for play,
> Their fortune, their time, and their life pass away:
> Just as mingled are PIGEONS; for 'tis no rebuke
> For a GREEK to *pluck all*, from a *groom* to a *duke.*

---

50   A gambling-house.

From the many *tricks* and *fancies* the inhabitants of this great Metropolis are subject to, it seems some poet has humorously described *London* as "*the Devil!*" The contrasts are so fine and delightful—so marked with light and shade—and, upon the whole, offer such an extensive volume of intelligence, that the peruser must be ignorant indeed if something of importance does not fasten upon his mind, and which may, at some future period, be applied with success. However, it is not from hearing the amateurs cry out, *"Bravo!"* and *"Encore!"* at the Hanover Square Concert Rooms, that a knowledge of music is to be acquired; and it is not in witnessing great numbers of society swallow *blue ruin* like water, at the *gin-spinners*[51] that the whole of the lower orders in the Metropolis are to be libelled and traduced; neither is it from beholding that description of *bons vivants,* whose peculiar enjoyment consists in *flooring* the watchman at midnight, that "seeing Life" can be said to have its advantages. And it is not because hundreds who have been locked out of their lodgings have praised the facility of a key that admits them without any reproof; nor is it in hailing a fountain where the streams of pleasure are of so accommodating and magical a nature that the HOT are ultimately *cooled,* but more frequently where the *cold* are soon made too hot. No. Life in London is intended to show that individuals ought not to be too confident or too precise; but, above all, it affords them the opportunity of appreciating the advantages that experience holds forth, not to look down upon their fellow-creatures with contempt; and also to avoid the following severe satire:—

> But then I'm told again that grandeur's sore
> At owning obligations to the poor:—
> Such favours cut no figure in discourse:
> She thinks she might as well thank dogs and cats
> For finding partridges and catching rats;
> And say "I'm much obliged t' ye," to a horse.
> Lo, to the great we breathe the sigh in vain;
> A zephyr murm'ring through the hollow walls;
> Our tear that tries to melt their souls, the rain
> That printless on the rock of ages falls.

---

51   Wine-Vaults

Chapter II.

Life in London is also to admire the good and to avoid the vicious; but, never to entertain an idea, that, however bad and depraved some individuals may appear to be, they are past any attempt to reclaim them from their evil ways; and likewise to bear in mind, that "it is never too late to mend."[52] To get "out into the world," or "seeing Life," is not merely an empty phrase upon every person's tongue, but it is an actual object in view. The father urges its necessity to his son—the uncle talks of its value to his nephew,— and the aunt mentions it to her niece as an object worthy of the highest consideration; and, in short, it is a paramount idea with all persons who have under their care, and who feel anxiously towards the promotion of youth. It is, however, not absolutely necessary to a man's salvation, or as the only road to

---

52   On the trial of *George Barrington,* a most celebrated *genteel* pickpocket, the Judge, in passing the sentence of the law upon him, a few years since, at the Old Bailey, observed, 'that after the abilities displayed on that and former days by the prisoner, and the numerous hair-breadth escapes by which his life had been saved, what important advantages they might have proved, if laudably exerted for the benefit of society; and yet the application of those talents had been perverted to his utter disgrace and the detestation of mankind." To which Barrington, with a deal of pathos, replied, "that, unfortunately for him, it had been admitted he possessed sufficient knowledge to convince him the mode of life he pursued was wrong—that he also was not destitute of abilities—yet, alas! he had never experienced any friendly hand held out to him, whereby George Barrington might have been enabled to regain *that* situation which he once possessed, but now, so unhappily was lost! No cheering asylum to receive him, where those vicious propensities might soon have been corrected, if not completely eradicated; and from whence he might have attained a CHARACTER. In joining society again, he might then have become, as it were a new man; but, instead of that much wished-for circumstance, the finger of scorn was pointed at him; shunned by the world, so as to preclude all possibility of an impartial intercourse with mankind, and his failings eternally blazoned abroad,—where was his alternative? Compelled to return to *that* way of life, which might even be disgustful and inimicable to his feelings. Had this not have been the case, he could assure the learned Judge with truth, that the afflicting and unhappy situation of which he was the miserable victim of that day be should never have experienced, in being torn from a beloved partner and innocent offspring, added to the dreadful recollection, in being transported from his native country, to spend the remainder of his days in bitterness and regret." On Barrington's arrival at Botany Bay, he obtained a situation of considerable trust, where his universal good conduct obliterated his former failings, and he lived and died regretted; portraying a striking example, that, however corrupt and infamous human nature may be at times, no channel should be left unopened, where at least REFORMATION may be attempted, if not completely effected.

make his fortune, that he should pay a visit to London, like the Mohammedans, who are compelled to undertake a pilgrimage once in their lives to do homage before the tomb of Mahomet at Mecca; any more than the assertion proves correct, that a man, born in England, who does not visit London, during his existence, dies "a fool."

It appears, then, that if a complete GRANDISON or a perfect *Joseph Andrews* are not to be met with in traversing the gay regions of St James's, nor a *Falkland* run against in the upper circles of fashion; yet, still it is a most instructive path for improvement; and the advantages of the *suaviter in modo* and the *fortiter in re* are discovered in the highest perfection. For more wit, higher learning, truer courage, superior accomplishments, better breeding, nobler souls, more splendid talents, greater liberality of sentiment, dignity of mind, and finer feeling, than adorn the nobility and gentry of the Metropolis of England, cannot be found, if equalled, in any nation of the world. Nor can it be refuted, that, throughout the middling classes of society in London, to the very brink of want and dire necessity, the highest independence of character is displayed. All of these classes are to be explored with the finest results to an intelligent mind; and while, on the one hand, *roars of laughter* are excited from the ridicule of surrounding circumstances; yet, on the other, traits of the highest sensibility have been discovered, and the *"big tear,"* rich in effect, seen silently stealing down the iron cheek of some debauchee, who had thought himself immovable upon all appeals to his feelings, yet found to be vulnerable when the secret and irresistible touches of nature have suddenly broke in upon his dissipated pursuits.

CHAPTER III.

A Short Sketch of the Author's Talents in taking a Likeness; or, in other words (and, perhaps, far more appropriate), a Pen-and-Ink Drawing of Corinthian TOM.

> 'Man may be happy if he will!'
> I've said it often, and I think it still:
> Doctrine to make the million stare!

IT IS NOT absolutely necessary to introduce our hero with a flourish of drums and trumpets; neither has it been thought essentially requisite that he should make his entrance upon the stage under the pompous *preparatory* air of—

"See, the conquering hero comes!"

yet, perhaps, it might be deemed equally as improper for him to *rush in,* from the side wings, abruptly, before the audience, without making some sort of a bow, or, like poor vulcan,[53] drop *ruddy* from the sky before the spectators; therefore, it may be presumed, that very few persons, if any, will have the temerity to deny the advantages resulting from *prepossession* or good-breeding; nor attempt to refute the incalculable benefits attendant on

---

53   This may perhaps rather prove an *ominous* simile. Vulcan, it is said, was thrown by Jupiter over the battlements of heaven; but let us hope that all "sorts of Life" may be completely at a *stand still,* and fun and gig be banished from all ranks of society, before TOM shares such a fate among the CORINTHIANS. But it cannot be.

a "good *introduction*"[54] to society in general. Indeed, *prepossession*, in many instances, has obtained such a strong hold-fast, that it is never totally erased from the *mind;* and even the recollection of it is frequently re-lighted up at the shrine of departed excellence with greater fire than such impression had first created. Then, if *effect* were my principal object in view, and I were permitted to make a choice of an impressive situation for CORINTHIAN TOM to take his stand, it should be after the manner of KEMBLE[55] in *Coriolanus*, at the base of the statue of Mars, in the hall of Tullus Aufidius, his greatest enemy:—

> Illustrious stranger, for thy high demeanour
> Bespeaks thee such,—who art thou? what is thy name?
> Thy face bears a command in't;
> Thou show'st a noble vessel.

CORINTHIAN TOM, it will be *ultimately* perceived, was not a mere hero on paper—he was not the refined, substantially correct (*imagined* being) Sir Charles Grandison, who, it should seem, was almost afraid of a splash of dirt operating against his person, and who also moved through society by rule and measure, and did nothing *wrong*. In fact such a character was never met with in real life. Neither was TOM a *Lovelace* in principle, or a *Joseph Andrews* from nature. No: he partook more of the qualities of a *Ranger;* and he even possessed some of the loose failings of a *Booth*. CORINTHIAN TOM was not as *invulnerable* as a CATO, nor as sentimental as a ROUSSEAU; but he would have kicked a *Joseph Surface* out of doors. To hypocrisy and cant he was a most determined enemy. The pure love of a *Clementina* would have overpowered his heart, while, on the contrary, TOM might have laughed at, and even quizzed

---

54   The Metropolis, after all its great bustle, variety, and attractions, is little more than a mere *wilderness* to an individual without an "*introduction*" to good company. In genteel life it is considered as a *desideratum*.

55   If it is possible that Corinthian Tom should fail in proving his *claims* to the above title as *valid,* all hands will unite in loud acclamations in admitting the appellation of Corinthian Jack to be genuine. Even our much-admired finished Tom cannot fill up the *chasm* left in the theatrical world, by the secession of this great performer from the stage. He was indeed a *Corinthian* of an actor.

a Miss *Byron*.⁵⁶ Although *One of the* FANCY, he was not a *fancy-man:* yet TOM was as much at home in blowing a cloud, listening to a night-row charge at a watch-house, as he proved himself an adept in all the luxuriant, voluptuous movements when waltzing at Almack's; yet our hero was no *Dandy;*⁵⁷ neither was TOM viewed as one of the wonders of the world; but he was denominated an *out-and-outer*⁵⁸ as far as the character of a man went. TOM was an only son, and became possessed of an immense property at the demise of his parent. His father was the architect of his own fortune; and had amassed together great quantities of wealth. TOM, according to the phrase of the nursery, was termed "a *darling;*" and while his father lost hours in calculating to a nicety the interest that a farthing might produce if well laid out, he was perplexing his brains after the newest fashion, or in humming the admired strains of the last new opera! TOM had been reared completely under the auspices of his *Mamma;* and his tender parent's ambition was, that her son, as she expressed it, should be the "finished gentleman!"—and that his ideas should not be restrained by the dry plodding of business, she encouraged as much as possible that he should mix with the upper ranks of society, in order that he might attain the completion of her most anxious project; and

---

56   Both of these heroines belonged to Richardson at one time; but, to speak like an artist, they were not both in KEEPING by him.
57   As I sincerely hope that this work will shrink from the touch of a pastry-cook, and also avoid the foul uses of a trunk-maker, but, on the contrary, that it may have "Life in London" long, very long after its author shall have been consigned to "that bourne from whence no traveller returns"—I feel induced now to describe, for the benefit of posterity, the pedigree of a Dandy in 1820. The Dandy was got by *Vanity* out of *Affectation*—his dam, *Petit-Maitre* or *Maccaroni*—his grandam, *Fribble*— his great-gran dam, *Bronze*—his great-great grandam, *Coxcomb*—and his earliest ancestor, Fop. His uncle *Impudence*—his three brothers *Trick*, *Humbug*, and *Fudge!* and allied to the extensive family of the *Shuffletons*. Indeed, this *Bandbox* sort of creature took so much the lead in the walks of fashion, that the Buck was totally missing; the Blood vanished; the Tippy not to be found; the Go out of date; the Dash not to be met with; and the *Bang-up* without a leader, at fault, and in the background. It was only the CORINTHIAN that remained triumphant—his excellence was of such a *genuine* quality, that all *imitation* was left at an immeasurable distance.
58   A phrase in the sporting world for *goodness;* a sort of climacteric— the *ne plus ultra.*

truth obliges us to declare, a readier scholar was never witnessed. Tom required no arguments to persuade or rod to enforce those precepts; as he seemed to feel all that his fond *Mamma* wished to inspire. His genius appeared directed to the same source; and Tom soon gave ample proofs of the rapid improvement he had made in the fashionable sciences. His Mamma just lived long enough to see him enter into the dazzling career with all the avidity and thoughtlessness of a youth at nineteen: his father survived his mother but a few years, and at the age of twenty-five Tom found himself in the possession of fine estates, plenty of money, and no one to control his inclinations. And largely did he participate in the pleasures of the great world. With a strong constitution, an ardent imagination, and full spirits, solicited and soliciting,—Tom was the gayest of the gay! Pleasure was his idol—novelty his ruling passion—and to gratify this propensity every avenue was traced that led to it. LIFE, in all its various shapes, he was determined to see; and whether he was animatedly engaged in squeezing the hand of some lovely countess at St James's, or passing an hour with a poor costard-monger in the back settlements of St Giles's, Tom was never at fault! Fastidiousness was not in his composition; and though he had numerous failings—yet he possessed many traits that were of the most pleasing and agreeable nature: MANKIND were his hobbyhorse—and however hard at times he rode them, still he kept in view that most liberal and dignified sentiment of one of the most unfortunate, but distinguished poets—

"A MAN is a MAN for a' that!"

Tom's time was so incessantly occupied, and his mind so overwhelmed with passing subjects, that reflection was quite out of the question. His decisions were too momentary, and his generosity was as often too much in the extremes, as his errors were multiplied by the instantaneousness of his disposition. CORINTHIAN Tom was not vicious from principle; although it might be urged his morals would not bear the strictest investigation of propriety, yet they were to be attributed more, perhaps, to the light and airy dispositions of his "companions," than as emanating from himself! Having no control to contend against, or being in dread of rebuke from dependent relatives, he ranged wherever he pleased, and anything like formality was never suffered to interfere with his pleasures. When tired of his excursions he retired to rest; and when recovered from the fatigues they might have occasioned, he rose to pursue them with fresh vigour.

> If e'er a pleasant mischief sprang to view,
> At once o'er hedge and ditch away he flew,
> Nor left the game till he had ran it down!

Tom's manners were pleasing, and he was possessed of that sort of ingenuous address and intelligent conversation (adapting it to the capacities of the various companies in which he intermixed), that lie scarcely ever . failed in prepossessing himself strongly in the favour of his hearers. His form, though it might not be compared with that of Adonis, was nevertheless manly and elegant: fashionable in his apparel, and always well-dressed, his appearance proved attractive. Neither was he destitute of what are denominated accomplishments, although some of them were not to be acquired at the CHARTER HOUSE, or the UNIVERSITIES of OXFORD and CAMBRIDGE; and, although this may perhaps call forth a sneer from the fastidious, the many "rows" in which TOM had distinguished himself by superior science, in rescuing himself from the rude grasp of the "guardians of the night," forcibly evinced the necessity of his taking those *degrees* termed *a la Belcher!* to prevent himself from being *floored* by those of a more athletic nature. He was fond of a little sport, and, at times, not very nice in *"kicking up a lark"* in order to produce it, and *"an ugly customer"* was frequently the result; but, to avoid being *"milled,"* it was expedient that he should be able to be on the alert, by giving the Marrowbone *stop*, or, if necessary, be *"missing"* before his antagonist had recovered the use of his pins from the shock. As an amateur in this Old English science, no one used the gloves with greater neatness than did TOM, and he has often puzzled some of the first-rate professors of the gymnastic art to be able to ward off the activity with which he could put in a one, two; and it was their opinion that, had TOM entered the ring as a public candidate for boxing fame, he would have proved himself nothing but a *good one!*

In handling the *ribbons*, and turning the corner of a street with his barouche and four, no mail-coachman, however experienced, could surpass him for the rapidity and neatness with which he executed this most *important* circumstance in the "annals of driving;" in fact, he was a perfect hero with the whip; a first-rate *Fiddler:*

> Prime of Life to "*go it!*" where's the place like London:
> Four-in-hand to-day, to-morrow you may be undone;
> "Where the duke and the'prentice they dress much the same,
> You cannot tell the difference, excepting by the name!
> Then push along with four-in-hand, while others drive at random,
> In buggy, gig, or dog-cart, in curricle or tandem!

and, upon the turf, there were few heroes who were better acquainted with the manoeuvres of the "sweaters and trainers," or was sooner "down" to a cross and jostle, than Corinthian TOM.

Though not a professed gamester, nor, indeed, addicted to gambling, or fond of it, still he had mixed among *professional* gentry enough to be "*up*" to their tricks and fancies, so as not to be made "*a pigeon.*"

However animatedly TOM might have sported his money on the race-course, upon a *Smolensko,* or backed the *Phenomena* trotting mare for a large stake; interested himself upon the *fleetness* of his greyhounds; admired and been delighted with the courageous properties of the English bull-dog; felt all alive when viewing the combats of the prize-ring; extolled the *staunchness* of his pointers, and praised the *well breaking-in* of his spaniels; or even *smiled* with indifference at the rolls of *soft* which his most captivating FANCY-PIECE[59] drew from him repeatedly; yet gambling-houses made no impression upon his feelings, as to the object of gain: he rose above this sordid passion, and felt that a real gentleman ought to have higher pursuits in view, in which he might wish to

---

59   A sporting phrase for a "bit of *nice* GAME," kept in a *preserve* in the suburbs. A sort of BIRD OF PARADISE!

excel. It was, however, true that curiosity had induced him to visit them; in fact, Tom had a great desire to *see* everything that gave a new feature to human nature; but he soon perceived that by one unlucky throw, even if the thing depended upon a *fair chance*, urged on in a desperate moment, he might have been obscured from the upper circles for ever! and this made him make up his mind, that, of all the "suits" he might be ruined upon, GAMING should be the last, and, in a *slangly* sarcastic manner, winding up the sentence, that it is "a *good flat* that is never *down*." But, as *accommodation* was Corinthian Tom's motto, in order to dissipate an idle hour, or to steer clear from proving disagreeable to a company who felt inclined for a little amusement by a friendly game, no one joined it with more alacrity than Tom did but he went no further.

Though he was not competent, perhaps, to have been made a Lord Chancellor, or to have been elected as one of the heads of a college, nor had he ability enough to fulfil the situation of a prime minister: yet Tom was not so totally absorbed by pleasure as to be indifferent to the means by which they acquired that great eminence in society; nay, on the contrary, he had paid every attention to passing subjects, in order to preserve him from the imputation of being ignorant as to the general movements of society. However, he made it an invariable rule never to profess a knowledge of any science or circumstance, from which, upon a more minute inquiry, he might be detected and held up to ridicule for his vain-boasting pretensions. He was also well aware, that, in PRIVATE, men were all alike subject to the workings of nature, irritated or pleased by the most trifling circumstances; and that SITUATION was every thing. "View," said Tom, "the judge, who, from his gravity and solemn demeanour upon the bench, imposed a reverential awe upon all those around him in public; look at him amidst his family and domestics, and even in the circle of his friends, you will find that his *feelings* are predominent. And, is it not well known, that a bishop, who, in an elaborate charge to a diocese, had exhorted the clergy to humility and temperance, and also his flock to patience, has been indicted for an assault? It has, likewise, been of considerable notoriety, that an eminent counsellor, who had endeavoured by the most energetic appeal to the feelings of a jury in calling down heavy damages for the enormity of *crim. con.* has proved himself an *automaton* to his own reasoning, and been found guilty of the same crime! Observe," said TOM, "the player, who has often and often electrified the audience, when in the personification of virtuous characters, by receiving tumultuous approbation for the dignified and inspiring sentiments which he has uttered—yet, as to *himself*, he has received no advantage from such experience, that 'virtue needs only to be seen to be admired;' but has thrown off the character with the dress, losing sight of all that he has so animatedly promulgated."

Among the modest fair ones, CORINTHIAN TOM was an object of more than a little attention; his extreme partiality for the ladies had introduced him to many singular adventures. He was polite, generous, and good-humoured; always lively in their presence, and abounding with that sort of "small talk" and anecdote which banished *ennui* from any place wherever he might be situated, and communicated pleasure to the female bosom; but as to deep research and scientific conversation, however they might exist in the company of some females, he did not look for such solid arguments in those circles, yet contented himself with the minor subjects of conversation, upon which he could descant with the tender part of the creation with ease and freedom.

> That I have often been in love, deep love,
> A hundred doleful ditties plainly prove;
> By marriage never have I been disjointed;
> For matrimony deals prodigious blows;
> And yet for this same stormy state, God knows.
> I've groan'd—and, thank my stars, been disappointed.

His pretensions, TOM, it seems, always wished it to be understood, were not to the title of "learned," but he had no objection to the appellation of "a merry fellow!" and if a neat pun, smart repartee, or jolly song were any proofs of it, he certainly possessed them in a tolerable degree. With a certain class of the sex, better known by the higher order of "*Cyprians*" the weight of TOM's purse had gone before him; and in his visits to the Opera, the Theatres, and other places of public resort, lures were held out to ensnare, captivate, and secure him; and if he was not steeled against the temptations he had to encounter, but became an easy prey by too great a liberality of disposition, it might, perhaps, be attributed more to a defect in nature than any radical system of depravity. However, be that as it might, his character was not exempt from the term of a LIBERTINE, and a title of that description, whether just or unjust, is very rarely erased from that person who happens to lay under its reproach; indeed, it too generally descends with him to the grave: but, whether the denomination of a *libertine* was to prove as a passport to future gallantries or to exclude him from the company of the modest and rational of mankind is yet to be inquired into.

> Money's a rattling sinner, to be sure:
> Like the sweet Cyprian girl (we won't say whore),
> Is happy to be frequently employ'd,
> And not content by *one* to be enjoy'd:
> Yet like the great ones, with fastidious eye,
> Seems of *inferior* mortals rather *shy*!

TOM was too much in the "hey-day of blood," it should seem, to be called aside from his favourite pursuits by casual remarks upon any particular part of his behaviour; and it might be observed, that, if his claim to *character* had ever been rightly appreciated, no question would have arisen but that he was certainly more entitled to be ranked among "choice spirits" than classed with "rigid moralists!" Like all other fashionable men, he *professed* to entertain the highest sense of honour, as being one of those most essential requisites that positively no gentleman can do without; and little doubt will be expressed but he felt its vast importance in society, except, perhaps, in that material point of view where it is so much *professed* and so little acted upon by *gentlemen*, to the—seduced female!

It is but justice to remark that, however TOM revelled away in all the luxuries of ease and fashion, on many prominent occasions, where actions speak instead of words, he never lost sight of that line of conduct which was necessary to constitute and support the character of A MAN.

This must suffice for a first *sitting:* in fact, it can only be looked at as a mere outline of CORINTHIAN TOM. The author must be upon "good terms with himself" indeed to have the vanity to suppose that he could have taken a *"finished likeness"* of such a hero the first time. No, no. His readers are too good judges to be imposed upon (if even attempted) by such an impudent artifice. The author, it is true, intends to do a good deal; but he does not mean to "out-Herod Herod!" He is also too anxious lest any sneer should escape from the critic, that the "mountain in labour" has only brought forth a mouse. CORINTHIAN TOM will, therefore, have the kindness to sit a second time; nay, a third, fourth, fifth, and even a sixth time, if it be thought necessary, in order to accomplish a perfect portrait. A PORTRAIT, it is hoped, that may bid defiance to the stare, the shrugs, the sneers, the ridicule, the grimaces, and the *cant* of criticism, *whenever* it has the honour of being placed in its "true light" by the hanging committee belonging to the Royal Academy.

One more observation, and this chapter is at an end. By way of an apology, or something like an excuse, for the delay of artists in general, it should be recollected, that the *likeness* of Corinthian Tom is not taken with a *machine*: and, notwithstanding the numerous lights and shades it may require—the frequent rubbings out—the various tints—the fine workings up, required to do justice to a head, nay a figure, altogether of no common quality, and the artist often out of humour with himself upon the arduous task he has undertaken, yet a promise is here given, and it will be fulfilled, that the likeness, such as it is, of Corinthian Tom, will be presented to his numerous friends, long, very long, before the usual time allowed to that most accomplished delineator of the "human face divine," Lawrence.[60]

---

[60] If report speak true, it is considered a great favour indeed to procure a likeness from this distinguished portrait-painter in less than five years. But then, when it is obtained, it is invaluable!

CHAPTER IV.

The great Advantages resulting from a Man's Father being "born" before him, illustrated with some curious Facts; and also pointing out, that a true Knowledge of the World is gamed only by Conversation, and that the Manners of every Rank must be seen in order to be known.

*The child who many fathers share
Hath seldom known a father's care!*

HOWEVER SINGULAR IT may seem, it appears the unfortunate SAVAGE attributed all his miseries to his having *too much* FATHER and literally *no* MOTHER. What pleasure might not the world have derived from his muse, if *they* had contended who should have supported or provided an ample fortune for him. His genius then might have soared above every obstacle, and his productions ranked him with the first poets of the age in which he lived. But that unnatural woman, to whom he owed his wretched existence, not only imbittered all his moments, and damped those ripening talents, which, notwithstanding the obscurity of his early days, burst forth with such uncommon ability, but also left him in the dark respecting the knowledge of his parent. In short, she ultimately rendered him a perfect outcast of society. Deprived of his *legal*[61] FATHER; tricked out of his *would-be*[62] PARENT, and debased and deserted by his

---
61   In point of law, the Earl of Macclesfield.
62   In point of fact, Earl Rivers.

mother,[63] who had a much greater claim to the title of tigress, the life of SAVAGE was one continued scene of misfortune and depravity. Presuming on the *nobility* of his blood, he was thoughtless, extravagant, dissipated, and insolent. His mind was alternately distracted with poverty and pride. It is true that his great talents gained him admirers, but his manners and satiric qualities never realised him a friend. He was a beggar in fortune, having no regular mode of subsistence without depending upon the charity of the great, or in trusting to his literary exertions for his daily support.

Widely different is the following circumstance, though equally important to our portraiture of LIFE IN LONDON. It is a pleasure to observe that, notwithstanding the *etiquette* of polished society, an instance is to be found in which the feelings of humanity triumphed over the baneful effects of prejudice, as will be seen in witnessing a contention displayed by two gentlemen for the title of *father* to a being whom the rigidity of the *law* allows to have no relation.

A Duke (once celebrated for his numerous gallantries, but who, within a few years past, has been consigned to the tomb of his ancestors), it seems, was so fascinated with the *agile* movements, united to other powerful charms, of a celebrated opera dancer, that he immediately offered her a *carte blanche*. The proposals were accepted without any hesitation; and this elegant "little bark" of *frailty* soon became the acknowledged *chere-amie* of the Duke. However the lady might be dazzled, in the first instance, with the grandeur of the Duke's title,— the splendour of his fortune,—the

---

[63] The Countess of Macclesfield. The infamous conduct of this woman towards her son is of so *fiend-like* a description that she appears more in the shape of an *imaginary* demon of romance, held up as an object of terror to deter other females from committing such outrageous acts against parental affection and humanity, than as an actual being, once moving in the upper circles of society. Indeed, if the cruel facts alluded to had not been the theme of public conversation at the time they occurred (1717), they would scarcely have obtained belief at the present period. It is one of the most diabolical portraits of a female ever seen; yet it is said that this countess, at one time of her life, was viewed as a most accomplished lady, and also entertaining the highest sense and notions of honour. It is rather singular to remark, that she proclaimed her own *infamy;* her marriage was dissolved by act of parliament, and the whole of her fortune, which was great, repaid her.

taste of his equipage,—the magnificence of his mansion, and with participating in all the luxuries of his enormous wealth; yet, it should seem, she was not totally *insensible* to the powerful attractions which graced the person of the late G. S———, Esq., of whom it was said, that, for elegance of manners and brilliancy of wit, he eclipsed every other competitor in the fashionable circles during his career. This *tender-hearted* Italian, possessing all the warmth of her native soil, and from not having clearly explained to her the *Old* English notions of *constancy;* neither restricted by any dull forms of propriety—but perfectly a free agent in regard to the softer passions, it is said, was not niggardly in bestowing her favours, in return for the polite attention of so accomplished a *gallant*.

> In vain I turn around to run away:
> Thine eyes, those basilisks, command my stay;
> Whilst through its gauze thy snowy bosom peeping,
> Seems to that rogue *interpreter* my eye,
> To heave a soft, desponding, tender sigh,
> Like gossamer, my thoughts of goodness sweeping.

The lady, at length, gave birth to a daughter; and, from the above intercourse, it appears, both of the heroes alluded to put in their claims to the title of "PAPA!" The Duke felt the weight of his own importance, and was completely satisfied in his mind that the "little innocent" belonged to his charge; and to his credit be it spoken, that whatever advantages were to be derived from education, good-breeding, and polite accomplishments, his grace most liberally bestowed upon his interesting *protégée:* nay more, he gave her a marriage-portion that few of the first ladies in the land could rival; and also united her with one of the highest families in the kingdom. At his death, he likewise left large fortunes for the whole of her children; besides rendering herself totally independent of her noble husband, from the immense estates and large sum of money he settled upon her. The late G. S———, Esq. at his death (which occurred several years before the noble Duke), to show that he possessed generosity as well as wit, also left the little "*love-child*" the agreeable present of £30,000, in order, it is said, that his *memory*, in whatever *doubtful* situation he stood towards her, might not be entirely forgotten by the child for whom he felt a parental affection.

The contrast between the above two characters is interestingly great. Poor SAVAGE, the *lawful* and un-lawful heir to a *peerage*, in consequence of his not being noticed by his relatives, was frequently glad to sleep night after night on a dust-hill, or to take refuge in a glass-house from the inclemency of the weather, having no regular place of residence to protect his unhappy frame. He also experienced all the horrors of mind in being sentenced to suffer death from an unfortunate quarrel, his life having been sworn away by a perjured prostitute; and the last scene of his "strange eventful history"[64] was wound up by an imprisonment, for a trifling debt, in Bristol gaol, where death put a period to all his calamities. While, on the contrary, the parental affection bestowed upon this unfortunate female, elevated her to the peerage, and she enjoyed a splendid situation in society as the Countess of———.

In the foregoing paragraph, it should seem, *too much* FATHER has been the subject; but in the following painful, yet interesting fact, it will be seen that an individual made his fortune without his knowing that he ever had had any "FATHER *or relative at all belonging to him*" Within the last fifty years, a person who had realised a fortune of upwards of £50,000, and who, it appeared, had been reared in the Foundling Hospital, felt such an unhappy *vacuum* in his mind, that he made known his distressing feelings by public advertisement; intimating that he wanted the society of some relative to enjoy his acquired wealth with him; and also offering a reward to any person who could give any information respecting his parents.

Not so with CORINTHIAN TOM; his father was born before him; or, as the old adage perhaps more tritely observes, TOM "was

---

64   The life and vicissitudes of this unfortunate poet, written by the late Dr Johnson, has long been pronounced to be one of the finest pieces of biography in the English language. It is a correct delineation of human nature, and ought to be read by every individual.

born with a silver spoon in his mouth;"[65] and POVERTY, that unwelcome visitor, was an unknown guest at the splendid mansion of his beloved sire. FORTUNE, it should seem, ushered TOM's entrance into the world: SPLENDOUR rocked his *cradle;* FUN, FROLIC, and FANCY, perched upon its top; and even LUXURY waited upon him in his *go-cart*. His golden leading-strings were under the guidance of TENDERNESS and REFINEMENT; and TOM could scarcely *lisp,* when ANXIETY, upon the utmost stretch, endeavoured to anticipate all his little wants. His infant tears too were instantly dried up by his attendant Acquiescence; and surly Contradiction[66] was forbid to cross his path, or even, upon any account, to thwart his wishes. Indeed, his childhood was one continued sunshine: no rude storms broke in upon his happy career; and, from the softness and serenity of his early days, his downy pillow might be compared to the exquisite repose of a bed of roses.

Year after year rolled on in the same luxuriant mode, and Tom had only to ask and to have! nay more, it was the study of all those persons placed around him to watch his motions and to provide everything that could, in the smallest degree, contribute to his happiness.

Tom was an only child, the heir to an immense fortune; but, by many of his parents' friends, Tom was characterised as a spoiled boy.

In short, Tom was born[67] to be a happy fellow, if the enjoyment of the "good things" of this world could have made him so. But some ill-natured or disappointed persons, it appears, assert these "good things" alone are not sufficient to ensure complete

---

65   It was Dean Swift's opinion that a fat sorrow is always better than a lean one! and, most surely, it will not be doubted but this authority is *orthodox*.

66   Lord Holland, the father of the late Right Hon. Charles James Fox, would never suffer that great orator to be contradicted in his infancy. The former statesman, it seems, entertained fears that it might break the rising spirit of his darling son. Some very curious and interesting anecdotes are extant respecting this mode of education adopted by Lord Holland. Corinthian Tom being also A LAD of great spirit, it is not unlikely but his father had a predilection for copying from so enlightened a *model*.

67   "*Born*" a gentleman. The mere idea is quite reviving, not merely to the lovers of pleasure, but also to the lovers of doing good.

happiness; more especially, if the proprietor does not know how to apply them to his own advantage.

> I like not the *blue-devil* hunting crew,
> I hate to drop the discontented jaw,
> Oh, let me NATURE's simple smile pursue,
> And PICK e'en PLEASURE *from a straw.*

If more riches are not the peculiar object in view, yet, perhaps, some trifling desire being left ungratified is too apt to create a degree of *restlessness* in the mind of the individual, that even the possession of the wealth of the mines of Peru could not remove. How frequently does it occur that the BOY *sighs* to become a man, under the anticipation of having his liberty, and being enabled to enjoy his *imaginary* pleasures uncontrolled; while, on the contrary, the MAN exclaims, with sincere regret, that "if his time was to come over again," with how much more profit, improvement, and happiness to himself, if not to others, would he employ it.

> The BOY and MAN an individual makes,
> Yet sigh'st thou now for apples and for cakes?
> Go, like the Indian, in another life
> Expect thy dog, thy bottle, and thy wife;
> As well as dream such trifles are assign'd,
> As toys and empires, for a godlike mind.
> Judge we by Nature? Habit can efface,
> Int'rest o'ercome, or Policy take place:
> By Actions? those Uncertainty divides:
> By Passions? these Dissimulation hides:
> OPINIONS? they still take a wider range:
> FIND, *if you can*, IN WHAT YOU CANNOT CHANGE.
> Manners with Fortunes, Humours turn with Climes,
> Tenets with Books, and Principles with Times.

The advantages resulting from "seeing the World," which had so often been the theme of discussion over the table of TOM's father, had, in a very high degree, excited the curiosity of our Hero. Mankind he had hitherto only seen in *perspective;* and that, added to ripening manhood and the close confinement, or rather unwearied attention of a private tutor, made him feel a most unconquerable thirst for a little practical experience with the human character. Tom's heart, in fact, panted for a more intimate connexion with society in general. It was most true, that he had nothing to render him unhappy; but still there was a something wanting that made him appear at times somewhat restless; notwithstanding, he had most liberally participated in every pleasure, as far as the limits of an anxious tutor and an amiable parent thought they could consistently allow. But this was not enough; and Tom ardently wished for the arrival of that day when he should be enabled to ramble amongst mankind without the fear of check or control, and also to shake off that restraint which had so strongly marked his boyish period,

Flattery, being so continually at Tom's elbow, operated rather as a kind of drawback to the exercise of his talents at this early part of his career; yet he was generally considered as a youth of great promise. NATURE, it should seem, had laid fast hold of him, and the impulse of the moment operated strongly upon his feelings: HUMANITY had instinctively showed itself in all his transactions, where this fine trait was necessary; and his composition and general deportment portrayed an active readiness to relieve the wants of his fellow-creatures.

> Sweet is the TALE, however strange its air,
> That bids the public eye *astonished* stare!
> Sweet is the TALE, howe'er uncouth its shape,
> That makes the world's wide mouth with wonder gape!
> Behold our infancies in TALES delight,
> That bolt like hedgehog quills the hair upright.
> Of ghosts how pleased is ev'ry child to hear;
> To such is Jack the Giant-killer dear!

Yet *distress*, to TOM, was like unto a pathetic tale which he had perused; and the mere idea of a hungry man, with no money in his pockets, counting the trees in St James's Park to beguile the *tedious* hour of dinner-time, to appease an empty stomach (which many worthy honest men have experienced), would have made TOM laugh heartily, as a sort of *creative* good joke, instead of believing that such *bitter* things could possibly have existence in a land of charity and benevolence.

Or, that a "*good fellow*," who, from the necessity of the moment, was compelled to *hide* his naked frame in bed, while some accommodating nymph of the tub *tenderly* [68] endeavoured, from the age and service of the article in question, to renovate the colour of an appendage once termed *a shirt*, that its owner might never have the appearance in public of wanting *clean linen* (which some wealthy men in the City of London nowadays would not hesitate to justify as fact, if the recollection of their poverty was not the most painful part of the memory), Tom would have asserted that any man who made so good a *shift* to obtain cleanliness ought never to want a piece of cloth to cover his body, or a bed to *hide* himself upon such a TRYING occasion.

On seeing the *soi-disant* "Bit of Blood," whose ideas of taste and elegance drove everything out of his head respecting the discharge of his expenses at a future period, but rendering his celerity necessary in crossing the streets to avoid the wandering

---

68   The following anecdote may, in a great degree, illustrate this *necessitous* point:—Mr Tony Le Brun, a *low* comedian, of some provincial notoriety, but particularly distinguished for his *dry* humour off the stage, and also for his *wet* qualities behind the glass, was engaged by the late Lord Barrymore, as Under-Prompter, to assist in conducting his Lordship's Private Theatricals at Wargrave, then in high repute in the fashionable world. With *ad*-dress Tony was abundantly supplied, but his *drapery* in general was rather *scanty*, and as to shirts in particular, he had but one, and that was literally a *unique*. As Mr Le Brun occasionally mingled in the dramatic scene as a *loathing* gentleman, it was expedient on such occasions to have that *solitary shirt* washed. Agreeably to such a measure, he leaped from his couch one morning in an unencumbered state of nature, and having dressed himself as genteelly as his wardrobe would admit (though his rotund body was unconscious of linen), and buttoned up his coat to his neck, to elude the *keen eye of impertinence*, he sent his shirt to the washerwoman to be got ready at a stated hour, and to be so highly *blanched* that it might rival snow. This indispensable point being settled, he attended the rehearsals as usual, and was very pompously giving his orders for the regulation of the devils in *Don Juan*, the stage being then crowded with ladies and gentleman (amateurs), when a little girl came behind the scenes with a message from the *blanchisseuse*, her mother:— "Mr Le Brun, my mammy has sent you your shirt." "What! has she washed it already, my dear, in two hours? damme, that is expedition!" "No, sir, she has not washed it," "Not washed it, you diminutive slut! what is the meaning of that!"   "My mammy says as how it is so old and rotten she is afraid it will rub to pieces in the washing-tub." "Poh, poh!" replied the abashed prompter, angrily, with a face as full of colours as a rainbow; "you are a very foolish child, and your mother is a greater fool who sent you: go back with it to your *soap-teazing dam*, and tell her, if she is ignorant of ways and means, I will instruct her; if the shirt is so *fine* that she is afraid of committing it to the tub with coarser vestments, bid her *pin it against the wall* and *throw water at it,*"

eyes of prying creditors, who not unfrequently pop all of a sudden on an old customer, and inquire after his long absence, with a familiarity rather embarrassing; CORINTHIAN Tom burst out in raptures, exclaiming, "that such a character ought to have been made an *Admiral*, for keeping so good a look-out after an enemy!"

On being told of "*a knowing Kid,*" whose desideratum in taking of lodgings was to have the accommodation of a key to let himself in, that he might not give any trouble; and then come home between two and three o'clock every morning, in order to avoid the pressing importunities of his talkative landlady, whose tongue was nearly worn-out in endeavoring to ascertain the finances of her most *interesting* lodger respecting the liquidation of her rent: such a hero, TOM observed, ought to have a PATENT granted to him for teaching women—*patience!*

And the "*White-washing* Buck,"[69] trying on his "ways and means," with the alluring sounds of a Nightingale, to *get the best,* in the first instance, of a few dashing tailors, bootmakers, and hatters, that he may be the better enabled, by his elegant "appearance," to impose, with the utmost *sang-froid,* upon society in general. *Punning,* with laughter, over his *cheap* wine, to his companions, at the *faith* of his tailor, in thus daily getting rid of both his *good* and *bad* habits; also at the almost forlorn-*hope* of the boot-maker, in ever expecting to overtake those *lively legs* he once had so accurately *measured:* and, likewise, in enjoying the idea of the *charity* of the hatter, whose anxiety chiefly consisted in showing his articles to be *waterproof,* in order that his customers might not be afraid of the *head-ache!* And then, by way of a *climax* to his wit, asking, with a *grin* upon his countenance, what man is worthy of existence in society who does not possess faith, hope, and charity. Such a *persuasive* genius, Tom asserted, who could thus *rig* himself out at the public's expense, could not fail in making a good *Prime*

---

69   A HERO (belonging to a most numerous family, in 1820), who gets *un-blushingly* rid of all his difficulties by a BILL OF INDEMNITY, granted to him for his *servitude* on board of "THE FLEET," for the short space of three months! WINE, of course, is *cheap* to such a hero; CLOTHES are of no expense to him; and as to *rent* and *taxes,* why he has nothing to do with them. He is an *invaluable* subject to his country, it must be admitted.

Minister! Or, a "SHABBY FELLOW" quilting a company where he had fared most sumptuously, when the *bill* was about to be settled, either by starting up and suddenly *boiling*, as if he had some prior engagement to fulfil; or, otherwise, shamming intolerably drunk, so as not to be *bored* by looking over long *items;* and also to prevent him from behaving *scaly* to the waiters by his getting rid of it altogether: TOM indignantly declared that such a contemptible *Sponge* ought always to be well *squeezed* in every company, and likewise *handed* out of society in general.

Nor did he forget the "NEAT ARTICLE," remarked for being a good time-ist in calling upon a very slight acquaintance at the juncture of meal-times, when good manners, though often painful in this case, compels the housekeeper to ask the "NEAT ARTICLE" to take a bit, after the well-known metropolitan compliment, "You may as well, as we have more than we can eat;" while his penetrating *liberal* rib, with looks as prepossessing as clouds before a thunderstorm, knowing the *value* of such *friendly* calls, fetches the "*Diddler*" a plate, to make him welcome, with activity like a person troubled with the gout, and observing by way of *sharpening* the appetite of the "NEAT ARTICLE," "that the lamb ought to be good, as it cost her husband the astonishing high price of per pound; but then he is so extravagant. Yet she did not mention it, very far from it, upon that account." He must be a "NEAT ARTICLE" indeed, TOM urged, that could endure such a *flattering* reception a second time.

But the history of the SPOUTERS,[70] and the various curious acts performed by this numerous class of persons in the Metropolis was a perfect *riddle* to Corinthian Tom. The idea of a mahogany table going up a *spout* to liquidate a man's rent, or a mirror to produce a joint of meat; and a new suit of clothes, after having given a hero a day's decent appearance, *vanishing,* by this sort of

---

70   TOM, it seems, completely mistook this term in the first instance, thinking it only applied to those persons who were attached to the drama, and who were, at different times, fond of declaiming detached sentences from SHAKSPEARE. But he was soon put right, on being informed, that it was a *long narrow spout,* which reached from the top of the house of the *Money-Lender* down to his counter, and through which the articles of property when *redeemed,* were conveyed, in order to facilitate business.

means, in order to make the first payment to a *tally* tailor, was a kind of *necromancy* he could not altogether comprehend, owing to Profusion and Elegance, his companions. It is true, Tom was as *learned* as the routine of a schoolmaster could wish him, respecting a *genteel* knowledge of languages; he was possessed of as much elegance and grace as a dancing-master could add to his exterior; but he was, at this period, as ignorant as a shepherd respecting the real traits and subterfuges of human nature in the Metropolis. The ties of *consanguinity* Corinthian Tom was no stranger to; but, it seems, he had yet to learn that, of all his *relatives*, experience would point out "HIS UNCLE"[71] to be of the most *feeling* and *accommodating* disposition; and who was ready at all times to supply his wants, provided he show cause why? His trees might be turned into cash, without *cutting* any of them down; his carriage might produce bank-notes, without coming to the hammer; and his wardrobe might not only make money, but he taken care of into the bargain. "This Spout," exclaimed Tom, "must possess the powers of Magic; and my UNCLE must be a liberal character indeed!" Yet when he heard of the independence displayed by this relative, in his not paying any sort of preference to society, and that the diamond necklace[72] of the duchess did not operate more strongly on his cocker feelings, than the poor market-woman's *flat iron*[73] to raise the needful to commence her daily

---

71   Cant term for a Pawnbroker: *this class now prefer the term* Silversmith!

> Who lives where hang those golden balls,
> Where Dick's poor mother often calls,
> And leaves her *dickey,* gown, and shawls?
> My Uncle.
> Who, when you're *short* of the *short* stuff,
> *Nose starving* for an ounce of snuff,
> *Will* "raise the wind" *without a* puff?
> My Uncle.

72   The history of the *"Diamond Necklace"* is well known at the West End of the Town.

73   It would be highly improper, even for an instant, to entertain an opinion that there are no honest, reputable, and even conscientious pawnbrokers in London. We trust there are very many; and though, perhaps, it may not be deemed by the feeling mind the most pleasant way of obtaining a competence, to do so from the distresses of the poor and unfortunate, yet, most undoubtedly, every man in this

happy country has a right to lay out his capital to the best advantage, provided it is done in a fair and honourable manner. But, that there is a class of swindlers who obtain licences to act as pawnbrokers, for the purpose of a disguise to their being the receivers of stolen goods, the Newgate Calendar can prove beyond all doubt; and such men, unfortunately, bring disgrace upon the respectable part of the profession. In this Metropolis there are upwards of two hundred and thirty pawnbrokers—in whose hands, at a very moderate estimate, there is generally property to the amount of seven hundred thousand pounds sterling, belonging to the poorest and most distressed part of the community! It is not our intention to deny the utility of such callings, as we are perfectly aware that, in some few critical instances, they have proved of considerable service. By preventing poor persons who are distressed from selling their goods and wearing apparel; or by assisting tradesmen with temporary loans upon their articles of furniture in time of need, with the advantage of redeeming them at a future period, when their circumstances were improved, pawnbrokers have often been of great benefit; for, if the articles in question were immediately sold, half their value might not be obtained, and they would be irrecoverably gone. So far, pawnbrokers may appear a useful class of society; but, on the other hand, in a large Metropolis like London, what a door is opened to raise money to support every species of vice! Fraudulent tradesmen turn their creditors' goods into money; servants pledge their masters' property; and mechanics their working tools and unfinished work. Money is so readily obtained at these shops, that they operate too frequently (in fact, it might be said daily) as an inducement to drunkenness, debauchery, idleness, and even prostitution. The business occasioned in this way by women of the town is scarcely credible, and pawnbrokers derive considerable emolument from this numerous and lamentable class of society. Their pledges are in general of the greatest value, and what articles are pilfered in the night are deposited the next day with the pawnbrokers; who, knowing their necessities, lend just what they please, and derive a wonderful profit from these articles being scarcely ever redeemed. The secrecy with which pawnbroking is carried on, admits room for great fraud on the part of the pawnbroker, respecting the interest of the pawns; and it is well known, that many persons, who have detected impositions in this respect, have preferred putting up with the loss, rather than expose the poverty of their situation in life, by appearing before a magistrate concerning such transactions. Those people who are continually in the habit of pawning are generally of such a description as to be entirely governed by the will of the pawnbroker, who takes and pays just what he thinks proper. Much evil arises too, from the negligence or design of these money-lenders, in not requiring a proper account from many of their customers as to their mode of obtaining the articles. Innumerable instances might be shown of the great disadvantages persons labour under in the Metropolis from jobbing tailors, who take in work; from laundresses, who have great quantities of linen to wash; from shoemakers that work at home, &c., who, even upon any imaginary want or pleasure, can have such ready recourse to these places for turning those articles into ready money. It has been related of a watchmaker, who was in the habit of having a great number of watches entrusted to his care to clean, that from idleness and drunkenness he had pledged most of them; and when any customer became so particularly pressing, that he could not put him off any longer, as soon as another watch came in to be cleaned, he took that to relieve the one wanted; till the business, it tickled CORINTHIAN TOM's fancy more than words can well express. But the *penetration* and *confidence* displayed by "*his* UNCLE" operated as a *climax* indeed, and struck him, as it were, all of a heap, when he learnt that an individual who had purchased a plate of *pork and greens* at a cook's shop, being overtaken by a hungry creditor on his road to the public-house, had this small debt discharged by the *Spout,* which gave him immediate relief, by taking in his hot dinner.[74] It was also made clear to TOM, that a man who had proved inflexible to all *dunning* at his residence, was, at length, suddenly stopped in the streets by the person to whom he was a debtor; and that, to get rid of his importunities, he

---

man was overwhelmed in distress, and the only return his employers experienced for their property was the duplicates. Numerous well-authenticated cases could be quoted, to show the alarming extent of pawnbroking in London. Every Saturday night, or till nearly one the next morning, are their shops crammed to excess with people procuring their clothes to make an appearance upon the Sunday; and on the Monday morning, crowds of men, women, and children, may be seen round their doors, frequently before their shops are open, that these deluded people may procure money to get a breakfast! The interest allowed by act of Parliament is sufficiently exorbitant, without any addition by the pawnbroker— but vast sums are obtained by charging an additional month's interest, after a pledge has gone two or three days over the date, which is scarcely ever disputed by the uninformed. It is from the weekly and daily pledges that the pawnbrokers amass such large fortunes. An anecdote has been related, that in a poor lodging-house, in which a single FLAT IRON was allowed for the use of its inmates, that the iron was pawned and redeemed eight or nine times in the week, and sometimes twice a day: the sum generally lent upon it was sixpence,—and if the interest is calculated, it will be found, that for the use of so small a sum, at a halfpenny each time, allowing it to be pawned four times per week, it will amount to eight shillings and eight pence per year! This is independently of the numerous pledges that are put in to redeem others, and the expense incurred by fresh duplicates. The pledges of poor women's aprons, towels, &c., are numerous in the extreme, and in general produce no more than fourpence, or sixpence, each article. If £10 only were employed in this lucrative way, it would, in the course of a twelvemonth, admitting that these articles were redeemed but once in a week, produce the enormous profit of £86, 17s. The great reluctance shown in general by pawnbrokers to persons who have lost their property, is of a most aggravated nature; as they well know that if any of the stolen articles are found upon their premises, they must restore them to the right owner, free of expense. In fact, the whole system of pawnbroking calls loudly for the interference of the legislature; particularly to protect the poorer classes of society, and prevent the immorality of the practice of taking pawns from children.
74   This occurrence is an undeniable fact, and took place in the neighbourhood of Smithfield, a few years since.

immediately went to his *Uncle,* pledged *himself* for the amount of the debt, discharged his creditor, and remained *ticketed* till he was *redeemed*[75] in the evening. In short, TOM was given to understand that "*his* UNCLE" did not turn a *deaf ear* to any articles of value presented to him, excepting young children, on whom, it is said, he could not place any precise *interest;* and that the calculations of "*his* UNCLE" were something like a game of balls, where the odds were TWO to ONE in favour of *winning!* "*His* UNCLE" was also a great man in being able to *accommodate* his friends with the loan of his *private boxes*[76] any evening, where more *original characters* might be witnessed than at either of the *Theatres Royal.*

The preceding, with many other circumstances of a similar description, which daily occur in "Life in London," it should seem, were wholly inexperienced by the affluent family of CORINTHIAN TOM, if not altogether unknown to them: but the mere recital of

---

[75] SHUTER, the celebrated comedian. This *funny* fellow, who was a perfectly original character *off* as well as *on* the stage, being well aware that the Managers of the Theatre could not do without him on the evening alluded to (SHUTER having been announced to perform), sent them the *duplicate* of himself,—when they, of necessity, sent and *redeemed* him accordingly. As a specimen of his *originality* of feeling, it may not, perhaps, be out of place to relate the following anecdote. It had been said of SHUTER, that he was descended from respectable parents: this he denied by public advertisement; asserting that he owed his existence to an Irish haymaker, from an amour with an oyster-wench. It appears he was very much attached to low company, and that his most intimate acquaintance was the then "JACK KETCH." Upon being rebuked by a friend, for his want of becoming pride, Shuter, in reply, told him he was completely in error, as his acquaintance had been highly born, was deeply educated, and that his father had made a great noise in the world. On explanation, it turned out—that "JACK" was born in a garret,—brought up in a cellar,—and his father had been a drummer in a marching regiment.

[76] A *poor* PUNSTER, who was hurrying through the streets one evening, was met by a friend, who asked him where he was going in such great haste? The *humorist* being rather *shy* in stating his errand, as well as anxious to conceal the *poverty* of his circumstances, and having only a few minutes left before his ticket expired as to *date,* which not being renewed, his property must have been forfeited, turned off the question, with a smile, observing, "To a place of *amusement*." "What part of the house?" "To the private boxes." "Is it a good piece?" "Excellent! It abounds with incident; and you cannot depart without feeling an *interest* in it." "What's the name of it?"—"JUST IN TIME!" "I should like to accompany you."—"No person," replied the Punster, "should I be more happy to take, if I did not feel a great *impropriety,* on my part, of introducing you to the company! This sufficed, and the PUNSTER got rid of his troublesome friend.

them occasioned our hero animatedly to remark, that, much as he had anticipated on the subject of "seeing Life," it now appeared to him more worthy of exploring than ever,—and he felt determined to pursue it, with increasing ardour, to the end of the Chapter.

> Happy the man who, void of care and strife,
> In silken or in leathern purse retains
> A SPLENDID SHILLING: he nor hears with pain
> New oysters cry'd, nor sighs for cheerful ale.

CHAPTER V.

Corinthian Tom's unceasing Anxiety to mix with the World uncontrolled. His Acquaintance with Young Logic, an Oxonian. Character of the latter. Death of Tom's Parents.

THE INCIDENTS AND diversity of human character, developed in the preceding chapter, it seems, had set Tom's mind on fire for a stroll to "see Life!" and he was continually on the *fret*[77] to obtain unrestrained liberty; in fact, to become his own master. This *thirst* for adventures was considerably increased, from his introduction to Robert Logic, Esq., who was the son of one of the most intimate friends of Corinthian Tom's father. The parents of Young Logic were both dead, and he was left in the possession of a considerable fortune.

LOGIC, as the phrase goes, had received a *College Education;* but those persons who were well acquainted with him seemed to *hint,* that he had rather been sent to Oxford to have the *character* of the thing, than to *astonish* the world at an after period with

---

77 This *expression* is frequently made use of by *natty* coachman, when the horses are so full of spirit that they will not stand still, and are in danger of *bolting* forwards almost every instant, in spite of the exertions of the driver to the contrary. Perhaps the following illustration may tend to render the above phrase more intelligible:—In taking up a *gouty* customer, who leaves his door, *limping* at the rate of half a mile an hour—or a *finicking,* fine, *half-bred,* lady, who, what with her maid fetching her *reticule* and other *fal-lals,* robs Coachey of several minutes, when the latter breaks out, "I should be much obliged to you, Sir, or *Marm,* if you would bustle a little, as you see my horses are on the *fret."*

any great works of intellectual profundity. Indeed, on the contrary, LOGIC had no pretensions to obtain one of *Literary* FAME's highest situations;[78] and he used frequently to laugh at the mere idea of his ever being distinguished at *Scapula Heath, Cape Hederic,* or *Lexicon Bay.*[79] To climb up the *Pindaric Heights* was not his forte; and it was also quite out of the question, he observed, that he should ever be chosen, from his talents, to become one of the inmates of *Convocation Castle*. But it should seem, if the CLASSICS had proved too *dry* a study for him within the walls of the College, he had, nevertheless, made some *amends*, as he termed it, for the *capabilities* he had displayed outside of them. LOGIC was as well known as a finger-post, for queering the *Gulls;* and the *notoriety* he had obtained in the *States of Independence,* and for the *Waste of Ready in Hoyle's Dominions,* was great indeed. In the *Kingdom of Sans Souci* he proved himself a *brilliant* of the first water; and from the figure he had cut in the *Province of Bacchus* and the *Dynasty of Venus*, LOGIC had been pronounced a hero. On the *Plains of Betteris* he had shown himself a general of no mean stamp: and his knowledge of *Navigation* was so good, that he had been enabled to steer clear of the shoals and rocks of *Dun Territory* and the *River Tick*. The aid of *Tomline's Light House* he never required; and the *Cave of Antiquity* he had no time to explore: but he was very fond of the *Salt Pits*. LOGIC had a complete map of the *Isles of Bishop* and *Flip;* and he was quite alive to all the movements upon these islands. For *Dodd's Sound* it seems, he did not care a *fig;* but he was very partial to the *scent* of *Codrington Manors, Mostyn's Hunting District,* and *Somerset Range*. He always made one in the sports at the *Hermitage, Port Meadow, Champaign Country,* and *Cape Negus*; and at the *Castle of St Thomas,* it is said, not a collegian was better known, or remembered for his generosity, than the lively dashing BOB LOGIC. With all his *nous,* however, it appears, he could not escape *rustication;* but his acquaintance with the *Cam Roads* soon put him to rights. LOGIC also had the good fortune to escape being *blown up* at *Point Non Plus*.

---

78   A *garret*,—the too frequent *reward* of genius and talent.
79   The *Phraseology* peculiar to the Collegians; quite of a local nature.

Added to his *University* knowledge of life and fun in the Country, his acquaintance with the Metropolis was extensive and accurate. LOGIC had been "*on the town*"[80] for several years; and no person had been more industrious towards *destroying* a fine constitution, or endeavouring to reduce a long purse, than he had. Such was the outline of his character. But those essential requisites for promoting the comforts and happiness of existence, lots of money and a vigorous stamina, seemed scarcely worthy of LOGIC's consideration, at least, if we may judge from the line of conduct he had hitherto pursued.

CORINTHIAN TOM and LOGIC not only became intimately acquainted, but something like friendship cemented their attachment. The generosity of the latter—his openness of character and liberality of sentiment—rendered him an object of attraction. The high spirit of which he was always master, his lively ideas of taste and style, and that complete possession of himself, which LOGIC had attained from his knowledge and experience of the various classes of life with which he was continually in the habit of mixing, made a deep impression upon the youthful imagination of CORINTHIAN TOM; more especially as the latter had scarcely heard anything but the sound maxims laid down by his father, and the cold routine discipline of his tutor, for his future progress in life. The light and airy mode of expression which invariably flowed from the tongue of LOGIC, stole so imperceptibly into the favour of CORINTHIAN TOM, that he drank largely of the intoxicating draught before he was aware of its delusive consequences. *Trifles* were dressed up with such extreme elegance, and *frailties* were disposed of with so much pleasantry, as mere matters of course,—incidental to human nature,—that anything like *criminality* was never thought of. PLEASURE was the word— GAIETY the pursuit—and LOGIC's meridian, the BEAU MONDE.

The contrast of characters was so great, and the attractions so powerful, that TOM might be said to be placed between two

---

80   "On the Town!" A man of the World. A person supposed to have a general knowledge of men and manners. In short, UP *to everything*!

magnets. To the parental and manly advice which had been so frequently bestowed upon him, aided by the solidity of deportment with which it was accompanied, TOM, it should seem, was by no means insensible; nay more, he felt tremblingly alive to its force and consequences. From its frequent *repetition,* however, its once strong effect was visibly obliterating from his memory. It was the same thing over and over again. TOM, with the levity of youth, thought he had got all his father's maxims by heart; and they grew *tiresome*[81] to him, in being continually thrust, as it were, upon his attention. How different were the recitals of LOGIC! With TOM, they operated upon his feelings like the anticipation of a pleasing journey, wherein he saw a fresh country, abounding with new scenes and prospects, with different manners and customs, and in which an intimate acquaintance might be gained with its inhabitants. This raised his curiosity to the highest pitch; and he panted with all the anxiety of a true sportsman in pursuit of game upon a new manor, or one eager to join in the pleasures of the chase.

Hitherto TOM had been restrained by the word of his father, and the influence that his mother possessed over him. He submitted to their advice without much reluctance; and various pleasures were abandoned, when suggestions were made to him of their being improper. But his acquaintance with LOGIC had rendered this *restraint* for the first time somewhat painful; admonitions now began to grow irksome, and were less attended to—and he imagined he was capable of *thinking* for himself, by falling into the too-much-to-be-lamented general error of youth, that his own opinion was equally as good as the experience of his parents. TOM,

---

81 Something after the manner of that inimitable comedian, Mr LISTON, in the character of *Gaby Grim,* in the laughable farce of "WE FLY BY NIGHT; OR, LONG STORIES." General Bastion, *Grim's* master, who bad gone blind in the service of his country, was very fond of relating the exploits of his youth over and over again, and invariably commenced his story with "When I was a Lieutenant in the 43d Regiment of Foot, in the year of our Lord, Anno Domini, at the siege of," &c. &c. *Grim,* who was always in attendance upon the blind General, it seems, grew so tired of his stories, that he frequently fell asleep; and on *Grim's* being called to account for his want of attention when his master's daughter eloped, he observed, that he had got them all by heart, having heard them & thousand times, and could not keep awake.

it appears, would often draw comparisons between the situations of himself and his friend LOGIC. LOGIC had no parents to call him to account for his levity of character, nor relatives to remonstrate with him on the impropriety of his conduct. The *object*, only, was before LOGIC, and not the consideration of the consequences that might follow. Perfectly free in body and mind, he gave full scope to his imagination; and the committal of many errors, perhaps, might have been saved, had some friendly monitor been near him, to point out the evils likely to occur from such a carelessness of disposition.

That LOGIC possessed numerous good qualities was never denied—but his mode of life caused him to be considered by many persons as a dangerous companion for youth. His conversation was so extremely fascinating, and his amours and adventures were related with such spirit and talent—calculated much rather to excite a sort of stimulus among his companions to similar achievements, than to operate at all as a check to such immoral and vicious propensities. It was in this point of view, that TOM experienced the general failing of human nature, which few men have sufficient strength of mind to conquer,—in imagining the situation of others much happier than their own. The exterior of men of fashion so dazzles and deludes the unwary, that even their most ridiculous foibles are looked upon *as fashionable,* and copied with as much accuracy, as if they were beauties,—at the expense of men of better judgment.

LOGIC was looked up to as a complete hero in affairs of gallantry, and his companions endeavoured to imitate his manners and style. TOM, who had not before been intimate with a person of similar habits, took him as a kind of model, and would often exclaim — "What a happy fellow BOB LOGIC is, in having no person to control or break in upon his pursuits and inclinations!"

Notwithstanding this exclamation of TOM, it is but justice to remark, that no child ever loved or respected his parents better than he was wont to do; or, perhaps, felt more forcibly persuaded, that no expense or exertions had been spared to improve his education or render him happy; in fact, he was their idol, being the only son left out of a numerous family. The smallest alteration in his health, created a thousand anxieties on their part; and if at any time he stayed out an hour later than usual, they were in a perpetual state of alarm, lest some accident might have befallen him,—till his return to them once more produced comfort and happiness.

Tom was fast advancing to manhood, and these tender cares, which had once proved so pleasing to his feelings, became now somewhat oppressive. His acquaintances were growing more numerous, and diversified in their notions; and the continual company of his parents was not quite so congenial as formerly,— which they perceived with no small degree of concern. Tom was also fast relaxing from that discipline of habit which had been imposed upon him; and lie frequently remonstrated with much warmth, when checked for a deviation from his hitherto general line of conduct. It had often been perceived, amidst all his regularity of behaviour, that he had a great thirst for company, and mixing more generally with society; but having a strict tutor, and being under the immediate eye of his father, this propensity was in a great measure suppressed, though not entirely eradicated from his composition. The correctness of his father upon all occasions, and the impressive amiability of his mother, had long restrained his natural inclination from displaying itself in those conspicuous colours in which it would have burst forth, had he been differently situated. But a number of his little foibles, from the great partiality of his father and mother towards their darling boy, it seems, had escaped their notice; and the extension of his acquaintance ultimately produced quite a revolution in his former scholastic ideas and habits. Indeed, so much, that the modest and diffident Tom at length began to assume an easy confidence, his embarrassment was fast leaving him, and he entered into company with a firm and prepossessing elegance.

Time rolled on fast and pleasantly; and as Tom and his friend Logic were almost continually together, scarcely any space could be allotted, even if it had been wished, for *reflection.* Indeed, the life of the latter might be said to exist only in one continued round of pleasure and enjoyment; and he would often good-humouredly tell Tom, in the Oxford phraseology, that he would soon get out of the *Land of Sheepishness*, and also get the better of *Pupil's Straits*. That, ultimately, Tom would not be troubled with DAD's WILL. A *New Guinea* would likewise give him pleasures beyond description; and LOGIC, in concluding his remarks, observed, with a smile, "My dear Tom, you will then be a happy fellow, and only have to beware of the *Fields of Temptation!*"

However, in the midst of CORINTHIAN TOM's pleasures, he received an unexpectedly severe shock from the death of his father, which shook him to the very centre. The recollection of all his father's kindness towards him,—the anxiety and industry of his parent, which had been manifested throughout the whole of his career, in realising a splendid fortune for him, —now burst upon TOM's feelings with redoubled severity; even his dashing friend LOGIC, for a time, was entirely forgotten in the paroxysms of his grief. Indeed, it was an epoch in his fate, that could not be passed over as a mere matter of course, when it was recollected, that the *entrance into life* of these two characters was marked with some *trifling* shades of difference. The SON participated in the pleasures of a splendid establishment, with a fortune more affluent than fell to the lot of many Noblemen, to gratify and foster his aspiring genius; while his FATHER, on the contrary, had gradually quitted the threshold of dependence, and, by perseverance, had mounted step by step, till he shook off his obscurity, and reached the summit of his wishes. He had realised a noble independence—performed one of the most important offices in the state—become the founder of a family—and without troubling the Herald's Office to pore over their musty records, or to cudgel their "inventive brains" to supply honours for his son with which to decorate his armorial bearings, his posthumous fame supplied TOM with an incitement, never in himself to sully his reputation, by forgetting the integrity, virtue, and benevolence of his deceased parent.

The mother of CORINTHIAN TOM, who had died some little time previous to his father, was in many respects the exact counterpart of her amiable partner; and although not so prominent a figure upon the canvass as either the "*Old or young* TOM," yet she could not be viewed in any other light, than as a most interesting

Chapter V.

portrait. An accurate likeness was not easily obtained, as it was one of those *rare* pictures, which are only now and then to be met with, and that seldom occurs for an artist to paint. A cursory view of this portrait, perhaps, might not cause any particular attraction; yet when its owner, who, from long possession, had been able to acquire a perfect knowledge of each various shade and delightful tint, expatiated upon its beauties, the beholder felt the most animated admiration. Although the *face* did not possess the unrivalled charms of a Venus—nor could the *eyes* boast of celestial blue—the *nose* was not aquiline—the *lips* were far removed from rubies —the *teeth* displayed no peculiar whiteness—the *cheeks* did not vie with roses—and her *figure* altogether was different from what a statuary would have chosen for a model; yet, notwithstanding, the *tout ensemble* was most truly pleasing. If her face was not gifted with those extraordinary requisites necessary to constitute a perfect beauty, yet it was not destitute of those fine traits, which are even more *beautiful* than beauty itself. In the happiness of her husband, *affection* strongly manifested itself; and in rearing a numerous offspring, her countenance displayed the *fond* and *anxious mother* in a most conspicuous light. The tale of the distressed, likewise, never failed to awaken the marks of a feeling and charitable mind. Such were the parents of Corinthian Tom, and such was the origin of which he had to boast.

> Why all this toil for triumphs of an hour?
> What, though we wade in wealth or soar in fame,
> Earth's highest station ends'in—here he lies!
> And *dust* to *dust* concludes her noblest song.

None of my readers, I feel assured, will complain of a loss of time, in witnessing Tom shed a few drops of sensibility over the remains of the authors of his existence,[82] whose lives were
devoted solely towards promoting his happiness, and placing him on an eminence even among the highest walks of society.

---

82   This conduct of Corinthian Tom is somewhat different from that of a person well known in a peculiar walk of society in the Metropolis. He is the son

> For the tear that bedews *Sensibility's* shrine,
> Is a drop of more worth than all Bacchus's tun!

---

of a gentleman, distinguished for his reputation, liberality, and talents, and who very *feelingly* wrote a letter to his father, stating "that IP HE THOUGHT HE WAS THE SON OF SUCH A MAN, HE WOULD INSTANTLY CUT HIS THROAT!" thus endeavouring to proclaim *his* MOTHER also an *infamous character I* The situation of his parents is not to be depicted— words cannot portray it; but the father, after giving vent to his grief and indignation, placed this written character under the portrait of his most beloved wife, whose virtuous conduct and disposition defied all censure. The female alluded to did not long survive this event, but departed this life broken-hearted; and the distracted husband has ever since, in the severity of his studies, endeavoured to banish from his mind that he -was ever the father of such a son. All attempts at reconciliation have failed; and the above portrait, to this day, remains in his study, with the son's
character attached to it. It ought to be observed, that the above young gentleman received a superior education at the expense of his father, and was brought up in the tenderest manner; a rebuke, however, from his parent, upon his deviation from supporting his character in life, was the origin of this *unnatural* letter.

CHAPTER VI.

A Word or two respecting "Architects of their own Fortunes." Tom out of his Leading-Strings. Poetic Invocation to the Pleasures of Life. His hurried Entrance into all Classes of Society. A few additional Touches of the Author towards finishing Tom's Likeness. The Impression Tom made upon the Town. Acquirement of his Title. A slight Glance at Tom's Choice of a Female— Corinthian Kate.

IN THE SPLENDID Metropolis of England there are numerous persons, who are termed the *"Architects of their own Fortunes."*[83] They have toiled incessantly throughout the whole of their lives; they have borne the severest privations

---

83   The acquirement of that immense brewery, which belonged to the late Mr THRALE, the former husband of the present Mrs PIOZZI (a lady highly distinguished for her literary talents), as related by Dr Johnson, is an anecdote well worthy the perusal of every person who feels any sort of anxiety to raise himself in society. Mr Thrale, to his great praise be it remembered, had but a salary of twelve shillings a week in the above large establishment, for many years after he had arrived at a state of manhood. His talents, however, enabled him to purchase that immense brewery. He also had a family of twelve children, which were brought up in the first style of elegance, and to whom, at his death, he left very large fortunes. Another instance of an enterprising mind is to be discovered in the person of the present Mr ROTHSCHILD, who, from being a clerk in a mercantile house in Manchester, has, in the course of a few fleeting years, risen so rapidly in point of wealth, as to have been enabled to take the whole of a Government loan of five millions without assistance from any other house: a circumstance never before accomplished by an individual. It is said, Mr Rothschild is worth three millions of money. He has, likewise, most extensive establishments in France, Holland, Germany, and Spain. Indeed, he may be considered as the first monied man in the world. It ought not to be forgotten that Mr Rothschild is one of the *first,* also, in support of all public

without a murmur; and by their industry and perseverance have surmounted almost giant-like difficulties, and ultimately accomplished the grand object in view—A large fortune. It has often been the subject of sincere regret, that such persons, with very few exceptions, have lived just long enough, according to a vulgar phrase, *to fill their pipe,* and leave others to *enjoy it.* [84] Just so with the father of CORINTHIAN TOM. The whole of his life was dedi-

---

charities. It is likewise worthy of remark, that the present LUKE HANSARD, Esq., the Printer to the House of Commons, treading in the steps of Mr Thrale, has equally distinguished himself. This immense literary establishment has been realised by Mr Luke Hansard, from his never-tiring industry ALONE! He arrived in London without a patron,—nay more, without a friend. With the world only before him as a guide to his future exertions, he has performed an Herculean attempt. Mr H. has also brought up a large family. His talents, as an expeditious printer, are so great, as to be without a rival. The House of Commons, for the last twenty-five years, have acknowledged the accuracy and expedition he has displayed, with the highest encomiums on his exertions. The above facts are introduced merely to show *what* HAS and *what* MAY be done with perseverance. Indeed, the Metropolis points out many *great men* in this respect—and surely such conduct is entitled to the term of *great:* volumes would not suffice to detail *how* many vast fortunes in London have been originated.

I am aware that some of my readers of a higher class of society, may feel, or seem to think, that I have introduced a little too much of the *slang*; but I am anxious to render myself perfectly intelligible to all parties. Half of the world are *up* to it; and it is my intention to make the other half *down* to it. LIFE IN LONDON demands this sort of demonstration. A kind of *cant* phraseology is current from one end of the Metropolis to the other. Indeed, even in the time of Lord Chesterfield, he complained of it. In some females of the highest rank, it is as strongly marked, as in *dingy* draggled-tailed SALL, who is compelled to dispose of a few sprats to turn an honest penny: and while the latter in smacking her lips, talks of her *prime jackey,* an *out-and-out* concern, and a *bit of good truth,* &c., the former, in her dislikes, tossing her head, observes, it was *shocking, quite a bore, beastly, stuff,* &c. The Duchess at an Opera, informs the Countess of "*a row*" which occurred on the last evening with as much *sang-froid* as CARROTTY POLL mentions the *lark* to a *Coster-monger* she was engaged in, at a gin-spinner's, and, in being turned out of the *panny,* got her *ogles* took *measure of* for a *suit of mourning.* Therefore, some allowance must be made for an author who is compelled to write under a subdued tone of expression, in order to keep his promise with the public,— that "the MODEST, it is trusted, will not have occasion to turn aside with disgust, nor the MORALIST to shut the book offended." In fact, in many instances, the language of real Life is so very strong, coarse, and even disgusting, that, in consequence of keeping the above object in view, the points of many a rich scene are in great danger of being nearly frittered away; nay, of being almost reduced to tameness and insipidity. My ingenious friends, ROBERT and GEORGE CRUIKSHANK, whose talents in representing "the living manners as cated to realizing an immense fortune,—while the whole existence of Tom was employed in spending it. This it was that gave rise to the expression of Tom's having been "born with a silver spoon in his mouth"—mentioned in a preceding chapter.

CORINTHIAN TOM had how arrived at the summit of his wishes; he had no check-string upon his inclinations—a plentiful fortune to gratify every propensity—a constitution in full vigour—and a disposition as lively and as gay as a disciple of Mirth could wish it; in short, he completely answered the description of the poet:—

> PARENT OF PLEASURE and of many a groan,
> I should be loth to part with thee, I own,
> DEAR LIFE!
> To tell the truth, I'd rather lose a *wife*,
> Should Heav'n e'er deem me worthy of possessing
> That best, that most invaluable blessing.
> I thank thee that thou brought'st me into *being*;
> The things of this our world are well worth *seeing*,
> And, let me add, moreover, well worth feeling;
> Then what the devil would people have,
> 'These gloomy hunters of the grave,
> For ever sighing, groaning, canting, kneeling.
> Some wish they never had been born, how odd!
> To see the handy works of God,
> In sun, and moon, and starry sky;
> Though last, not least, to see sweet woman's charms,—
> Nay more, to clasp them in our arms,
> And pour the soul in love's delicious sigh,
> Is well worth coming for, I'm sure,
> Supposing that thou gav'st us nothing more.
> Yet, thus surrounded, LIFE, dear LIFE, I'm *thine*,
> And, could I always call thee mine,
> I would not quickly bid this world farewell;
> But whether HERE, or LONG or SHORT my stay,
> I'll keep in mind for ev'ry day
> An old French motto, *"vive la bagatelle!"*
> MISFORTUNES are this lott'ry-world's sad blanks;
> Presents, in my opinion, not worth thanks.
> The PLEASURES are the TWENTY-THOUSAND PRIZES.
> Which nothing but a *downright ass* despises.

---

they rise," stand unrivalled in this peculiar line, feel as strongly impressed with the value of *delicacy* as I do. But if some of the plates should appear rather *warm*, the purchasers of "Life in London" may feel assured, that nothing is added to them tending to *excite*, but, on the contrary, they have most anxiously, on all occasions, given the preference rather to "*extenuate*" than to "set down aught in malice." All the Plates are the exact representations, as they occurred, of the various classes of society.

Logic had let his friend indulge himself in all the luxury of grief before he made his bow or offered any sort of condolence on the loss he had experienced. At length he left his card[85]— and a messenger was soon despatched after him.[86] Sorrow was on the wane, and Tom had sincerely performed all the duties required from an affectionate son. The "time *for everything*" had also passed away. Pleasure now knocked at his gate for admittance.—Mirth likewise waited in the hall to obtain an audience.—Fun was in attendance for his turn to pay respect to Tom.—Messrs Sprees and Rambles were only waiting for the signal to be *off*— and *l'argent* was in readiness to put *movements* and life into the whole of the group, previous to starting.

Tom, under the influence of Logic, it should seem, proved himself an apt scholar indeed; and the pupil, it is said, in a very short time out-stripped his Master. The *Land of Sheepishness,* as Logic termed it, was now out of sight; and Tom, he observed, had weathered *Pupil's Straits* with great success. In short, Tom appeared determined to bring up his lee way, as the sailors express it, with a wet sail; or, was rather more like a bird that had escaped

---

85

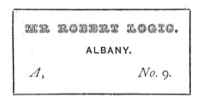

On the back of the above card was written:—
Dear Tom,

Bob's *alive!* But you had nearly lost your friend last night, as I was *cast-away* after taking in a good *cargo* at the Isle of Bishop.* I was rather *bosky,* and could not manage the *helm* at all, and must have *foundered* had it not been for the assistance of a *pilot*† who safely towed me into the *light-house.*‡

* A phrase among the Collegians at Oxford for petting *jolly* over port wine and roasted oranges and lemons.
† A watchman.
‡ Watch-house.

86   Dear Bob,
Tom's afloat! And will soon set sail. You must have more ballast aboard next voyage. Be quick Bob. *Tempus Fugit*!

from its cage. There was no discrimination at his onset. All places, both high and low, were visited by Tom in such rapid succession, that anything like their merits or demerits were out of the question. The ardour too with which he pursued his career, astonished every one; and Logic was at length not only so *dead beat* as to be compelled to cry for quarter, but to seek a temporary retirement, in order to renovate his constitution.

Tom, however, did not require the aid of a Gentleman-Usher to announce him to the Upper Walks of Life. His splendid fortune had now been *buzzed* about from one end of the town to the other; and wherever he went, *that* circumstance alone was *weighty*[87] enough to give him attraction even in the highest circles of society. But it was not from the length of his purse, that Tom obtained his *notoriety*. He possessed genius and talents, backed by an *understanding* that operated upon his mind like a rallying-post, whenever his senses got into disorder. His GENIUS, however, was rather of a different sort from that possessed by a *Squire Groom*;[88] and his TALENTS were of a higher cast than those evinced by a *Charles Goldfinch*;[89] although he was quite as *au fait* in describing the merits of a horse-race, as either of these two celebrated heroes of the Turf. His understanding was not made up of *technicalities* and *precedents*—it was not the *borrowed light* of some sensible and learned companion, nor did it consist in *retailing* the sentences and maxims belonging to another person. No; his understanding was *intuitive*—its corner-stone was common sense—and its application, Tom found, in most cases, was of so decisive a nature, as scarcely ever to call for a *reverse* of judgment. Most certainly, his claims to attraction did not rest on the casual advantages of

---

87 *Robin Roughhead.* First, then, you must know that I'm the cleverest fellow in all these parts.
Dolly. Well, I know'd that afore!
Robin. But I'll tell you how it is—it's because I'm the richest fellow in all these parts; and if I hav'nt it here *(pointing to his head),* I HAVE IT HERE *(slapping his pocket).—Fortune's Frolics.*
88 I can't write; but I tell you what I'll do; I'll poison her parrot, and cut off her squirrel's tail, dem me.—*Love a-la-Mode.*
89 A gentleman like me—a useful member of society!—bet the long odds; nobody ever heard of such a thing.—*Road to Ruin.*

inheritance. Corinthian Tom derived them from a higher source.

Nature had undoubtedly marked him as one of her favourites, and gifted him with some of her rarest qualities. She had bestowed on him an uncommonly fine person, the elegance of which was prepossessing in the highest degree. A face, if the term of very handsome did not belong to it, which was *illumined* with the brightest rays of intelligence, portraying an openness of countenance, that indicated its owner possessed of a generous and sensible *mind.* An eye which, while it penetrated almost the inmost recesses of the object before it, was completely free from that sort of disdain which too often accompanies high birth and pretensions,—with a mildness overspreading the whole, at once disarming and interesting the spectator. Indeed, his whole HEAD was such, that though it might not be *worshipped* in the vast extent of the Metropolis, yet was of that class, that, meet it wherever you might among other HEADS, however surrounded by importance of situation, you could not contemplate it with indifference. It fastened upon your fancy; and if ever comparison came across your argument, it stole upon your remembrance with the emphasis of its fine and expressive character. It has been remarked, that the *wig* placed upon the head of the *Counsellor* gives importance to his station; while the *Divine* often acquires a degree of solemnity, by such an addition to his person. The *Player*, likewise, imposes upon the audience from the numerous revolutions which his head assumes. But this HEAD required no artificial aid to make it *impressive;* it was all *character.* Indeed, it was wholly indebted to Nature, who had worked it up in her best manner. She had also bestowed upon it some of those exquisite touches, which render her works so beautiful and varied, and confer a superiority on her compositions which art can never attain. *Gaiety* enriched the harmony of its features, and never left its situation for an instant, except to give place to the greater ornament of *feeling*. In short, Corinthian Tom's *exterior* was the theme of universal admiration, and its effect was considerably increased by his interesting *deportment.* United, he never failed to impress his beholders with the conviction, that his attractions were far above mediocrity, and demanded for him a degree of consideration and respect, that must always cause him to appear CONSPICUOUS.

Tom's box at the Opera caused many a languishing eye and palpitating heart to wander towards its elegant owner. His *stroll* through the Theatres caused a different sensation among another class of females, and no lures were neglected to decoy and entrap him. In the Parks, Tom was the GO among the "GOES!" His *peep* into the *Stews* was merely *en passant;* and the knowing, enticing, Mother DISH-*ups* something "*new*" was tried on in vain to "have the best" of our Hero only for a single *darkey!* Upon his descending into the *Hells,* if he did not prove himself as troublesome an inmate as the *dramatic* Don Giovanni, or possess the icy qualities of Signor Antonelli, the fire eater and hornpipe dancer upon red-hot iron bars, he nevertheless had found out the *secret,*— which, if it did not altogether prevent him from being *scorched* a little, yet saved him from being *burnt to death!* At Newmarket, Epsom, and Doncaster Races, Tom was viewed as the *tulip* of the turf. He not only took the shine out of the *Prime Ones* at *Tattersall's,* but his *nod* for decision of judgment was the *fiat* of taste. In showing himself at the *Fives Court,* all the *peepers* of the *Fancy* were on the stretch to *ogle* his beau-ideal form and appearance. At *Moulsey Hurst* he sported his *blunt* with all the confidence of "Carlton House to a Charley's Shelter," on his favourite pugilist. At *Almack's,* Lord Stair,[90] in his best days, could not have acquitted himself with more grace, politeness, and elegance, than did Corinthian Tom; and viewed as an amateur, De Hayes, Vestris, or Oscar Byrne, did not eclipse him. At the Dog Pit, his judgment respecting the canine race was so clear, that even *Bill Gibbon's* and *Caleb Baldwin* yielded the palm to him without a shrug of the shoulder or a *sneer* upon their *mugs?* In short, there was no place that could afford the slightest touch of pleasure and amusement, from *Blue Blazes* to the Royal Institution and Outinian[91] Lectures,

---
90 When the Earl of Stair was at the court of that distinguished monarch, Louis XIV., he was pronounced to be the most accomplished man in Europe.
91 This word is derived from the Greek pronoun *outis, nobody,* of which the genitive is *outivos.* The origin of this institution appeared very much

but what was ransacked again and again,—till finding anything "*new*" was hopeless.

The *unique* appearance of our Hero, at all times,—his corresponding vehicles,—his elegant high-bred cattle,—and his servants, displayed such a unity of mind and taste, that he was christened by the *Beau Monde*, CORINTHIAN TOM. In fact, his *set-out* altogether was of so fascinating a description that he had no competitor in the ranks of fashion. The coach and harness-makers took him for a *model*, and were upon the alert in copying all his designs. TOM could teach his tailor with as much ease the advantages of an elegant *fit*, as he could point out to his coachmaker the true principles of taste. It was his Mind that made him a leader in the upper circles, seconded by his eye, which might be called *microscopic*, as he viewed everything with a critical severity. In all that he did, he was pronounced *out-and-out*.

Notwithstanding all this high-sounding praise, which TOM realised in his pursuit of "*seeing Life!*" it seems, he felt a considerable *vacuum* without the society of some superior female. He entertained the idea that his *character* was not altogether *complete*, without having such a *tender* companion to occupy and interest his leisure moments.

> SWEET NYMPH of rosy cheek and sprightly mien,
> Who, vagrant, playful, on the hills art seen,
> E'er Sol illumines the gray world below;

---

to please Corinthian Tom, and he spoke of it in terms of the highest satisfaction. The idea of what is every-BODY'S business being NO -*body's* business is here demonstrated in lectures of considerable talent, elegantly written, and which are also delivered with much emphasis and eloquence. And however singular to relate, yet such is the fact, that NO-*body's* business is performed at the OUTINIAN INSTITUTION by SOME-body, who has not only a head and a heart, but a purse attached to it, in the cause and service of mankind. Most certainly it should be EVERY-body's business, if possible, to lend a hand towards the improvement of society,—which No-BODY, till now, seemed inclined to put in practice. This paradox, however, is put to rest by the OUTINIANS taking up this most laudable cause, with spirit of mind, energy of talent, and great liberality as to expenses. The visitants are of the highest order in society; who are also supplied with refreshments gratuitously. The Institution, which is held in the founder's house, it seems, also originated with him: a gentleman more distinguished for his general philanthropy and benevolence of character, than even for the possession of immense wealth and splendid establishments.

> Now, doe-like, skipping wild from vale to vale,
> Enamour'd of the rills and fresh'ning gale,
> From whose mild wing the streams of fragrance flow.
>
> Oh! 'midst those hills and vales contented stray,
> Thou wilt be *ruin'd* if thou com'st away,
> Doctors, too much like man traps, lie in wait;
> They'll tell thee, beauteous nymph, TEN THOUSAND LIES,
> That they can mend thy bloom, and sparkling eyes;—
> Avoid, avoid, my dear, the dangerous bait!
>
> Like the first woodcock of the year,
> The instant that he dares appear,
> The country's up to kill him—dog and gun!
> So when thou showest, nymph, thy rosy face,
> I see at once an Æsculapian chase;
> And, oh! IF CAUGHT, thou wilt not find it *FUN!*

But the difficulty of selecting a female to correspond with his critical ideas of taste and elegance, so as not to reduce the reputation he had acquired in the *Beau Monde,* was not to be viewed as a mere matter of course: indeed, it was very far from anything like *routine* to TOM. Numbers were not wanting, it appears, out of which he might have made a choice. But it was an *article* that could not be ordered according to any particular *pattern*,—neither was it the sort of *Smithfield bargain* HEROINE, that was to be taken with *all her faults,* at a certain price. No; it was a being the very counterpart of himself that he wanted; one who seemed to feel, or pretended to feel, *intuitively* upon all the subjects of taste and elegance. One, also, who gave a *character* to all her actions. This was the sort of almost fairy creature that he wished to fill up the little vacancy he had left, and give *eclat* to his curricle. It was after the manner of the poet:—

> Sure such a pair were never seen,
> So justly form'd to meet by nature.

But, to a *mind* like TOM's, difficulties were only to be opposed to be conquered; and as the proverb informs us, every *Jack has his Jill*, so CORINTHIAN TOM liberally admitted the truth of its latitude to the fullest extent. He set out with all the ardour of a *Don Quixote,* although without a lance or a target, in quest of this beloved heroine of his finely-wrought imagination. TOM was a host in himself, and required not the aid of a *Sancho Panza* to second his efforts. The *Paradise* of the West soon stopped his career,—and his penetrating eye, like a staunch pointer, made a *dead set* at the object that crossed his path. He could not leave it. He was *entranced,* as it were, on the spot. The beauty and style of the *Fair One* even exceeded his anticipation: and, like a true sportsman, his shots told, and the prize was borne off in triumph.

> Let me confess that beauty is delicious:
> To clasp it in our arms is nice—but vicious:
> That is to say, *unlawful* hugs—caresses,
> Which want those bonds which God Almighty blesses.
> I do not say that we should not EMBRACE:
> We MAY—but then it should be done with GRACE:
> The *flesh* should scarce be thought of—there's the merit:
> Sweet are the palpitations of the spirit.
> WOMAN's a lovely animal, 'tis true,—
> Too well, indeed, the lawless passions know it;
> Unbridled rogues, that wild the charms pursue,—
> And madly, with the *scythe* of RUIN, *mow it!*
> Thus giving it of death the wicked wound,
> A tender flow'r stretch'd sweetly on the ground!

CORINTHIAN TOM might now be said to have arrived at his grand climacteric. In matters of masculine taste and elegance he was decidedly the hero of his day: and in his choice of a female, his judgment, it was thought, had even outstripped his previous outdoings. Upon her first appearance in the Park, the *Pinks* not only sighed after her, but cast many a longing —lingering look behind; and even the ladies were compelled to acknowledge her beauty, and join in the praises of her delightfully fine Grecian form. TOM was the admiration and envy of the *Ton;* and his *chère amie* the acknowledged *Venus de Medicis* of the circle of the *Elegantes!* The *acmé* was now complete,—and the lovely *Miss Catherine* was soon distinguished by the denomination of CORINTHIAN KATE.

CHAPTER VII.

Corinthian Tom's Excesses render Rustication necessary. A Visit to Hawthorn-Hall. Jerry Hawthorn's Introduction to Tom. Character of the latter. A Day's Sporting. A Jollification at Hawthorn-Hall. Tom's descriptive Song of the Metropolis. Jerry's Arrival in London.

> Calmly let ME begin and end Life's chapter,
> Ne'er panting for a HURRICANE of rapture;
> Calmly let me walk—not riotous and jumping:
> With due decorum, let my heart,
> Perform a sober quiet part,
> Not at the ribs be ever bumping—bumping.
>
> RAPTURE'S a charger—often breaks his girt,
> Runs off, and flings his rider in the dirt.

THE POET'S ADVICE, it should seem, was not heeded by Corinthian Tom: *advice*, indeed! to a *Sprig of Fashion*, just starting with four-in-hand, that did not value either turf or turnpike, and who flattered himself that he could with his whip take a fly off the tip of his leader's ear, with as much nicety as the renowned William Tell shot the apple off his son's head! No, no: *advice* was out of the question. Heroes *give*, not *take* it,—or wherein consists the *heroism?* Tom plunged into everything: he commenced his journey, as if existence depended upon his celerity;[92] and never stood still till he was *dead beat!* [93]

> These violent delights have violent ends,
> And in their triumph die, like fire and powder,
> Which as they meet consume.

The grand *secret*, at length, unfolded itself to Tom, that "*the Constitution*," sooner or later, must be obeyed; which, not all the hints, caution, or advice, given to him by his acquaintances, it seems, could effect. This high-mettled Corinthian also found, that a little relaxation from his incessant "DAY and night scenes" was absolutely necessary to his health. It is true, Tom might have been such an expert charioteer, as to have "got over the ground without breaking his neck or, as his friend Bob Logic good-naturedly observed to him, that he also possessed *nous* enough to "*weather Pupil's Straits, without being blown up at Point Nonplus!*" Yet, with all his first-rate talents towards perfection, he could not escape from the haggard face, the squeamish appetite, and the debilitated frame, which *excess* never fails to implant on the *peep-o'-day* gay votary of Pleasure. Though our hero had not received a positive *notice to quit*;[94] or even so much as the first of the THREE WARNINGS,[95] yet the token was sufficiently impressive to remind him, that if the *loose screw*[96] was not attended to the *hinges* would be ultimately out of repair. The old proverb whispered to him, that a "stitch in time" might soon put all to rights again; and TOM, who had formerly laughed heartily at the idea of LOGIC's retirement from the busy world, for a few days, in order to renovate his frame,

---

92   In the slang of the day, the phrase is, "Get over the ground if it breaks your neck!"
93   "*Dead beat!*" or "*beat to a stand still!*" Common phrases in the Sporting World, when a man or a horse is so completely exhausted from over-exertion, or the constitution breaking down, as to give up the object in view, not being able to pursue it any further.
94   A cant phrase, applied to any individual who appears to be in a state fast approaching towards dissolution.
95   Mrs Thrale's celebrated tale.
96   A "loose screw," or a "*screw loose:*" *i.e.* meaning something wrong. To such heroes as CORINTHIAN TOM, perfectly intelligible.

now felt that, without the enjoyment of HEALTH,[97] even pleasure itself not only grows tiresome, but becomes painful.

TOM, however, was too *game* to acknowledge any sort of *alarm* at this slight visiting of the *penetralia;* but, finding himself rather "out of sorts," as the phrase goes, called, as it were, with a friendly "How do ye do," on the celebrated Doctor PLEAS'EM. This dashing disciple of Æsculapius, though not exactly after the manner of *Colman's* Doctor *Bolus,* whose poetic talents raised his fame:

> Apothecary's verse—and where's the treason?
> 'Tis simple honest dealing, not a crime,
> Where patients swallow physic without reason,
> 'Tis but fair they should have a little rhyme.

Yet it was urged, that he nevertheless *cured* more persons by his pleasing address than his prescriptions, however skilfully applied. It was said of him, that his *tongue* had been his fortune. He had *talked* his way through life to a good purpose. He had not only procured himself a practice of ten thousand pounds per annum, from the humble situation of an apothecary; but he had also gained for himself a *Title;*—not merely that of a "*great Physician*" yet one that his heir could enjoy without the slightest knowledge of physic.

> His fame for miles through all the squares ran,
> In reputation none could exceed him:
> The Belles and Beaus call'd him "a fine man!"
> His name was—"*Doctor* PLEAS'EM!"

Indeed, so high was his skill in public estimation, that, upon the slightest twitch of uneasiness, the Doctor was always alongside the *pulse* of royalty. No man, it is said, was better read in the science of physiognomy than Doctor PLEAS'EM. His manners, too, were of so interesting a description, and his affability and condescension

---

[97] It was the opinion of STERNE, that the enjoyment of HEALTH was NINETY-NINE blessings out of *one hundred.* "Grant me but health, thou great Bestower of it," says he, "and, if it seems good unto thy Divine Providence, shower down thy Mitres upon those heads which are aching for them."

so universal, that an individual was half cured at the first visit. His penetration and knowledge of characters were so extensive, that he could distinguish with the utmost facility, from a touch of the pulse, between a vulgar plebeian habit of body, and the imaginary, refined, elegant creature of the upper circles of society. United to his other accomplishments, Doctor PLEAS'EM was also a man of the world. His mansion was truly imposing; the interior of which, to have witnessed, was quite a treat. It contained as many rich presents from those patients who had been indebted to his skill for a restoration to society, as would have made a distinct room to have been shown at Bullock's Museum. But who would not have given a silver inkstand for the preservation of a beloved wife—or a golden cup to Doctor PLEAS'EM for deceiving the grim King of Terrors, in carrying off a *tender* husband? The numerous *coughs* and slight indispositions which he had removed in the Fashionable World, furnished his tables with as much GAME as if he had been in the possession of several manors. The frequent dinners given by Doctor PLEAS'EM were so excellent in their style, as to be the theme of praise with all the epicures at the West End, although, in himself, he was abstemious to a fault, and a staunch devotee to regimen. In fact, so many great persons were under, or thought themselves under, obligations to Doctor PLEAS'EM, for the numerous cures he had performed in their families, that all his sons were provided with valuable official situations, even without any solicitation on the part of the Doctor.

Corinthian Tom, in his gay career, it seems, had crossed Doctor Pleas'em's path several times, and the polite *nod* had passed between them as often as daylight, but nothing in the *counting*[98] way had yet occurred; and Tom wished it now to appear, that he merely called, *en passant*, to inquire after the health of the Doctor, and, in the course of conversation, slightly to introduce the state of his own. The Doctor, who was quite alive to these sort of visits, always kept anything like *alarm*[99] from the minds of his visitors,

---

98   *Money matters* are not alluded to in this instance, but merely the simple *pulse.* It, however, must be admitted, that both of them are *feeling* subjects.
99   An anecdote has been related by a medical man of celebrity, that an

never noticing any alteration in their appearance, unless he was applied to in a *professional* way. He was also totally different from many others of the faculty, whose distinguished talents have placed them in an eminent point of view, and who *rudely* tell individuals applying to them for relief, that *nothing* is the matter with them; and at other times, with equal abruptness, nay, unfeelingly, reply, that *relief* is out of the question. No! Doctor Pleas'em was a hero of another school. He well knew that, in the upper circles of society, *illness* was perfectly necessary towards health; and that it would be quite *barbarous* to deprive any fashionable lady of the enjoyments resulting from an *elegant*[100] indisposition. In short, it was admitted on all hands, that no person was so well acquainted with the various species of ILLNESSES, from what is termed *political*, down to the *rheumatism in the shoulder*,[101] than Doctor Pleas'em.

Tom at length made his visit *intelligible* to the Doctor, who was no stranger to the spirited career which his visitor had been pursuing in the *beau monde*, and, with his usual smiling *naïveté*, told him "he had been a little too *rackety;* or rather like a bird confined in a cage, who, finding his door open, had flown about indiscriminately from bush to tree, till it had scarcely any strength left to reach a sprig to perch upon. "Perhaps," added the Doctor (shaking Tom by the hand), "I have been rather too severe in this remark; but, my dear friend, you stand in no need of the aid of physic. A few days' rustication, and partaking of the enjoyment of the sports of the field, will not only renovate the system, but you

---

individual in good health, but of a nervous habit of body, was frightened to death, in consequence of a person meeting him, and observing, "he looked so very ill, that it was much more requisite for him to be in bed than out of doors." The individual alluded to immediately fancied himself *ill*, took to his bed, and died accordingly. Numerous other instances might be quoted, if necessary, in the Metropolis.

100   This *innocent* stratagem, it is said, has often been tried in the Fashionable World, to ascertain "of what weight and importance the individual is held in the *scales* of society, from the number of inquiries and cards that are left respecting their health."

101   In both of these disorders, it operates as a good *ruse de guerre*, if a doctor only calls in the character of a friend. It also gives an effect to a previous impression that might have been *imposed* upon the public. But against the disciples of *John Doe* and *Richard Roe*, it has been known, in several instances, to have put them off their guard, and allowed time for an escape.

will return to town with an increase of spirits.

> Let sloth lie soft'ning till high noon in down,
> Or, lolling, fan her in the sultry town,
> Unnerved with rest; and turn her own disease,
> Or foster others in luxurious ease;
> I mount the COURSER, call the deep-mouth'd HOUNDS.
> The FOX, unkennell'd, flies to covert grounds;
> I lead where STAGS through tangled thickets tread,
> And shake the saplings with their branching head;
> I make the FALCONS wing their airy way,
> And soar to seize, or, stooping, strike their prey.
> To snare the FISH, I fix the lurking bait;
> To wound the FOWL, I load the gun with fate.
> 'Tis thus through change of EXERCISE I range,
> And *strength* and *pleasure* rise from every change.
> Here beauteous HEALTH! for all the year remain.
> When the next comes, I'll charm thee thus again."

"Bravo, Doctor, that will do," exclaims TOM; "there is *novelty* in the sound. It is true, a few days in the country will brace up the system; my mind will also be engaged with the diversity of scene and new characters; and I shall then return with the advantages of fresh vigour to enjoy the pleasures of LIFE IN LONDON. Besides, the experience I have had will teach me not to push along so *harem-scarem* as heretofore, but to pause a little, in order that I may *cull* those sports which may appear the most acceptable and congenial to my desires." TOM had scarcely finished these remarks, when he took a most friendly leave of *Doctor* Pleas'em, highly delighted with his *prescription;* and, on his way home to *Corinthian House,* called in at the *Albany,* to pay a visit to BOB LOGIC. Our hero explained the nature of his journey into the country; but BOB observed, he had other *game* in view, and must therefore beg to decline, for the present, accompanying his elegant friend in his *rustication.*

On TOM's arrival at CORINTHIAN HOUSE, he immediately repaired to his library, to look over the invitations which he had received from his friends in the country, whenever he might find it convenient to absent himself a few days from London; but among the number he found two of a very pressing nature from the Countess of TRUMPS and my Lord BUMPER. "It will not do," says TOM, "to spend more than a single day at his Lordship's seat, for there the remedy would prove worse than the disease. His Lordship is a four-bottle man, at least, and his principal enjoyment consists in challenging his company to keep pace with him, glass for glass, till he sees the whole of his guests drop under the table, or otherwise disposed of, and then exulting in the words of *Hipocrates*:—

> The only health to people hale and sound,
> Is to have many a tippling health go round.

But the mansion of the Countess of TRUMPS was pronounced by TOM to be even of a worse quality for a visitor to encounter than Lord BUMPER's *Chateau*. The dinners given by the Countess to her guests, it was said, were positively not to be excelled; indeed, so much were they in repute, that even the most fastidious epicure united in the general praise, for the superiority of style with which they were served up on all occasions. TOM maintained there was only one little drawback against paying his respects to the Countess of TRUMPS, which was, she played her *cards* so well, that every mouthful taken by any of her visitors was sure to cost them *five guineas!*

"I have it," cries TOM, "I will look for *Old* HAWTHORN's letter, which I received at the death of my father, but at that painful moment I then hastily threw it by, having no leisure or inclination to pay any attention to its contents. Mr HAWTHORN was a brother of my mother's; and I have often heard my father speak of him as being one of the most generous and best-hearted men of his day. If I am now fortunate enough to lay my hand upon it, from the slight recollection I have of Mr HAWTHORN's request to me, I shall most certainly embrace its invitation to spend a few days at his farm." After *rummaging* over a number of epistles, TOM's eye, at length, caught hold of the letter in question, which, in all probability, had it not been searched after under the present peculiar circumstances, might have remained unopened or unperused till doomsday. TOM read the following lines with great eagerness and pleasure:—

Hawthorn Hall.
DEAR NEPHEW,
  I am sincerely grieved, believe me, for the very great loss you have sustained in the death of your worthy and honourable father. He was one of my oldest friends and acquaintances: and it is but justice to his memory to state that, through a long and meritorious life, I never heard the slightest reproach levelled against his character. May you, my dear Nephew, be like him in every respect. I cannot wish you better. Whenever inclination suits, or when you can spare a few days from town, no one, rest assured, will endeavour to make you more welcome, comfortable, and happy, than I shall. If you are fond of hunting, shooting, &c., we have plenty of it at your service. My son, Jerry, who I must inform you, is a tightish clever sort of a lad enough, will be proud to wait upon his cousin, I am sure, when you please to arrive at Hawthorn Hall, which I hope will not be long first.

  Believe me, dear Nephew,
   Yours sincerely,
    JEREMIAH HAWTHORN.

Tom's sensibility was keenly touched, and the tear stood in his eye, as he glanced over the disinterested character given of his father by *Old Hawthorn*. All the scenes of gaiety and fun, that it might be said he had plunged into almost headlong since the death of his worthy sire, added to the great variety of new acquaintances he had also formed, had not as yet obliterated one tittle of that feeling and respect, whenever it flashed across his recollection, which he had always entertained for his dearly-beloved parent. Indeed, it had broke in upon his memory with redoubled affection and delight, and, in the words of *Hamlet*, as it applied to himself, he warmly exclaimed—

> Take him for all in all,
> I shall not look upon his like again.

HAWTHORN HALL was now the only object in view. It was new: it was delightful: and TOM pictured to his glowing mind, a few days at least of sport and merriment among the country folks. "I am *off,*" said he to LOGIC. But to part with CORINTHIAN KATE, aye, there was the rub! Pausing on the subject was dangerous; the thrilling tone of "*Don't go, my dear* TOM," from the persuasive tongue of KATE,—one who had hitherto but to name a request to have it granted,—might not only have placed HAWTHORN HALL out of TOM's sight for ever, but have prevented poor JERRY from the pleasure of his elegant friend's company in his *Rambles* and *Sprees* through the Metropolis: he, therefore, kissed her coral lips with an adieu that bespoke a speedy return. His prime *bit of blood* was crossed without delay; but he had scarcely proceeded a few yards, when he turned, as it were, involuntarily round for a parting gaze on the lovely figure of KATE:—

————————This is a creature,
Would she begin a sect, might quench the zeal
Of all professors else; make proselytes
Of who she but bid follow.

TOM clapped spurs to his steed to overtake his carriage, which he had sent forward to wait for him at a short distance on the road. He was out of sight in an instant; and all the pleasures of the Metropolis were left behind him for a short period.

TOM now thought of nothing else but *Old* HAWTHORN and *Somersetshire;* and pursued his journey with all the expedition of a stage-coach, taking refreshments merely when necessary. So much was CORINTHIAN TOM in haste to arrive at HAWTHORN HALL, that, although he had numerous acquaintances living at *Bath,* he stayed no longer at this elegant city than to allow time for changing horses at the *York Hotel*, and then galloped off in full speed for the house of his friend. Of *Old* Mr HAWTHORN, TOM had but a very slight recollection, having only seen him once at his father's residence, when he was quite a boy; but, nevertheless, the high approbation which his parent had bestowed upon the general conduct of his uncle, had not, in the slightest degree, escaped his memory. TOM had now nearly mastered his journey, being within a few paces of the object of his wishes—HAWTHORN HALL, the approach to which was rather rude and uninteresting than otherwise. It would have puzzled an *Inigo Jones*, or a *Christopher Wren*, to have demonstrated to what order of architecture the building belonged; or, more properly speaking, whether it belonged to any *Order* at all. NASH, with a shrug of his shoulders, would *instanter* have pronounced it horrid and *barbarous.* Its interior was not more fascinating as to decorations. *Useful* articles were to be found in abundance; but no Grecian sofas for luxurious lolling *tete-a-tetes* were to be seen; neither had the modern taste of the stylish furnishing upholsterer from the Metropolis yet made any progress in altering the venerable appearance of HAWTHORN HALL. The antique jovial fireside, with its roomy corners, that made all its inmates cheerful and warm when taking their humming stingo *October*, had also resisted the innovating hand of time, and remained in *status quo* for upwards of a century. This residence, however, had one qualification to boast of, which every visitor felt impressed with in an eminent degree on entering its doors. It was *cleanliness* to the very echo: the white cambric handkerchief might have been applied to every part of it, and not have lost a single particle of its colour. This *simplicity* operated as a fine contrast altogether, for the elegant and tasteful review of Corinthian Tom. As a building, Hawthorn Hall was never mentioned; it had no comparison about it, although the house was as well known in Somersetshire as a finger-post that directs the traveller on his journey. But as to its proprietors, who had descended from father to son for the last two hundred years, the case was materially different—a CHARACTER had been established by the Hawthorns for their generosity, hospitality, and charity, which was the pride and theme of the village in which they resided, and which had never been *sullied* from one generation to the other. The name of Hawthorn was in high repute in Somersetshire; nay, more, it was the passport to friendship and humanity.

> How often have I loiter'd o'er thy green,
> Where humble happiness endear'd each scene!
> How often have I paused on ev'ry charm,
> The shelter'd cot, the cultivated farm,
> The never failing brook, the busy mill,
> The decent church that topt the neighb'ring hill,
> The hawthorn bush, with seats beneath the shade,
> For talking age and whisp'ring lovers made!
> How often have I blest the coming day,
> When toil remitting lent its turn to play,
> And all the village train from labour free,
> Led up their sports beneath the spreading tree,
> While many a pastime circled in the sh

CHAPTER VII.

> The young contending as the old survey'd;—
> And many a gambol frolick'd o'er the ground,
> And sleights of art and feats of strength went round.
> And still as each repeated pleasure tired,
> Succeeding sports the mirthful band inspired;
> The dancing pair that simply sought renown,
> By holding out, to tire each other down;
> The swain mistrustless of his smutted face,
> While secret laughter titter'd round the place;
> The bashful virgin's side-long looks of love,
> The matron's glance that would those looks reprove.
> These were thy charms, sweet village! sports like those
> With sweet succession, taught e'en toil to please;
> These round thy bowers their cheerful influence shed.
> THESE WERE THY CHARMS—

TOM had now crossed the threshold of HAWTHORN HALL, where his anxious uncle was in attendance to hail his arrival. Reciprocal congratulations passed between them, when Mr HAWTHORN, in the ecstasy of the moment, grasping TOM's hand with great fervour, observed, "I am heartily glad to see you, my dear friend; and you are welcome a thousand times over, for the sake of your amiable father." TOM's heart was almost too full to reply to this kind sentiment—a slight tinge overspread his interesting countenance—and for an instant he felt a slight embarrassment at the gratifying reception he had thus met with from Mr HAWTHORN. JERRY, who was as bold as brass among his companions in the village, now stood almost on tip-toe peeping at the door of an inner apartment, afraid, as it were, of encountering the elegant impressive appearance of TOM, till he was summoned to come forth by the voice of his father, in order to be introduced to his London cousin, of whom FAME had already given so high-sounding a character. JERRY was somewhat *shy* upon this occasion, but not *sheepish*; it was that sort of *bashful* modesty, which an individual is sometimes apt to feel, when he is aware of coming in contact with a person of acknowledged superior talents. JERRY was no *Johnny Razo* either—he was not a staring, gawky, grinning country bumpkin, who laughs at he cannot tell what; and who is *astonished* at everything that he sees! No; he was a creature of another cast. JERRY was fond of a bit of fun—as gay as a lark—open-hearted, generous, and unsuspecting—and the life and soul of the village in which HAWTHORN HALL was situated. In all the sports and pastimes of the place, JERRY was the hero of the tale. At *hunting* and *shooting* he would not yield the palm to anyone. Over a five-barred gate he would *leap* without the slightest hesitation; and a wide ditch he would *jump* across, divested of anything like terror. For a *race* of a hundred yards, his speed was so excellent that he had no competitor; and to *trot* his pony, against "anything alive," he had taken the *conceit* out of all his opponents for miles round the country. In throwing a *quoit* he exhibited great strength and dexterity. At awake or a fair, in *cudgelling* or *wrestling,* JERRY had none of the worse of it. In the art of *self-defence* he showed such traits of the clearing-away system, that it was evident he had not visited Bristol and Lansdon Fair for nothing. In convivial scenes, no one made himself more jolly than JERRY; and his song always proved acceptable, nay, frequently an *encore.* With the *tender-hearted souls* of the village, his generosity and good-natured intention rendered him a great favourite; indeed, if a chapter were necessary in this work to be written on Rural Amours, perhaps no hero would cut a more prominent figure than JERRY HAWTHORN. But as this subject is too far removed from LIFE IN LONDON; and as he did not possess the advantages resulting from the tuition of a *Thwackum* and a *Square*, to point out at all times the evils attached to youth in partaking of the *forbidden fruit*, it will be much better to let the curtain remain down. However, at all events, this is not the time to *draw it up.* At a harvest-home, or a merry-making at Christmas, JERRY exhibited as much, perhaps more, natural taste and agility in his dancing than those persons who could boast of the advantages of having had Opera teachers to instruct them. In short, he was the very *double,* or *counterpart*, of CORINTHIAN TOM; making an allowance for the different spheres in which their various talents were exercised.

CORINTHIAN TOM's *perception* soon enabled him to enter into all the ideas and pursuits of those persons around him at *Hawthorn Hall.* So much so, that in the course of a day or two he was like "*one of themselves* ." There was not the slightest *reserve* about TOM's character; and it was his maxim, at all times, to accommodate himself, as much as possible, to the dispositions of the company in which he might be situated, *i.e.,*

When at ROME to *do* as ROME does!

Intimacy had now removed JERRY's *bashfulness;* and TOM and his merry cousin were almost inseparable. The unsophisticated manners and ingenuous disposition of JERRY had made TOM quite attached to him; and the former had already laid open all those little secrets which occur on the sly, "*that* DAD *ought not to know,"* as JERRY said, with as much frankness as if he had been intimate with TOM for twenty years: and all the tricks and fun of the village were disclosed to the latter hero without the least disguise. Indeed, JERRY appeared particularly anxious to make the time of his guest pass pleasantly and comfortably; and every little thing was produced that was thought would in any way afford amusement to CORINTHIAN TOM; while JERRY, in turn, treasured up almost every expression that fell from the lips of his elegant friend. He also looked up to him as a great master, and his arguments operated upon the mind of JERRY like the decisions of a Judge.

That Tom, who was the GO among the GOES, in the very centre of fashion in London, should have to encounter the *vulgar stare* of this village; or, that the dairy-maid should leave off skimming her cream to take a peep at our hero, as he mounted his courser, is not at all surprising: and Tom only smiled at this *provincial* sort of rudeness. In fact, he was Jerry's idol; and the latter, on looking at himself, began to make comparisons upon the different *cuts* of the apparel which decorated their persons. Indeed, the contrast was so striking, that an individual of less lively disposition and taste for dress than Jerry must have perceived it. "I should like," said Jerry, half checking himself, for fear of giving an affront. "Speak out, why this hesitation, my dear Coz?"[102] replied Tom. "Why then, upon your return to town, if you will let your tailor send me down a suit of clothes, according to your order, it will

---

102   Although this sort of relationship may be considered as *obsolete* in the Metropolis, it is not so in the country; and the affectionate term of *Coz* is often applied to each other.

be conferring a lasting obligation on your humble servant." "But why not return with me to London, Jerry? It was my intention, previous to quitting *Hawthorn Hall*, to have requested the favour of your company to spend a few months with me at *Corinthian House*. Everything that is worthy of being seen in the Metropolis you may depend upon my services to point out to you." "I should like it of all things," Jerry answered, in great raptures, "if Dad has no objection to it. It is true, I have been in London, and took a look at the Monument, Westminster Abbey, St Paul's, &c.; but, in other respects, I am almost as ignorant as if I had never been there. With such a friend as you at my elbow, who could introduce me to all the *prime* places, Oh, it would be glorious! I must try to get *Dad* in the humour to give his consent, and if you only second the proposition, it is done." Tom, smiling, assured Jerry he should not want his support.

The various exercises which Tom had taken with Jerry, during his residence at *Hawthorn Hall*, added to the rides over the velvet turf on Claverton Downs, had now so completely renovated his health[103] that his return to the Metropolis was decidedly fixed upon, and nothing occurred to delay his journey, but a day's fox-hunting with Sir *Harry Blood's crack* pack of hounds, Jerry's praises of which had so excited his curiosity, that Tom declared he would not miss such a day's sport on any consideration. He felt an additional interest in it, in consequence of Jerry's having frequently burst forth upon his ears with the *view-halloo;* the fine musical tones of which, it was generally admitted, no huntsman in Somersetshire could give in such rich style as young Hawthorn;

---

103   It should seem, that Doctor *Pleas'em* was a great advocate for *exercise*, and not much of an admirer of *medicine;* indeed, it appears to be the opinion of the learned, that, amidst the great discoveries and improvements made in the various sciences, most unfortunately for the benefit of mankind in general, *Physic* has not kept an equal pace. In a *consultation* of eight of the most *skilful* physicians of the Metropolis, who were called in to give their opinions upon the complaint of a person of high rank (a female of great beauty), it was clearly demonstrated, after her death, upon an investigation that could not fail, *five* of them were absolutely in the *dark,* and the other *three* had shown very little more *light* upon tho subject. It was rather sarcastically remarked, at the time, 'that her relatives could not complain that she had not been well-doctored!!!"

and we regret that we have no means of communicating its *excellence*[104] to our readers.

Tom now expressed to Jerry's father his intention of quitting *Hawthorn Hall*, who declared he would not suffer his departure on any account, without inviting a few friends to partake of a *jollification*, and a "parting cup" on the occasion. Tom, after expressing his thanks for the kindness he had received from Mr Hawthorn and his son, declared himself highly pleased with the project, from the amusement such a treat must afford him.

Tom and Jerry had been so much together, that the former might be said not to have been *alone* since his arrival at *Hawthorn Hall;* and, indeed, he would not have been so *now*, had not Jerry taken a ride over to Sir *Harry Blood's* park, to ascertain particulars respecting the time of the Fox-hunt. *London* and Logic now flashed across Tom's recollection; but more especially his lovely Kate, who appeared so distinctly before him, that, having a few minutes' leisure previous, to being summoned to dinner, he sat down, and composed the following stanzas:—

> While *Chloe's* lip, or *Rufa's* hair,
> Some favour'd poet's theme supplies;
> Tho' not a fig for me she care,
> Be *mine*, My Kate's bewitching EYES.
>
> Witches by various signs we trace,
> Howe'er imposing their disguise;
> 'Tis thus My Kate, with angel face,
> Betrays *her* witchery in her EYES![105]
>
> One for a *snowy bosom* pleads;
> "Give me *round arms,*" another cries:
> For me, no bliss on earth exceeds,
> To meet My Kate's bewitching EYES.

---

104 Those persons who recollect the *view-halloo* given by Mr Incledon, in his song of *Old Towler* (to acquire the tones of which, it took the above incomparable singer upwards of sixty rehearsals under an old huntsman, before he could venture a public performance of it), may form some sort of a comparison of its excellence, when informed that the superiority was allowed to Jerry.

105 The eyes of Corinthian Kate, it was said, equalled in brilliancy those of a late celebrated Duchess: of whom it is related, that a dustman, whose short pipe was out, with much *naivete* asked her to let him *light it* with the *fire* of her EYES.

> Uplifted looks, demurely sad,
> Preacher or Puritan may prize;
> I love the twinkling lustre glad,
> That gilds MY KATE's bewitching EYES.
>
> Long may those orbs unclouded shine!
> Youth's sunny weather swiftly flies;
> Nor all, with hearts like her's benign,
> Wear like MY KATE's bewitching EYES!
>
> Whene'er a glance of love she throws,
> I know the meaning it implies;
> For language no expression knows,
> To match her *eloquence* of EYES.
>
> By night they pierce my very dreams:
> And wakeful fancy,—when I rise
> Still warm, in *fascination* seems
> To paint MY KATE's bewitching EYES!

On the morning appointed for the Fox-hunt, JERRY placed himself under TOM's bed-room windows long before day-break, and, with his melodious *view-halloo*, aroused him from his slumbers. TOM was soon up; and, having equipped himself in the true Sportsman's style, was ready to start to join the party of Fox-hunters at Sir *Harry Blood's*. "Here, my dear *Coz*," said JERRY, "take your choice of two as fine hunters as ever leg was laid over, and which were never yet thrown out. But, before we go, let us fortify our stomachs with a slice or two of hung beef, and a horn or so of humming stingo!"

> Scarce the hounds were in cover, when off REYNARD flew.
> Not a sportsman who view'd him a syllable spoke;
> The dogs remain'd threading the thorny brake through.
> But at length in a *burst,* from a deep thicket, broke!
>
> The Fox knew his country, and made all the play,
> Whilst many a stubble and meadow were cross'd;
> O'er valleys and woodlands he kept on his way;
> When, lo! with the pack of his brush—he was lost.

Soon after their arrival at *Sir Harry's* park, the fox was turned out, and afforded one of the most delightful day's sports ever witnessed. It was not till after a chase of twenty-six miles, without the least check, that they ran into him, as Reynard was attempting to make his escape into a gentleman's garden; and TOM and

JERRY were both in at the death. Here JERRY again displayed his musical talents in the *death-halloo*, and remarked to TOM, what a *crack* pack of hounds Sir *Harry's* were, as in their pursuit of the fox through several herds of deer, and an amazing number of hares, their steadiness of conduct had been such as could not be surpassed, *if equalled*, by any pack in the county of Somerset.

On their return to HAWTHORN-HALL, they found the company, invited to take their farewell of CORINTHIAN TOM and JERRY, assembled in an apartment, termed the "SPORTSMAN'S CABINET;" the upper part of which was hung with the fox- skins of several past years killing; here and there a martin- cat intermixed, and gamekeepers' and hunters' poles in abundance. In the windows, which were rather large, several arrows, cross-bows, and other accoutrements were displayed; the walls also were decorated with numerous paintings connected with sporting subjects. Dinner was scarcely over and the cloth removed, when several of the old Sportsmen struck up in a loud chorus *"No mortals on earth are so jovial as we;"* at the conclusion of which, the health of CORINTHIAN TOM, as a sportsman, was drunk with loud cheers. Here JERRY got up, and assured the company that his *Coz.* loved a chase of *twenty-six* miles on end as well as any of them; and, without further ceremony, presented TOM with a pint bumper of port, with the fox's brush dipped and squeezed into it to give a zest to the liquor, who, in return, drank the healths of all the person present.

Bill Pointer, as keen a sportsman as ever followed a pack of hounds, and who was never known to refuse a leap in the severest chase, now proposed the following bumper toast— "HORSES *sound*, DOGS *healthy*, EARTHS *stopt, and* FOXES *plenty."* As many *chases* were talked over as the intervals between the songs and toasts would permit. *Tom Moody*, *the High-Mettled Racer*, *Hunting the Hare,* the *Jolly Falconer*, and

> A southerly wind, and a cloudy sky,
> Proclaim a hunting morning,
> Before the sun rises, we nimbly fly,
> Dull sleep and a downy bed scorning.
> To horse, my boys, to horse, away,
> The chase admits of no delay, &c.,

were not given, it is true, in the *refined* style of a stage performance; but they had to boast of a peculiar *character*, which actors cannot acquire. Jerry's *"Bright Chanticleer,"* with its *halloo* accompaniment, made the "Cabinet" ring again with applause; and at the express desire of Farmer *Corn*, he was pressed to favour the company with the late Charles Dibdin's delightfully descriptive song of the "Labourer's Welcome Home," which he, with the utmost good-nature, immediately began:—

> The ploughman whistles o'er the furrow,
> The hedger joins the vacant strain,
> The woodman sings the woodland thorough,
> The shepherd's pipe delights the plain.
> Where'er the anxious eye can reach,
>
> Or ear receive the jocund pleasure,
> Myriads of beings thronging flock,
> Of nature's song to join the measure;
> Till, to keep time, the village clock
> Sounds, sweet, the LABOURER'S WELCOME HOME!
>
> The hearth swept clean, his partner smiling,
> Upon the——

Here JERRY's recollection failed him; or, the *bumper toasts* had made such an impression upon his intellectual faculties, that he was unable to proceed. He was therefore compelled to apologise. By way of a *set-off,* he begged the attention of the company for his *Coz,* who, he was persuaded, would give them a *prime London touch.* This *notification* of JERRY's was received with great approbation, when his relative immediately began the following rhapsody,—entitled:

LIFE IN LONDON.*

London town's a dashing place, For ev'rything that's going, There's gig and fun in ev'-ry face, So nat-ty and so know-ing, Where

* A New Song by Pierce Egan, set to Music by A. Voight.

CHAPTER VII.

CHAPTER VII.

CHAPTER VII.

CHAPTER VII.

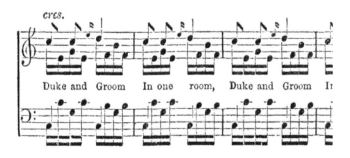

CHAPTER VII.

Chapter VII.

CHAPTER VII.

107

Chapter VII.

town for me! Danc-ing, sing-ing, full of glee, O London, London

town for me! *ff*

(The first and last strains of these three verses are not
original.—A. Voight.)

A DESCRIPTION OF THE METROPOLIS:
written by
Corinthian Tom.

London Town's a dashing place
For ev'ry thing that's going,
There's *fun* and *gig* in ev'ry face,
So natty and so *knowing*.
Where Novelty is all the rage,
From high to low degree,
Such pretty *lounges* to engage,
Only come and see!
What charming sights,
On gala nights; Masquerades,
Grand parades,
Famed gas lights,
Knowing fights.
Randall and Cribb
Know how to *fib!*
Tothill Fields

Pleasure yields;
The Norwich bull
With antics full.
Plenty of news,
All to amuse;
The Monkey "JACCO"
All the crack O!
Ambroghetti's squall,
Match girls bawl!
Put on the *gloves.*
Playful as doves,
Then show your *forte*
At the FIVES COURT;
Conjurers rare
At *Bartlemy* fair;
Polito's beasts,
See city feasts,
Lord Mayor's day—
Then the play,
Adelphi Theatre;
Pretty feature!
Rotten Row
Is all the Go!
In the Bench,
Keep your wench.
When next you roam,
Matthews "AT HOME!"
Such prime joking,
Lots of smoking,
Here all dash on
In the fashion!

CHORUS—Dancing, singing, full of glee,
O London, London town for me!

From ev'ry part the natives run.
To view this spot of land;
All are delighted with the fun,
Astonish'd 'tis so grand!
To VAUXHALL haste to see the blaze,
Such variegated lights;
The ladies' charms are all the gaze—
No *artificial* sights.
Lovely faces
Full of graces,
Heav'nly charms
Create alarms!
Such glances
And dances,
To the sky
See SAQUI fly
In a blaze.
All to amaze.
Cyprians fine,

Kids full of wine;
Orchestra grand
Pandean Band;
Charming singing,
Pleasure bringing;
Great attraction And satisfaction;
Plenty of *hoaxing*,
Strong coaxing;
Beautiful shapes,
Beaux and apes,
Prone to quiz
Every phiz!
Dashing glasses,
Queering lasses;
Flashy cits,
Numerous wits;
Loud talking,
Thousands walking,
Rare treating,
Numbers eating,
Punch and wine,
Ev'ry thing prime;
Grand CASCADE,
Once display'd;
Duke and groom
In one room;
Here all dash on
In the fashion!

CHORUS—Dancing, singing, full of glee,
O London, London town for me!

Such various *fancies* there display'd
To please and cheer the mind;
They captivate both man and maid
All polite and kind.
See fashion driving through each street,
With splendour and renown;
Pedestrians, too, with *shining* feet,
O, what a charming town!
Four-in-hand,
Down the Strand;
Funny gigs
With knowing wigs;
BAXTER's hats[106]
That queer the flats;
Flashy whips
With silver tips;
Leathern breech,
Pretty stitch!

---

106   *Topper-maker* to the FANCY; brother of *Ned Turner,* the celebrated pugilist; in high repute with the amateurs, in respect to giving the *knowledge-box* an important *look!*

High-bred cattle,
Tittle-tattle;
TATTERSALL sell;
Peep into *"Hell!"*
Full of play,
And make a stay;
Hear KEAN speak,
GRIMALDI squeak!
Courts of law,
Full of jaw;
BROUGHAM plead;
MACAULAY read;
And Old Borum
At the Forum:
To Opera prance,
See Vestris dance;
At Free and Easy
Full and greasy
Prime song and catch;
Then trotting-match;
London cries,
O rare hot pies!
Sadler's Wells
In summer tells;
Quick approach
In hackney coach;
Take your *Daffy*
All be happy;
And then dash on
In the fashion.

CHORUS—Dancing, singing, full of glee,
O London, London town for me!

The company, who had not been idle with their glasses, had now got rather freshish.[107] Old Hawthorn and his visitors appeared highly delighted with Tom's descriptive song of the Metropolis; indeed, several of the party wished for an encore. Jerry whispered to his cousin, that he thought a better opportunity could not occur for putting the question to his father about his intended journey to London. Tom fulfilled his promise, and acted as an able second upon the occasion; and Farmer Stubble, one of Mr Hawthorn's most intimate friends, unexpectedly declaring that it might tend towards Jerry's improvement—under the tuition of such a gentleman as Corinthian Tom—the motion was carried without a divi-

---

107   In a fair way to become *intoxicated:* but a country phrase altogether, as "I was rather *freshish!*"

sion. The scene altogether was happiness and good-humour; and the old Farmers, anxious to have a bit of fun among themselves, gave each other the wink to ply the Gentleman Londoner, as they termed him, with plenty of drink, that they might send him merry to bed. This, how ever, was useless, as Jerry put Tom on his guard respecting their intention; and, both uniting against these jolly fellows, they soon had the laugh against them.

Farmer Stubble now rising, with a glass in his hand, recited, in rather a discordant voice, the following verse from the Tippling Philosopher:—

> Democritus always was glad
> Of a bumper to cheer up his soul,
> And would laugh like a man that was mad.
> When over a good flowing bowl.
> As long as his cellar was stored,
> The liquor he'd merrily quaff;
> And when he was drunk as a lord,
> At those that were sober he'd laugh.

Mirth and harmony enlivened the company till a late hour: *how* several of them got to bed, it is not worth while to inquire. Suffice it to say, CORINTHIAN TOM "saw them all out"—when he retired to rest, highly delighted with his day's sport and his evening's entertainment.

The morning having arrived for TOM and JERRY's departure for London, all was hurry and bustle at *Hawthorn Hall.* The latter got up rather early, to take leave of his numerous friends in the village; but more especially to bid "good-bye," and to take a parting kiss, *on the sly*, of those *tender* companions who had so pleasingly occupied his softer hours. Several of the farmers' daughters, it appears, had "*set their* caps" [108] at JERRY, whose situ-

---

108   Something after the manner of *Molly Maybush* and *Jemmy Jumps,* in "The Farmer":—

"MOLLY.—Did I think you ever could forget the day you left our village. Don't you remember, as you were stepping on the coach roof, as I stood crying, you with one foot on the little wheel, and t'other just on the boot; your right hand you stretched to the coachman, and your left as I held in mine, washing it with my tears, the postman at that moment sounding his horn:—'Gee-up!' says the coachman, and I soon lost sight of my JEMMY.

ation in life rendered him rather an enviable object in their choice of a husband. The thought of losing him operated strongly on their feelings; and particularly as he was going up to London with such a gay gentleman as CORINTHIAN TOM, it was but natural to expect, that all of them would soon be forgotten, in the blaze of female attraction which he would have to encounter during his stay in the Metropolis. All this was done even without the knowledge of his clearest friend and confidant, TOM; but, in these occurrences, few persons like to have any witnesses of those precious moments, when the hand is squeezed with ecstasy—the love-sick sigh half suppressed—and the pearly drop steals down the cheek of beauty, at the departure of a favoured lover. Upon these points, SHAKSPEARE observes, with great truth, that—

> Friendship is constant in all other things.
> Save in the office and affairs of love:
> Therefore all HEARTS in love use their *own* TONGUES.
> Let every EYE negotiate for itself,
> And *trust* no AGENT; beauty is a witch,
> Against whose charms faith melted into blood.

The coach at length drew up to the hall-door, when TOM took a polite farewell of the party, accompanied with many thanks for the sports that had been selected for his amusement. The tears stood in Old HAWTHORN's eyes, when he grasped the hand of his son, and faintly articulated, "*Goodbye!*" JERRY felt rather ticklish, but endeavoured to preserve his firmness. The domestics also respectfully wished him a pleasant journey; when off they started, bowing to their friends, till they lost sight of *Hawthorn Hall*. LONDON now was the only object before them; and the anticipation of enjoying the company of his lovely KATE, and the facetious BOB LOGIC, in a few fleeting hours, stole across TOM's mind with increased effect; while JERRY, in raptures, frequently

---

"JEMMY.—*Have me!* certainly, they were all upon the *scramble* for me, as if I was a tit-bit for a city feast. I was such a neat—tol lol! hey! BETTY dressed at me—JENNY skimmed the cream—MOLLY robbed the hen roost—SUSAN baked the round little hot loaves for my breakfast—BECKY sung to me—SAL hopp'd—and POLL bobb'd at me; but, poor things! it wasn't on the cards—cou'dn't be."

burst out, humming the last line of his Cousin's song of "*London, London town for me.*" They pursued their journey as fast as the horses could go; and every milestone was hailed with pleasure, as it brought them nearer to the Metropolis. Nothing of importance occurred on the road; and, after a few changes of horses, JERRY found himself sitting comfortably by the side of TOM, at *Corinthian House.*

CHAPTER VIII.

Jerry an Inmate of *Corinthian House*—Its Taste and Elegance described—Useful Hints from *Tom* to *Jerry*—The latter in training to become a *Swell*—His Introduction to Bob Logic—A Ride in Rotten Row.

WITH MANY PERSONS, it should seem, to "KNOW THE WORLD," consists in knowing now to get money; to know HOW to purchase annuities and estates; to know HOW the stocks fluctuate; to know HOW to *juggle*, with the *Jugglers* of 'Change Alley; and to know now to make a large fortune: with others, the *grand secret* appears to he, to know HOW *to keep it,* after it has been obtained. This sort of *knowledge,* however, was not the *forte* of Corinthian Tom, nor of his friend Logic; on the contrary, no persons knew better than they did, how to *spend* a fortune. "Seeing Life," was their object. To keep all sorts of company—to admire an accomplished mind, whenever they found it—to respect and follow notions of real gentility—and to select the most sensible and agreeable persons in society as their companions; to see this sort of *"Life"* was what induced Jerry to leave Hawthorn Hall. There was no *sophistry* attached to his character; he came to *London* with an impatient ardour to join in the *fun*— to enjoy the *lark*—to laugh at the *sprees,* and to be *alive* in all his Rambles. It appears, however, his *highest object* was improvement; intending to return to Hawthorn Hall somewhat wiser than when he left it—to possess a more correct knowledge of the various classes of society, and a more enlarged acquaintance with men and manners.

To "See Life," then, was the primary consideration of Jerry Hawthorn—but it was not to agree with every disposition, and conform with every species of behaviour totally inconsistent with the tenets of reason, prudence, and good manners; neither was it to ridicule all sober, well-disposed persons, as people wholly unfit to live in the world. It was not that "sort of Life," that encouraged individuals to drink very hard—to swear a good round hand—to sing an indecent song—or to be smutty and fulsome in discourse.

IT WAS NOT to mimic and take off such as have, unhappily, an impediment in their speech; to be excessively droll in remarks on those who are disfigured through any natural defect; or to look on every person as a FOOL that has any regard for religion.

IT WAS NOT to be loose in morals, wanton in debauchery, and horrid in imprecations; to appear learned in everything allied to obscenity and lewdness, and in everything else to appear as ignorant as a person might please.

IT WAS not to know, or pretend to know, all the young ladies in town; and should you discover any one, two, or three of them to have conceived an affection for you, to endeavour to debauch them all; and if you are so happy as to succeed, then to forsake and expose them, by way of gratitude for the favours they had bestowed.

IT WAS NOT to belong to drinking clubs, sporting clubs, or debating societies. To go often to the playhouses, and there always to distinguish yourself as highly as possible in assuming every freakish air and saucy attitude; and, when profound attention is required for the hearing of any fine and pathetic speech, to be suddenly seized with a loud fit of coughing; to clap like a hero at what you should not, and hiss at what you do not understand.

IT WAS NOT to go to taverns, coffee-houses, and places of ill- fame, to commit every sort of outrage and disorder; such as jumping about the rooms, putting out the candles, spilling the liquors, breaking the glasses, kicking the waiters, &c., &c.

IT WAS NOT to frequent places of fashionable resort, and to

keep it up all night in drinking, swearing, and singing; and when fair morn makes her approach, then heroically to sally forth into the street, *reel* about like a RAKE of the first magnitude, insult all you meet, knock down an old woman or two, break a few windows, stagger to another tavern for a fresh supply of the juice of the grape, and finish your glorious frolic in being sent home in a hackney-coach, senseless, speechless, and motionless, more like a beast than a rational intelligent human being.

> The passions are all prone to sad disorders,
> Whose objects never should approach their *borders!*
> "O lead us not into temptation!"
> Is a choice prayer, and which I much admire—
> So *many things* are dangerous to desire!
> So ripe for foul assassination!
>
> O youths! whene'er the wishes warm of nature
> *Tumultuous rise*—destroy their dangerous dance;
> The curb of reason to your aid advance,
> And *souse them* with her *buckets of* cold water.
> No harm is in the passions, to be sure,
> But then they must not gallop wild to door;
> Close keep them, just like hounds that long for hare,
> Or muzzle them, indeed, like ferrets,
> And thus suppress their wanton spirits,
> That, lawless, wish to be as free as air.
>
> The passions, as I've said, are far from *evil.*
> But if not well confined they play the devil.
>
> Learn from *that* candle—mark its *govern'd* flame,
> How in its lustre—gentle, steady, tame,
> So mild, such trembling modesty, so quiet!—
> But let him touch your curtains on your bed,
> Who on such stuff delighteth to be fed,
> Lo! in a brace of minutes what a riot!
> He pulls (for nought the unbridled rogue reveres),
> Like SAMSON, *an* OLD HOUSE *about his ears.*

JERRY had now realised the summit of his wishes, in being happily situated under the roof of his relative at CORINTHIAN HOUSE. The elegance of his cousin's appearance had often excited his praise and admiration; but he was now altogether as much delighted, nay, astonished, at the superlative style which TOM had displayed in *decorating* the interior of his mansion; and some little time had elapsed before JERRY's eyes grew familiar to the

CHAPTER VIII.

grandeur and dazzling objects with which he was surrounded. Indeed, to describe the numerous beauties CORINTHIAN HOUSE contained would require a complete and extensive catalogue. It was a perfect model; a combination of taste and excellence. There was nothing superfluous about it, yet nothing was wanting. All that ART could produce had been effected, regulated by a sound and critical judgment. Every room had its CHARACTER; and all of them were *emphatic*. In the selection of paintings, exhibited upon one side of the PICTURE GALLERY, a correct knowledge of the *old masters* had been displayed it was admitted by all the connoisseurs who had seen them. Upon the other side of this splendid apartment the contrast was equally fine and attractive. The beauties of the MODERN SCHOOL OF PAINTING, rising proudly in an improved state of grandeur, were viewed, challenging, as it were, the OLD MASTERS to the scale of *competition*. The works of Sir Joshua Reynolds, West, Lawrence, Fuseli, Opie, Westall, Gainsborough, Loutherbourg, the eccentric Barry,[109] Beechy, Turner, Wilkie, Haydon, &c., &c., shone forth in all that vigour of expression, softness of touch, and brilliancy of colouring, which gave a *character* to that era of painting, so highly distinguished during the reign of our much-lamented and revered Monarch, George the Third, the founder of the Royal Academy. JERRY was at a complete *standstill* between these two great magnets of attraction. He was no connoisseur, yet he used to observe to TOM there was a "certain something" about the paintings that seemed almost to fasten him to the spot.

In the SKETCH-ROOM, which was principally dedicated to

---

[109] The works of this distinguished painter, and his great eccentricity of character, were often the subjects of conversation between CORINTHIAN TOM and his visitors. JERRY laughed heartily on being told by his Coz that BARRY, who lived like a hermit, entirely by himself, in a very capacious house, on the Adelphi Terrace, in order to save the expense of repairing a broken pane of glass, placed a most beautiful painting, of the value of five hundred guineas, against the window, to keep out the cold and the rain! This great artist was the intimate friend of the late Edmund Burke, Esq.; and so delighted was Barry with the work on the *"Sublime and Beautiful,"* when it was first shown to him in manuscript, that he literally copied every word of it for his own use.

the productions of the late GEORGE MORLAND, JERRY was rather more if not quite at home, almost skipping with rapture as his eye ran over the subjects of that unrivalled genius of the pencil. NATURE was seen so strongly at every touch that JERRY nearly fancied himself again at HAWTHORN HALL, looking at his dogs, pigs, and horses.

It was the opinion of CORINTHIAN TOM, in his remarks to JERRY, when the latter first entered this apartment, that if MORLAND had only painted half the number of subjects which are now before the public, their value might have been enhanced twice as much; and *finished* pictures, instead of *sketches,* most likely would have been the result. This was the reason TOM assigned to JERRY for having it called the SKETCH-ROOM. "Nine times out of ten," said TOM, "dull matter-of-fact calculation is not allied with genius." *Money,* to GEORGE MORLAND, was a *colour* that he did not paint with; and, therefore, respecting its *value,* he seemed to know nothing. *Embarrassment* and the catch-poles first drew up the curtain and showed him the iron bars which stopped his thoughtless career. They also explained to him, in the most feeling manner, the *uses* of a strong lock. They likewise pointed out to GEORGE the difference of his *prospects,*—not in an artist-like manner to his "mind's eye," but in a clear distinct way of business, that *twenty shillings* make a POUND. For the *moment,* he keenly felt the disgusting *cramped* situation of Carey Street, which compelled him to *peep* at his objects through the iron rails of his apartment: for the *moment,* also, he felt the immediate *necessity* of procuring the gold *talismanic* key to give him once more his liberty, again to wander amidst the beauties of nature: it was then that MORLAND painted for *money:* it was then that GENIUS was in fetters: it was then that rapid *exertions* got the better of his *taste.* The instance speaks forcibly for itself. "The sooner you paint me a picture, Mr MORLAND," said the *leary* Bum-trap, "the sooner the door will be open to you. Freedom is in view,—and I'll discharge your debt." No skilful angler ever threw his line into the water with a more *coaxing* bait to hook the poor fish, than Mr *Screw* "tried it on" with his prisoner. It was plausible: it was better,—it gave no trouble to his acquaintance: it also prevented *shyness* or REFUSAL from his friends. The lock-up house, by such means, lost its terrors. Employment was found for the mind and pencil of *Morland*. He experienced no *shiverings* of the body—no feverish *parched-up* tongue, waiting with the most anxious suspense for the return of the messenger to bring the NO, which ultimately sent him to jail, or the delightful YES, that set the prisoner once more at liberty. On the contrary, GEORGE was quite at home. He did as his inclinations prompted him. Jolly fellows called on him in abundance; and the song and the glass went round with the freedom of a tavern. All his wants were supplied, and the *misery* of a spunging-house was not seen in MORLAND's apartment. In fact, he was better attended than when out of it. From the *top screw* to the *stamper*-cleaner, all of them felt an interest in waiting upon the "GREAT GENIUS," as he was termed, in order to take a sly peep at his paintings. *Here* GEORGE set no price to his pictures; but when he was tired of his companions, and his confined situation, he then industriously, and in a short time, *painted* himself out of the lock-up house. *Lumbering*[110] him never afterwards gave MORLAND any horrors: and, whenever he was again in *trouble*, the same kind of *judgment* was repeated, time and often, till Mr *Screw* had realised a tolerable collection of valuable paintings. This officer was rather fond of pictures himself; but when any gentleman took a fancy to purchase any of them, Mr *Screw* never betrayed a want of knowledge of their value, by the *prices* he affixed to them, MORLAND died at a premature age;—dissipated habits proved his *quietus*. The ruder scenes of Nature were his hobby. *Genteel* Life was too dull, too insipid, for his pencil. But a more independent mind never had an existence; and his good qualities were numerous. The lap-room he preferred to the parlour. Too much assumption of would-be politeness and self-importance he thought frequently decorated the latter, while the former furnished nothing else but originality of character. The *coal-heaver* cooking his own meat, and taking the *lining* out of a pot of porter at one *pull*—the carman tossing off a

---

110   *Being* arrested.

glass of gin like water—and the needy woman ballad-singer going from house to house attempting to get a halfpenny out of some poor tradesman for a song, were the sort of groups that fastened on the mind of MORLAND. He never felt more happy than when he was seen amongst them: he depicted their various traits and peculiarities in the most glowing colours; and he has left them behind him, living as it were on his canvas, a monument of his unrivalled talents in a peculiar style of painting.

To the Saloon,[111] the walls of which were completely covered with the most highly-finished engravings executed in the Metropolis, Jerry often repaired, when a few leisure moments offered, to contemplate such an inimitable collection of portraits of public characters. Over Harlow's[112] trial scene of Queen Katherine before Henry the Eighth, and Wilkie's Blind Fiddler and the Rent-day, JERRY was frequently witnessed rubbing his hands with delight at their excellence.

The DRAWING-ROOM was noble, grand, and impressive. The LIBRARY, however interesting, was attractive from the superior bindings of the books, which caught the eyes of the spectators upon their entering it; yet, upon a more close examination, by the lovers of literature, it discovered that a MIND had not been wanting in the proprietor, in the selection of the works it contained.

The portfolio of *caricatures*, including the whole of the fine and extensive collection of GILRAY's works, often afforded great fun and laughter for JERRY; while the inimitable wood-cuts, which Tom had been rather prodigal in getting together, by way of a *set-off*, astonished JERRY at the great perfection which had been attained in this curious and interesting branch of the arts.

---

111 This apartment had been christened, a long time before JERRY arrived in town, by LOGIC, the "ACQUAINTANCE ROOM." BOB would frequently catch hold of JERRY by the arm, after they had become intimate, and ask him to take a turn among their acquaintances; for so he denominated most of those characters, such as Mr Kean, Mr Brougham, Miss O'Neill, Miss Kelly, &c., who were continually appearing before the eye of the public. It was from the remarks of LOGIC that JERRY picked up considerable information respecting the above sort of persons.
112 The death of this young artist, from the extraordinary talents he possessed, has been considered an irreparable loss to the arts.

CHAPTER VIII.

The CONVERSATION ROOM was equally as elegant and impressive as the other apartments. It was the "gig-shop" of the visitants, but denominated by BOB LOGIC the *Bay of Condolence*.[113] In short, the *tout ensemble* of CORINTHIAN HOUSE operated so imposingly upon the feelings of those persons of fashion who had been permitted a sight of its interior, that in their instructions to the upholsterer, as far as the inside of this magnificent dwelling could be imitated, the general expression was, "I should like to have my house fitted up exactly after the style of CORINTHIAN TOM's!"

JERRY was taking a sly peep at himself in an elegant looking-glass that reflected his whole length of person, when TOM suddenly broke in upon him, and, clapping his hand upon his Cousin's shoulder, exclaimed, with a smile—

"We must assume a STYLE if we have it not!"

JERRY, rather confusedly, replied, "I understand you; I must send for your tailor to give me a *new* touch." "That shall be done without delay," said TOM. Mr PRIMEFIT, of Regent Street, was immediately sent for, and ordered to attend upon Mr HAWTHORN, with his pattern-card, to take orders.

> But how shall I, unblamed, express
> The *awful* MYSTERIES OF DRESS;
> How, all unpractised, dare to tell
> The art sublime, ineffable,
> *Of making* MIDDLING MEN *look* WELL;
> Men who had been such heavy sailors
> But for their shoemakers and tailors!
> So, by the cutler's sharpening skill,
> The bluntest weapons wound and kill:
> So, when 'tis scarcely fit to eat,
> *Good cooks*, by DRESSING, *flavour* MEAT.

---

113   This room had a variety of names. Its godfathers were also numerous. The *Bay of Condolence*, as Logic termed it, had afforded him consolation from his *pals* during the relation of many of his nightly adventures and misfortunes. JERRY used to style it "Harvest Home," from the numerous good things which were served up in it. And from the continual *buz* he had to encounter when any of the *bon vivants* dropped in to have a bit of chit-chat, Tom designated this apartment the *"Chaffing Crib!"* But it derived its *climax* from the *high-life-below-stairs* gentry who *whispered* it one to another, as "Hell broke loose!"

> And as by steam impressed with motion,
> 'Gainst wind and tide, across the ocean,
> The merest TUB will far outstrip
> The progress of the slightest ship
> That ever on the waters glided,
> If with an engine unprovided;
> Thus BEAUX, *in person* and in *mind,*
> Excelled by those they leave behind,
> On, through the world, undaunted, press,
> *Backed by the* mighty power *of* DRESS;
> While folks less confident than they,
> Stare, in mute wonder,—and give way.

"My dear Coz," said Tom, "we shall soon intermix with the various classes of society; and although it is not absolutely necessary that you should be able to dispute the accuracy of a *Greek quotation* with a Porson—contend with a Mozart upon the fundamental *'principles of harmony*—enter into a dissertation on the properties of *light and shade* with a Reynolds— quote *precedents* with a Speaker of the House of Commons— argue *law* with an Eldon—display a knowledge of *tactics* with a Wellington—write *poetry* with a Byron—relate *history* with a Gibbon—contest *grammatical points* with a Horne Tooke—*wit* and *eloquence* with a Canning—support the *Old English Character* with a Windham—dance with an Oscar Byrne—*fence* with an O'Shaunessy—*set-to* with a Belcher —*sing* with a Braham—contest the *law of nations* with a Liverpool—*erudition* with a Johnson—*philosophy* with a Paley—the *wealth of nations* with a Smith—*astronomy* with an Herschel—*physiognomy* with a Lavater—*equity* with a Romilly—and so on to the end of the Chapter of Talents in the Metropolis;—although it is not necessary, I again repeat, my dear Coz, that you should be able to rival all the traits of excellence possessed by the above characters, yet it is essentially requisite that you should have some knowledge of their respective qualities, and be sensibly alive to their immediate value, and the impression they have made on the minds of mankind." "Hold, hold!" said Jerry, smiling, and making a low bow at the same time; "there is one person among these distinguished men that you have forgot to mention—Who shall dispute *taste* with Corinthian Tom?

The latter hero gave rather a graceful *nod* in return for this unexpected compliment, which, it should seem, augured to TOM a kind of budding of the lively genius of his Cousin's mind. The CORINTHIAN had just ordered his servant to bring him "*The Weekly Dispatch*," to see how sporting matters had been going on in the Metropolis during his absence from town, when Mr PRIMEFIT was announced to Mr HAWTHORN to be in waiting to receive his commands.

Mr PRIMEFIT, according to the "*counter-talking* part of the community," had done "all his dirty work;" and among the *needles*[114] at the West End of the Town, who must sport a genteel *outside,* no matter at whose *suit,* it was observed, between a grin and a pun, that he had not only got rid of all his "*had habits*" but had likewise outlived his *sufferings.*[115] It was said of this celebrated "apparel furnisher," that, if he received the cash for ONE coat out of *three,* nothing was the matter! In his *intercourse*[116] with people of fashion, the character that ran before him was a perfectly gentleman tradesman. He had one *point* in view on setting out in life, and he never lost sight of it. To ask his customers for payment was to *lose* their custom. Though for the first seven years DICKEY PRIMEFIT was engaged in *cutting-up* his cloth, hurried beyond measure, yet those "troublesome customers," *John Doe* and *Richard Roe,* were continually at his elbow, *nudging* him to take "measure of their suits" in preference to every other person; his law expenses and "MUM *tip,*"[117] in consequence, were frightful; yet DICKEY braved the fury

---

114   Otherwise *Sharps.* I have not been exactly able to ascertain whether this phrase originated with a *Punster;* but it must be admitted it does not want for *point.*
115   "*Tom Simpleton.*—Just as we talk to one another about our coats:— We never say, 'Who's your tailor? 'We always ask:—'WHO SUFFERS?'"
                                                                                        —JOHN BULL.
116   This, certainly, must be viewed as an improvement in phraseology. *Intercourse* is a soft, stylish, and pleasant word. There is nothing *plebeian* or waiter-ish about it.
117   *Silence!* How extremely *polite* and *gentlemanly* to inform an individual that he will be "*wanted*" on such a particular day, instead of dragging him away from his business and family, and locking him up like a felon, besides making a *buz* about his premises, which not only knocks up his credit in his neighbourhood, but spoils his reputation at a distance. Why, SUCH *accommodation* is *worth* any TIP. It is a *multum in parvo* trait of "Life in London."

of the woollen draper's "storm" with the utmost composure. With a placid countenance he never refused credit to any British officer, either in the sea or land service, let the distance or uncertainty of the expedition be what it might. The *reference* of one gentleman to another was quite sufficient to Mr PRIMEFIT; and the *garments* were made and sent home without further inquiry or delay. Of course, in return, the *charges* of DICKEY were never overhauled; indeed, what GENTLEMAN would have behaved so *ungentlemanly* to a tradesman who was all civility, politeness, and *accommodation*, from one end of his pattern-card to the other. The business of Mr PRIMEFIT, therefore, became so extensive, that he sent clothes to all parts of the world. In *London,* no gentleman, who had been once in the books of DICKEY, would listen to the name of any other tailor, which rendered PRIMEFIT the "*go*" for a tasty cut, best materials, and first-rate workmanship. DICKEY had a "soul above buttons;" he had no narrow ideas belonging to him; and he flattered himself that, ultimately, it would *all be right.* "*No gentleman*" Mr PRIMEFIT would often assert, when he has been blamed for giving such an extensive loose sort of credit, *"I am convinced, but will act as such, sooner or later, towards me!"* So it proved. Things, at length, took the expected turn. Many long out-standing bills came in. His capital accumulated. His business also increased in so extraordinary a manner that several clerks were necessary to keep it in order, and ensure *punctuality.* DICKEY was almost as true as a clock to his time, in attending to orders. His character for fashion was so *emphatic,* that numbers of stylish tradesmen, who found it necessary to have a "bettermost coat" by them, for "high days

---

'Tis GOLD

> Which buys admittance; oft it doth, yea, make Diana's rangers false themselves, and yield up Their deer to the stand o' th' stealer; and 'tis *gold* Which makes the true man killed, and saves the thief—
> Nay, sometimes hangs both thief and true man; what *Can it not* DO, *and* UNDO?

But after all, it must be viewed as a most liberal *accommodation* to the unfortunate but embarrassed debtors, and such *secrecy* has rendered the most important services to thousands of persons in the Metropolis.

and holidays," regardless of the charge, employed Mr PRIMEFIT. The sunshine of prosperity was now so complete, that not a single *bum-trap* had crossed the threshold of DICKEY's door, in the way of *private* business, for many a long day past. In short, Mr PRIMEFIT had realised the climax of his exertions—he had *measured* his way into a carriage. DICKEY was principally distinguished for the *cut* of his coats. To CORINTHIAN Tom he was peculiarly indebted, as a leader of the fashion. It was owing to this circumstance that Mr PRIMEFIT waited in person at *Corinthian House;* indeed, the active use of the scissors and parchment had long been removed from the hands of DICKEY, and his principal occupation now consisted in *talking* over the versatility of fashion to his customers, and giving directions to his men. But the slightest idea that might drop from CORINTHIAN Tom respecting the advantages of dress was what DICKEY could not resist, and he, therefore, ordered his carriage immediately to attend upon our rustic hero.

Tom and JERRY, previously to the arrival of the *apparel-furnisher*, had been discussing the advantages resulting from *dress* and ADDRESS; and the CORINTHIAN had also been pointing out to his Coz not to *skim* too lightly over so important a subject, but to peruse with the most marked attention that *grand living* BOOK *of* BOOKS—

MAN!!!

"It is worthy, my dear JERRY, to cherish the Poet's observation to its utmost extent," said TOM, "that the consideration of that noblest of animals is one of the most PROPER STUDIES which belong to the education of an individual. It is our duty to trace him through the various avenues that lead to his *elevation*, and it is also incumbent upon us to penetrate into the dark paths which ultimately bring MAN into a degraded state. The *comparisons* of many MEN, so often impressed on my memory by my late worthy father, now flash across my recollection so strongly that I will repeat them for your instruction, JERRY, and though rather odd, were not altogether, perhaps, UNJUST. Some of them he thought bore a likeness to a badly-written dramatic piece, decorated with the most fascinating scenery and captivating music, and many of the audience, upon retiring to their closets, have felt a sort of vexation in being lulled off their guards by such gaudy allurements, or that *delusion* could have been dressed up so speciously as to have overcome the advantages of common sense. Just so, it was my father's opinion, concerning *dress, address*, and ELOQUENCE; and he thought Lord Chesterfield had too often been prophetic in declaring a prepossessing appearance to be very imposing, and capable of performing wonders, as it proved frequently the fact, that mankind are so much dazzled with the exterior as not to trouble themselves about any further consideration of the object before them. Have we not experienced, said my father, that many of our most trifling *scribblers* have found their way into splendid mansions, and, in luxuriant bindings, gained prominent situations in elegant bookcases; while, on the contrary, numerous EMINENT AUTHORS have been consigned to moulder on the shelves in the warehouses of the booksellers, not even partaking of the friendly shelter of *boards*. Strip, says he, many ORATORS of their *eloquence*, and that *glare* which has misled our feelings, *ignis fatuus* like, at the moment, and, when leisure occurs to ascertain their real character, it will be found that little more than a *mask* remains to cover their deceptions. *Tear* aside the FLATTERER's *art*, and a composition of more flimsy materials never appeared to public view. *Dissect* the *plausible* MAN of his seeming candour, and *pretence* will be his most prominent feature. *Trace* the VIOLENT politician through his approaches to patriotism, and you will rarely find that he gains the summit of your expectations—A TRUE PATRIOT: the fiery ordeal of place, pension, or sinecure, to *check* his violence, creates so strong a blaze on his feelings, that few heroes have escaped its scorching rays! VIEW the SECTARIST, who preaches, prays, and exhorts his fellow-creatures, that meet weekly to unburden their overloaded consciences, to obtain a crumb of comfort from his exertions—behold this leader of piety, this *monument* of righteousness, too frequently the slave of avarice, and his ambition prompted more in being the acknowledged head of a party than actuated by those pure motives which true religion never fails to inspire. Analyse the

CHAPTER VIII.

pleadings of some learned counsel, whose highly-coloured description of his client's virtues would almost extort admiration from the hearers for so good a man,—yet be not surprised if, at some future period, on a more intimate acquaintance with the person who has been so brilliantly described by a *well-rewarded* brief, he turn out in reality as different in character as LIGHT is to *dark*.

"So numerous are the instances which might he displayed, my dear Coz, 'to hold the mirror, as it were, up to Nature,' that volumes would not suffice to portray the various characters which *cross our path* DAILY *in* LONDON. A *theoretical* inquiry will not go far enough in ascertaining the real features of society in the *Metropolis*. You are now on the *primest* SPOT in all the world: it may be a prejudice,[118] but I will show fight in support of tins assertion, with the last drop of my blood. I would, therefore, advise you to make the best use of your time. I have seen a great deal of LIFE myself; but I have a great deal yet to *see!* However, I am by no means *invulnerable;* and shall, in all probability, be yet '*had*' upon many *suits*, that at the present moment I am not *awake* to. Then let me impress upon your feelings, not to be TOO CONFIDENT; and do not think that in a little time you will be 'UP to *everything;*' or, to use a current expression among the *knowing ones,* do not let it be said of you, *sneeringly,* that you are *quarter* FLASH, and *three parts* FOOLISH!!! This is the common error most of the '*darlings*'[119] and *swell kids* of the Metropolis *split* upon. In *flattering* yourself that you are KNOWING, *whisper* into your own ear, and make

---

118   I cannot but think that this expression of CORINTHIAN TOM's must be viewed as "a prejudice;" though it might claim pardon as an honourable one. Would not *La Fleur* have expressed himself as warmly in favour of *Paris?* Who's to decide? But, to cut the matter short, the *Spaniard* would doubtless give the preference to Madrid; the Italian, German, &c., in favour of their native homes, to the end of the chapter; without poor PADDY's *bothering* his head in favour of Old Ireland; or TAFFY *spluttering* about the beauties of Wales. Sir WALTER SCOTT might say something handsome about the new Capital of the North. If the expression had been the *primest spot* for FUN, London would have been backed at least *even*, if not at high ODDS.
119   Too many of the young *Swells* are ruined in disposition, from their cradles, by their fond Mammas. The child of a gentleman must not be *contradicted!*—it would *spoil* his *temper!*

an allowance that there are to be found in company persons as *knowing* as yourself, if not more *knowing!* by which you will avoid the application of the poet:-

> "I am Sir Oracle,
> And when I ope my lips let no dog bark!

"Yet be the REAL thing or nothing: if you are University *bred,* be able to show your *passport* when it is demanded of you at the turnpike-gate of Learning. Rather, at all times, *plead* ignorance than show it. Better to adopt the ingenious mode of *Rosencrantz* and *Guildenstern* in their answers to *Hamlet*—

> *HAM.* Will you play upon this pipe?
> *ROS.* My Lord, I cannot; I know no touch of it!
> *HAM.* 'Tis as easy as lying.

"But, if there is one observation more than another that I wish to impress indelibly upon your mind, my dear Coz, it is —never to disgrace and injure the character of a friend in that family where you have been introduced as a friend. Let the *honour* of the husband and the father be preserved inviolable. Never let the once-friendly door be shut against you, as a scoundrel and a hypocrite, and you only be remembered as *infamous.* It may be *sermonising,* I admit, but it is highly worthy of your best attention; and, for my own part, amidst my numerous failings, I trust I may, without any egotism, pride myself, in the above instance, in having strictly adhered to an honourable line of conduct. I have only one more remark, by way of a *finisher,*" said Tom, smiling; "when once, Jerry, you have been *queered* upon any event, remember it in future; for, as my friend Bob Logic says, IT IS A GOOD FLAT THAT IS NEVER DOWN.[120] By-the-bye, I wonder I have not seen him since my return to London. I shall introduce you to him. You will find LOGIC a most interesting, humorous fellow;

---

120   There are numerous persons in the world, that never can be convinced of their errors. These are the sort of *flats* that the cup and ball *chaps* like, who will play and stand the *grin,* till they are completely *cleaned* out, and have not a *mag* left to help themselves with.

full of anecdote: and, having mixed with all sorts of society, quite at *home* in all of them."

Mr PRIMEFIT was now ushered into the *Chaffing Crib*, to receive the necessary instructions for the *swell suit*[121] from the CORINTHIAN; and JERRY was also in preparation to undergo the *tactics* and "small talk" of the above celebrated artist.[122] The *choice* of the pattern-card had already been disposed of; but to procure that "certain sort" of a cut, which tends to give the hero the *look* of a gentleman, was rather of too important a nature to be despatched without some consideration. It was however obtained. But Mr PRIMEFIT was longer than usual in his operations, as his eyes were continually wandering among the great variety of new paintings which had been introduced since his last visit to *Corinthian House*. Indeed it was a most attractive apartment; and some little allowance might be made for the unsteadiness of the tailor's optics. The plate,[123] without any further comments on the subject, is sufficiently glowing in its representation to give the spectator some idea of its imposing appearance. During the time Mr PRIMEFIT was applying the measure to ascertain the frame of young HAWTHORN, the CORINTHIAN smiled to himself at the lusty, unsubdued *back* of his merry rustic Coz, at the same time making comparisons, in his own mind, at the vast difference of the hinder parts of his *dandy*-like friends at the west-end of the town,

---

121   Under such hands, JERRY bid fair soon to get rid of his rustic *habits*, or (perhaps, it might be more correct to observe), in TRAINING, under the auspices of CORINTHIAN TOM, in order to become a *Swell*. A "good appearance," of all other considerations, IF not absolutely the *first*, is, however, deemed one of the principal requisites, in high life, to *look* the *character* of a GENTLEMAN.

122   This term, it should seem, had given great offence to several gentlemen of the *brush* who frequented the *Chaffing Crib*. But LOGIC insisted that the *point* of the thing bore him out. Mr PRIMEFIT was a person that made use of *colours* in his profession; and about his WORKS *light* and *shade* wore also skilfully displayed. He was, likewise, a man of *taste;* and that he possessed a knowledge of the *human figure* could not be denied.

123   It was considered a good idea of the CORINTHIAN, to have every article that was NEW first placed in the *Chaffing Crib*, to undergo the ordeal of the visitors, and then, if pronounced *"the thing!"* it was removed to another apartment, to remain as a fixture; while, on the contrary, if the article excited no interest, it was removed altogether. But, nine times out of ten, the *taste* of TOM was admitted to be GENUINE.

when put into the scale against the country breed of JERRY. TOM laughingly told PRIMEFIT, that he had not been so well *backed* for a long time. The knight of the thimble gave a polite nod of assent; and he had scarcely *obscured* his card, made his *exit,* and *popped* into his carriage, when LOGIC, with the freedom of an old friend, came running into the room, and *sans ceremonie*, began addressing the *Corinthian* with "My dear TOM, I am glad to see you returned to town. Positively, your absence has made a complete blank in the fashionable circles. But I have to congratulate you upon your looking so well. This journey has put you all to rights." "It has indeed," replied TOM; "but let me first introduce to your notice, my doctor,[124] JERRY HAWTHORN, Esq., to whom I am indebted for a principal part of my renovation; and, for the possession of a good heart, an excellent pair of heels, with hands not idle nor deficient, when any occasion may require the use of them, you will find my cousin not wanting. And JERRY, in your becoming acquainted with my friend, ROBERT LOGIC, Esq., I have to inform you, that his *head* contains all the *treasures,* I beg pardon *(smiling)*, all the *'Larks'* of Oxford. You will not only find in him a complete map of the Metropolis, as to peculiar points and situations; but likewise a pocket-dictionary respecting many of the living characters it contains. Therefore, between you both, you may *chaff,* hit, and run with the gayest boys in our circle of acquaintances. But use him well, BOB, and remember that he is not yet out of *Pupil's Straits,* and must not, as you say, be blown up at *'Point Nonplus.'*" JERRY was quite in the dark as to these latter phrases, and appeared rather embarrassed, till LOGIC gave him a friendly grasp of the hand, and told him, he should soon be quite *au fait* with them and many more in less than a month. He then took his leave in the same light, airy, and gay manner that he entered; observing, he should expect to see them both in the Park on the following

---

124   To the cheerful pleasant exercise which TOM enjoyed in the company and sporting pursuits of JERRY, during his residence at Hawthorn Hall, the Corinthian attributed the speedy renovation of his health.

Better to hunt in fields for health unbought,
Than *fee* the *doctor* for his *nauseous* DRAUGHT!

Chapter VIII.

Sunday. "We shall be there," replied Tom.

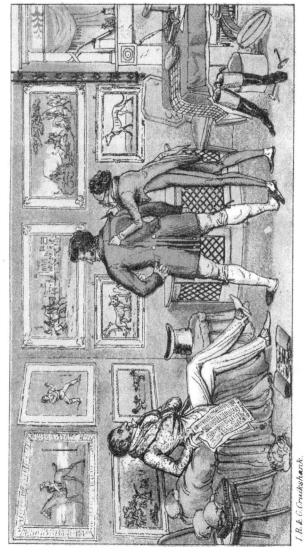

"JERRY IN TRAINING FOR A "SWELL"."

The "*swell suit*" had been received at *Corinthian House;* and the "rustic habits" of Jerry were removed altogether. Mr Primefit had most satisfactorily performed his task; Tom also expressed his approbation that so much attention had been paid to his orders; and Hawthorn felt quite pleased with the talents displayed by his "apparel furnisher," and he scarcely knew himself, as his eye ran over the mirror which reflected the elegant metamorphose he had undergone.

"My dear Jerry," said Tom, "our horses will soon be ready, and we shall then start off for what I term the *Show-Shop* of the Metropolis—Hyde Park; which is, in my opinion, one of the most delightful scenes in the world. Indeed it is a fine picture of the English people.

> "Can Europe, or the world produce,
> Alike for *ornament* or use,
> Such models of stout active trim men,
> Or *samples* of such lovely women!
> Such *specimens* of order, dress,
> Health, comfort, *INBRED* cleanliness,
> As here displayed, the summer sun
> Lingering seems proud to shine upon?

"It is in this Park, Jerry, that the Prince may be seen dressed as plain as the most humble individual in the kingdom; the *Tradesman* more stylish in his apparel than his Lordship; and the *Shopman* with as fine clothes on his person as a Duke. The Countess not half so much 'bedizened' over as her own *Waiting-Maid;* the *Apprentice Boy* as sprucely *set off* as a young sprig of Nobility; while the *Milliner's Lass* in finery excels the Duchess. But the air of independence which each person seems to breathe renders the *tout ensemble* captivating.

> "The same pursuits together jumble
> The rich and *poor*, the proud and *humble*.
> The enfranchised *tradesman,* if he stirs,
> Here *jostles* half his customers;
> Here, in a rage, the *Bond Street* spark
> Is *bearded* by his father's clerk;
> "While yon proud dame (O sad event!) is
> *Out-elbowed* by her own apprentice.
> And since, like others less polite,

Chapter viii.

> *Fine* FOLKS have lungs, and limbs, and sight,
> All destined to the same employment,
> All eager for the same enjoyment;
> Here sense and nature have it hollow,
> And FASHION is constrained to follow,
> To join the *vulgar* happy crew,
> And FAIRLY do as others do,"

The servant announced the horses to be in waiting at the door, when TOM and JERRY without delay started off to join the "gay throng," promenading up and down in the SHOW-SHOP. As they rode along through the streets, the CORINTHIAN good-naturedly hinted to JERRY, to avoid, if possible, the too common but vulgar practice of turning round to look back after any person whom he might point out to his notice. JERRY returned his Coz thanks for his friendly and well-timed advice, and TOM pushed forward,

> To join his cronies in the Park,
> "Fellows of likelihood and mark,"
> In trot or canter, on the backs
> Of ponies, hunters, chargers, hacks,
> Proud to display their riders' graces
> Through all imaginable paces,
> From walks and ambles up to races;
> By dint of leather and of steel,
> His bridle *up,* or *down* his heel;
> Now dashing on, now lounging slow,
> Through the thronged ride, to Rotten Row!

This grand circle of fashion, which suddenly burst upon JERRY, as he entered the gates of the Park, operated rather strongly upon his feelings.[125] The long line of splendid equipages, rattling along, passing and repassing each other, under the guidance of charioteers of the highest blood and pedigree. The prime "*bits of blood,*" from the choicest studs in the kingdom, prancing about as proud as peacocks, and almost unmanageable to their dashing riders. The *Goldfinches* of the day trying to excel each other in point

---

125   The Emperor of Russia, when on a visit to the King of England, was particularly partial to a ride in Hyde-Park. The *simplicity*, united with the elegance of the scene, delighted the Emperor beyond measure; and in the warmth of his observations on this occasion, asked, "*Where he could see the poor people of England?*" Is it possible that a *finer,* unstudied, more home *felt* compliment, yet true, could have been paid to the English Nation.

of coachmanship, turning their vehicles rapidly—almost to the eighteenth part of an inch, and each priding himself in having obtained the character for displaying the most elegant *"set-out,"* The Man or TON *staring* some modest female, that attracts his attention, completely out of countenance; while the *Lady of Rank,* equally *delicate* in her ideas of propriety, uses her *glass* upon the same object till her carriage removes her out of sight. The Debauchee endeavouring to renovate, or brace himself up with the fine air of the Park, *ogling* all the girls that cross his path. The Swell Dandy could not exist if he did not show himself in the Park on a Sunday. The Gambler on the *look-out* to see if any new pigeon appears in the circle, in order to plan future operations that may turn out to his advantage. The *peep-o'-day* Woman *of Quality*, who, night after night, disposes of all her hours of rest in card-parties and routs, is here to be seen riding round the circle to *chit-chat* and nod to her friends, in order to get rid of her yawnings, and to appear something like being *awake* at dinner-time. The Peer relaxing from his parliamentary duties, and the Member of the Lower House, here take a ride among the various parties in the circle to hear their conduct and measures descanted upon, and likewise to "pick up" a little information respecting the buz on public affairs. The scheming *Procuress* sporting some new-caught lady-birds in a splendid carriage, in order to excite attention and to distribute her *cards* with more effect. The wealthy CIT, whose *plum* has rendered him *sweet* among his grand next-door neighbours at the west-end of the town, here shows himself with all the confidence derived from a splendid fortune. The extravagant *Fancy*,[126] making use of a

---

126 "*O, damn the expense!*" used to be a favourite phrase of a well-known high-sporting character of great notoriety, a few years since, in the gay world, so the object in view was accomplished; to the effect of having it said of him, that "he had one of the finest women in the kingdom under his *protection,* and that he had never denied her a single request, although *ruin* ultimately stared him in the face," in spite of his having one of the most splendid fortunes of the day. But then it was *his* fancy: and some of these *fancy articles,* it needs no "ghost from the grave" to prove, have been so *expensive* in "Life" in London, that even the almost inexhaustible *purse* of a personage of very high rank was found to be insufficient to support the wants of a certain *lady-bird,* long since consigned "to that bourne from whence no traveller returns;" and the female in question was compelled to retire from such

thousand little arts that she is mistress of, trying to take the *shine* out of all the other females in the circle, merely to show the *taste* and liberality of her *keeper*. The *flashy Tradesman*, who laughs at the vulgar prejudices of old sayings and propriety about "keeping your shop and it will keep you," here pushes along in his *natty* gig and prime trotter, and appears upon as "good terms" with himself as the richest banker in London, laughing in his sleeve at the idea that, if anything goes wrong from his stylish pursuits, a temporary absence from his friends, united with the aid of *white-washing*, will soon make him "all right" again. The *Warrior*, too, who has rendered some services to his country, may here be seen prancing up and down on his charger, *secretly* receiving the praises and admiration of the passing crowd. PAINTERS on the look-out for *characters*, and *Authors* for the purpose of gaining a knowledge of real life. It is here that the really "GREAT PEOPLE" are to be met with, as well as the "*soi-disant* GREAT" are to be witnessed aping and mimicking the airs of persons of quality on this grand drive of fashion. It ought, however, not to be forgotten, that everything which is lovely, interesting, honourable, virtuous, generous, feeling, witty, elegant, and humane, which tends so much to give the English females a proud superiority over those of most other nations, is here to be met with in a transcendent degree; and it should also be remembered, that everything which is designing, crafty, plausible, imposing, insinuating, and deluding, is likewise to be run against in these gay paths of pleasure. The passions are all *afloat*, but GAIETY of disposition overtops the whole. *Observation* is upon the stretch,—and SCANDAL, *en passant*, is in full swing, at the rate of twenty miles an hour. NOTORIETY here is everything, and the various modes to obtain it are so numerous that the eye is fatigued with the contrast of the *elegant* and *ridiculous* forms which so rapidly assail it: and, after all, it is of so fleeting a nature in London, that very few persons can flatter themselves on having NOTORIETY long in their possession.

---

high protection, *on that account* alone. But more on this subject, anon!

TOM & JERRY, SPORTING THEIR "BITS OF BLOOD" AMONG THE PINKS IN ROTTEN ROW.

CHAPTER VIII.

The PROMENADE, or "*Grand Strut,*" is equally interesting and attractive, from the numerous characters of both sexes, *ogling* each other, as they frequently come in rude[127] (but fashionable) contact. The *Tailor*, confined to his shop-board all the week, enjoys the double advantage of gaining a little fresh air in the Park, as well as admiring some of his own performances on the backs of many of the dashing crowd; and the *Milliner*, also upon the same errand, not only to improve her health, but to retain in her eye the newest fashions sported in this hemisphere of the GREAT. The pleasure, too, of being known and recognised by your friends and acquaintance. The numerous bows and friendly How d' ye do's? With that admired sort of LIFE in London, all jostling against each other in the Park with the utmost *sang-froid*. The NOBLEMAN and the *Yokel*—the DIVINE and the "*Family-man*"—the PLAYER and the *Poet*—the IMPURE and the *Modest Girl*—the GRAVE and the *Gay*—the FLASH COVE and the *Man of Sentiment*—the FLAT and the *Sharp*—the DANDY and the *Gentleman*—the out-and-out SWELL and the *Groom*—the real SPORTSMAN and the *Black Leg*—the HEAVY TODDLERS and the *Operators*—the dashing BUM TRAP and the *Shy Cove*— , the MARCHIONESS and her *Cook*—the DUKE and the "*Dealer in Queer*"—the LADY and her *Scullion*—the

---

127   To "*be comfortable*" indeed, is altogether an obsolete phrase, nowadays in the Walks of Fashion. To be invited to a party where plenty of room is allowed to cut the victuals—*stretch* yourselves at your ease— and be attended upon in calling for anything you might want, would be considered a dull routine sort of entertainment. Quite shocking! It might do for a "*comfortable*" farm-house *squad*. But for Life in London —it must be crowded walks, positively a well-dressed mob of persons, treading upon each others heels. An overflowing theatre, where it is necessary to fight for the places after they have been taken. And a rout, so oppressed with company, that the ladies and gentlemen are obliged to *scramble* and *snatch* for refreshments, and consider it quite a *treat* if they have the good luck to procur" only a *mouthful!* Then it is *the thing*—the go—quite the Ton! It is above the low and vulgar ideas of "comfort!" So emphatically described by the Countess of *Fal-lal!* "O my dear Lady *Finnick*, the Marchioness of Diamond's rout, last night, exceeded everything of the kind since the *Flood*. To say it was crowded, would be a *stupid,* indefinite term. All the world was there; no *delicate* walking up and down the rooms; all *squeezed* together in one mass; the ladies' dresses nearly *torn off* their backs. There was no such thing as being able to procure the slightest refreshment. The panels of my carriage were broken to pieces in reaching the door of the Marchioness. But I would not have stayed away for the expense of twenty carriages. O! it was delightful."

PINK OF THE TON and his *"Rainbow"*—the *Whitechapel* KNIGHT OF THE CLEAVER and his fat *Bib*—the BARBER'S CLERK and the *Costard-Monger*—the SLAVEY and her *Master*—the SURGEON and *Resurrection Man*—the ardent LOVER to catch the smiling eye of his *Mistress*—the young BLOOD in search of adventures, and to make assignations:—

> ALDERMAN CRAMP, anxious to take the air,
> With his young bride so lovingly and fair,
> While a *gay* RAKE who sees the happy pair,
> A bliss so *wonderful* resolves to share.
> *He whispers, "Madam,* you've a charming spouse,
> So neat in limb, and then so smooth his brows!"
> "Sir, I don't understand you."—"What's say, dove?"
> "Nothing, my duck; I'd only dropt my glove."
> "To-morrow, at the fruit shop, will you come?
> At twelve o'clock."—"Lord, Sir, how you presume!"
> "Who's that that *scroudges!*—you shan't shove my wife."
> "I shove her! a good joke, upon my life!"
> "Leave him to me—how dare you thus to treat me?"
> "I dare do any thing, if you'll but meet me."
> "Me meet a man? I shouldn't have thought of you.
> At TWELVE indeed! I can't *get* OUT *till* TWO."

TOM and JERRY had scarcely got into the ride, in *Rotten Row*, when TOM received a host of nods and smiles from his acquaintances. But who had the CORINTHIAN with him was the question. That was the *puzzle* to be solved. "He is not of London growth, I'm sure," said the lively *Lady* WANTON to her sister, the Hon. Miss SATIRE, as TOM and JERRY rode by her carriage. "His ruddy, unsophisticated, Huntsman's face, bespeaks him of the *Tally-ho* sort. He is rather a handsome, well-made fellow, an't he?" "Handsome, indeed!" (echoed Miss SATIRE, accompanied with a most disdainful toss of her head, and putting up her glass and surveying poor JERRY from head to foot with a microscopic eye). "You mean, Sister, that he is decked out in elegant clothes; but, from the awkwardness he displays in them, the wearer seems quite a stranger to such sort of apparel. Indeed, I think he looks like one of the *Tally-ho* sort, as you call it; one who has left the rude company of hounds and horses to mix with genteel society, under the patronage of the CORINTHIAN!" "O he!" replied *Lady*

Wanton, "you are, as usual, ill-natured in your remarks, without a cause. But I dare to say he is rich: however we shall know more about him when we see *Trifle*." These, and a thousand other whisper comments, or rather private attacks, had Jerry to encounter, unknowingly, as he passed up and down the ride.

The Duchess of Hearts, in her open barouche, came dashing along the ride; and, upon her Grace perceiving the Corinthian, she gave him a most gracious smile. Tom instantly made up to her carriage, and, with his usual happy talent, introduced to the Duchess of Hearts, his cousin, Jerry Hawthorn, Esq. All eyes were now fixed upon the carriage of the *Duchess*. Jerry came in for his share of the *gaze*, as a new hero in the Park, and the crowd began to assemble round her barouche. Poor Jerry, who could take the most dangerous leaps without the slightest hesitation or fear wrestle, sing, dance, and talk with all the merry lads of his village—squeeze the hand and steal a kiss from the vermilion lips of Mary Rosebud, in the vicinity of *Hawthorn Hall*, with all the confidence of a Tom Jones—could not *look* upon the "face divine" of the Duchess. The rustic hero was almost struck dumb, and he appeared shy and embarrassed. The blaze of *beauty* was too much for his feelings—but it was not beauty alone. It was not the *still-life* beauty of the Sculptor and the Artist,—there were no touches of tameness and insipidity about it. It was not merely a beautiful index; it had a corresponding heart. The eyes spoke volumes of intelligence; but the smile that animated the features threw such a bewitching fascinating air over the whole of them, as to enrapture every beholder. It was one of Nature's highly finished pieces; it was a composition of excellence. Wit and good-nature were seen as playful dimples; and sensibility and harmony gave a delightful lustre to every part of the countenance. Satire and *Art* did not belong to this face; indeed, the slightest glance of it evinced that the outline was talent. The *tout-ensemble* was a spell that operated like enchantment on the spectator. But poor Jerry was not the only man who had felt embarrassed on being introduced to the Duchess of Hearts. Ho, no. Numerous confident heroes, men of the world, too, distinguished for superiority of talent, and who had played the "first fiddle" in most other companies, felt so great an awe in her presence, that long, very long, after they had been permitted to mix in her circle of friends, they looked upon a *second* situation, in comparison with the witty, enlightened, elegant, and susceptible DUCHESS, as almost above their grasp. The splendour of riches, as riches, gave no title to pre-eminent attention in her presence: the passport was talent. The MIND was the object looked at, and the DUCHESS was always surrounded by the first wits of the age. She was a female of great literary attainments, and also a warm admirer of them in other persons.

TOM and JERRY had scarcely taken their leave of the DUCHESS when they came up with the splendid carriage and retinue of the MARCHIONESS OF DIAMONDS. JERRY had to undergo the *ordeal* of another introduction: but in this instance he assumed greater confidence. He was not overwhelmed with beauty. The MARCHIONESS wanted that "*certain sort of something,*" so easy to be impressed with, yet so difficult to describe. Everything that ART could supply was employed to embellish and set off her person with effect. The *mantua-maker* had to alter her dress a hundred times, if it did not make the *bust* of the MARCHIONESS a perfect model for a statuary to copy from. The *taste* of the *milliner* was *tortured* again and again, to produce unrivalled, exclusive, novelty for the head of this great female leader of the fashion; and the *invention* of the jeweller was never allowed to be at *rest*, in order to give a *richness* to her person which otherwise could not have been acquired. In short, STYLE was her *idol*. To gain the name of being the best-dressed lady, and to have her routs the most numerously attended, were the darling themes of her conversation, and the limit and extent of her ideas. That such a one was denominated a CORINTHIAN,—a dashing *fellow*,—a *buck*,— a *blood*,—the GO,—a leader of fashion, &c., was of itself a sufficient recommendation to her notice. She was restless and uneasy except when engaged in some fashionable bustle. Change of scene, to her feelings, according to the fashionable calendar, such as being at Bath, Brighton, Cheltenham, &c., in their seasons, was as necessary as change of apparel. It was too great a *bore* to the *Marchion-*

ess to inquire about the mind or talents of her acquaintance; but, if he were rich he was sure of the *entrée* to her parties. She had abundance of *sentiment* attached to her *character*, but not a grain of *feeling*. The pathetic imaginary tale of distress, highly wrought up in a novel, was delightful,—it was exquisite; but an account of real poverty was excruciating to her mind,—it was horrid,—quite disgusting,—shocking, and must not be repeated in her presence. She was entirely made up of ART; anything like unsophisticated nature was brutish, barbarous, and low. Such was the contrast between the above two ladies to whom poor JERRY had been introduced. On turning his head, HAWTHORN felt quite delighted to perceive LOGIC, at no great distance, among the crowd of horsemen; and, with a smile on his countenance, he gently touched the arm of the CORINTHIAN, and observed that his friend BOB was making his way to join their party. The TRIO was soon complete, and the comical face of LOGIC prepared them to expect some fun and good humour. "Have you seen the *Divinity?*" said the *Oxonian* to Jerry. "Whom do you mean?" "Why, the Duchess of Hearts! Isn't she a delightful creature? and, but for that one *failing!*" "Hush!" cried Tom. "Well, never mind, JERRY," said BOB, "more on that head anon!"

In going down the ride, Logic pointed out to Jerry the Rich Old Evergreen. "No general in the army, however attentive to his duty," said Logic, "ever kept a more active foraging party than did this amorous hero. Notwithstanding his allowance of four most splendid establishments to different women, at one period of his life, every *pretty face* that was *comeatable*, and every female possessing charms, which could excite any emotion in his amorous breast, was presented at his mansion by his male and female procurers. Old Evergreen was considered as the most *systematic* debauchee on the town; and although he had injured the peace of mind of *lots* of most interesting girls, he was never *injured* in his life. The extent of his purse carried everything before it. He was one of the deepest *files* in London: indeed, he was *awake* upon every suit. On the *turf*, or at the *table*, he was quite at home; and more young noblemen fell sacrifices to his schemes than to those of any other person who knew how to *cut* a DUCE or *slip* a tray. To the houses of ill-fame he was a contributor that defies description. To relate the manner in which Maria was *deceived*—Betsy *decoyed*—Pamela *entreated*—Agnes *persuaded*—Charlotte *inveigled*—Louisa *cajoled*—Nancy *tricked*—Fanny *amused*— Caroline *played with*—Polly *shuffled*—Kitty *cheated*—Susan *imposed upon*— Jane *hummed*—Sally *deluded*—Ellen *seduced* —Lucy *betrayed*— Peggy *debauched*—Sophia *duped*—Rachel *frightened*—and Emma *coaxed*,—would be utterly impossible; but that OLD EVERGREEN fulfilled what SHAKSPEARE has so emphatically described, was never doubted, to those he

> "Op'd the chamber door,
> Let in a maid, that out a maid
> Never returned any more!

"My dear JERRY," continued BOB, "it was the pride and boast of *Old Evergreen* that the finest females of this kingdom had, at various times of his life, either adorned his mansion or *graced* his coach; and from his *cabinet of rarities* two great personages had not only been furnished with mistresses, but also several of the most conspicuous characters in the blaze of fashion. So *keen* a sportsman was *Old Evergreen*, and so well acquainted with the manoeuvres of the course, that he was not easily *jockeyed;* but, when a new object appeared in view, no one knew better how to *hedge-off* than he did, in having no objection that his OLD *fillies* should run under other names. *Old Evergreen* had ample resources in replenishing his stud."

"Who is that sprightly-looking young man, with a pretty girl with him, in the single-horse chaise,"[128] said Jerry to Logic, "that gave you a nod when he passed us just now?" "He is called Bill Dash," replied the *Oxonian,* and I assure you he is a *Swell* of the first magnitude, and *well breeched.* He is one of those characters that will have everything *prime* about him. He is always talking of behaving like a gentleman, *i.e.,* to do what is right one man to

---

128   See the right-hand side of the plate, where the little boy is running to get out of the way of the horse.

another. For instance, if he makes a bet, to pay it also, if he says a thing, to keep his word; and if he promises a handsome present to a female, it is done. He is as independent as the wind. He does not care for any body. Fond of joking; but as coarse as a fishwoman at Billingsgate. *Propriety* he laughs at; and the company of *modest* women he absolutely ridicules. The *ladybird* you see with him he has taught to *spar;* and they frequently have a *set-to* together with the gloves, by way of amusement. Nevertheless, she is a woman of very superior accomplishments. Yet Dash, notwithstanding his eccentricities, has numerous good qualities,—he hates *canting* and hypocrisy beyond expression, but he never wants to be twice asked to relieve the really unfortunate, and drops his *blunt* like a generous fellow. I will, Jerry, introduce you to him the first opportunity; and you will find that, in exploring the *character* of Bill Dash, your time may be employed to advantage."

Logic had scarcely concluded his remarks on Dash, when the Honourable Dick Trifle, in his phaeton and four, rapidly passed them. Bob was also known to Trifle; and received the friendly nod from this first-rate hero of the *Dandies.* "How strangely he is dressed!" exclaimed Jerry, in an undertone, laughing, to Logic. "Why, he looks as prim as a lady's maid! What a fine shape too!" "Yes," said the *Oxonian;* "you must not expect every person, Jerry, to have such a jolly back as you have got, Trifle, you must know, descended from rather a different stock than you did. His father was one of the completest *petit maîtres* ever beheld; and his *delicate* mamma was *affectation* personified. It was an *attorneyship* marriage on both sides. The only union between the parties was a contiguity of estates. To have made *love* to each other would have been too much *trouble;* and therefore they dispensed with it. But the issue of this marriage was the Hon. Dick Trifle—a character strongly depicted by Shakspeare, as one of the

> "*Tribe of* Fops,
> Got 'tween sleep and wake!

"But Dick eclipsed his parents, in being the most *trifling* subject of the three. *Study,* to Trifle, was the greatest *bore* in the world, and he, in consequence, preferred an *opinion* ready *cut* and *dried* for him to giving himself any *trouble* upon passing events. He was one of the completest *smatterers* of the day; and employed an intelligent person who read everything for him, and accordingly furnished him with a little 'small talk' for the companies he mixed with. But he was like a clock that was wound up for a certain number of hours; if the argument lasted longer, or went beyond his morning's preparation, he was directly at a stand-still. TRIFLE was prodigiously fond of everything new. He was like a child with a plaything, *tired* of it in a few hours. His acquaintances were numerous, but they seldom lasted longer than a few days, when he made no hesitation in giving them the '*cut direct*.' His splendid fortune gave him rather an air of importance in some peculiar respects; and for *bronze*, he was equal to anything in the whole list of fashion! He was fond of knowing something about the *pedigree* of every new hero or heroine that crossed his path, and he employed scouts for that purpose; for this feature, TRIFLE was distinguished in the higher circles. His dress, upon all occasions, partook of the extremity of fashion, and however ridiculous it might be, he heeded it not, so he could boast of its being NEW. Indeed, my dear JERRY, it is too true, that in this great Metropolis there are thousands of the above sort of '*apologies*' for men to be met with in a day's walk; fellows who do not possess one original idea, whose *intellectual* faculties do not extend beyond the length of their noses, and who are made up of *imitation*, from the beginning to the end of that *Chapter of Caricatures* upon the human race; sullying the dignity of a man, and reducing his character to the degradation of the *vain butterfly*, or more gaudy *peacock*."

"Do you see that well-dressed man, with his hair powdered, standing very near Trifle's phaeton," said Logic to Jerry, "as I perceive he has been *marking you down* as a bird of good plumage, and who may, at some future day, perhaps, answer his purpose for *plucking*. He is well known at all the tables; and always on the look out for a 'good customer.' He however prefers '*pigeons*' He does not want for address; and his manners are also extremely insinuating. His *plausibility* of attack is generally so well managed, that strangers are got '*into a string*' before they are aware of their danger. He prides himself always in being worth *a thousand pounds;* and, likewise, in never being without it. This large sum principally consists in the value of his articles of dress: and which tend to render his appearance more imposing, and to give *effect* to his deeply-laid plans. He is as deliberate as a lawyer; uniting the talents of a good actor. His gold watch, chain, and seals are of the first workmanship; and which he soon contrives to give the stranger a sight of. A diamond shirt-pin, of considerable brilliancy, dazzles the eyes of the spectator. On his little finger he sports a diamond ring, which gives a sort of action to his eloquence, as he is sure to give a flourish with it. His gold-headed cane, finished off in a most attractive style, he always brings into play. He is a complete master of all those 'little arts,' which are so well calculated to prepossess strangers in general that he is a man of considerable importance and property. In point of *finesse*, he is admitted to be one of the greatest adepts on the town; and from his 'getting the best' of most of his opponents, he has been long designated Plausible Jack. He lives in good style; owing to the great success he has had in repeatedly *blowing up* both the young and the old at *Point Nonplus.*" "I am quite astonished," said JERRY, "and I feel much indebted to your kindness for the hints you have given me,"

TOM, who had been engaged for a short time with some of his acquaintances, now joined Jerry and Logic, and observed to Hawthorn they might as well leave the Park; and also invited Bob to dine and spend the evening with them at Corinthian House.

As our heroes were quitting the ride (but owing to some little irregularity which had taken place at the gates leading to Piccadilly, the long string of carriages were for a short time prevented from proceeding), they passed a dashing equipage, in which were seated a plump, rosy-faced, middle-aged female, richly attired, accompanied by three young beautiful girls of the most attractive appearance, and decorated in the highest style of fashion. LOGIC, being close to the window of the coach, which was open, was soon recognised as an old friend by the *Gouvernante,* as she seemed to be, who addressed him in rather an under-tone, with

"How do you?—you are quite a stranger;" at the same time almost *staring* poor JERRY out of countenance. The "Three Graces," as HAWTHORN thought them to be, with their playful eyes also gave him such good-natured *looks,* almost *winking* at him, that JERRY appeared fixed to the spot, as if held by some powerful *magnet.* LOGIC gave a nod to the plump lady in return, and, as he did not wish to attract the gaze of the spectators by keeping up a conversation, he kept moving onwards, to get up with the CORINTHIAN, who was about a hundred yards before them; when, by way of a good-bye, the *Gouvernante,* smiling, observed, "I suppose, it will not be long first, Mr L., before you give us a *look* in, and perhaps you will bring your friend along with you."

The carriages were now again in rapid motion, which circumstance relieved JERRY, as it were, from his temporary trance. "What lovely girls!" exclaimed HAWTHORN; "I suppose that is the Mamma, and her three daughters. I declare I was quite struck with their pleasant countenances. You seem an old acquaintance of theirs." LOGIC said, laughing outright, "Yes, yes; they are good-natured enough, if you will furnish the means."

> "Hang all the bawds; for where's a greater vice
> Than taking in young creatures all so nice?
> And yet to them,'tis merely knitting, spinning—
> No more!
> Although the *innocent* is made a whore:
>
> With just as much *sang-froid* as at their shops
> The butchers sell rump steaks or mutton chops,
> Or cooks serve up a fish, with skill displayed,
> So an *old* Abbess, for the rattling rakes,
> A tempting dish of human nature makes,
> And dresses up a luscious maid:
> I rather should have said, indeed, un-dresses,
> To please youth's *unsanctified* caresses.
>
> I like examples of a wicked act,
> Take, therefore, reader, from the bard a fact.
> An old PROCURESS, groaning, sighing, dying,
> A rake-hell enters the old beldame's room—
> 'Hæ, mother! thinking on the day of doom?
> Hæ—dam'me, slabb'ring, whining, praying, crying?
> Well, mother! what young filly hast thou got,
> To give a gentleman a little trot?'

'O CAPTAIN, pray your idle nonsense cease.
And let a poor old soul depart in peace.
What wicked things the DEVIL puts in your head,
Where can you hope to go when you are dead?'

'How now, old beldame? shaming heaven with praying!
Come, come, to business—don't keep such a braying;
Let's see your stuff; come beldame, show your ware:
Some little *Phillis*, fresh from country air.

'O Captain, how *impiously* you prate,
Well, well, I see there's no resisting fate;
Go, go to the next room, and there's a bed,
And such a charming creature in't—such grace!
Such sweet simplicity! *such* a face!
CAPTAIN, you are a *devil*, you are indeed.

'I thank my stars that naught *my* conscience twits;
"Which to my parting soul doth joy afford;
O CAPTAIN, CAPTAIN; what, for nice young *tits*,
What will you do, when I am with the Lord?"'

"What do you mean, Logic?" said Jerry. "I mean to inform you," answered the *Oxonian,* with a grin on his face, "that those three nymphs, who have so much dazzled your optics, are three nuns, and the plump female is *Mother*... of great notoriety, but generally designated the Abbess of ... Her residence is at no great distance from one of the royal palaces; and she is distinguished for her bold ingenuous line of conduct in the profession which she has chosen to adopt; so much so, indeed, that she eclipses all her competitors in infamy. Honour, however singular it may seem, *Mother*...lays claim to as the key-stone of her *character.* She certainly must be considered as a female of singular pretensions; and materially different from the 'frail sisterhood' in general. *Mother*...is also very anxious to preserve something like *'a reputation;'* that, when she is spoken of amongst the gay votaries of pleasure, it might be said, that the *'devil is never half so black as he is painted.'* This desire of *reputation* it ought to be observed, does not originate from the *qualms of conscience,* but arises from her peculiar sagacity to prevent interruptions to the business of her house, in order that her visitors may not be 'broken in' upon, or overhauled by the unmannerly intrusion of the officers of justice, accompanied by distracted parents seeking their deluded children. It is the greatest boast of *Mother*… that she is an open and avowed enemy to *seduction,* also that the cries and lamentations of *ruined* girls shall not echo along the walls of her mansion. Her maxim is, that good order must be preeminent. Force or squeamishness are contrary to her plan; and the most ready compliance to her wishes, by those persons she admits into her house, must never be lost sight of for an instant. For the better regulation of her mansion, *Mother*… has established a code of laws, which, without hesitation, must be agreed to, before any girl can be taken under protection. She is likewise candid and sincere in her professions; and will not suffer any damsels to enter her service under any species of *delusion.* It is the general plan of *Mother*…to reason with all those females who claim protection, respecting the course of life they are about to embrace. She points out to them the vicissitudes they are likely to meet with in such an uncertain career; but particularly to bear in mind, that, whatever disasters may ensue, it is solely attributable to themselves. It must also be well understood, that, in connecting themselves with her *household*, it is entirely from their own preference and adoption! and those girls who cannot comply with her *dictates* had much better relinquish their intentions. *Mother*…is completely a woman of business. She also makes known to those females who apply to her for places, that those girls who conduct themselves well will meet with every indulgence: no pleasure is denied to them; besides, having the pleasure and enjoyment of an elegant carriage, and livery servants to attend upon them to all the public places of resort. But their characters for *honesty* must bear the strictest investigation: this point, *Mother*… is very scrupulous in ascertaining: as her house is not only furnished abundantly with plate, but the trinkets necessary to be displayed on their persons, when she sends them to the Opera, the Theatres, Masquerades, &c., require on her part some little caution. *Mother*… always pays great attention to the health of her ladies, as a Son of Æsculapius belongs to the establishment. The above preliminaries being adjusted, no time is lost in conducting the '*new inmate*' to a most elegant wardrobe; where the metamorphose is soon rendered complete; and BETTY, who perhaps had but recently *scoured* the dirty floor of some humble dwelling, now becomes the fashionable *Cyprian*, to take wine from the hands of a gentleman. Everything that art can devise to improve the shape; cosmetics to heighten the complexion; and dresses of the most fascinating description, to render the *tout ensemble* luxuriantly captivating, are resorted to with the utmost anxiety. No woman knows the taste of her visitors better than *Mother*… It is her peculiar study, and she is considered to excel in all her entertainments: but in keeping her eye towards the 'main chance,' those fashionables who participate in her midnight revels will soon be taught the necessity of having a long purse. Though *modesty* is not the motto of *Mother*… , yet she is a woman of discernment and polite behaviour. She is not to be easily duped, and before she introduces her 'new inmates' to the gallants, she deems it necessary to give them a few instructions, to put them on their guard against many impositions that novices are liable to in the various walks of life. Her particular injunctions to her pupils are, 'However, my girls, you may be amused, never suffer yourselves to be *bilked*.' With this advice, the thoughtless girls make their appearance in her *'Show Room,'* not with the coyness inherent to modesty, but with the loose manners of Bacchantes, singing,

> 'From tyrant laws and customs free,
> We follow sweet variety.'

This apartment is particularly calculated, from its elegant embellishments, to co-operate in setting-off to great advantage the charms of its female visitors; and to these regions of pleasure all the gay boys of the Town occasionally resort. *Mother*… is indefatigable in her selection, and keeping up her stock of beautiful females. An admittance to her Mansion requires but little introduction; yet her visitors consist principally of the higher classes of society. However, my dear JERRY, you must excuse me in making any of them public, lest some of the *tender* part of the PEERAGE might feel a little *squeamish* in having the names of their partners brought upon the carpet, as well as a small portion of *grave* SENATORS appear rather *hurt* at their *amusements* being called in question, though many of them might assert, that they only went, as it were, to take *a peep* at the *Curiosities* in the ABBEY."

"Look, look!" said JERRY, whose attention was suddenly arrested by a row on the path, as the crowd were pushing forward to get through the gate. On inquiry, it turned out, that some thieves, dressed in the first style of fashion, had attempted to pick the pockets of the passengers. Nothing further now transpired, and, in a short time, our HEROES arrived safely at *Corinthian House*.

CHAPTER IX.

Tom and Jerry visit the Playhouses. A Stroll through the Saloon of Covent Garden Theatre. Taking "Blue Ruin" at the "Sluicery" after the "Spell is broke up." A Peep into a Coffee-Shop at Midnight. Tom and Jerry in "Trouble" after a "Spree." A Night-Charge at Bow Street Office; with other matters worth knowing, respecting the unfortunate Cyprian, the feeling Coachman, and, the generous Magistrate.

CORINTHIAN TOM, WITH all his romantic notions, was not a *Don Quixote* in his chivalrous exploits; neither was his *protégé* JERRY, a *Sancho Panza* in his adventures. Windmills were not the objects of their research and attack; but the *gallantry* they possessed stood upon higher ground than to suffer *distressed* damsels to be in want of protectors. MUNCHAUSEN was however considered too *great* a traveller to be admitted of the party in their *Rambles* and *Sprees* through the Metropolis; but yet Tom's *golden* key operated like *magic* in opening all the doors that opposed his progress; and his showers of silver were of so pelting and penetrating a nature, that few persons could be found, who possessed courage enough to resist the powerful effects of such a storm.

The rusticity of JERRY was fast wearing off, and he was gaining confidence every day, under the auspices of TOM, who had taken some pains to make his Coz somewhat *au fait* upon most of the subjects that had come before him; and which, added to the assistance of LOGIC, he bid fair, in a short time, to become as *prime* an article in the "gay throng" as either of the above heroes in *kicking up a lark*, or to *mill* his *way* out of a *row*; to pay compliments to the *Swell* high-bred fair ones at the West End of the Town; to *chaff* with the *flash Mollishers*[129] and in being at home to "a peg" in all their various SPREES and RAMBLES. JERRY was an apt scholar; and, in some particular instances, it was thought, he had already made a "tie" of it with both his "great" masters.

To most of TOM's acquaintances he had been introduced; but an introduction to the lovely, fascinating, *Corinthian Kate*, it seems, was reserved as a high treat for JERRY, when a more congenial opportunity offered.

TOM, having pushed the glass about briskly after dinner, proposed a visit to the Theatres. JERRY was all alive, in an instant, at the sound; but the fine old wines of the CORINTHIAN had made him a little "bit on the *go*" and TOM was also in high spirits. LOGIC (who was a great lover of the bottle) was too *bosky*, as he termed it, to accompany them to the *Fields of Temptation*. The *Oxonian* had been quite full of Oxford all the evening, and drinking bumper-toasts to all his friends, the "good fellows" at that University; but more especially to all the "*Unfortunates*" at the *Castle of St Thomas*. LOGIC had been explaining to JERRY the nature of *Pupils Straits*. That at present JERRY was also out of *Dad's Will*. The *States of Independence* were likewise before him; but, above all, to keep a good look-out after the *Waste of Ready*. Logic's comical mug was here so twisted with the *hiccough*, that he could scarcely articulate, "Jerry, my boy, you have gained a little knowledge respecting the *Province of Bacchus*; and you are now *(hiccoughing)* under the *Dynasty of Venus*"—The CORINTHIAN observed to his Coz, that, as the "*Dustman*"[130] was getting fast hold of LOGIC, they would be off without him.

Upon their arrival at Drury Lane Theatre, the performances did not operate on their feelings as a source of attraction. It is true they took a *glimpse* at the play; but as they did not go for anything

---

129   A slang term made use of by thieves and police-officers for low prostitutes.
130   *Sleepy*. When a person cannot keep his eyes open, it is said, he has met with the *dustman*.

like *criticism* on the abilities of the actors, or to descant upon the merits of the pieces, it was merely a *glimpse* indeed. Our heroes went upon another errand. Their eyes were directed to different parts of the house: and Tom not meeting with any of his acquaintances at "Old Drury,"[131] as he had anticipated, they immediately pushed off to take a peep at Covent Garden Theatre. A *look* at the Stage was quite sufficient for their purpose; and, without any more delay, the Corinthian and Jerry soon *bustled* into the Saloon.

Tom and his Coz, had scarcely reached the place for refreshments, when the *buz* began, and they were surrounded by numbers of the gay *Cyprians*, who nightly visit this place. Some of these *delicate* heroines, which the plate represents, soon began to jeer the Corinthian on the *cause* of his absence; while others of these *Lady-birds* were offering their congratulations to him on his restoration to Society. Jerry being in company with so distinguished a hero as Tom was of itself a sufficient source of attraction to these *Fancy Pieces* (who have an eye to *business)* to pay their court to Hawthorn; and, accordingly, their cards were presented to Jerry, in order to grace their lists with the addition of a new and *rich Friend*[132] These cards rather puzzled Jerry, who appeared astonished that such dashing females should keep *shops*. Upon HAWTHORN giving a *hint* on this circumstance to Tom, the latter immediately put an *extinguisher* on the conversation, with *"Hush!"*

---

131   Notwithstanding the last two erections of this Theatre, the phrase is so familiar with almost every person acquainted with Theatricals, that it is a question whether it will ever lose the title of "Old Drury."
132   An universal phrase with the girls of the Town for "their *Keepers,"*

TOM & JERRY, IN THE SALOON AT COVENT GARDEN.

The scene altogether made a strong impression on the lively *senses* of poor JERRY; and more animatedly, perhaps, than if he had not been *flushed* with wine before he entered the SALOON. He not only asked a variety of questions concerning those girls that took his attention, either on account of their beauty, fine figure, or dress; but also, respecting many of the male promenaders, who appeared to him quite at home, as to a knowledge of and intimate acquaintance with most of these unfortunate females.

"My dear COZ," whispered the CORINTHIAN, "it would be a most interesting, as well as an extensive work to detail anything like the histories of the LADIES that visit here, accompanied also with the memoirs of their GALLANTS. But take notice of any *characters* that may appear prominent to you here, and at some future period, if it is in my power, and you remind me of the circumstance, I will give you all the necessary information you require."

"Who is that fashionably-dressed gentleman, that seems almost *twisted* into the form of an S?" said JERRY. "He was once a distinguished leader of fashion," replied TOM, "but he is on the *shelf* now." "I think so, indeed," echoed JERRY, "if form has anything to do with it."

JERRY, who had just entered into a little *chit-chat* with "*Fair* FANNY," suddenly recognised a tall thin gentleman, with powdered hair, and about thirty years of age, that passed him, as a person he had seen several times at Bath. "Do you know him?" said FANNY. "With all his demure looks, he is a precious hypocrite, and expends thousands a-year upon the women. But he will have nothing to say to us girls of the Town. He is only fond of the *Slaveys!*[133] (*laughing heartily*). I imposed myself upon him once as a *Slavey!* It is true, Sir, I assure you, that he keeps a man and his wife in London, to whom he allows £500 a-year, for the sole purpose of collecting *Slaveys* for him; and they are accordingly sent down once or twice a week, as it may happen, to a receiving-house he has for that purpose, kept by an old woman in Bath. But it is all done upon

---

133   A *slang* term for servant maids: being servants of all work; and also in allusion to their laborious employment and hard work.

the sly; and the greatest secrecy is preserved throughout all the transaction. Indeed, I could not learn his name, nor his residence in that city, it is so well managed. The *Slaveys* are all well paid, besides their expenses up and down to Bath. He, however, does not make choice of one out of six that is sent to him; and he never will, on any account whatever, see a girl twice. But *modest* SLAVEYS are so scarce an article," said FANNY, laughing outright, "you know, Sir, in the Metropolis, that his procurers in London are obliged to *queer* him, and they are compelled to resort to some of the new girls of the Town, and to put them up to the secret before they leave London, to behave themselves *modestly* upon the occasion. The sums of money that he gets rid of in this way are immense." JERRY appeared so much astonished at the recital of the above circumstances, that he could scarcely give credit to his own ears—

> Can such things be?
> And overcome us like a summer's cloud,
> Without our special wonder!

The strange tales which JERRY had heard, and the extraordinary characters that he had been made acquainted with in the course of the last few days, made him exclaim, "This, indeed, is LIFE IN LONDON!"

In the recess, allotted for refreshments, the Plate discovers a rich *Old Debauchee*, with his finger up, in a sort of *"hush"* manner, inquiring after *"Brilliant* FANNY."[134] The fruit-woman[135] is off like shot to search the Theatre for the Ladybird in question, to inform

---

134   Several of the girls are here known by what are termed "nicknames," according to circumstances, or after their persons. Such as *"Brilliant* FANNY!" The *friend* of FANNY was a gentleman who hated the *trouble* of having money about him; indeed, he was of so extravagant a disposition, that he always "lived in credit!" *i.e.*, he received his money quarterly, from a large Jewellers' firm; and his creditors, to an accredited amount, were paid one quarter under the other. FANNY never received from "her friend" any *cash* for her favours, but plenty of *Jewellery*. Her person was always elegantly decorated with valuable necklaces, ear-rings, &c., which gained her the appellation of *"the* BRILLIANT!"

135   These persons are of the most accommodating description about the Theatre. They will fetch and carry like a spaniel; answer any questions about the girls, &c., provided the *tip* is forthcoming.

the Brilliant" that "her friend" has been inquiring for her. FANNY, decked out with an elegant muff and dashing plume of feathers, is seen skipping along to take a jelly with her Old Gallant. The young *Sprig of Nobility,* in black, with his glass, is surveying "the Brilliant" as she passes him. Near to Fanny is a gay young fellow, fashionably dressed in blue, arm in arm, with "an antique *remnant* of fashion," one of the *Lord Ogleby* tribe, and who has been repeatedly quizzed by "the Brilliant" as being neither "ornamental nor *useful.*" But the Antique asserts, if he stays at home a single night, he is devoured with *ennui*, and that, by way of apology[136] for his appearance in the Saloon, he *merely* "looks in" to see an old acquaintance, or if anything "new" appears among the stock of *Frailties!* The "*Fair* MARIA,*" dressed in a blue riding-habit, seated on a chair in a corner, near the recess; and the "*pretty* Ellen" standing behind her, are throwing out "*lures,*" in order to attract the notice of the Corinthian and Jerry. The "Old Guy," on the top of the stairs, with his spectacles on, fast sinking into the "lean and slippered pantaloon," is gently tapping, in an amorous way, the white soft arm of "lusty *black-eyed* Jane;" and inviting her to partake of a glass of wine, to which she consents in the most "*business*" *like* manner. Indeed, "Black-eyed Jane" has often publicly remarked, that it is immaterial to her whether it is a Duke or his *Groom*, so that she receives her *compliment*.[137] Several Jewesses may also be recognised promenading up and down the Saloon. In the motley group are several *Coves* of *Cases*[138] and procuresses, keeping a most vigilant eye that none of their "decked-out girls" brush off with the property intrusted to them for the night;[139] and other persons of

---

136   The "qualms of conscience" will sometimes intrude, however persons may try to push them off. As King *Richard* observes—
        "O Tyrant Conscience! how dost thou afflict me!"
137   This lady has such an eye to the *"main chance,"* that, unlike the "frail sisterhood" in general, she has saved a considerable sum of money, which has been placed out at interest in the Bank of England; and to which sum "*black-eyed* JANE" is continually adding.
138   The proprietors of houses of ill-fame.
139   Several persons near the theatres get their livelihood by letting out dresses to these unfortunate women, at a certain price for the evening; but, notwithstanding all their "eyes of Argus," they are sometimes duped, by the girls running

the same occupation, may be *seen* closely WATCHING the females belonging to their establishments, that they are not idle,[140] as to the purposes for which those unfortunate girls are sent into the SALOON. The Artist has been uncommonly happy in his delineation of the above characters, who made their appearance when the sketch was made.

Jerry did not feel any inclination to quit the Saloon, from the great attraction and novelty which it had afforded him. He, therefore, kept promenading up and down, indiscriminately *chattering* with one or other of the girls, till the usual mode was adopted of putting out the lights, as the only effectual method of getting rid of *such* company, who never stand to any consideration about *propriety* or time. The Corinthian suggested to his Coz, that, as the Spell[141] was *broken up*, and he could visit the Saloon as often as he thought proper, for further observations, they would take a *turn* to a "*Sluicery*"[142] to have a *bit of fun*. JERRY, who was now *ripe* for anything, took hold of TOM's arm, and they immediately left the Theatre.

This is a fine sketch of real life, and the lovers of *character* may trace it in every figure in the plate before them. Tom is *sluicing* the *ivory* of some of the unfortunate heroines with *blue ruin*, whom the breaking-up of the Spell has *turned-up* without any *luck*, in order to send them to their *pannies*[143] full of *spirits*. Jerry is in *Tip*

---

off with the clothes, &c.

140   Others board and lodge the girls in their houses, who are generally kept as dirty as *sweeps* all the day, but decked out at night like *Duchesses*. It is also no uncommon thing for many of these unhappy girls, who are not "in luck," as it is termed, or, more properly and intelligibly speaking, if they do not bring home money, the wages of their prostitution, to be sent to bed supperless, and frequently beaten into the bargain. Their mistresses likewise *search* them immediately after their *gallants* have left them, so that these wretched girls are scarcely ever in the possession of a single shilling. The life of a PROSTITUTE is of itself a most severe *punishment*, independent of *disease* and *imprisonment*. A volume would not unfold the *miseries* allied to such a character.

141   So termed from its attraction. A species of enchantment!

142   A gin shop—from the lower orders of society, and women of the town, *sluicing* their throats as it were with gin.

143   Apartments

Street upon this occasion, and the *Mollishers* are all *nutty*[144] upon him, putting it about, one to another, that he is a *well-breeched Swell*[145]. The left-hand side of the Bar is a "rich bit of LOW life; and also points out the depravity of human nature. *Gateway* Peg has just entered for her *ninth* glass. This "*lady-bird,*" who has not only disposed of many an *unruly customer* in her time, but *buzzed* them into the bargain, is taking her drops of *jackey* with Old MOTHER BRIMSTONE, who has also *toddled* in to have a *flash of lightning* before she goes to *roost*. Both these fair ones (who are as *leaky* as sieves, from turning their money as fast as they get it into liquor) are *chaffing* at "FAT BET," in consequence of the pretended *squeamishness* of the latter to Tom, that she had a great objection to every sort of *ruin*, no matter how it was *coloured,* since she had been once *queered* upon that suit. Peg has just given the following toast to *Old* Brimmy, "*Bad luck to the* Hussey *that would not wash her cap in it, sooner than wear a dirty one.*" MOTHER BRIMSTONE, an old *cadger,* and a *morning-sneak* covess,[146] who is pouring some *blue ruin* down the baby's throat to stop its crying, has borrowed the *kid*[147] in order to assist her in exciting charity from the passing stranger in the street. GATE-WAY PEG is a fine but an afflicting portrait of the rapid degradations from virtue to vice. This *lump* of infamy, disease, and wretchedness, was once a well-known toast among the *bons vivants* for her elegance of person, and has passed some of her thoughtless, but fleeting and splendid hours, in a chariot. The little *urchin,* who has been *dragged* out of bed by his mother, and who is seen offering the *butter-boat*, and begging "that he may be served immediately with a quartern of the best gin, to cure his mammy's pain in the stomach," has scarcely any covering on his back except his father's waistcoat, which has been hastily

---

144 Very Fond
145 Pockets full of money.
146 Thieves that, just as day begins to break, *sneak* into the passages of houses, if the servant maid has left the door open by accident, and take anything within their reach.
147 It is a very common practice in London for women to borrow young children to go out begging with.

put on him by his thoughtless parent. The *Cove* and *Covess*[148] of the *Sluicery*, with faces full of *gammon*, and who are pocketing the *blunt* almost as fast as they can count it, have just been complaining of the *wickedness* of the times, and the difficulty of "*paying their way.*" Swipy Bill, *a translator of Soles*[149], who has been out for a day's *fuddle,* for fear his money should become too troublesome to him, has just called in at the *gin Spinners* to get rid of his last *duce*[150] by way of a *finish,* and to have another drop of *blue ruin.* This last glass would have *floored* him, had it not been for the large butt of liquor which he staggered against. Hiccoughing, he swears, "he'll stand by Old Tom while he has a *sole* left to support such a good fellow." *Kit Blarney*, who has just got rid of her *sprats,* which had been "up all night" and rather the *stronger* for the day or two she had had them in her possession, though she had assured her customers all the day they were as fresh as a *nosegay,* as she had just got them from Billingsgate, has dropped in for the purposes of lighting her short pipe, to get a *drap of the* CRATURE, and to get rid of the *smell* of the fish, which remained about her olfactory nerves! The above scene may be nightly witnessed after the Spell is dissolved, but in much more depraved colours than is here represented. It is, however, Life in London.

---

148   The master and mistress of the house, &c.
149   A cobbler that can *vamp* up old shoes to look like new. A *prime* piece of deception; and those persons who purchase secondhand shoes soon find it out on a wet day.
150   Twopence.

Chapter IX.

TOM & JERRY, TAKING BLUE RUIN, AFTER THE SPELL IS BROKE UP.

MIDNIGHT. TOM & JERRY AT A COFFEE SHOP NEAR THE OLYMPIC.

CHAPTER IX.

The CORINTHIAN and JERRY, who had got rather "a little funny" by this time, from the *lots* of wine and *blue ruin* they had drank in the course of the evening, were recommended by FAT BET to take a cup of coffee, as it was getting late, which would put them all to rights. Our heroes, on leaving the *Sluicery*, were not long before they *strolled* into a Coffee-shop.

This group (which the plate so correctly delineates, and in point of *character*, equal to any of HOGARTH's celebrated productions) displays a complete picture of what is termed "Low LIFE"in the Metropolis; drunkenness, beggary, lewdness, and carelessness, being its prominent features. It is, however, quite *new* to thousands in London. TOM and JERRY have just dropped in, by way of a *finish* to the evening, in their route towards home, and quite *prime* for a *lark*. Knowing the use of their *morleys,* fear is out of the question; and coffee or a *turn-up* is equally indifferent to them. Upon the entrance of these *Swells*, a general *stare* is the result: the *Cyprians* are throwing their *leering ogles* towards them, in hopes of procuring a *Cull;* and if the latter are caught any ways inclined to *roosting* from being *swipy,* the young *buzmen* will make them pay dearly for the few *whiles* they may enjoy. "*Mahogany Bet,*" so termed from her *never-fading* colour, who has braved the wind and weather, night after night, under some gateway, for succeeding winters, but quite done up as to *matters of trade,* and as hoarse as a raven, is now glad to *singe* a muffin, by way of *sarvitude,* to prevent total starvation; and "*Pretty Poll,*" on the right- hand side of the fireplace, *gulping* down some coffee, once the boast of the Garden for her beauty, is now so bloated and loathsome as to prove disgusting even to the lowest visitors of a coffee-shop. Over the fire-place, as if in *contempt* of the subjects, the *Cove* of the Ken, has placed the portraits of INNOCENCE and VIRTUE. *Squinting Nan,* full of *lush*[151], jealousy[152], and indignation at *Dirty Suke,* for seducing her *fancy-*

---
151   Drink.
152   To describe this "*sensation,*" in the instance alluded to, is totally impossible; but, however degrading and repugnant it may appear to the feelings of human nature, it is too true, that there are to be found in the Metropolis thousands of men who exist entirely on the *prostitution* of women. Females, who daily and nightly walk

man from her, is getting over the box to *sarve the hunter out* for her *duplicity,* which tends to kick up a general row. SUKE swears by her precious *sparklers* that she will have a fight for *Jem.* KAN has nearly knocked the coffee out of the *black diamond's* hand, who is growling like a bear at losing a *drap* of it. *Ugly Bob,* a waterman to the *Jarvies,* is endeavouring to obtain a "chaste salute" from the lips of *Frowsy Sail;* but she is *blowing up* the nasty fellow for his *imperance;* and says "she will *smash* his *topper,* if he attempts to take any more liberties with her person." The little *mot* who is *trying it on* upon JERRY's *clie,* to feel if any *blunt* is to be had, has just turned round to *the flue-faker,* begging the dirty fellow to keep his *distance;* and JEM SPENDALL, almost in the last stage of a consumption, of a shabby genteel appearance, standing up, with a pot in his hand near *Squinting* NAN, was once one of the gayest young *swells* upon the town, whom TOM has just recognised. But owing to a combination of unfortunate circumstances, such as *gambling,* dissipation, &c., he is so *cut up,* that all his *old pals* have turned their backs upon him. The *chap* in the corner with his hat on the top of his head and his arms crossed, near *Mahogany* BET, has been *chaffing* SPENDALL the whole of the evening, about his being so *cucumberish* as to be compelled to *gammon the draper,*[153] making the room ring again with noisy peals of laughter at the distress of the unfortunate *homo.*

---

the streets of London, for the sole purpose of getting a livelihood, and to support such a set of wretches. But the most extraordinary circumstances attached to these disgusting fellows are (so finely described by the poet,

All are not men that bear the human form!)

that these unfortunate women suffer themselves to be beaten by them; and also carry their *fondness* to such an excess for those "petticoat pensioners," that, if they catch them with any other girls, their jealousy is so great, that they will fight and tear off the clothes of the suspected females, in order to be revenged for the *inconstancy* of their "fancy-men," although in the habit of *prostitution* themselves. It is impossible to account for this *inconsistency* of feeling.

153   When a man is without a shirt, and is buttoned up close to his neck, with merely a handkerchief round it, to make an appearance of cleanliness, it is termed, "*gammoning the draper!*"

Chapter ix.

TOM & JERRY IN TROUBLE AFTER A SPREE.

Some of the *kids,* anxious for a *lark,* are determined to serve out the *Swells,* as they term TOM and JERRY and the *office* has been given to *shove* the poor *flue-faker* against TOM's light drab coat. The CORINTHIAN, being no *novice* in these matters, *floored* two or three of the *musty coves* in a twinkling. The *row* then became general—the *glims* were all *darkened,* and the whole of the party were soon out in the street to settle their differences. JERRY proved himself a *trump;* and TOM told him not to give a *chance* away, when they *milled* all the *chaps* that opposed them. The tables being thus unexpectedly turned upon those *midnight birds*, "Watch, watch," was vociferously called—the rattles were all in motion—and lots of *Charleys* came *toddling* up to the spot. The CORINTHIAN ultimately was overpowered by numbers, and *lugged off* to the Watch-house.

Our heroes were soon in "*trouble*" after this *spree;* and the plate is an exact sketch of a Watch-house scene at midnight. This feature is what the *bons vivants* term being *pounded; i.e.*, being caught *astray* from propriety; or, in other words, when the *wine* is in the *wit* is out. The CORINTHIAN is "trying it on" to get out of *trouble*, and to *gammon* OLD SNOOZY, the night-constable, that his word must be taken because he is a *gentleman*.[154] JERRY, on finding his Coz in danger, endeavoured to rescue him from the rude grasp of the guardians of night; and, as he was now getting a little *flash*, he *tripped-up* two of the *Charleys*, as he said, without charging them "*a halfpenny for it;*" but, as he could not fight a *mob*, he was obliged to give way to numbers, and also suffer himself to be *dragged* into the Watch-house. All TOM's eloquence was of no avail, as OLD SNOOZY would not dismiss the complaint *"at any price,"* On the left side of the plate, one of the coffee-shop party is *tipping* a *Charley* to *buff*[155] it strong against TOM and JERRY, as they are first-rate Swells, and that "something may be made of them." JERRY appears so strong, that half a dozen of these *old cripples* can scarcely hold him. The bleeding *mug* of the watchman,

---

154 OLD SNOOZY asserts, that they have nothing else but *gemmen*, Members of Parliament, &c., who kick up rows and are brought to the Watch-house. But it's all *gammon*—it won't do.
155 To try it on.

together with his *broken lantern*, were such strong evidence against the muscular powers of our heroes, that OLD SNOOZY observed, he could only befriend the gentleman so far as to admit them to bail; but the charge against them must be entered in the book, and be disposed of the next morning before the Magistrates at Bow Street. *Bail* was accordingly procured; and our heroes, in a *rattler*, arrived at an early hour at CORINTHIAN HOUSE once more in safety, but rather in a sleepy, worn-out condition.

By the time that TOM and JERRY had taken their breakfast, and dressed themselves, the dial pointed out to them it was near one o'clock, the hour appointed for their *appearance* at Bow Street. Upon the arrival of our heroes at this public office, several night-charges, besides matters of felony, were waiting for the decision of the Magistrates; in consequence of which, the CORINTHIAN and JERRY seated themselves till it came to their turn to be heard. HAWTHORN was so much taken up with the novelty of the circumstances before him, that it nearly escaped his memory that he attended at Bow Street on purpose to answer for his breaking the peace.

During their stay, the following interesting scene took place. An elegant but unfortunate young female, it seems, whom poverty had reduced to its lowest ebb, had, in a fit of desperation, almost as her last resource, called a hackney coach, and drove to a house in a respectable street near Grosvenor Square, to solicit relief of a friend who had known her when Virtue and Prosperity shone upon her. But, alas! the door was shut against her, and she was ordered to depart without delay. This shock was almost too much for her already agitated frame, but the relief of a few tears enabled her to order the coachman to proceed to an elegant mansion in Portland Place. It was the residence of her *seducer*—the origin of all her misfortunes;—it was also the dwelling of her *keeper,* who, when satiated with her lovely person, had abandoned her to the wide world. To him she now applied for a few pounds, in order to escape the horrible life of a *street walker*—and, like a humble penitent, to return to her home, and to sue for forgiveness, even at the feet of her agonised and distracted relatives. Upon her sending a message to see this *gentleman,* the answer returned to this unfortunate creature produced so violent a fit of hysterics, that the coachman could scarcely restore her to her senses:—it was *"that if she did not instantly quit the place an officer of justice would be sent for, and herself given into custody."* She then drove to one or two other houses with no better success. On her arrival at Lincoln's Inn Fields, in a state of frenzy, she wished to quit the coach, but only gave the coachman three shillings. Some little altercation ensued, as the long time the coachman had been employed made his fare amount to a heavy charge. *Jarvey* finding no means of settling the dispute, took the summary mode of driving this unfortunate girl to Bow Street Office, and represented his complaint to the Magistrate. The latter person informed her that if she did not pay the coachman he must be under the painful necessity of committing her to prison. Her elegance of deportment— her manners, so truly interesting—and her tale of the injuries and misfortunes she had sustained, was so artlessly told, that not a dry eye was to be seen in the Office. In a tone that penetrated every heart, she represented to the Magistrate, *"that she was now quite indifferent as to what might become of her!"* "Can you take any less, Coach man?" said the Magistrate. "No, sir; I am but a poor *sarvant,* with a wife and family to support; and my master is a very *hard* man, who will make me account and pay for my time; or else, I would not say anything about it for myself!" After a short pause, and in great agitation of body and 'mind, she took out of her pocket-book two shillings, and, putting them down on the table, scarcely able to give utterance, *"that it was* ALL THE MONEY SHE POSSESSED IN THE WORLD. She was sorry for the Coachman:he was not to blame; indeed, he had been more kind to her than otherwise. She had never cheated any person in her life, and it was the first time she had ever appeared before a Magistrate:"—her tears now prevented her from proceeding. JARVIS took up the two shillings by the order of the Magistrate; but instantly throwing one of them out of his hand (the tear starting from his eye), exclaimed (with as fine pathos as Mrs Siddons in the best of her performances,—but it was Nature that spoke), *"It shall never be said* that Bill—— took the last shilling from a woman in distress. *No, no. I'll manage it somehow with my master. And, my girl, if you will but tell me where you live, I will also drive you home, if you live as far off as Barnet!*" "I have *no residence*!—I am *without a home*. I sold all my clothes yesterday to discharge my lodgings; I have not a friend in the w-o-r-l-d!" *(sobbing violently)*. The Magistrate was overcome; and Justice was never seen to greater advantage. The scene was affectingly impressive. The hand of the Magistrate, as if involuntarily, produced the purse out of his pocket in an instant, but his tongue could scarcely articulate—"No, MY GOOD FELLOW, YOU SHALL NOT LOSE YOUR EXPENSES—THERE THEY ARE FOR YOU" *(putting down the money)*. "Your generous and manly conduct DESERVES MORE than YOUR fare!" To the unfortunate female, who had nearly fainted away, he observed, "*My* poor girl, I am sorry for your situation. There is a three-shilling piece for you. Let me entreat you to return to the path of virtue. Repent of what is past; and you may yet become, by your future conduct, a useful and a good member of society." This admonition, although delivered in the most expressive manner, had not a single harsh accent of reproof connected with it. The generous conduct which this unfortunate girl had experienced, both from the Magistrate and the Coachman, seemed to have fixed her to the spot: but, when she recovered the possession of herself, the superior manners she displayed in returning thanks to the worthy Magistrate and honest *Jarvy*, and the way in which she took her leave of the Office, *touched* every one present. Indeed, it was a fine scene altogether. It was one of Nature's richest moments. Description, either from the pencil or the pen, must fall short in communicating it. My Uncle Toby would have *hobbled* on crutches one hundred miles to have witnessed it; and *Corporal* Trim would never have related the circumstance without *blubbering* over it for an hour. Sterne would have made a complete chapter of it. The *Dead Ass* at Nampont— the *Friar*— and *Maria* of Moulines, were not finer pictures of the human heart, either in richness of colouring, grandness of design, or softness of touch, than the eloquence of Nature displayed in the unfortunate Cyprian's case at Bow Street.

BOW STREET. TOM & JERRY'S SENSIBILITY AWAKENED AT THE PATHETIC TALE OF THE ELEGANT CYPRIAN, THE FEELING COACHMAN, & THE GENEROUS MAGISTRATE.

CHAPTER IX.

JERRY at the request of TOM, endeavoured to overtake the coach, in order to ascertain its number: but the idea struck TOM too late to give HAWTHORN an opportunity of coming up with the vehicle. Upon JERRY's returning, he observed, the Coachman was out of sight. This was a great disappointment to CORINTHIAN TOM, and he exclaimed, "I am very sorry for that; but I trust, my dear friend, that so generous and feeling a fellow will never be OUT OF SIGHT of the liberal and good-hearted of mankind!"

The plate is an accurate representation of the Public Office, Bow Street: and the portrait of *Coachy*, is a fine specimen of the talents of the artist in his *personification* of CHARACTER.

The countenances of the prisoners, as standing in the felon's box with irons on their legs, are also depicted with great felicity of expression.

The CORINTHIAN and JERRY were now called upon to defend themselves against the charge made by *Barney O'Bother,* the watchman; who may be recognised in the plate, standing near the unfortunate Cyprian, dressed quite *theatrically*[156] for the part he was about to play. *Barney's* head was tied up with a handkerchief; in his right hand he held a broken lantern, a sort of stage property, that had been brought forward on many similar occasions; and in his left a damaged *rattle,* also an old performer at Bow Street. A threadbare coat, torn in slits, likewise ready for any emergency, completed the *denouement.* Barney told a prime "tough story" to the Magistrate, laying it on rare and *thick* against the CORINTHIAN; and as to the country-looking gentleman, *Barney* observed, "that he had not only *spoilt* the look of his face; but had nearly knocked out one of his eyes. That he was as strong as a lion, as he had *bate* down, with as much *ase* as if he had been mowing of grass, *Pat Sullivan, Tim Ryan, Roger M'Carthy,* and *Dennis O'Bryan,* whom

---

156 *Nine* times out of ten the Watchmen "get the best" of the night-charges. They are frequently in the right, there is no doubt; but, as they always have a broken lantern by them, with the other little *et ceteras,* ready cut and dried, to produce, if necessary, in order to give a kind of *emphasis* and *character* to their statements, besides having "the pull" in their favour in opening the charge and *colouring* it as they think proper, little hopes can be entertained of any one, who unfortunately may be engaged in a *night-row,* getting through "the piece" before a Magistrate.

he had called in to assist him in keeping the *pace;* and *plase* your honour, when I talked to the *jontleman* about it, he said he would not *charge them a halfpenny for it.* My coat, your worship, has also been torn into *paces,* and my rattle and lantern broke into the bargain." The CORINTHIAN endeavoured to refute the charge made by *Barney*, by stating that the principal part of it was a "*made up*" ONE. The Magistrate observed, that he had no alternative but to order the expenses of the watchman to be paid, for the damage he had received, as the latter had sworn to it. He, therefore, advised them to retire and make it up. TOM and JERRY took the *hint,* made their bows to the Justice, settled the difference with the *Charley,* and soon returned to *Corinthian House,* where LOGIC had been waiting their return for a short time, in order to have a bit of fun with them on their *night's* SPREE,

CHAPTER X.

Tom and *Jerry* at a Masquerade Supper at the Opera House. An Assignation. A Lounge in Bond Street. A Visit to Mr *Jackson's* Rooms. *Tom, Logic,* and *Jerry* call upon the *Champion of England,* to view his Parlour and the Silver Cup. A Turn into the Westminster Pit, to sport their Blunt ON the Phenomenon Monkey. Finishing the Evening, and "getting the best of a *Charley*."

JERRY FREQUENTLY HAD a hearty laugh at the *Coffee-Shop Row,* whenever it came across his mind; indeed, the incidents of the night were of too comic a description easily to escape from his memory; but, in repeating the unfortunate Cyprian's case at Bow Street to his acquaintances, in which Jerry took great delight, he was considerably affected. Often would Jerry break out in raptures "that Coachy was a *trump* indeed!" and Tom, equally animated, exclaimed, "There was a fine heart under a rough garment; and if I did but know where to find the generous fellow, I would make him a present of as good a coach and horses as could be purchased."

> Worth makes the man, and want of it the fellow;
> The rest is all but leather or prunella.

LOGIC was so often at the elbow of HAWTHORN, that the latter was rapidly getting *awake* to the tricks and fancies of London, and could appear at almost any place without showing symptoms of the *Johnny Raw!* Tom, therefore, proposed, as a diversity of scene, that Jerry should go with him to the masquerade, at the

Opera House. The only difficulty which existed on the subject was—what *character* Jerry could *personify* to the most advantage and with ease to himself. Logic, with a grin on his face, suggested that Jerry would be quite "at home" if he went as a *Huntsman*. It was a sure place to *turn-up* plenty of *game;* and, with his whip in his hand, he would have an opportunity of *lashing* all the folly that might surround him. The *"view halloo"* (of which he was so complete a master), now and then introduced, would give such a *finish* to his character, that he might *hunt* the place with all the confidence of an old masquerader. "Bravo!" cried Tom, "I like the idea. What do you say to it, Jerry?" "Under your direction, my dear Coz," replied Hawthorn, "I cannot fail. Give me but a few hints before we start, and I will do my best to play my part to your satisfaction." "It shall be so; and what *character* do you intend to personify, Logic?" said the Corinthian. The *Oxonian* thought that he should merely parade the room in a domino for the first half hour; and if he then felt himself in a humour to have "a bit of fun," he would attempt to assume a *character*. Dresses were procured without delay, when Tom soon became attired as the gay libertine, *Don Giovanni;* Jerry was metamorphosed into the *Huntsman;* and comical Bob obscured in a black domino. All being ready, this prime trio started off full of spirits, determined to have a complete night of it at the Masquerade. Logic had made up his mind to *quiz* and *teaze* both his friends; and his intention in going in a domino was, that he could slip out unobserved, change his dress, and return in a *character,* in the assumption of which he might be less liable to meet with detection from the CORINTHIAN and JERRY. LOGIC felt quite pleased at the *fun* which he had pictured to himself he should experience in crossing his two friends, while their minds were entirely engaged in the surrounding scene, and, perhaps, thrown off their guard; and, also, in being frequently at their elbows when they thought that he was placidly pacing up and down the rooms as a silent spectator, in an insignificant domino.

Chapter X.

TOM & JERRY LARKING AT A MASQUERADE SUPPER, AT THE OPERA HOUSE.

177

JERRY had received his *cue* from the CORINTHIAN; and he also picked up a few loose hints from LOGIC, as they rode in the carriage through the streets. BOB screwed up his comical face, assuming a sort of gravity, and assured HAWTHORN that a *Masquerade* represented one of those luxurious moments when scarcely anything but the passions prevail. It is also a fine picture of "*Life*" in the Metropolis. It has its attractions and its drawbacks. "For my own part," said LOGIC, "I have been delighted beyond measure at the extraordinary talents that I have met with at this species of amusement, as well as having been disgusted with witnessing *impudence* substituted for ABILITY; but, nevertheless, the contrast is not only entertaining but profitable, as it affords degrees of comparison towards acquiring a more intimate acquaintance with the various classes of society. A MASQUERADE, at all events, gives an opportunity for the exhibition of talents. The *searchers* after *fun* may either *find* it or *create* it. The MAN OF WIT may *show* it. The PUNSTER be quite 'at home,' The SATIRIST have full scope for his powers of ridicule. The DANCER may sport a *toe* with effect and applause; and the LOVERS OF MUSIC enjoy a treat. The SINGER can amuse the company and be amused in return. The SERIOUS hero can scarcely be *serious* at a Masquerade, but then he may keep his *laugh* to himself under his mask-: and, however strange it may appear, yet such is the fact, that the FASTIDIOUS person may still remain *fastidious* in the motley group by which he is surrounded, under the protection of his disguise. It is true, the dashing *Cyprian* here sometimes throws her *bait* to inveigle the gallants *flushed* with wine, tossing her head, and passing herself off as a woman of quality, to make a better bargain for her favours. The *Man of the World* repairs to a Masquerade in search of adventures. The *modest folks,* but yet *curious* ones, who may have felt a wish just to have it to say in company, 'they have been at a Masquerade once in their lives;' yet, perhaps, have reason to repent it as long as they exist. The *genteel* thief, in order to rob the *unwary* under the appearance of a person of rank; and whose *assumption* of *consequence,* if detected in the act, is almost enough to appal an OLD TRAP, under the fear that he has laid hold of the wrong person. The *decked-out*

PROCURESS, parading up and down, to keep a sharp *look-out* after her young brood, that none of them might fly off with her *finery*, which she has lent out at above 100 per cent, profit, to embellish their unhappy frames. The *dissipated* of all ranks drop in here, by way of an excuse to try to get rid of their *ennui* for *half an hour*, in search of NOVELTY: and the wind-up of the critic is, 'that a Masquerade in England[157] is one of the *dullest*-species of amusement; and that though the room is full of *characters,* in point of fact, it really possesses no *character* at all for merit and talent:' nay, he terms it shocking, and quite a *bore."*

"A view hallo for the critic," interrupted JERRY. "So say I," rejoined LOGIC, "and you may travel from Dan to Beersheba and cry 'all is barren!' But I am not one of that description. I am for life and a curricle: and, as it is the *opinion* of a noble Law Lord,[158] given without a *fee* (a man of the most distinguished talents and eloquence), *'that a little* MIRTH *in this* MELANCHOLY LIFE *is a good thing,'* I mean to act upon it. The *unmasking* at the supper-table, my dear boy, you will enjoy, as it is often a great source of laughter and surprise, when it discovers the faces of numerous acquaintances, who have been playing off their wit and raillery against each other all the evening, under their various disguises. A MASQUERADE is an *unsorted* class of society, I readily admit; but are you not liable to mix with bad persons in the best-regulated companies? Even robberies have been frequently committed in churches; and if you keep *aloof* from mankind on that account, you may soon become a crying philosopher, afraid to stir from your own fireside, in order to prevent *contamination,* and be devoured by hypochondriacism the remainder of your days. It principally depends, in my humble opinion, on the strength of mind possessed by the persons themselves." Here LOGIC was

---

157 Notwithstanding the great vivacity of the French people, the Masquerades in England have been considered, with all their defects, by most travellers, to be, in point of spirit and characters, much superior to such amusements in France. *Punch* and *Punchinello* being by far the most numerous personages at a French Masquerade.
158 J Erskine.—This opinion is certainly a good one, either in point of law or fact.

interrupted by their arrival at the Opera House. "Well done!" cries the CORINTHIAN; "most impartially argued, BOB. Now for it, JERRY; remember, that

> All the world's a stage,
> And all the men and women MERELY players;
> They have their exits and their entrances,
> And one man in his time plays many parts.

"Enough," replied HAWTHORN; "I shall do my best."

It was about twelve o'clock when our TRIO entered the Masquerade: they were in a right humour for fun and the scene before them, having taken a glass or two of TOM's rich old wines, the vivifying qualities of which would almost make the *dumb* to *chatter*. The stage exhibited a most extensive motley group. The illuminations were not only splendid, but profuse, in all parts of the house; the bands of music all in full sound; and the gallery, opened for the admission of spectators, displayed a most brilliant assemblage of company. Indeed, it was an imposing scene altogether, however familiar the eye might be with amusements of this kind. The activity, life, fun, frolic, gaiety, mirth, and good humour which presented itself, gave it that peculiar sort of interest which renders description imperfect to a person who never witnessed the variety of incidents that occur at a Masquerade. Country dances were well executed by some of the characters: others portraying their knowledge of attitudes in the elegant but *lascivious* waltz: quadrilles were performed with great taste: *heavy*-heeled HARLEQUINS in abundance; and plenty of CLOWNS not possessing sense enough to play the *fool!* SAILORS ignorant of the difference between larboard and starboard, and who never had had even a glimpse of the ocean: Ballad-singers without the slightest knowledge of music, yet with pockets full of NOTES: ORANGE-GIRLS more *civil* than their oranges, and far more inviting than their fruit —though not exactly after the manner of—

> As saucy, leering, playhouse Nan,
> A plump and forward wench,
> With basket hanging on her arm,

> Came striding o'er each bench:
> With notes so shrill her fruit she cries,
> To tempt the beaux and belles,
> "Do you not want any oranges,
> Or some choice nonpareils?"
> A BUCK observed the sparkling nymph,
> And as she sidled by,
> He squeezed her hand and praised it much,
> And kiss'd her on the sly.
> The girl to freedoms such as these
> Had been accustom'd long;
> She let him do whate'er he pleased,
> Nor thought him in the wrong!

Lots of *Domino* heroes, *courageous* in their attacks upon CHARACTERS, yet not possessing courage enough to attempt a *character*. *Country Bumpkins*, who never lost sight of *Lunnun*, with a *Cockney* dialect. COUNSELLORS, with wigs and gowns, but no lawyers. DOCTORS, full of prescriptions, in search of patients, without troubling themselves about a knowledge of the *pulse*. ABBESSES without nunneries; and NUNS who despised "the veil" altogether. Yet here and there this *insipidity* was relieved by a sprinkling of talent,—a lively repartee,—a *bonne bouche*,—a character almost without a fault, —elegantly attired females, witty and interesting, singing three or four lines of some well-known airs, with such delightful melody, as to leave a regret that the ear could catch no more of them; and comical fellows exerting themselves to promote mirth, continually passing and repassing each other, to render this diversified assemblage, with all its defects, nevertheless prominent and attractive.

Such a lively scene could not but operate upon the mind of JERRY, although he had been in a great degree prepared for it by TOM and LOGIC, and he seemed so dazzled for the instant, that he was in the act of drawing backwards, as if afraid to proceed, when LOGIC whispered into his ear to "GO IT!" JERRY soon started from his surprise, and gave the *view-halloo* so loud and fine as to attract the attention of most of the company towards him, and then dashing into the thickest of the group, with so much life and spirit, as if determined to keep up the delusion, with all the animation of a real fox-chase, with a fine country before him, and the dogs and horsemen at his heels.

From the flattering reception JERRY met with in traversing these regions of frolic and fun, he soon overcame his fears; and the CORINTHIAN felt quite pleased that his *protege* had acquitted himself with so much talent. Indeed, from the vivacity he exhibited, JERRY appeared more like an "*old stager*" in these revels than the inexperienced fearful *debutant:* in fact, HAWTHORN was so much alive to the scene before him, that he hallooed, sung, and slashed along with his whip, till he was almost exhausted, and compelled to sit down. TOM (as his *Donship*) had been also actively engaged in distributing a thousand elegant compliments to the lovely *fair ones;* and LOGIC, under the *domino*, had been *u* "*going it*" upon a few of his friends with much humour. The time of TOM and JERRY had been so pleasingly occupied, that neither of them had bestowed one thought about LOGIC. The *Oxonian*, taking advantage of this circumstance, had slipped out to the wardrobe, and changed his black dress for a pink one. He now approached JERRY, and, altering the tone of his voice, observed, "*Mr Huntsman,* you seem to have been upon a good *scent:* have had rare sport: and met with *finer* game here than ever you turned up in the neighbourhood of *Hawthorn Hall!*" "Who the deuce is that," cries HAWTHORN, "that knows me here?" But LOGIC had dashed into the midst of the crowd of masks, and was lost sight of before JERRY recovered from his surprise. The *Oxonian* soon afterwards came across TOM, who was surrounded by a host of ladies, listening to the following song, which the CORINTHIAN had nearly concluded:—

> Go not yet, for now's the time,
> The "*boys*" are all bang-up and prime,
> Full of *spunk*—ripe for a *lark*—
> "Damn the expense!" exclaims each spark,
> In *spirits* every one.
> My dears, you know, you need not *blush*,
> Nor be afraid, or cry out "*hush!*"
> Then grant the favour that I ask,
> No one knows you under your mask.
> Then stay! Oh, be gay.
> Away with *coyness* and parade,
> 'Tis all fair at a MASQUERADE,
> Or wherefore do we come?

CHAPTER X.

> The hours fly, the Poet sings,
> And SCANDAL here has got no wings;
> For here we meet "upon the sly,"
> And all too GAME to cry "*O fie!*"
> A truce to love's alarms.
> "*Good* characters" *here* consist in dress,
> Your lovely charms then let me press;
> Your *honour's* safe, my life, my heart,
> Then be not *cruel* e'er we part.
> Oh, be gay! Then stay.
> Away with *coyness* and parade,
> 'Tis all fair at a MASQUERADE,
> Or wherefore do we come?

LOGIC stopped TOM's career all of a sudden, with "Mighty Don, if you are so very liberal to those ladies, you will not have left the hundredth part of a compliment for poor CORINTHIAN KATE, who is now closely besieged by the Grand Turk, on yonder seat." LOGIC could scarcely articulate the words for laughter; when he was off again like a shot. TOM blushed under his mask, and felt rather mortified for the neglect he had shown to KATE; and instantly went in pursuit of her. LOGIC, who well knew TOM's feelings on this *tender* subject, thought this would be the case, and stationed himself near the *Turk,* to witness his manoeuvres, and to enjoy the *hoax* he had practised on his friend. The CORINTHIAN approached the lady under the protection of the *Turk,* and, rather in an agitated soft tone, said, "My dear KATE!—*Kate!*—*Kate!*— my love!" but receiving no answer, he was about to take hold of her hand, when LOGIC started forwards, and assuming a solemn tone of voice, articulated, "Hash man, beware! you know not what you do. Have you no regard for your life? You are sure to be strangled if the Grand *Turk* perceives your attack upon this favourite lady of his Harem, and to whom he has just thrown the handkerchief." "A fig for his bowstring, scymitar, poison-bowl, guards, and all," said TOM; then, turning towards the lady, with a touch of the pathos exclaimed—

> "There is more peril in thine eyes, KATE,
> Than twenty of their swords!"

Logic could not contain himself any longer at this piece of

fun which he had made; but, bursting out into a hearty laugh, and, making use of an old pun, told Tom "that he was Miss-taken; it was all a *hoax:* and asked him if he did not know his old *Pal* Bob Logic?" "Confound you," replied the Corinthian, "you had nearly brought me into a troublesome scrape, and made me feel for the moment rather uncomfortable; but no matter now as you have explained it. Where's Jerry?" Our heroes immediately went in search of Hawthorn, whom they found animatedly pressing the hand of a *Nun,* and soliciting with great ardour, a sight of her face, her name, &c., praising her shape and make, and saying how much he admired her. Logic and Tom did not interrupt the *tete-a-tete,* but kept aloof, waiting to see the *denouement.* The lady, it seems, having caught sight of Jerry's countenance, unknown to him, at an early part of the evening while he was taking some refreshment, recognised him as the *protege* of the Corinthian, and with much *naiveté* asked Jerry, if he followed all his sporting pursuits with so much ardour. "You certainly, Sir," said the lady, *laughing,* "appear to be an apt scholar, and have done credit to the instructions of your master; and as *hunting* seems to be your *forte,* I flatter myself I can afford you the pleasures of a long *chase.* But you must not hold me any longer, as I really must endeavour to join my company." "My dear lady," in a most impassioned manner, replied HAWTHORN, still pressing her hand, "let me not be *at fault*—let me obtain the right *scent,* favour me with your card, and upon my"—"Hold, Mr TALLYHO! no professions, the only *clue* you will obtain from me is—No! no! you shall have no *clue* at all from me. What am I about? A complete stranger, and to—O dear, Sir! how can you make such an improper request?" But JERRY was too much of a sportsman to quit the field, at least, without "marking down his bird;" and therefore pressed his request with redoubled ardour. "Well, then," said the lady, "since you are determined not to receive any denial, and will not let me go without an answer, take the first letter from the solution of each of the following sentences, and you will not need any further information." JERRY was all attention to derive the *secret* of his inquiries.

> What men love;
> What very few ladies can do without;
> What they like dangling after their trains;
> What they cannot resist;
> What they never like to be called;
> And what the ladies are always in search of.

"Cruel fair one, to impose on me a task only fit for a conjurer to resolve!" exclaimed JERRY; "and thus to tantalise and perplex me. But surely you will not leave me thus in the dark to"—"*O fie*! Mr TALLYHO. Cruel, indeed! Have I not *(smiling)* been very explicit, and liberal in my information towards you? Well, then, one word more: if you should obtain the *clue*, you will also derive a *term* from which every lady wishes to escape.

> Then *hunt* it out; I will you greet,
> Kindly welcome, when next we meet.

"Good-bye, good-bye." JERRY felt so surprised at this unexpected adventure, that he stood like one in a *trance*, contemplating the wit and talents displayed by his *incognita*, while the lady, with a graceful nod, skipped off; and in all probability he might have remained in his reverie for some minutes, if the laughter and two hearty slaps on the shoulder from TOM and LOGIC had not brought him to his recollection. "What!" cries TOM, "at *fault*, my dear Coz, and the *game* in view?" "To her, to her, my boy," said LOGIC. "I am completely *thrown-out*," replied JERRY; "and if you, LOGIC, and the CORINTHIAN, do not lend me your assistance to expound a *riddle* the lady has left me, I shall never be able to *run her down*." "Let us hear this *riddle?* said TOM. "LOGIC is a good hand at making out conundrums." JERRY then repeated to them the sentences from the answers to which he was to take the first letter. "It is more like an ACROSTIC than a riddle," exclaimed the *Oxonian;* "and I have no doubt 'we three loggerheads' can make it out. But I think I know the lady." "Who is she?" asked JERRY, with great earnestness. "Do not be in such a hurry," replied LOGIC; "it requires some little caution before I mention the name of any female. I may be very wrong to judge from the mere *shape* of a lady in disguise; but the voice seemed familiar to me, as I caught the last sound of 'Good-bye.'" Here the conversation was interrupted by one of the characters, as a ballad-singer, amusing a group of masquers with the following comic song:—

> To the Masquerade we go,
> To meet with fun and gig;
> But it often proves our woe;
> I'll instance DICKY Fig.
> Mrs Fig did sob and sigh To see the Masquerade;
> But DICKY cried "O fie!"
> 'Tisn't fit for us in trade. CHORUS—
> Then all run
> To see fun
> At a MASQUERADE.
>
> Now DICKY was a rover,
> A gallant, gay young man;
> He sent his wife to Dover—
> Then called upon his NAN:
> Saying now I'll please my fancy.
> For I have lost my wife;
> Then come, my dearest Nancy,
> The comfort of my life.
> CHORUS—Then all run
> To see fun
> At a MASQUERADE.
>
> Mrs FIG *vou'd* not be cheated,
> Out of *"this here"* treat;
> In the country, defeated,
> So *"hid"* in the next street—
> For she had a lover,
> As I heard 'em talk;
> A sprightly dashing Glover,
> She didn't like to balk.
> CHORUS—Then all run
> To see fun
> At a MASQUERADE.
>
> To the MASQUERADE they went,
> Quite charmed with the sight,
> BUT soon they did repent,
> With sorrow and affright!
> Miss NANCY lost her lover.
> In confusion of the place;
> Mrs FIG miss'd the Glover,
> And couldn't him trace.
> CHORUS—Then all run
> To see fun
> At a MASQUERADE.
>
> They ran about distracted.

CHAPTER X.

> Seeking of their loves;
> By every mask attracted,
> Like two unhappy doves.
> When full of wine and fire,
> This frisky little gig;
> Wish'd a lady to retire,
> Behold! 'twas Mrs Fig.
> CHORUS—Then all run
> To see fun
> At a MASQUERADE.
>
> Thus FIG made love to wife,
> The wife to DICKY FIG;
> Producing blows and strife,
> Turn'd out a funny rig:
> Mrs FIG did cry and pout—
> "O you *naughty* rover!"
> Yes, *Marm*, I've found you out
> Is *this* the road to Dover?"
> CHORUS—Then all run
> To see fun
> At a MASQUERADE.
>
> So good people come and see, And don't be afraid;
> Your sure of fun and glee At a MASQUERADE.
> But to avoid all strife,
> Tho' you be a ROVER;
> Don't make love "to wife,"
> "*Think of the road to Dover!*"
> CHORUS—Then all run
> To see fun
> At a MASQUERADE.

"I saw Sir RICHARD WANTON here," said LOGIC, "and I have no doubt, the *Old Flat* has come to the Masquerade to please and humour his wife, whom he is doatingly fond of. There is a great disparity of years between them; it is almost JANUARY and MAY: but the immense fortune of Sir RICHARD, I am well assured, was the only attraction that obtained the hand of the lady, backed by her parents, as being a most excellent match. As to *love* on her part, psha! But the old boy can refuse her nothing; and upon several occasions she has made him look perfectly ridiculous."[159] "If she

---

159   When the Countess of ——, a lady eminently distinguished for the propriety of her conduct, and the mother of a once beautiful Duchess, complained to the Duke of —— respecting her daughter's wearing such out-of-the-way high feathers—that it was perfectly ridiculous—the laugh and talk of the whole town; and, as her daughter's husband, she begged of him to remonstrate with

has done nothing more than that," said TOM, "it is of no consequence. Only *ridiculous*, BOB, is a mere *bagatelle*. But, JERRY, how did you get into *chat* with her?" "The *Nun,*" replied HAWTHORN, "had lost her party, and I caught her on the wing, and promised to assist her to find them; but there was something so witty and interesting belonging to her, that instead of angrily telling her

> 'To go to a nunnery, go!
> That heaven had made her one face,
> And that she had made it another."—

No, no! I am not so much out of temper with the fair sex; but I strove gently to detain and amuse her; and, as she did not seem very anxious to rejoin her party, I endeavoured to make the most of my time by pressing her for a meeting at some future period, in case her friends should come upon us suddenly, and I might, in consequence, be separated from her without obtaining the desired information." "Very gallant, indeed," said LOGIC, "and perhaps if you had personified *Don Quixote* here, it would have been a more appropriate character for you. But do you recollect anything particular about the dress or the person of the *Nun?*" "Yes, yes, I do; she is very prominent about——," JERRY whispering into the ear of the *Oxonian*. "That's enough, I am off," observed LOGIC; "and I will ascertain, if possible, if I am right in my conjectures." "Success attend you," said JERRY, taking hold of the arm of TOM, and once more joining the motley group. Their progress was soon arrested by the sounds of the favourite air from *Guy Mannering*, as they anticipated, of "*O slumber, my darling!*" However, on going into the crowd, they were not only surprised, but amused, with the following parody on that delightful piece of music by a female character, habited *a la Poissarde,* and who, *disdaining* any *imitations* of those celebrated singers that have

---

her on the folly and levity of her behaviour, the Duke, with a good-natured smile on his face, replied, "I thank your Ladyship for the anxiety you have expressed on my account, and also for your feelings as a parent; but if her Grace does not *put anything upon my head* to make it *uncomfortable*, I cannot refuse her the liberty to decorate her own as she pleases."

distinguished themselves in the execution of this delightful ballad, *chaunted* it in all the richness of *slang* that characterises the neighbourhoods of Nightingale Lane and Tothill Fields.

> O slumber my *Kid-wy*,[160] thy *dad* is a *scamp*,[161]
> Thy mother's a *bunter*[162] brush'd off on the *tramp;* [163]
> She's sold all her *sprats,* and left nothing for thee,
> And got *lushy*[164] with *daffy,*[165] and out on a Spree![166]
> Then rest thee, *Kid,* rest thee, *Kid, snooze*[167] while you can,
> If you open your *peepers*[168] you'll go without *scran.*[169]
> O slumber, my *Kil-wy,* I no longer can stop,
> For to-morrow poor *Jemmy* will be *topp'd*[170] on the *drop;*[171]
> Though I'm *napping* my *bib,* [172] yet I hope he'll die *proud,*[173]
> And all the PRIGS[174] *shell out* [175] to buy him a shroud!
>   Then rest, &c.
> Then, my *Kid,* if you live, I trust you'll prove *game,*[176]
> An *out-and-out*[177] good one, and true to your *flame;*[178]
> But cut all the *buzmen,*[179] and do the thing right,
> Learn the use of your *morleys,*[180] and show the *traps*[181] fight.
> Then rest thee, *Kid,* rest thee, *Kid, snooze* while you can,
> If you open your *peepers* you'll go without *scran.*

The *trio* was once more formed by the return of LOGIC. "It is all up," said he to JERRY, "I have lost all traces of the fair *Nun:* but

---

160 A young one.
161 Footpad
162 A low loose woman
163 Walking.
164 Drunk
165 Gin.
166 Out on a bit of fun.
167 Sleep
168 Eyes
169 Victuals
170 Hung.
171 Gallows.
172 Crying, and wiping the eyes with an apron.
173 An expression among abandoned women of the town, when any of them lose their flash man, as "Well, how did BOB die?"
174 Thieves
175 Subscribe, or club their pence together.
176 Courage.
177 Complete-perfection-nothing wanting
178 A girl.
179 Pickpockets.
180 Hands
181 Police-officers.

a truce to grieving; you are a good sportsman, and will soon turn up more *game!" (laughing.)* "Come, come," replied HAWTHORN, "no more of your fun: I am sure you have accomplished your errand; therefore, keep me no longer in suspense." "Well, well," answered the *Oxonian*, "1 think I have; but first we will retire to a seat in yonder corner, and, over a cup of coffee, let us all cudgel our brains to expound this riddle, as you call it, to see whether the application of the letters bears any analogy to the name of the lady I have in view." Both TOM and JERRY immediately acquiesced with this proposition. LOGIC, who was rather clever in giving explanations to matters of this kind, and with some little assistance from TOM, after a short period, pronounced it most certainly to be as follows:—that

		ACROSTIC.
What all men love	is	W omen!
What few women can do without	is	A rt!
What they like dangling after their trains	is	N UMBERS!
What they cannot resist	is	T IME!
What they never like to be called	is	O LD!
And what ladies are always in search of	is	N ovelty!

"And what female who possesses anything like a *character*, that does not wish to escape being termed *a Wanton*!" "Excellently well made out!" said TOM: "you have not, LOGIC, thrown away *all* your time at the University, I must confess." JERRY rubbed his hands with glee, and joined in the praises of the CORINTHIAN that LOGIC was a clever fellow. The *trio,* after some little consultation on the subject, decided that the *"fair Nun,"* from the questions she had given to JERRY, answered the description, and could be no other person than the lively Lady WANTON.

On the supper being announced, the rooms were thrown open for the reception of the company; but the rush of both male and female characters was so great, to obtain good seats, that it should almost seem three parts of them had been without food for a week,[182] from the very eager and hungry mode of attack they

---

182 The vulgar phrase of *"I'll have my whack, if it makes me sick!"* is in most of the above instances completely verified. The emptying of plates, —the cutting

commenced upon the dishes which were placed before them. TOM (as may be witnessed in the Plate) displayed the utmost gallantry in his attention to the ladies; and JERRY, perceiving that some of the company were disposed to have a little fun, was determined not to be a jot behind-hand with any of the most lively heroes connected with the motley group. A strong Clown began the *lark*, after the manner of a *"comic bit"* [183] in a Pantomime, by jumping on the table, and nearly upsetting one of the glass chandeliers, then sticking a knife into a fowl, which a *Counsellor* was cutting up, bore it off in triumph, and asked the Lawyer, if he had not *cut* his client? When a *Punster*[184] thought he had said one of his best things, by observing, that it was most certainly *"foul"* play. Another hero, of the same class of would-be wits, urged it was, however, completely in point, as *Counsellors* were generally concerned in most cases of robbery; and JERRY, to give a *climax* to the thing in question, laughingly told TOM, that, in suiting the action to the word, by flogging the Clown off the table, if he had not used Mr *Merryman* according to his deserts, it could not be said, that he had 'scaped a *whipping*.— Hem! SHAKSPEARE! The "knight of the woeful countenance" appears to be quite exhausted with his search after windmills, and is lying on the ground. The NUN, who is seated between the *Coalheaver* and the *Fireman*, does not seem very scrupulous about taking *"her drops;"* and is also laughing to herself at the row which is likely to take place between her *hele-*

---

and coming again,—tossing off the wine like water,— demolishing the tarts,—and swallowing the jellies, not only exhibits such a *taste* for gluttony, but evinces that most of the supper folks are determined not to pay HALF-A-GUINEA for *nothing*. Yet to the lovers of life and observation, the witnessing of such a scene, where so many mouths are all actively employed, and the remarks which also occur on such an occasion, is worth half-a-guinea at any time, without partaking of the slightest refreshment.

183   Without attempting anything like a *pun* upon this theatrical phrase, performers in general are so fond of "comic bits," as to admit they are *food* to them. Ask *Joey Munden, Emery, Matthews, Liston, Harley*, &c., or any of the heroes belonging to the *Mug-cutting* company?

184   There are many unfortunate *cripples* in this WALK OF FUN, so very *lame* and *distorted* upon every subject, that, instead of creating a laugh, they mostly claim our pity, if not excite our disgust.

gant admirers; both of whom have been *labouring* to say something handsome to her respecting her charms. The *Coalheaver*, rather angry at the supposed advantage his opponent has got over him with the lady, and valuing himself on his strength, is pulling the *Fireman's* long snout; while the latter, as he termed it, in consequence of the *rudeness* of such a fellow, threatens to *spoil* his fingers with his *chiv*.[185] The flinty MORDECAI, who would sooner "lose his life than his *propertish*" on most occasions, but amorously inclined in the present instance, is giving way to his feelings, and don't care a single farthing about his *"Monish,"* so he can but gain his object; but, nevertheless, he cannot persuade the pig-faced lady to unmask, "at any price." The JACK TAR is quite pleased with his night's cruise, and is continually singing out, "What a prime *Shindy*, my Messmates." HARLEQUIN is "trying it on" with the lady near him to become his *Columbine;* and, if she will but consent to his wishes, he declares, that, with only a touch of his *bat*, he can make her happiness complete. The wine had been pushed about so briskly during the time of supper, that the most numerous part of the company, from its potent effects, were fast losing their diffidence and reserve, which had rendered them so dull and flat the previous part of the evening, and were getting as lively and as gay as could be wished, each contributing *somehow* or *other* towards the mirth and variety of the scene.

Supper being over, the stage once more became thronged with characters, that might be said to be more alive than heretofore; and *reeling* with several of them required no assumption to execute new steps. Tom, as *Giovanni*, amorously paid his court to all the ladies that crossed his path, from the *squeamish* Nun to the *saucy Poll Slammerkin;* and, being elevated with wine, the various modes he took of introducing himself to the females, according to the difference of the characters they represented, produced considerable mirth and laughter. JERRY was also *'primed* for any pursuit, and he hunted up the *game*, throughout all the groups, with the true spirit of a sportsman, almost splitting the ears of many of

---

185   Knife.

the delicate "fair ones," who complained of the loudness of his *view-halloo.* LOGIC, by this time, was completely in for it; and rather troubled with the *hiccough,* which was fast increasing upon him, from the copious libations he had taken at the supper-table, drinking to the shrines of Venus and Bacchus, till he had become quite comical, and, with a bottle and glass in his hand, was dancing and singing, though a little *faulty* in his recollection:—

> Then all get drunk if you wish to be happy;
> To shun pleasure that courts you is stupid and sappy:
> Drink away, you'll be nobly repaid for your labour;
> Why, 'twill make you as happy again as your neighbour.
>
> Since friendship's so rare and so bright a jewel.
> To the fire of life that kindly adds fuel;
> With wine make your clay so moist and so supple,
> Instead of one friend, why you'll meet with a COUPLE.
>
> Thus, were the world drunk, 'twould double their pleasure;
> The drunken miser would double his treasure;
> A city feast would have double the covers;
> And ladies would double the lists of their lovers;
>
> The drunkard two bowls, as he's drinking and roaring;
> And if you were all drunk, you'd my song be encoring.
>   Then all get drunk," &c.

JERRY, dashing along in his hunting career, was so intent upon the scene before him, that he had nearly passed his "fair *Nun,*" who was in company with another female, without observing her, when his eye suddenly caught sight of her lovely shape, as she was about to quit the Masquerade. HAWTHORN, in an instant, was all raptures; and, with more boldness than prudence, he immediately made up to her, and in a low tone of voice, almost a whisper, said, "My fair *Nun,* I have made out your riddle. I beg your pardon, I ought to have addressed you as my dear Lady WAN——" "Hush! for heaven's sake, hush!" replied the lady, dropping the arm of her companion, and retreating a few steps; "the Baronet is near at hand; and if you expose me here, I shall be ruined for ever!" "Only let me, fair *Nun,* claim your promise of—

> "Then *hunt* me out, I will you greet

> Kindly welcome, when next we meet,

and I'll be as silent as a *poacher*" cried JERRY. "Not now, —you must not press it at the present moment,—indeed you must not," answered the lady. "Time is precious," said HAWTHORN, "and I cannot part with you without I have your promise fulfilled. Let us meet at ——,on——." "Quit me instantly, then," replied the lady, as she perceived the Baronet coming towards her, "and it shall be so." JERRY immediately seized her hand and kissed it, when the "fair *Nun*"joined her companion, and the eyes of JERRY never lost sight of them till they left the MASQUERADE.

JERRY was now tired of his *character*, and went in search of TOM and LOGIC, to communicate this second adventure; but the TRIO, by this time, was too much out of joint to be made up for any active pursuits again during that evening; and they had even separated without LOGIC's usual comic "good-bye" of—

> When shall we three meet again,
> In lightning, thunder, hail, or rain?

Where they *went*, or *how* they spent their time, is not worth the trouble of inquiring; let it suffice it to state that neither TOM, JERRY, nor LOGIC, found their way to *Corinthian House* on bidding adieu to the MASQUERADE.

However, a day had scarcely passed over before our TRIO again collected together, and, in their morning's lounge, took a turn into *Bond Street*. As several of the "Public Characters" passed through this fashionable place of resort, LOGIC pointed out most of them to JERRY, and related a variety of anecdotes concerning their importance and their different walks in society. "There is one of the most amiable and worthy of her sex,' said the *Oxonian,* as a lady, in company with an elderly gentleman, rode by them in their coach-and-four; "and some twenty years ago, she was distinguished at one of our theatres-royal as a most lively and interesting actress. Her talents were acknowledged to be of the first order, and she was a great and deserved favourite with the public. Her humour was intuitive,—it was genuine; but it was not that sort of *caricaturish grimace* which disgraces several of our present comic performers, who, in too many instances, appear to prefer raising a laugh at their own expense, rather than not provoke one at all. This lady, if my recollection serve me, was a pupil of the representative of the Comic Muse, at that period; a most finished actress in her peculiar line, and in her zenith quite an idol. For years she lived in the utmost splendour, from the exercise of her extraordinary and delightful talents, and brought up a numerous family; but the remembrance of her cruel, wretched, unmerited, neglected exit, cannot fail in eliciting a tear from the admirers of unrivalled abilities and lovers of the drama. But I am wandering from my previous subject," observed LOGIC! "The fame of the lady I was first talking about was not confined to the Metropolis alone; she was equally an object of attraction in all the great provincial towns in England: and in her visits to Dublin she took the lead in her profession. But this lady has retired from the stage for several years; and is now the affectionate wife of the elderly gentleman you saw her with, one of the most eminent and wealthy bankers in the Metropolis. By this marriage, she has become related to three of the most distinguished families in the state, who, at different periods, as to political matters, have been considered as highly important; in fact, she may be viewed as the mother-in-law of a MARQUIS, an EARL, and a BARONET, one of the oldest and most independent in principle of that rank in the kingdom. It is true, there is a vast disparity of years between the parties; but the propriety of conduct observed by the lady, united with real love and attachment which she possesses for her husband, is the subject of praise by all those persons who are in habits of intimacy with them: indeed, in their behaviour towards each other, they represent a second DARBY and JOAN, in spite of a once celebrated poet's satire on MATRIMONY:—

> HAIL, wedded love! the bard thy beauty hails!
> Though mix'd, at times, with cock-and-hen-like *sparrings:*
> But *calms* are very pleasant after *gales,*
> And dove-like peace much sweeter after *warrings.*
>
> I've written—I forget the page, indeed;
> But folks may find it, if they choose to read—
> That marriage is too *sweet* without *some sour*—
> VARIETY oft recommends a *flow'r.*

> Wedlock should be like *punch,* some sweet, some acid;
> Then life is nicely *turbulent* and *placid.*
>
> A picture that is all light—
> Lord, what a thing! a very fright!
> Ho, let some darkness be display'd;
> And learn to *balance* well with shade.

"The husband of this lady, although so nearly allied with political families so diametrically opposite to each other, yet he has decidedly nothing to do with politics. His character shines as a connoisseur in pictures, possessing a fine taste—an ardent admirer of music—a most lasting and impassioned attachment for the drama; with a sensible head, and a feeling heart to direct the whole of his pursuits. The sons of Royalty have often been regaled at his festive board; and even the KING himself, in the most affable manner, has graced this couple with his presence.

"But Mrs ——, however highly distinguished by her performances on the stage, has proved herself a much greater actress on the large theatre of the world. One of her principle STUDIES is to do good:—to relieve the really distressed family—to succour and cherish the unfortunate—to make old age happy and comfortable—to raise drooping merit, and to rescue it from oblivion—charitable and humane upon all occasions—dignified without pomp—and feeling and honest without any marks of ostentation. An open and an avowed enemy to silly upstart pride—a charming and interesting companion, possessing an enlarged mind—a most sincere friend—an honourable and highly-gifted acquaintance—a lady at all times, and a real ornament to her sex. Her elevation and the enjoyment of immense property," said LOGIC, "has taught Mrs —— to know the advantages of riches; to distribute them with a sensible and feeling discernment for the benefit of mankind; and, instead of becoming the hatred and envy of surrounding circles, to obtain the praise of society in general, acting as a model for those females who sincerely wish to do good to others as well as to themselves. Such is the character of that lady, Mrs——. May her charitable hand then," said JERRY, "never be in want of supplies."

The CORINTHIAN now proposed to introduce JERRY to Mr

CHAPTER X.

JACKSON, as they were so near his rooms; and also to become a subscriber. "You are an old acquaintance, LOGIC," said TOM; "and, if you like, we will have a little *exercise* together?" "No, not to-day, I thank you; I am too *ticklish* in the *wind* at present," replied the *Oxonian*. Without farther delay our heroes paid a visit to this celebrated teacher of the Art of Self-Defence. The room (which is most accurately represented in the annexed Plate) might be deemed a CORINTHIAN *set-out* altogether; and no man is more deserving of the appellation of CORINTHIAN JACK than Mr JACKSON. Indeed, he is acknowledged to be such by the very first classes of society, from that self-knowledge of propriety, gentlemanly deportment, and anxiety to please, which plays round his character at all times. Servility is not known to him. Flattery he detests. Integrity, impartiality, good nature, and manliness, are the corner-stones of his understanding. From the highest to the lowest person in the Sporting World, his *decision* is law. He never makes a *bet;* therefore, he has no undue influence on his mind. There is nothing *"creeping"* or *"throwing the hatchet"* about this description. It is the plain and naked truth. The writer of it fears no refutation: and those persons who are acquainted with "Life in London," he feels confident, will back it to the very echo. His room is not common to the public eye; but, nevertheless, the taste of it is not *caviare* to the million. No person can be admitted without an introduction. As a teacher of the Art of *Self-Defence*, Mr JACKSON has no competitor.

While TOM was engaged in setting-to with Mr JACKSON, JERRY, in order not to pass his time in idleness, was weighed, to decide a bet between him and LOGIC for a rump and a dozen. JERRY lost it; having proved 6 lbs. above 12 stone. BOB was in high glee, having *queered* the countryman, as he termed him. In one corner of the room a picture is to be seen, framed and glazed, with the following inscriptions painted upon it, and which is a present:—"FROM THE RIGHT HON. W. WINDHAM, M.P., TO MR JACKSON.

ART OF SELF DEFENCE. TOM & JERRY RECEIVING INSTRUCTIONS FROM Mr JACKSON, AT HIS ROOMS IN BOND STREET.

"The fatal effects of a Roman quarrel, in the Piazza del Popoli la Coltellata, in the Roman costume." The subject in question represents a person lying dead, killed by an assassin, who is seen making his escape, with the dagger in his hand. Women and children are shrieking with agony over the body. Several men, in cloaks, looking at the deed, terrified, as it were, yet all afraid to stop the flight of the assassin.

"Humbly recommended to the consideration of those who are labouring to abolish what is called the brutal and ferocious practice of boxing" "When comparisons are made," said LOGIC to JERRY, "the above plate speaks volumes in favour of the manly and generous mode resorted to by Englishmen to resent an insult or to decide a quarrel."

On quitting Bond Street, TOM asked his companions if they would go with him to the city, as he had a purchase to make at a jeweller's upon Ludgate Hill; to which they both acquiesced. It was to choose a diamond-necklace for CORINTHIAN KATE, in order to make up for the *neglect* which TOM felt he had committed, in not taking her with him to the Masquerade. TOM spared no expense in the purchase, which was soon made; and upon the return home of the *trio* through Fleet Market, on passing the prison, LOGIC said to JERRY, "If ever I am *screwed* up within these walls, I hope you will not forget to call and see an old friend" *(smiling).* "There is many a true word spoken in jest," replied the CORINTHIAN. "But come, let us make haste home: we will take an early dinner, and, if you have no objection, I will introduce you to the CHAMPION OF ENGLAND, as it will be in unison with our morning's visit, and, most likely, it will also lead to another jolly night," "I am always ready for anything you propose," answered LOGIC. "And I should like it of all things," replied JERRY. "Let us then be off, as soon as you please, my dear COZ." It was not long after dinner when the *trio* repaired to the house of the CHAMPION; and JERRY and LOGIC were introduced by TOM to this pugilistic hero. HAWTHORN was particularly pleased with the appearance of the parlour (which the Plate represents), it being filled with numerous portraits and other sporting subjects. The CORINTHIAN is showing the silver cup to

JERRY and LOGIC which was presented to the CHAMPION, from the Sporting World, of the value of eighty guineas, on Monday, the 2d of December 1811, at the Castle Tavern, Holborn, by Mr EMERY, of Covent-Garden Theatre, accompanied by the following complimentary address:—"THOMAS CRIBB, I have the honour this day of being the representative of a numerous and most respectable body of your friends; and, though I am by no means qualified to attempt the undertaking which has devolved on me, by a vote of the subscribers, yet the cause will, I am confident, prove a sufficient excuse for my want of ability. You are requested to accept this CUP, as a tribute of respect for the uniform valour and integrity you have shown in your several combats, but, most particularly, for the additional proofs of native skill and manly intrepidity displayed by you in your last memorable battle,[186] when the cause rested not merely upon individual fame, but for the pugilistic reputation of your native country, in contending with a formidable foreign antagonist. In that combat you gave proof that the innovating hand of a foreigner, when lifted against the son of Britannia, must not only be aided by the *strength* of a LION, but the HEART also.

"The fame you have so well earned has been by manly and upright conduct, and which I have no doubt will ever mark your very creditable retirement from the ring or stage of pugilism. However intoxicated the *cup* or its *contents* may at any future period make you, I am sufficiently persuaded the gentlemen present, and the sons of John Bull in general, will never consider you have a *cup* too much." [187]

LOGIC, whose comic mug was always on the *grin*, filled out the punch, and gave as a toast, in compliment to the CHAMPION, "May true courage never want supporters." "Bravo!" cries JERRY; "here goes! It is the most pleasant mode of *cupping* a man that I ever heard of." The room speaks for itself—it can be seen at all times, and, therefore, it may be *identified* when any person thinks

---

[186] With Molineaux, at Thistleton Gap, in the county of Rutland, on Saturday, the 28th of September 1811. The Champion has not fought any battle since that period.
[187] For more detailed accounts, see BOXIANA, vol. i., p. 419.

CHAPTER X.

CRIBB'S PARLOUR.— TOM INTRODUCING JERRY & LOGIC TO THE CHAMPION OF ENGLAND.

proper. The CHAMPION was blowing *a cloud*, always happy and contented—and had just taken off those *Jack Boots* which stand at the bottom of the table, and which weigh twenty pounds; at the same time observing, "If they can't use their fists quicker in France than they do their legs, the Lord have mercy upon them." TOM observed to JERRY, "it was evident the CHAMPION had no predilection for the French.'"

The *dog-fancier* in the corner, behind the CHAMPION, as soon as an opportunity offered itself, sidled up to the *Swells*, touching his *castor*, and thus addressed JERRY. "Mayhap, as how, Sir, you *vou'd* like to see a bit of *fun* to night *vith* this here little *phenonmy* Monkey. He has *spoilt* all the dogs that has fought him. *Jacco Maccacco* is nothing else but a *hout-and-houter*, Sir; and is *veil vorth* your notice, you may depend upon it." "Where is he to be seen asked JERRY. "Here's a card,[188] Sir, *vith* all the *partiklers*" O, it is at the Westminister Pit I preceive," said TOM. "Come, LOGIC, push about the punch; and we will go and have a look at him. I have been informed, this circumstance has been viewed by all the amateurs connected with the sports of the day as one of the most

---

188
AN ITALIAN TURN-UP.
Surprising Novelty in the Sporting Circle.
On Tuesday next, September 5, at Seven o'Clock in the Evening,
A special grand Combat will be decided at the WESTMINSTER PIT,
FOR ONE HUNDRED GUINEAS,
Between that extraordinary and celebrated creature, the famed Italian Monkey,
JACCO MACCACCO,
of Hoxton, third cousin to the renowned Theodore Magocco, of unrivalled fame, and a Dog of 20 lbs. weight, the property of a Nobleman, well-known in the circle.

N.B. The owner of the Monkey having purchased him at a great expense, on account of his wonderful talents, begs to notice to his friends of the FANCY that another person has started a match, with a common Monkey, on the day preceding this match, with an intent to injure him and deceive the public.

After which, a DOG-FIGHT, for Ten Pounds, between the CAMBERWELL BLACK AND TANNED DOG and the well-known STRATFORD DOG; and a match between two Bitches, the property of two Gentlemen well known in the Fancy. To conclude with BEAR-FIGHTING.
†††Regular Nights, Mondays and Wednesdays.

Chapter X.

TOM & JERRY SPORTING THEIR BLUNT ON THE PHENOMENON MONKEY, JACCO MACACCO, AT THE WESTMINSTER PIT.

extraordinary features in the Sporting World. *Jacco,* only weighing twelve pounds, and fighting dogs of twice his own weight, with all the skill of a prize pugilist, and ultimately being the death of them." The punch was soon finished; LOGIC puffed out his segar: and upon fat *Bob,* the guard, roaring out in a hoarse voice, like thunder, to his companion, "I say, come *lush, Jem,* and let us *toddle,* or else you see *ve* shall be too late, for I know there's a precious *mob* going from our yard." This hint, though not meant to do any injury, was not very friendly towards the landlord, but it was quite sufficient to clear the room of all his customers in a twinkle, who brushed off as fast as possible towards the Westminster Pit.

On the arrival of the *trio* at the Pit, JERRY expressed his surprise at the crowd of persons, which had assembled round the doors, anxiously waiting to obtain an admittance. "What a motley group," exclaimed HAWTHORN to TOM, as he surveyed *flue-fakers,* dustmen, lamp-lighters, stage-coachmen, bakers, farmers, barristers, swells, butchers, dog-fanciers, grooms, donkey-boys, weavers, snobs, market-men, watermen, honourables, sprigs of nobilty, M.P.'s, mail-guards, *swaddles, &c.,* all in one rude contact, jostling and pushing against each other, when the doors were opened to procure a front seat, "Yes, my dear Coz, it is a motley group," replied TOM; "but it is a view of real life; and it is from such meetings as "these, notwithstanding they are termed very *low,* that you have a fine opportunity of witnessing the difference of the human *character.* In the circles of fashion you scarcely meet with any contrast whatever. You will recollect, JERRY," said TOM, *smiling,* "they are all sporting characters, and are all *touched,* more or less, with the scene before them; and the *flue-faker* will drop his *bender* with as much *pluck* as the *honourable* does his *fifty,* to support his opinion. The *spirit* is quite the same; and it is only the *blunt,* upon subjects like the present, that makes the difference between the persons in question."[189] "No box-keepers are here, JERRY, to keep places till the first act (fight, I mean) is over," exclaimed LOGIC, with a prime grin on his face. The loud barking of the dogs, the

---

189   "My money is no fool, if I am," says a *Sweep* to a DUKE.

singularity of the remarks, and the confidence and ease with which every *greasy* hero or *sooty chief* placed himself by the side of the Swells without making any apology (as feeling that he had a right so to do), in treading upon a coat, or dirtying the apparel of the person next to him, *tickled* the feelings of Jerry more than he could express. The Plate is a correct representation of the *animation* displayed upon this subject by the gay tyke-boys; and most of their *nobs* for *low* cunning are able to get the "best of" the *keenest* barristers in the kingdom, and would form a fine subject for a *Sporting* Lecture upon Heads. It may also be seen that quite as much anxiety prevails in this Pit, on the termination of an event, as upon the decision of the Derby Stakes at Epsom Races. Upon entering the above *Canine* Theatre, Jerry's *sneezer* was touched with some *convulsive* efforts, so that his *fogle* was continually at work, which Corinthian Tom observing, asked Hawthorn, with a *smile* upon his face, "if he did not like *Perfumery*, as the Pit was as highly *scented* as Gattie's. What! you a sporting man, Jerry, and not love a good *scent*? O fie! Keep no more dogs then!"

The Dog-Pit was filled in a few minutes, and numerous persons went away *grumbling*, as if they had lost the finest sight in the world, at the disappointment they had met with in not being able to procure places. Some little delay having occurred before the performances commenced, a costardmonger, from the upper story, roared out, "I say, governor, how long are *ve* to be kept in this here *rookery* before you give us a sight of this *Phenomony?*" Jacco Maccacco was at length produced in a handsome little wooden house, amidst the shouts and loud whistling of the audience. But he was not *polite* enough to bow in return for this mark of approbation paid to him. Jacco had a small chain of about two yards in length placed round his loins, which was fastened to a strong iron stake, drove a considerable depth into the ground. He was then let out of his house. The dog was immediately brought and let fly at him; but the monkey, previous to this attack, gathered himself up with as much *cunning* as a prize-fighter would do, in order to repel the shock. The dog immediately got him down, and turned him up; but the monkey, in an instant, with his teeth, which met together like a saw, made a large wound in the throat of the dog, as if done with a knife; and from the great loss of blood the dogs in general sustained who were pitted against Jacco Maccacco, several of them died soon afterwards. The monkey seldom met with an injury in any of these contests; but he is of so ferocious a nature that his master deems it prudent to have a plate of iron before him, in case he might make a mistake and bite his legs. "*What a deep covey!*" said a greasy butcher with his mouth open, a red night-cap on his nob, and pointing towards JACCO MACCACCO. "I'll bet a thigh of mutton and *smash*,[190] that the monkey wins. Blow me tight, if ever I saw such a thing in my life before. It really is wonderful. And what a *punisher* too! Why he seems to *mill* the dogs with as much ease and sagacity as if he had been fighting matches with them for years." A small volume might be filled with the singular remarks and gestures made by this noisy motley group on the *finishing* qualities possessed by JACCO MACCACCO. Some laughed; others shouted vehemently; and numbers of them were continually jumping up and down in a sort of ecstasy, knocking their sticks against the ground, not unlike the inmates of the lunatic asylum when free from their strait-waistcoats. The matches being over, some clean water was thrown over the monkey, in order to refresh him, when he appeared little the worse from the effects of his battles; and was immediately put into his wooden house. "I would not," said JERRY to TOM, "have missed this curious scene for a trifle; but, if you had not given me the *hint*, I should most certainly have lost my money. I had not the least idea that so small a monkey, nay, if any monkey at all, could have done such terrible execution." "Then make haste, and draw the *blunt*" urged LOGIC, "or perhaps, as you are an entire stranger to the stakeholder, he soon may be *non est inventus!* Such things, I assure you, have happened in pits of a better description than Westminster."

On quitting this Dog-Fanciers' theatre, the *Oxonian* observed to his companions, that the neighbourhood of Tothill Fields was so truly prolific of life and fun, that, as they were on the spot, it

---

190 Turnips and caper sauce. A prominent article among *pot-house* gamblers.

would be a pity to lose the opportunity; therefore, if they had no objection, he should like to take a *peep* into several of the houses, merely to see what was going on. "We may as well finish the night gaily," said Logic. "With all our hearts," answered Tom and Jerry. "Lead on, Bob, and we will follow." Public and other houses were explored without loss of time: and it was a "poor *shop*"[191] indeed, that did not produce some little *amusement,* and even something of *character.* In most of the instances, the CONTRASTS were fine, interesting, and profitable. The soldiers and their *trulls* were seen tossing off the *heavy wet* and spirits, and feeling, perhaps, more *actual* enjoyment than their generals and their ladies, who have all the advantages of riches and fortune to produce them comforts and to make them happy. "The dissipation of the Guards," said Tom, "I have heard, is equal to anything you can mention in the Metropolis. Many of them are tradesmen, who work hard when off duty, earn a great deal of money, but spend it as freely as princes; they also live on the best of provisions, are full of gallantry, and keep their girls: yet, it is true, however extraordinary it may appear, that no soldiers in the British army are better *disciplinarians* than the Guards; men who have endured the greatest fatigue and privations when in actual service; and who, upon all occasions, have performed prodigies of valour; yet, when at home, and in quarters, they are determined to *enjoy* all the good things belonging to society, singing—

> How happy's the soldier who lives on his pay,
> That *spends* HALF-A-CROWN *out of* SIXPENCE a day;[192]
> He fears neither bailiffs, nor yet any dun,
> But he rattles away with the roll of his drum.
> The king finds him money, quarters, and clothes,
> And he cares not a *marvedy* how the world goes!
> But row de dow, &c.

---

191   A cant phrase for a public-house. For instance,—Such a "*shop*" is a prime place for fun.
192   This is frequently done by many persons in London; but for further particulars, or an explanation upon this *paradoxical* subject, *how* it is to be accomplished, an inquiry at the Fleet, King's Bench, Newgate, Whitecross Street, and Marshalsea prisons, will no doubt prove satisfactory, even to the most *sceptical.*

Costardmongers and *flying dustmen* were also "blowing a cloud" with their fancy *vomcn; cadgers* enjoying a good supper, laughing at the *flats* they had imposed upon in begging for "charity's sake" in the course of the day; *fish-fags* who had turned their marketings to a good account; and the *prigs* with their *blowens,* spending the produce of the day; and all, in appearance, as happy and comfortable in their minds as if they were in the possession of thousands a year. "The more scenes I witness," said Jerry to Logic, "the more I am surprised. I have heard *talk* of the *varieties* of 'Life in London,' but what I have already seen beggars anything like attempt at description."

Jerry had scarcely uttered these words when in rushed *Chaffing Peter*, well known in Tothill Fields as the oracle of the dustmen, piping hot from the Old Bailey, with an account of one *Lummy,* belonging to the flying squad, who had been tried for stealing a pair of breeches. *Dirty Suke,* whose face had not had anything like a piece of soap across it for many a long day, and who had a sort of sneaking kindness for *Lummy*, began now to *nap her bib*, but the tears could not roll down her cheeks for the dirt. *Lummy* was reckoned a *trump* among the costard mongers; and some sorrow was excited upon his *werry* hard fate. "Peter," said Suke, "did not *Lummy 'sert* his innocence? come, tell us *vat* he said for himself to the judge." "If you'll keep all your *chaffers* close, and put your *listeners* forward, you shall hear all about it." Silence was called, when Peter began to relate what *Lummy* had said:—"So help me bob, my Lord, you must know, my Lord, that me and *Neddy* had done a *werry* good day's *vork,* my Lord; and as ve vere coming through St Giles's, my Lord, who should ve meet, my Lord, but *Tinker Tom, Dirty Suke,* and bogle-eyed *Jem,* the dustman, my Lord, who vere all rather *lushy,* my Lord. 'I say, you *Lummy,'* says *Jem,* roaring out to me, my Lord;— my name you must know is *Lummy,* my Lord;—'Vy, you are getting proud, *Lummy,* because your hampers are empty, and you vas going to pass us. Come, *Lummy,* von't you stand a *drap* of *summut,* as you are in luck, and it's a wicked *could* day?' 'No,' says I, my Lord, 'I vasn't a going for to pass you,' 'Vell,' says *Jem* to me, 'I have got a *duce,*'—I suppose, as how, my Lord, you knows what a *duce*[193] is,—'and *Tom's* got a *win*,[194]—and *Dirty Suke* can flash a *mag*,[195] and I dares to say ye can make it out amongst us to have a *kevarten* or two of gin, before we does part. Come, *Lummy*, let us *toddle* to the *Pig and Tinder-Box*,[196] they have got a *drap* of *comfort* there, I knows.' It's all true, every vord of it's true, so help me bob, my Lord. So avay we goes to the *Pig and Tinder-Box*, my Lord, and I did not like to look little, my Lord, as I vished to be a little *nutty* upon *Dirty Suke*, you see, my Lord; so I *gov'd* her a '*shove in the mouth,*'[197]. 'Come, *Covey,*' says I to the landlord,—ve always calls the landlord *Covey,* my Lord,—'Come, bustle, and let's have half a pint of your *stark naked.*' Vell, my Lord, ve had it: ven *Dirty Suke* says to me, my Lord, after I had had a *buss* at her, though she vas werry shy, my Lord, yet she needn't, my Lord, for I *viped* my *chaffer* first. 'Vy, *Dummy,*' says she, 'so help me bob, you have forgot poor Neddy,—you ought to have given him a *drop*, he's a good hard-vorking creature, that's vat he is.' Everybody loves my Neddy, my Lord. 'Vell,' says I to *Suke*, and I endeavoured to snatch another *buss,* but she vouldn't stand it, my Lord, so help me bob it's true, 'so he is a good *hanimal,* and Neddy shall have a *drap.* Come, *Covey,*' says I, 'let's have a *kevarten* of gin;' and, so my Lord, so help me bob it's true, I gave the whole of the *kevarten* to Neddy. 'Vy,' says *Dirty Suke,* 'it's a mere thimblefull in his *gills;*' and so it was, indeed, my Lord. 'Give him another *kevarten,*' says she, 'and if you are too scaly to *tip* for it I'll *shell* out and shame you.' 'Now I likes that,' says I to *Suke;* it's true, so help me bob, my Lord; 'if you loves me, love my ass.' And so, my Lord, as Neddy had done an out-and-out day's work, I giv'd him another *kevarten* of gin. But, my eyes, my Lord, no sooner had he swallowed it, than he began to kick and f——,— but I begs your pardon, my Lord. Neddy now, my Lord, was so full of *frisk,* that off he bolted, my Lord,

---

193	Two-pence
194	Penny.
195	Half-penny
196	Elephant and Castle.
197	A glass of liquor.

when *Dirty Suke* stood laughing at the door, with the gin-glass in her hand, till she almost, my Lord, was ready to—but, my Lord, I von't mention it. Vell, my Lord, Neddy brushed into *Monmouth Street* all amongst the *Barkers*, my Lord; and vat does I do in this here *dilemmy*, my Lord, but run as hard as I could after my ass, my Lord; and my ass, having lost poor *Lummy*, was running after me. Veil, my Lord, just as I caught hold of my ass, a squinty old apple-woman came between me and my ass, and she tripped me up, my Lord, so help me bob it is true; ven I, to save myself from falling into a cellar, my Lord, I caught hold of a pair of breeches that vas hanging upon a nail. But the *traps*, my Lord, immediately took me into custody, and said as how I stole'em. So help me bob, my Lord, I did not vant any breeches, I only vanted my ass. It is a very hard case, my Lord, that an innocent man, my Lord, should be *lagged,* my Lord, because he vas so unfortunate for once in his life to be found in low company, looking after his ass. My Lord, if I am to stand *seven-pence,*[198] my Lord, I hope you'll take it into your consideration, and not let me go without MY ASS!"

From the repeated *"flashes of lightning,"*[199] and now and then a "clap of *thunder,*"[200] with a *damper*[201] to make all *cool* again, which Tom, Jerry, and Logic, were compelled to *swallow* in treating several of the characters they had accidentally mixed with, the trio were getting rather *funny;* indeed, Logic was so taken with the rolling eye, the plump wanton figure, and *slang chaffing* of Slippery Sall, in the oyster line, that the Corinthian had some difficulty in *stalling him* off, he was so *nutty* upon the *charms* of

---

198   Seven years transportation.
199   Glasses of gin.
200   Brandy.
201   Most persons who are in the habit of going from one public-house to another, and drinking a number of drams in the course of a day, in order to allay the heat or thirst arising from the pernicious use of such quantities of ardent spirits, frequently take a glass of porter, which is termed a cooler, a damper, &c.; and too many individuals, hard drinkers, flatter themselves that, from such sort of CARE, they are keeping the nails out of their *coffins** till the trembling hand, the diseased appetite, and the debilitated constitution, lamentably point out the fatal error, too late to be corrected.
*A glass of spirits is termed, among the wet ones, adding "another nail to the coffin."

this "fair one of the tub." The *Oxonian*, with a half hiccough, was continually singing out, "Here's a champaign country, as we say at Oxford!"

In one house, at which the TRIO called in their road home, a dustman's wedding was being celebrated, with all the low peculiarities belonging to that class of society; and Jerry laughed heartily at the following old flash song, which one of the party was roaring out, with a voice like a *stentor,* to some of the *ladies* of the dust-hill.

You gentlemen give ear unto my ditty,

> It's as true a *chaunt* as ever you did hear,
> It's concerning the *scouts* of the city,
> And those rascals you never need to fear!
> You must know from a *rum Teen* we bundled,
> O the *glims* we all darken'd in a trice,
> When turning the corner of Old Bedlam,
> A *scout* laid me flat upon my face.
>   Fal de dal, de dal, de dido.
>
> No sooner the blow I had recover'd
> Than up I got and stood upon my *pins,*
> Crying, b———t you, you old blind b———,
> I'll make your lantern jaws for to ring:
> O I took him such a *lick* of his *mummer*,
> And ding'd his rattle clean out of his hand;
> That I soon had him down in a minute,
> When his *canister* came slap against his stand.
>   Fal de dal, de dal, de dido.
>
> One of my companions coming up,
> When he heard the report of the blow,
> Saying, "Well done, *my nice one,* you have done it,
> To another of these rascals let us go!"
> And as we were rolling it along, Sir;
> A NIGHT GUARDIAN we found fast *asleep,*
> When we DOWN'D WITH HIS BOX in a minute.
> *And* tumbled the OLD CHARLEY in the Street!
>   Fal de dal, de dal, de dido.

TOM GETTING THE BEST OF A CHARLEY.

"Well thought of," said TOM, smiling; "this song has reminded me of a bit of fun which I had intended, JERRY, to have shown you before you left London. It is *'Getting the best of a Charley;'* and I will put you *up* to it before we go to sleep to-night." After one or two more flashes of lightning, the TRIO were again on the *toddle*, and LOGIC *reeled* his way through *Parliament Street*, after his companions, without any music; and also *stumbled* through some part of the *Strand;* but he was missing before TOM and JERRY arrived at *Temple Bar.* "Never mind," said the CORINTHIAN; "there is no danger of BOB's being lost; he may be trusted alone;[202] he knows too well the advantages of a KEY to be locked out of a lodging."

TOM, finding the OLD CHARLEY fast asleep, laughingly observed to JERRY, who was in *Tow Street*[203] with a couple of Cyprians, "Now we'll have the best of him. I'll soon *wake,* this dealer out of time from his dream;" and, as the Plate so admirably delineates the scene,—

> 'Twas silence all around and clear the coast,
> The WATCH as *usual,* DOZING on his post!
> And scarce a lamp display'd a glimmering light!

TOM had the CHARLEY in his box down in an instant. HAWTHORN laughed immoderately at the dexterity of TOM, and with the utmost glee said to the CORINTHIAN, "My dear Coz, the CHARLEY had the 'best of us' last time, at Bow Street, but we have got the best of him now, and therefore let us keep it!" The above *cant* phrase puzzled JERRY considerably when it was first made use of by TOM, but, on its being *practically* illustrated, he observed, "that person must be a *cripple* indeed, if ever the watchman overtook him on such an occasion." Indeed, it is totally impossible, under such circumstances, for a *Charley* to extricate himself, without the assistance of some of his brother "guardians of the night." The noise made by the watchman to get out of his box broke in upon the ears of another *old scout*, across the road, who, half asleep

---

202   A knowing one; a man not to be imposed upon.
203   Being decoyed or persuaded by any person.

and without knowing what was the matter, sprang his rattle for assistance. "Let us be off," said TOM; "it won't do to remain here any longer." The two *Cyprians*, in the most *tender* and persuasive manner, now endeavoured to *gammon* JERRY and the CORINTHIAN up *Shire Lane* to a place of *safety*, as they termed it. "No," replied TOM, "I rather think not! your house, I am afraid, is not *insured;* but, I must admit, your *policy* is not a *bad one* neither!"

It is quite immaterial how our heroes eluded the pursuit of the *Charleys*, or in what manner they spent the remainder of the night; they were out on a "*spree,*" and were determined to finish it. They were not immaculate. One circumstance, however, is very clear, LOGIC found his companions in a "whole skin," on paying a visit to *Corinthian House* the next morning

CHAPTER XI.

The Contrast—*Country* and *Town*: Evil Communication corrupts good Manners. A "Look-in" at *Tattersall's.* Gay Moments; or, an Introduction of *Jerry* and *Logic* by *Tom* to *Corinthian Kate.* Tom exhibits his knowledge of Fencing in an "Assault" with Mr *O'Shaunessy*. *Kate* and *Sue* caught upon the Sly, on their visit to the Old Fortune-Teller, by *Hawthorn* and the *Corinthian*. The "Ne plus ultra of *Life in London*." A visit to Carlton Palace by *Kate, Sue, Tom, Jerry,* and *Logic*.

JERRY, WHO USED to rise with the lark when at *Hawthorn Hall*, to join his brother sportsmen, singing—

"When ruddy Aurora awakens the day,
Bright dew-drops impearl the sweet flowers so gay,"

had, since his arrival in London, reversed the scene altogether. His acquaintances, TOM and LOGIC, had bid adieu to anything like *regularity* of living long before HAWTHORN made up the *trio;* and had only gone to *repose* or left their beds as circumstances required. *Daylight* had frequently ushered both of them into their apartments before *sleep* had overtaken their eyes; and they had as frequently, in succession, got up by candlelight in the evening to *enjoy* their breakfasts. JERRY, under such *masters,* soon became an apt pupil, or rather caught the contagion: the sweet notes of the lark had now lost their effect on his once delighted ear; and he was so repeatedly wrapt up in the arms of *Somnus,* from the fatigues of the over-night, that the loud, noisy, unwelcome, intruding "*Cries* of London" did not *break* in upon his slumbers:—

> Like a lark in the morn with early song,
> Comes the sweep, with his "*Sweep! soot, ho!*"
> Next the cherry-cheek'd damsel, she trips it along,
> "Any milk, pretty maids below!"
> "Any *dust?* any *dust?*" goes the tinkling bell,
> While sharp in each corner they look;
> Next the Jew with his bag, "*Any cloash to shell?*"
> "*Any* hare-skins, *or* rabbit-skins, cook?'
>   Let none despise
>   The merry, merry cries,
>   Of famous LONDON TOWN!
>
> Thus the various *callings* in harmony blend—
> "Come, here is your nice *curds* and *whey!*"
> "The last dying speech of——" "Old chairs to mend!"
> "Choice fruit, and a bill of the play!"
> "Here's three for a shilling, fine mackerel, O!"
> "Any phials, or broken flint glass?"
> "Come break me, or make me, before I go!"
> D'ye want any fine *sparrow*-grass?"
>   Let none despise
>   The merry, merry cries,
>   Of famous LONDON TOWN.

The clock had struck one at *Corinthian House* before our heroes descended into the "*Chaffing Crib*" when Tom, with a smile, observed to Jerry,

> "We take no note of time, but by its loss!"

The tea-things were scarcely removed before the door opened, and again presented the comical face of LOGIC to his merry companions. "Why, BOB," said JERRY, laughing, "if I am not mistaken, you were lost in the 'Fields of Temptation' last night. You stole a march upon us. No good-bye." "No, no," answered TOM; "LOGIC was very busy in the oyster line; only look at him; he appears quite *harassed*." "I must confess," replied the *Oxonian*, "that I have not exactly recovered from the severe effects of the repeated 'flashes of lightning' and strong 'claps of thunder' with which I had to encounter last night; indeed, I could not resist the fury of the *storm;* and, ultimately, my little frail bark was *Strand-ed* and went down!" "Well done, Master LOGIC," observed JERRY;

Chapter XI.

A "LOOK IN" AT TATTERSAL'S.—TOM TAKING JERRY'S JUDGMENT IN PURCHASING A "PRAD."

"so you think to *creep* out of it by *punning*; but it won't do; you are caught." "Come," said the CORINTHIAN, "it is getting late, and I have no time to spare. I am going to TATTERSALL'S to purchase a *prad* upon the judgment of JERRY, and you may as well go with us, BOB." LOGIC acquiesced, when the *trio* were off like a shot, and soon arrived at the above grand sporting rendezvous, which the print so clearly illustrates.

This scene is so very familiar to a certain part of the public, and can also be identified at any period, that it scarcely requires a comment. But to a great portion of Society in the Metropolis, who are quite aloof from sporting transactions, a short account of this most celebrated repository may prove not altogether unacceptable. The group of *characters* speaks for itself. But it is impossible to pass over the "*I's Yorkshire Cove*" endeavouring to *gammon* JERRY about the fine *action* of the horse before them. HAWTHORN, with a smile on his countenance, in return, asked YORKSHIRE, "if he saw anything *green* about him?" This hint was quite sufficient for TOM; and the CORINTHIAN informed TATTERSALL that he would not have the *prad* in question "*as a gift.*" LOGIC laughed at the *rotundity* of *paunch* of a person near JERRY, and, by way of a PUN, said he supposed it was "the *great* horse-dealer!"

JERRY expressed himself so much pleased with his visit to TATTERSALL'S, that he observed to LOGIC, during his stay in London he should often frequent it. "I delight," said HAWTHORN, "to be in the company of sportsmen; and no objects afford me greater satisfaction than the sight of a fine hunter,— the view of a high-mettled racer,—and the look of a *perfect* greyhound."[204] "I admire them also," replied the CORINTHIAN; "and TATTERSALL'S will always prove an agreeable lounge, if no direct purpose call a person thither. If nothing more than INFORMATION be acquired, that *alone*, JERRY, to a man of the world, is valuable at all times. Besides, TATTERSALL'S gives a *tone*[205] to the *sporting* world, in the

---

204 After *seven descents,* Lord Orford, it is said, obtained the object for which he had been so solicitous, without any diminution of speed or the beauties of shape and symmetry—a perfect greyhound.

205 It is a common expression among sporting persons—"How do they

same way that the transactions on the ROYAL EXCHANGE influence the mercantile part of society. It has likewise its *'settling days'* after the great races at *Newmarket, Doncaster, Epsom, Ascot,* &c. I do not know about the *bulls* and *bears*;[206] but if it has no *lame duels* to *waddle* out, it has sometimes *Levanters* that will not *show* for a time, and others that will *brush off* altogether. But this does not happen very often; and TATTERSALL's has its 'good! MEN' as well as the *'Change;* and whose *'word'* will be taken for any amount. It has also its 'subscription room,' which is extremely convenient for gentlemen and other persons who feel any inclination to become acquainted with the events of the sporting world, at the moderate charge of *one guinea* a year. Indeed," continued TOM, "there is an air of sporting about this place altogether; elegance, cleanliness, and style, being its prominent features. The company, I admit, is a *mixture* of persons of nearly all ranks in life; but, nevertheless, it is that sort of *mixture* which is pleasingly interesting: there is no *intimacy* or *association* about it. A man may be well known here; he may also in his turn *know* almost everybody that visits TATTERSALL'S; and yet be quite a *stranger* to their habits and connexions with society. It is no matter who *sells* or who purchases at this repository? A *bet* stands as good with a LEG, and is thought as much of, as with a Peer,— MONEY being the *touchstone* of the circumstance. The 'best judge' respecting sporting events is acknowledged the 'best man' here; every person being on the 'look out' to see how he *lays* his *blunt*. The DUKE and the *Parliamentary Orator,* if they do not know the properties of a horse, are little more than *cyphers*; it is true, they may be *stared* at, if pointed out as great characters, but nothing more. The *nod* from a *stable-keeper* is quite as important, if not more so, to the Auctioneer, as the *wink* of a RIGHT HONOURABLE. Numbers of persons, who visit TATTERSALL'S, are or wish to appear *knowing;* from which *'self'* importance they are often most egregiously duped. In short, if you are not as familiar with the *odds* upon all events as

---

bet their money at TATTERSALL'S?"
206   CORINTHIAN TOM, it appears, was rather in doubt whether *bulls* or *bears* were disposed of by Mr TATTERSALL.

CHITTY in quoting precedents—show as intimate an acquaintance with the *pedigree* and *speed* of race-horses as a GULLEY—and also display as correct a knowledge of the various capabilities of the prize pugilists as a JACKSON;—if GAIN is your immediate object, you are 'of no use' at TATTERSALL'S." "Yes," says LOGIC, with a grin, interrupting TOM; "there are to be found here as many *flats* and *sharps* as would furnish the *score* of a musical composer; and several of these *instruments* have been so much played upon, and are so wretchedly out of *tune*, that the most skilful musician in the world cannot restore them to perfect *harmony.*" 'It is," resumed the CORINTHIAN, "an excellent mart for the disposal of carriages, horses, dogs, &c., and many a fine fellow's *stud* has been *floored* by the hammer of Tattersall. There is a capacious TAP attached to the premises, for the convenience of the servants of gentlemen in attendance upon their masters, or for any person who stands in need of refreshment. Tattersall's, for the purposes intended, is the most complete place in the Metropolis; and if you have any desire to witness 'real life'—to observe *character*—and to view the favourite *hobbies* of mankind, it is the resort of the *pinks* of the SWELLS,—the *tulips* of the GOES,—the *clashing* heroes of the military,—the fox-hunting clericals,—sprigs of nobility,—stylish coachmen,—smart guards,—saucy butchers, —natty grooms,— tidy helpers,—knowing horse-dealers,—*betting* publicans,—neat jockeys,—sporting men of all descriptions, —and the picture is finished by numbers of real gentlemen. It is the tip-top sporting feature in London." "It must have been the work of some time," said Jerry, "to have formed such a famous connexion." "Yes," replied Tom; "you are quite right. It is not the *work* of a day. The name of Tattersall is not only high, but of long standing in the sporting world; and everything connected with this splendid establishment is conducted in the most gentlemanly manner. The founder of these premises was, during his time, viewed as one of the best judges of horse-flesh in the kingdom; and, as a proof of it, he made his fortune by a horse called Highflyer."[207]

---

207   In remembrance of whom the following epitaph was written:—
    HERE LIETH

CHAPTER XI.

The trio, upon quitting Tattersall's, took a walk into Hyde Park, when Logic hinted to his companions, that, by way of a *contrast* to their last night's excursion, an hour or two in the evening might very well be disposed of at the Italian Opera." "I should not have the least objection," said Tom, "but I have made an engagement to drink tea with Kate. She wishes me to hear her sing a new song she has recently acquired, and I cannot disappoint her; indeed, since Jerry has been in town, she has had very little of my company." "Apropos," exclaimed Logic, "I claim your promise of an introduction to Corinthian Kate." "And I too," urged Jerry, eagerly. "It shall be so, my friends, if you promise to '*keep the line*'[208] answered Tom; "you shall be admitted into the *preserve*, but, remember, no *poaching*. Logic, you have an excellent touch on the pianoforte; Kate is excessively fond of music, and you will therefore be a most welcome visitor. Jerry's merry song and lively company will also ensure him a good reception. I shall do everything in my power to promote perfect harmony, and I think we may, at least, picture to ourselves a few '*gay moments*' But let us return home as soon as possible, as I have ordered an earlier dinner than usual, that I might keep to my appointment."

The progress of the trio was interrupted for a short period, in their way to Corinthian House, through the streets, with the following dialogue between a costardmonger and "his voman" whose donkey had accidentally slipped one of his feet into a plug-hole.

JERRY laughed as heartily as if he had been witnessing a pantomime; indeed, the scene altogether was highly ludicrous.

The perfect and beautiful symmetry
Of the much-lamented
HIGHFLYER;
By whom, and his wonderful offspring,
The celebrated TATTERSALL acquired a noble fortune.
But was not ashamed to acknowledge it.
In gratitude to this famous
STALLION,
He called an elegant mansion he built
HIGHFLYER HALL.

208   To behave in a becoming manner: not to forget one's self!

Tom smiled; and Logic was on the broad grin. "*Vy* don't you mind *vat* you're *arter*," said Poll, "instead of rolling your *goggles* about after all manner of people; it *voud* be much better for you if you did, I knows. Here, don't you see all the carrots and greens, that cost me every *mag* I *coud* raise last night, will be down in the dirt and not *vorth* one brass *farden*." "Burst you," replied Bill, angrily, "if you don't hold that are *red rag* of yours, I'll *spoil* your mouth for a *munth*. You are always making a bad matter *vorse*, that's *vat* you are, so help me God." Then turning to the *donkey*, and roaring out, "*Vat!* you've got your foot in a plug-hole, and be damned to ye, have ye? Didn't I buy you last night—pay for you this morning—and brought you home in a hay-band? *Vat* more d'ye want, heh? Such obstinate devils as you are, are never satisfied; but I'll *sarve* you out for it, that's *vat* I *vill*," Bill, at length, released the donkey's *toddler* out of *trouble*, and giving the poor animal some terrible blows with a stick, roared out to him,— "If you don't mind *vat* you're *arter* now, I'll cut your precious rump off." The *donkey* soon mended his pace, and our heroes kept laughing at the circumstance till they arrived at *Corinthian House*.

The cloth being removed, and after the circulation of a few glasses of wine, Tom observed it was time to be off. The carriage was immediately ordered; and in a very short time the TRIO found themselves in the presence of the heroine of the tale. Tom was the master of the ceremonies upon this occasion, and Logic and Jerry received a flattering smile on their introduction to Kate; when the latter, without delay, presented to the notice of her visitors her companion, the lovely Susan. Matters of etiquette being adjusted, it was not long before "the *tea*" was introduced. Logic, who was never at a loss for conversation, was gay and witty upon the passing occurrences of the day; *i.e.*, such occurrences as were most likely to please females. Sales by candle—prices of hay—and the value of shares in the different canal companies, did not intrude upon the *Oxonian's* mind. It was in a much lighter field of conversation that he played off his artillery with success. It was in praising the sylph-like figure, attitudes, and admirable dancing of Miss *Tree*—the ballad-singing of Mrs *Bland*—the inimitable pathetic touches of Miss *Kelly*—the plaintive, heartfelt, musical notes of Miss *Stephens*—the acting of Miss *Taylor* [209] —the modest, unassuming Miss *Smithson*—the bewitching Madame *Vestris*—and the captivating Miss' *O'Neil*, that LOGIC commanded attention. BOB knew the time when to be a *lady's man*, as well as to be without the *streaming* qualities of a *lady's maid* in a row. He was well aware there was a time for everything; and no one knew better how to accommodate himself to all sorts of company than the lively intelligent *Oxonian*. TOM was equally elegant, but so *finished* in all his remarks, that *decision* seemed to rest upon his lips. JERRY, though not quite so eloquent as his two friends, nevertheless contributed with much humour towards the *chit-chat* of the tea- table. If a horse, a bird, or a dog, could have been cleverly introduced, JERRY would have shown himself a first-rate hero: however, his *eyes* had been sufficiently opened, in his *Rambles* and *Sprees* with the CORINTHIAN and LOGIC, to *see* his way more clearly upon the present occasion than he otherwise could have done. KATE, highly attractive from her fine person and superior manners, soon convinced the *Oxonian* and JERRY, that it was not from her *decorations* alone she became an object of attention: and SUE, interesting from her loveliness and simplicity, made a much greater impression upon the surrounding group than all the art in the world could have done towards elevating her in the minds of the persons present. Such was the *"gay party"* assembled; nay, more, it was a liberal one. It was, most certainly, a party with too many faults belonging to it, but yet not a single *absent* friend or a neighbour were served up as a *dish of scandal,* where every person present could help himself to a *slice!*

Both LOGIC and JERRY had only seen CORINTHIAN KATE, *en passant*, amidst the bustle and gay throng of the Park, and they had yet to encounter the danger of her charms and fascinat-

---

209   In the character of *Jeanie Deans,* in the "Heart of Mid-Lothian," as dramatised by T. Dibden, Esq., that individual who can witness the exertions of Miss Taylor without shedding a tear, must be made of *inflexible* stuff indeed! It is one of the finest triumphs of the art of acting. The delusion of the "stage effect" is so far forgotten, that the powers of NATURE only seem to prevail.

ing attractions when increased from the advantages of dress, and heightened by the most lively and impressive talents. During the *chit-chat* at the tea-table, JERRY could scarcely keep his eyes off KATE. HAWTHORN, in consequence, at times blushed, appeared confused, was aware it was extremely *vulgar*, knew that such conduct was wrong, and, also, that it was not the behaviour of a gentleman; but, above all, that it was acting unkind towards his friend and cousin: yet, in spite of all these honourable feelings and checks, which he endeavoured to keep upon himself, he often transgressed into a downright *stare,* as if under the influence of some powerful magnet that he could not resist:

> For her own person,
> It beggar'd all description;
> O'er picturing that VENUS where we see
> The fancy outwork nature.

The *Oxonian* too, with all his experience in these matters, would have been equally at a loss to have known what to have done with his *optics* (as he afterwards remarked), if his *green specs* had not operated as a prime *hedge* [210] for him: and in all probability, had not the CORINTHIAN been present, the gallantry of LOGIC would have tempted him to have repeated the words of the poet as a compliment to the mistress of his friend:—

> Angels were painted fair to look like you!

Upon the removal of the tea-things, very little time was suffered to elapse, before TOM gave the *hint* to LOGIC, that "*gay moments*" were too precious to be wasted, the pianoforte was at his service, and the company were anxiously waiting to hear him commence the harmony of the evening. LOGIC required no further invitation, and immediately took his seat at the instrument; but before he had half finished the air of—

---

210 To "*hedge off,*" or "*it's a prime hedge for me,*" are phrases repeatedly made use of in the Sporting World, when an individual wishes to save himself from any serious consequences.

> When to lovely woman's powers
> Man submits his enraptured soul!
> He culls life's sweetest flow'rs,
> His hours in pleasure roll!
> No other joys invading,
> Tempts deluded man to stray;
> Blest alone, with love, pervading,
> She bends him to her sway,
>   Lovely woman!
>   Lovely, lovely woman!
> Man's best and dearest gift of life!

Kate and Sue complimented the *Oxonian* on his musical talents; indeed, these "*gay moments*" of the party were enriched by each of them displaying their various talents, to prevent the intrusion of *ennui;* or, in other words, to avoid the *bad* manners of looking at their watches—lolling and yawning, and picking their teeth—which too often occur when time hangs heavy on the hands of a company destitute of abilities.

The eloquence of Jerry was not the worse for a few glasses of wine, and Logic very frequently turned round, full of humour, bidding his companions to "keep time," and to pay attention to the man in the orchestra. Tom, who had already *plied* the *Oxonian* with several bumpers, handed him another glass of wine, and observed, with a smile, "that it would be impossible to neglect a man of his *great* taste!"

If ever time had passed merrily in any company, it might be said to have positively *flown* away among this *gay* party. Pleasure was their idol; it was the creature of their imagination: and no heroes ever offered more sacrifices at its attractive *shrine* than did our trio. They were devotees to Pleasure, morning, noon, and night. Logic, at all times, possessed so much *gaieté de cœur,* that no assemblage of persons could be dull for an instant in his presence. The CORINTHIAN was equally so in disposition, if not gifted with talents even of a higher cast to amuse and interest a company; and Hawthorn, the laughing, good-natured Jerry, if he could not *chatter* like a magpie upon all subjects that were introduced into conversation, yet no one departed from his society with an impression that a *dummy* [211] had taken his seat amongst them.

Equally devoted to gaiety and pleasure were our heroines; but the *dispositions* of Corinthian Kate and the lovely Sue were diametrically opposite to each other. KATE was proud, yet dignified; commanding, but polite; and, conscious of her own fine person, and its powerful influence upon the opposite sex, she left nothing untried that could tend to *improve it*. She could smile at a comic incident, and shed tears over a pathetic tale; but it was more from the impulse of the moment than any deep impression they had made upon her feelings; and when these convulsive efforts had subsided, they were nearly forgotten by her for ever. Kate, too, was fond of ACCOMPLISHMENTS, not precisely as *accomplishments*, but on account of their commanding attention; and, under this idea, she had been actively industrious to make herself mistress of everything that could add to her importance. She could sing well—dance elegantly—was a proficient in music—an adept at drawing—a delightful scholar, and the *tout ensemble* completed with the manners of a lady. The Corinthian was her idol, but it was not from all-powerful love,—it was not that tender symptom which operates so *penetratingly* on the *first sight* of an individual, that agitates, produces tremblings, palpitations of the heart, and creates confusion in the breasts of females, and yet cannot be accounted for, but so it is! No; it was her ambition that had sealed the *contract*. It was the splendid fortune of Tom, his elegant figure, his superior abilities, his great character, and his being the TON, that had fastened upon her eye; and Kate preferred the *envy* of her sex, in securing such a hero to herself, rather than to be *pitied* for loving him without obtaining a *conquest*, being lost, as it were, to the world, and sighing and pining in some private corner. Propriety, and even *character*, had been leaped over in order to gratify her ambition; and even sinning with her eyes open: but—

> The world was never wickeder than now—
> WEDLOCK abused—her bond pronounced a jail
> A WIFE call'd vilely 'ev'ry body's cow,

---

[211] A cant phrase for a stupid fellow; a man who has not a word to say for himself. The family of the *dummies* is very numerous.

> A *canister*, or *bone* to a dog's tail!'
> What dare not knaves of this degenerate day
> Of Marriage, decent hallow'd marriage, say?
> 'Wedlock's a heavy piece of beef, the rump
> Returns to table, *hash'd,* and *stew'd,* and *fried,*
> And in the stomach much to lead allied,
> A hard, unpleasant, undigested lump:'
> But fornication ev'ry man enjoys—
> A smart anchovy sandwich—that ne'er cloys—
> A *bonne bouche* men are ready to *devour,*—
> Swallowing a neat half dozen in an hour.
> 'Wedlock,' they cry, 'is a hard pinching boot,
> But fornication is an easy shoe—
> The first won't suit;
> It won't do.
>
> 'A girl of pleasure's a light fowling-piece—
> With this you follow up your game with ease;
> That heavy lump, a wife, confound her!
> Makes the bones crack,
> And seems upon the sportsman's breaking back,
> A lumb'ring eighteen pounder!
>
> 'One is a summer-house, so neat and trim,
> To visit afternoons for Pleasure's whim;
> So airy, like a butterfly so light:
> The other an old castle with huge walls—
> Where Melancholy mopes amid the halls,
> Wrapp'd in the doleful dusky veil of night!'

But, to use Jerry's own words, respecting the lovely Sue, he has often since been heard to remark,—"What a vast difference appeared between these two females. While Kate," said he, "has excited your astonishment, from her dignity, grandeur, and self-possession,—the tenderness, solicitude, and anxiety to please, portrayed by Sue, has interested every one in her behalf beyond description. Unconscious of the influence which her lovely person and beauty had upon her beholders, she required not the aid of art to render it more effective, but which tended to make her simplicity doubly captivating." The mildness of Sue's disposition was unfortunately the means of her becoming a sacrifice to her designing protector. Sincere, in her own professions of love, she believed the emphatic vows of her hero to be equally true; and therefore, had yielded to his entreaties; but, in return, Sue found herself deceived for her generous, unlimited affection. She had not one grain of *harshness* in her whole composition. She could, also, boast of accomplishments equal to CORINTHIAN KATE, but SUE was more reserved in displaying them; as *ambition* did not fire her *brain* to excel other females in beauty, grandeur, or talents. In short, lovely SUE partook more of the interesting tender companion than the high-notioned, extravagant, dashing mistress. The dispositions of our heroines not coming in contact with each other, they were intimate friends; and KATE was extremely partial to SUE, who was her neighbour and also a frequent visitor. Females, in general, it should seem, are not very fond of introducing pretty women to the company of their male acquaintances; but SUE was viewed more in the light of a pretty *foil*, by CORINTHIAN KATE, than in the dangerous character of a powerful RIVAL. It was under this impression that the LOVELY SUE was invited to meet the TRIO.

After the *Oxonian* had played several pieces of lively music, he requested as a favour that KATE and his friend TOM would have the kindness to preform a waltz. KATE without any hesitation immediately stood up; TOM offered his hand to his fascinating partner; LOGIC struck up a favourite air, when this *lascivious* dance took place. The Plate conveys a correct representation of the "gay scene" at that precise moment. The anxiety of the *Oxonian* to witness the attitudes of this elegant pair Lad nearly put a stop to their movements, on his turning round from the pianoforte, and presenting his comical *mug* to their notice, crying out *"Bravo!"* It was with the utmost difficulty that KATE could suppress a laugh, it had such a risible effect upon her countenance; and it was impossible for the CORINTHIAN to assume anything like an air of gravity upon this occasion. JERRY was too much attracted by the charms of lovely SUE to notice the above circumstance, or even to spare the *corner of one* of his eyes to view the superior dancing of KATE and TOM, his time being completely occupied in singing, more after the style of INCLEDON than BRAHAM, to the interesting object before him—

> "When I gazed on a beautiful face,
> Or a form that my fancy approved;
> I was pleased with its sweetness and grace,
> And falsely believed that I loved;
> For I could look, I could like, I could leave.
> But I never loved any till now."

Chapter XI.

I.R. & G. Cruikshank
AN INTRODUCTION. GAY MOMENTS OF LOGIC, JERRY, TOM & CORINTHIAN KATE

As lovely Sue was only a visitor like himself, and not under the immediate influence of any person present, JERRY thought there was no bar to his saying a thousand civil things to her; and more especially as she did not appear offended at any of his remarks.

None of the company were *starters*,[212] and both Kate and SUE sang some delightful airs during the evening. The song and the glass had also passed very briskly round between the TRIO, till the face of LOGIC had assumed a shining aspect: JERRY was getting very merry; and the CORINTHIAN, quite full of spirits, was laughing at a small piece of torn paper, which he had just picked up off the carpet, and respecting which both KATE and SUE had denied having any knowledge. It contained the following sentences, which TOM read aloud: — "*Mary Devis* begs leave to inform the ladies in general that she answers all sorts of difficult questions proposed to her, in a satisfactory manner; nativities cast, &c., and is to be heard of." "This is some old Fortune-Teller, I'll be sworn," says TOM; "and if I knew the direction, JERRY, you and I would pay her a morning visit. Come, ladies, do not be so unkind; give us the *Old Hag's* direction!" Both KATE and SUE blushed with confusion, but again denied any knowledge of the circumstance.

LOGIC, at length, grew tired of performing on the pianoforte, and, having no other *companion* to engage his attention, begged leave, that the "*odd one*" as he termed himself, might retire. The lovely SUE also proposed taking her departure, when JERRY, with a squeeze of the hand, insisted upon seeing her safe home. Thus it was the TRIO separated, and finished their "GAY MOMENTS!" for that sitting, but under a general promise that they would have

---

212   The *lateness* of the HOUR never had any influence upon the minds of our TRIO while "mirth was afloat;" and neither TOM, JERRY, or LOGIC came under the denomination of *starters!* Our heroes were too fond of PLEASURE to lose a single atom of it: and, therefore, they left it to the REGULARS (the *eleven* and *twelve* o'clock sort of people, who would not stay a minute longer for the world) to *break* up the *links* of HARMONY. Indeed, it is very often experienced in society, that, when any person has taken his departure, who had contributed, in a great measure, to the mirth and amusement of the evening, a degree of *flatness* has instantly pervaded the scene—the remaining company become dull, and the frequent result is a general SEPARATION. The "*good-nights*" and the "*good-byes*" so *unsettle* the party, that it is impossible to keep them *steady* afterwards.

CHAPTER XI.

another meeting the first opportunity.

LOGIC, according to promise, kept his appointment to meet our heroes at the Rooms, in St James's Street, to witness "the assault" between CORINTHIAN TOM and Mr O'SHAUNESSY. JERRY expressed his admiration, and LOGIC was also loud in his praise, at the superior style displayed by TOM in the *ornamental parade of quarts and tierce;* and also at the coolness and skill exhibited by the CORINTHIAN in the *grand assault.* "Indeed," said LOGIC, "as an amateur, I never saw any one equal to him; and I really think that he would *puzzle*, if not be a competent match for many persons who call themselves professors. JERRY, you really must take a few lessons from Mr O'SHAUNESSY before you return to *Hawthorn Hall.* It is an elegant accomplishment, and no gentleman ought to be without some knowledge of it.[213] If it were not for my *"green specs'"* (smiling), "I should like to have a bit of a flourish, and demand a 'taste of your quality' before I suffered you to depart." "I cannot, my dear BOB," replied JERRY, "expose my *ignorance* of fencing here; but, next time I meet you in the *Chaffing Crib*, if you like it, I will show you *how* to *use* a *cudgel.*

Only a small *taste."* "No, no," answered LOGIC, "that won't *fit!*" The Plate is an interesting pretty picture altogether; and, it must be admitted, the fencers display great ease and elegance in their attitudes. Mr O'Shaunessy not only met with a most flattering reception, but he was pronounced a complete master of the art.

---

213 "There is no exercise," says SIR JOHN SINCLAIR, in his code of *Health and Longevity*, "with a view to health, better entitled to the attention of those who are placed among the higher classes of society than that of FENCING. The positions of the body, in fencing, have for their objects erectness, firmness, and balance; and in practising this art the chest, the neck, and the shoulders, are placed in positions the most beneficial to health. The various motions of the arms and limbs, whilst the body maintains its erect position, enables the muscles, in general, to acquire vigorous strength; and, in young people, the bones of the chest and thorax necessarily become more enlarged, by means of which a consumptive tendency may be prevented. Various instances may be adduced where FENCING has prevented consumption and other disorders. It has been remarked, also, that those who practise this art are, in general, remarkable for long life and the good health they have enjoyed. These considerations, combined with the graceful movements which it establishes, and the elegant means of self-defence which it furnishes, certainly render the art an object of considerable importance."

FENCING.—JERRY'S ADMIRATION OF TOM IN AN "ASSAULT" WITH Mr O'SHANNESSY, AT THE ROOMS IN St JAMES'S STREET.

CHAPTER XI.

On quitting the Fencing-Rooms, TOM and JERRY accompanied LOGIC to the Albany, where they bid good-bye to the *Oxonian:* and, in their way towards Bedford Square, having an appointment at that place, HAWTHORN espied, at a short distance before him, in Russell Street, KATE and SUE tripping it along, as if in great haste. JERRY instantly mentioned the circumstance to TOM, but the CORINTHIAN had scarcely caught a glimpse of their persons, when they quickly turned down an obscure narrow street; and if the curiosity of our heroes had not been strongly excited, so as to give them a run for it, they must have lost sight of the ladies altogether, having only turned the corner of the street time enough to, witness their entrance into a very shabby, dirty-looking house. JERRY and TOM soon approached it. The door being open, *sans ceremonie* they ascended the stairs, upon which a *brush* did not appear to have been used for many a day; and, indeed, they were now so covered with mud, that a *shovel* would have been a far more appropriate article, before any water could have reached the boards so as to restore them to anything like a decent appearance. Our heroes, however, were not to be deterred in their ascent, and they arrived at the top of the house. "It must be the Fortune-Teller's," TOM whispered to JERRY. The Old *Impostor* (which the Plate represents), was "*laying out the cards,*" as she termed it, to *tell* the "fortunes" of SUE and KATE: but, it appears, she possessed no *knowledge whatever of her* OWN FORTUNE, when she was apprehended by the police officers, and afterwards tried at the Sessions House, Clerkenwell Green, and sentenced to six months' imprisonment. Of the above *punishment* that was in *store* for the OLD HAG, her cards were so unkind to their mistress as never to give the least *hint*. This circumstance *alone*, respecting the *ignorance* of fortune-tellers, speaks volumes to the unwary. But such is the credulity of mankind, that nothing can allay the *thirst* for a "peep into futurity!"[214] KATE and SUE had fallen into

---

214   Between thirty and forty years since, a woman of the name of Corbyn resided in a very small house, which she kept to herself, next door to the sign of the Bricklayers' Arms, in King's Gate Street, Holborn, who, at that period, and for several years afterwards, was in high repute as a fortune-teller, or *"cunning woman,"*

from her printed hand-bills, which she had well circulated in the areas of houses belonging to noblemen, and other persons of rank, at the west end of the town, and in various parts of the Metropolis, in order to decoy the women and men-servants to have their fortunes told; also, that they might put these bills into the hands of the daughters of their masters; in which she set forth "that she could give satisfactory answers to all questions respecting persons at a distance, either upon the sea or land,—cast the nativities of individuals,—resolve difficult points," &c. This bill had the desired effect, and Mrs Corbyn carried on a roaring trade. She was an extremely ignorant woman, but really a *cunning* one, so far as to cheat those persons who came to see her out of their money; and although she could not *read* a book, yet she could *converse* with the planets fluently. Neither had Mrs Corbyn the slightest knowledge of arithmetic; but she was quite expert, or pretended to be so, in calculating *nativities*. She, however, was a bold, confident woman, and well knew the method of *working* upon the *credulity* of the female sex in particular. Mrs Corbyn was no stranger to the impression made upon the mind by *stage effect;* and therefore, the *room* which individuals were ushered into by her servant, was so darkened as to produce a solemn and appalling appearance upon the stranger, who, in general, was left alone for about a minute: the walls were covered with the sun, moon, stars, &c., painted in black, for the visitor to contemplate. This sort of suspense had its importance; when all of a sudden, out popped the *"cunning woman"* dressed in a corresponding style, and in an assumed tone of voice, well calculated to excite fear in the breast of a female, demanded to know the nature, of the inquiry? If the lady wished to be informed respecting persons at a distance, then the *"cunning woman"* opened a large black book, full of hieroglyphic characters, which she pretended to consult upon the subject; and also pointed with her wand to the stars, uttering some incoherent expressions, till she derived the information to *humbug* the suitor. But, if it was about getting a husband, and in what time, *then the cards were laid out.* And by way of a grand *climax,* if more money was advanced (for Mrs Corbyn had always an excellent practice of being paid first), she offered to, show any female the exact likeness of her future husband? If the person acquiesced, Mrs Corbyn bid her not to be frightened, in order to increase the effect of her arts, and immediately she drew aside a curtain, which discovered a large square of clear glass, behind which was a narrow passage, parted off from the room, and a man whom she employed for the purpose, as a confederate: on Mrs Corbyn uttering a few cabalistic sounds, totally unintelligible, the confederate would show his face, and then *vanish* in an instant. This piece of deception, which was well managed, operated so strongly upon the feelings of many of her *tender* visitors, that they have not only *screamed* out with terror, but several have actually fallen down in fainting fits. When any man wished to see his future wife, she had also a confederate female to play the part. Mrs Corbyn increased so rapidly in property, that she was enabled to leave her obscure dwelling for a more capacious respectable house, which she had elegantly furnished, in Store Street, Tottenham-court Road; and where she carried on her deception in high style, laughing in her sleeve, till she was ultimately routed by the police. An impostor, of a similar description, also lived in the Old Bailey, under the denomination of a *"cunning man,"* about the same period; and within the last five-and-twenty years, another hero of this class dwelt in the neighbourhood of Bethnal Green, who was known by the appellation of the *"straw man."* This fellow this error; and TOM and JERRY thus traced them into the OLD HAG's apartment, when the hearts of the ladies were beating pit-a-pat to hear the important secrets of their fate unfolded to them. The Plate sufficiently bespeaks the poverty of the HAG's garret; an old rug answered the double purpose of keeping out the cold, and serving as a door, through a hole in which TOM tickled SUE with his whip, in order to attract her attention, and accompanied it, in a solemn disguised tone, with the words of MACBETH to the Witches:—

> "I conjure you, by that which you profess,
> (Howe'er you come to know it) answer me.
> Though you untie the winds," &c.

Sue, starting from her seat, trembling at every joint, exclaimed, "What shall we do? my patience! here is the Corinthian!" Kate, afraid to turn her head round, to meet the countenance of our hero, blushed, and felt ashamed on being caught in so ridiculous a situation. But while Tom and Jerry were laughing heartily at the confusion they had made, Kate, followed by her friend, immediately ran downstairs, were in the street in an instant, and walking off as fast as possible towards their residence, before the Corinthian and his Coz had recovered themselves from this ludicrous scene. Tom went in pursuit of the fair ones, leaving Hawthorn behind to compose the feelings of the *Old Hag*, who was in a dreadful state of agitation, not only from the sudden interruption which she had experienced, but under the fear that our heroes were two officers of justice in search of her. "What!" said JERRY,

---

had little figures made of *straw*, which, in order to elude the pursuits of justice, it was his practice, before he opened his *"cunning lips,"* to make his visitors purchase. But, at length, "the man of straw" was tried and convicted as a rogue and a vagabond, and sentenced to six months' imprisonment; and for a second offence he received the *correction* of the house. But, thanks to the vigilance of the police, most of these bare-faced impostors have been obliged to put down their *"callings;"* and it is now principally practised by a few gipsy women, who go about early in the morning under the pretence of purchasing clothes from the servant maids, before their masters or mistresses are up; and who prevail on these thoughtless, indiscreet girls to have their fortunes told, in order to get them off their guard, that some of their gang may, in the interim, rob the house.

smiling, "you a fortune-teller! and your *cards* not to tell you that you would have a great *surprise* before long?" "Oh, dear! no, sir," replied the old impostor; "my cards never tell such things as *them are;* but I hope you will have some compassion, and do not mean to take me before a justice." HAWTHORN convinced this *cunning* woman of her error by taking his departure, and using all the speed he was able to overtake his party. JERRY soon came up with them, when KATE and SUE, on finding the laugh against them, acknowledged their error. "Say no more about the *Old Hag*" said the CORINTHIAN; "and as she is now Out of your *sight*, so let the *impostor* be also out of your *mind*. I have got a fine treat in store for you, that will excite more astonishment, and give you more pleasure and satisfaction, than fifty visits to all the *cunning* women in the world!"   "But pray tell us what it is, that we may, in some degree, prepare ourselves for it," replied KATE, backed in the most persuasive manner by the lovely SUE. "Is it a Ball—a Masquerade— a "visit to the Opera— the Theatre— or"— "You need not proceed any further, my dear creature, with your questions," said Tom, "as it will remain a profound secret with me till to-morrow morning, eleven o'clock, when my Coz and I will call for you and your friend; therefore, as a favour, I must request that you do not keep us waiting a single instant, as we are compelled to be at the place by a specific time, or we shall not be admitted." "You are a cruel, very cruel man!" exclaimed KATE, "thus to tantalise us: indeed, you are almost as bad as *Blue Beard* with his *blue chamber;* but, nevertheless, you may depend upon our being ready to a minute." SUE likewise endeavoured, with all the playfulness she was mistress of, to obtain the *secret* from HAWTHORN; but the latter, with a smile, impressively gazed on her sweet face, squeezing her hand, and with a theatrical sort of dignity, declaimed, "I must be *cruel*, only to be KIND!" Prior engagements, on the part of our heroes, compelled them to apologise for taking rather an abrupt leave of the ladies for that evening; but pledged themselves to pay them an early visit the next morning.

Chapter XI.

TOM & JERRY, CATCHING KATE & SUE, ON THE SLY, HAVING THEIR FORTUNES TOLD.

The CORINTHIAN and JERRY, accompanied *by* LOGIC, were punctual to their appointment; and KATE and SUE were dressed long before the time, waiting with the utmost anxiety to receive them. No delay now occurred, and the "gay party" were in the carriage and rattling through the streets before the *fair ones* had scarcely time to inquire after the nature of the *secret,* or the name of the place they were about to visit. "To CARLTON PALACE, ladies," replied TOM; "and if you do not, on your return home, all of you say, that it eclipses every house you have previously witnessed in the Metropolis, I will forfeit anything you may be pleased to inflict upon me, in thus highly raising your anticipation." "Indeed, we will not let you off," cried LOGIC, "if we find that you have *imposed* upon us; and JERRY shall be the *judge* upon this occasion." "Agreed," observed the CORINTHIAN. The footman announced, by his handy work at the knocker, that the party had arrived at CARLTON PALACE.

TOM, JERRY, LOGIC, KATE, and SUE, immediately entered the GREAT HALL, which is extremely capacious, being forty-four feet in length and twenty-nine in breadth. It has a noble effect, is embellished with columns of beautiful Sienna marble, and is also decorated with a variety of bronzed antique busts, by *Nollekens.* It is well lighted by an oval skylight, and displays numerous sculptural ornaments. The pavement is of marble, chequered with black; and six superb lanterns are suspended in various parts of the Hall.

The VESTIBULE is a fine apartment, which leads to the centre of the suite of rooms. The ceiling is delightful. The rich velvet draperies, a superb chandelier, and marble busts of the Dukes of Devonshire and Bedford, Lord Lake, and the late Right Honourable Charles James Fox, all executed by *Nollekens*, tend highly to interest the attention of the visitors.

The GREAT STAIRCASE, which is extremely grand, is divided into arches, in the niches of which are two bronzed colossal figures: one, as Atlas, supporting a circular map of Europe; and the other, as Time, holding up a clock of singular construction. On the walls of the staircase is an equestrian portrait of King George II. It is impossible to pass this staircase without admiration.

CHAPTER XI.

The WEST ANTE-ROOM is spacious, and is used as a waiting- room for persons of distinction. It is well adapted for such a purpose, as it contains whole-length portraits of the Duke of Cumberland, uncle of his late Majesty; Henry Frederick, Duke of Cumberland, brother of the late King, painted by *Sir Joshua Reynolds*, in a style of excellence equal to any of the tints of Reubens or Vandyke; also a portrait of the late Duke of Orleans, by *Reynolds*. There is likewise a portrait of the Duke of Clarence, in naval uniform, by *Hoppner*, which is much admired. Portraits of Louis XV., King George II., and Queen Caroline, are also to be seen in this apartment.

The CRIMSON DRAWING-ROOM is splendid indeed. It is a fine combination of art and effect; and undoubtedly a proud trophy of the superiority of the manufactures of Great Britain. The draperies are of crimson satin, and the walls are also covered with the same article. The carpet, which is of a light bluish velvet, is a fine piece of workmanship, on which are the crest and coronet of the present King, when Prince of Wales. This apartment is also distinguished for a superb font, a present from his Holiness the Pope. The centre chandelier, it is said, in point of grandeur, cannot be equalled in Europe. It also abounds with fine portraits of the late Dr Markham, Archbishop of York, tutor to his present Majesty, painted by *Hoppner;* Lord Erskine, by *Reynolds;* Lord Thurlow, by *Sir T. Lawrence:* the celebrated Marquis of Granby, by *Reynolds;* the Jewish Bride, by *Rembrandt;* and the picture of St George's Interview with the Princess, after having killed the Dragon, by *Reubens*, which give a climax to this apartment, that must be seen to be fairly appreciated.

The CIRCULAR-ROOM is a fine relief to the preceding one, having a tent-like appearance, from the suspension of Roman drapery of light blue silk, with which the walls are in part covered. The ornaments are numerous; and the ceiling is painted to represent a sky. A very large cut-glass chandelier is reflected in four pier-glasses opposite; added to which magical effect, the pier-glasses also reflect each other. The sensation it has upon the visitor is not to be described.

The Throne-Room, which the Plate represents, conveys all the magnificence of Royalty. The draperies are of crimson velvet, ornamented with gold-lace fringe, &c. Jerry was quite absorbed in thought with the grandeur by which he was surrounded, till Logic, smiling, tapped him on the shoulder, and asked him, "if he called the position he then stood in *backing* the Throne?" Jerry started from his reverie, and laconically observed, "I am astonished!" "This very large, handsome carpet, on which we now tread," said Logic, "I understand, is all in one piece. It weighs more than a ton, was originally an inch in thickness, and made in Spitalfields." The attendant rather animatedly observed, "Sir, all the carpets throughout the Palace are of English manufacture. The King will not suffer anything else to remain here, except presents."

Ante-Chamber, formerly the Throne-Room. This is also a very interesting and elegant apartment. The draperies are blue velvet, and the walls covered with the same, gold lace, fringes, &c., sofas and chairs of gold to correspond. This room contains a rich crimson-coloured carpet, the centre of which is embellished with the Royal arms. An exquisite chimney-piece of white marble, decorated in the most superb style. Pier-glasses reflecting each other; and on the panels of the doors gilt ornaments in carved work, representing the orders of the Garter, Bath, St Andrew, and St Patrick. This room is embellished with whole length portraits of the late King in his coronation robes, and her late Majesty Queen Charlotte, as a companion, painted by *Ramsey.* Also the portraits of the present King, in the robes of the order of the Garter, by *Hoppner;* and, as a companion, the Duke of York, by the late *Sir Joshua Reynolds.*

The Rose Satin Drawing-Room is fitted up in the Chinese style, and the walls are covered with rose-coloured satin damask, with gold mouldings. The chimney-piece is also in the Chinese style; but a splendid looking-glass, and the hangings and furniture are all English. It abounds with beautiful China ornaments, valuable stones, &c.

Chapter XI.

I. R. & G. Cruikshank.

THE "NE PLUS ULTRA" OF "LIFE IN LONDON".— KATE, SUE, TOM, JERRY AND LOGIC, VIEWING THE THRONE ROOM, AT CARLTON PALACE.

It is also conspicuous for a circular table, presented by Louis XVIII. to his present Majesty, which is one of the finest pieces of art of the Sevres manufacture ever seen. It is painted on porcelain, and set in a rich mounting of gold; in the centre of which is a painting of Alexander the Great, surrounded with profiles of all the great heroes of antiquity. To the lovers of painting, this apartment affords a rich and interesting treat. Two three-quarter portraits of Henrietta Maria, Queen of Charles I. by *Vandyke*, exquisitely finished. Two large Landscapes, by *Cuyp;* three cabinet pictures also by the same artist. A Hawking Scene, by *Adrian Van de Velde.* The Manteau Bleu, by *Metz.* Sportsmen Regaling, by *Paul Potter.* The Coup de Pistoler, by *P. Wouvermans.* Children with a Guinea-pig and a Kitten, by *Adrian Van der Werf.* Interior of a Kitchen, by *Mieris.* Cavaliers preparing for Riding, by *Cuyp.* Crossing the Brook, by *Adrian Van de Velde.* The terrified Boy, by *Potter.* This and the above painting are so truly excellent as to defy an accurate description of their merits. An Interior, by *Peter Van Slingelandt.* Portrait of George I. by *Sir Godfrey Kneller;* also of George II., unknown. The Village Festival, by *Teniers.* A Herdsman and Cattle, by *Adrian Van de Velde.* The Hay-Field, by *Philip Wouvermans.* Several more cabinet pictures also form such a source of attraction to the admirers of the fine arts and old masters, that it is a matter of sincere regret to leave them, to attend upon the call of the person who shows the visitors these unrivalled suite of apartments.

The Ante-Room, from the Entrance-Hall, an octagonal vestibule, leads to the suite of state apartments on the right, and operates as a sort of prelude to the above magnificent rooms. Between the windows, that are opposite the doors of entrance, is a large pier-glass, which reflects the objects before it, and produces a most interesting effect. The chimney-piece of white marble is very fine; and over it is an oval portrait of the celebrated Madame Pompadour. This room is distinguished for a fine collection of bronze statues; among which is William III. in Roman armour, crowned by Victory, and tramping Rebellion under his feet. It has also two small antique bronzes of the Venus de' Medici; likewise one of Louis XIV. in Roman armour. Over the panels of four doors are portraits of the Princesses Augusta, Elizabeth, Mary, and Sophia, painted with great delicacy, Louis XV. when a youth, by *Vandyke;* Henry, Prince of Wales, son of James I. Another oval portrait of Madame Pompadour, after the manner of the French school, is also placed in this apartment.

The BLUE VELVET ROOM is the private audience chamber of the King; and its decorations are of the most magnificent description. The ceiling is painted in imitation of a sky, at the corners of which are representations of British naval and military triumphs. The panels of the walls are dark blue velvet, with gilt mouldings. The draperies and the carpet are likewise blue. The state chairs, and also the sofas, are covered with blue satin, and a superb cabinet mahogany table stands in the centre of the room. Numerous pier-glasses, in gilt frames, and paintings of the finest class render the *tout ensemble* enchanting. The Shipwright of Antwerp, by *Rembrandt;* a Boat Piece, by *Albert Cuyp;* the Baptism of the Eunuch by Philip, painted by *Both;* and Christ restoring the Paralytic, by *Vandyke*, are among the finest compositions of the old masters.

The BLUE VELVET CLOSET is a corresponding appendage to the preceding room, and is of the same elegant description. A superb chandelier of cut-glass is suspended from the ceiling, and the paintings are equally attractive. A Party returning from Hawking, by *P. Wouvermans.* A Camp Scene, by *Cuyp.* View of a Town in Flanders, by *Vanderheyden.* The Haunted Cellar, by *Maas,* a German story, is a master-piece of the art. It portrays the mistress of the house stealing as it were down the ladder that leads to a vault, with her fingers on her lips, indicating her wish to be silent, to find out the ghost; when she discovers, at the extremity of the vault a light, and her maid-servant, with her lover and a friend, drinking her wine. There is also an excellent companion-picture by *Metzu.* A View in Holland, by *Vanderheyden.* A Landscape, by *Ruysdael.* And also a cabinet picture containing portraits of King Charles I., his Queen, and the Infant Prince, afterwards Charles II., by *Mytens*, render the BLUE VELVET CLOSET a most conspicuous apartment, notwithstanding the fascinating rivalry by which it is surrounded. This closet produced considerable mirth between our "gay party;" TOM whispering to KATE to bear in mind the *secret* of the *Blue Chamber*. JERRY also observed to LOGIC, that he never saw *"blue* look *so pleasant* before!" when the *Oxonian* retorted, with a grin, that he would bet ten to one "there was nothing like *Blue Ruin* about it."

The LOWER SUITE OF APARTMENTS is entered, after descending the grand staircase, by a vestibule, the windows of which open to the lawn. This room has a double row of Corinthian columns and pilasters, forming a colonnade, at the ends of which, and between the pilasters on both sides of the apartment, are splendid looking-glasses, which, from their reflection, produce the appearance of an interminable colonnade. The effect is delightful. The walls are covered with scarlet cloth, with gilt mouldings, and the window-curtains and draperies correspond. The chimney-piece is of statuary marble, over which is a clock that has neither dial, face, nor hand, and is viewed as a great curiosity. China ornaments, slabs, and bronzed figures, candelabras of superior workmanship, are numerous indeed. The pictures are also selected with great taste, and a composition of Roman architecture is an object of great admiration. The following pictures embellish the LOWER VESTIBULE. A Landscape with Figures, by *David Teniers*. A Family Piece, by *Grant*. A Castle Piece, by *Nicholas Bexhem*. A Water-Mill, by *Holbina*. A Stag Hunt, by *Hackaert*. An Old Woman buying Fruit, by *Gerard Douw*. Horses, by *Vandyke*. Two Landscapes, by *Teniers;* and a River Scene, by *Cuyp*. "The whole of these paintings are so delightfully finished, that it almost seems a libel on the visitor's taste, from the hurried manner he is compelled to pass them over," said LOGIC to the CORINTHIAN; "indeed it cannot be termed any thing more than merely a *glance* at these royal apartments."

The LIBRARY is large, and has five windows in it, which look into the garden. The books are handsomely bound and arranged in classes, under the Librarian, Dr STANIER CLARKE. The appearance of the Library not only displays considerable taste, but convenience has also been consulted. A fine collection of maps, concealed by the cornices of the book-cases, on spring rollers, can be referred to without the least trouble. The doors of the Library are also, concealed by imitative books. Here are, likewise, several groups of figures, busts, and horses, and some fine miniature pieces of Roman sculpture. Ebony chairs, of the time of Henry VIII., with scarlet cushions, and the furniture, &c., to correspond. The chimney-piece is supported by four columns of the Corinthian order, and on which is placed a curious clock, constructed by Sir W. CONGREVE, Bart. "A great respect is paid to *Time*" said Jerry to Logic, "as I have remarked, in the apartments we have gone through, several magnificent clocks." "It is highly necessary in a Palace," replied the *Oxonian*, "for the sake of example. Our late revered good old King was a great *timist*, and, upon all occasions, he was *exactly* to the *minute:* and believe me, my dear Jerry, it is one of the best traits about a gentleman to keep his *time,* for there is no *harmony* about the *composition* without it." "Well said, Bob," observed the Corinthian.

The GOLDEN DRAWING-ROOM, which is entered from the Library by folding doors, is a splendid specimen of the Corinthian order of architecture; the columns of which are entirely gilt with burnished and matted gold. The panels of the doors contain whole pieces of looking-glass from the top lo the bottom, and are likewise so judiciously placed in various parts of the room as to reflect each other, which has an effect not to be described, representing *no end,* as it were, to this magnificent apartment. It would require the extent of a small volume minutely to describe the draperies, the curtains, the China jars, the candlesticks, the tables, sofas, &c. All that *invention* could suggest, all that the powers of ART could master, and all that *talents* could supply, have been united with such a felicity of effect in this GOLDEN DRAWING-ROOM, as proudly to bid anything like competition defiance. It has also to boast of the following rich subjects of the pencil:—Village Fetes, by *Teniers.* A Horse-Market, by *P. Wouvermans;* and a Laboratory, by *D. Teniers.* A beautiful time-piece, of white marble, induced the lovely SUE, with a smile, to observe, on quitting this enchanting place, "Mr

HAWTHORN, you seem to have passed over 'Time,'" "Indeed, madam," replied JERRY, "I think, my friend LOGIC, with all his knowledge of *harmony*, would not be able to 'keep *time*' on entering this golden apartment." "I am inclined to agree with you, Coz," said the CORINTHIAN. This GOLDEN ROOM positively *electrified* JERRY—*surprised* TOM—*delighted* KATE— put SUE into *raptures*— and the *Oxonian*, with ecstasy, vowed "there was nothing like it on the earth!" The looking-glasses on each side of the entrance of it made this small gay party appear like several hundred persons.

The GOTHIC DINING-ROOM operates as a fine relief to the preceding one. It is divided into five compartments, or Gothic arches, with gold mouldings. The windows, which correspond, have rich crimson silk draperies; and the marble chimney-piece is also designed in the Gothic style. At the east end is a screen of four arches, each containing splendid looking-glasses, with a magnificent side-board; and the west end of the room is nearly similar. It also abounds with characteristic embellishments, and on the panels are emblazoned shields of the royal arms of England from the reign of Edward the Confessor to the time of Queen Anne.

The BOW SITTING-ROOM, which forms the entrance from the grand staircase to the lower suite of apartments, is covered with scarlet cloth, with gold mouldings. It has several rich cabinets, gilt tables, China vases, and elegant candelabras. But it is attractive from its fine collection of cabinet pictures from the Flemish and Dutch masters.—The Wise Men's Offerings, by *Rembrandt:* the excellence of this painting challenges criticism. Two Interiors, by D. *Teniers.* Boy with an Ass, by *Adrian Van de Velde.* Sleeping Pigs, and a Lady at a Window, by *Gerard Douw.* A Portrait of a Painter, by *Metzer.* A Landscape, by *Poelemburgh.* A Landscape, by *Berghem.* A Landscape, by *Karl du Jardin.* Two Interiors, by *Ostade.* The Assumption of the Virgin, by *Reubens.* A Castle-Piece, by *Jardin.* Robbers attacking a Waggon, by *P. Wouvermans.* Portrait of Reubens, by *himself.* Vandyke, by *himself.* "The above paintings alone are quite sufficient," said TOM, "to occupy more than the attention of one day; and then they might be reviewed with even greater delight."

CHAPTER XI.

The ANTE-ROOM to the Dining-Room is extremely interesting from its fine chimney-piece, magnificent clock, set in marble, cabinets of ebony, valuable stones, slabs of red porphyry, and a great variety of superb porcelain vases. The sofas and chairs are richly gilt and covered with scarlet cloth, as are also the walls of this room. It has also numerous paintings. A Conversation-Piece, by *Mieris.* Pan and Syrinx, by *Reubens.* Hawking, by *Wynants.* Blind Fiddler, by *Ostade.* A Farrier's Tent, by *P. Wouvermans.* Cavaliers, by *Cuyp.* Lady and Parrot, by *Mieris.* Maternal Affection, by *Mieris.* Cattle, by *Paul Potter.* The Drummer, by *D. Teniers.* Returning from Hawking, by *P. Wouvermans.* An Interior, by *Ostade.* Cattle, by *Karl du Jardin.* Milking, by *Adrian Van de Velde.* Fishermen, by *D. Teniers.* Domestic Employment, by *Gerard Douw.* An Arbour, by *Ostade.* A Poulterer's Shop, by *Mieris.* A Village Fete, by *D. Teniers;* and a Conversation-Piece, by *Mieris.* "The principal part of these paintings, which are such fine studies for our rising artists," said TOM, "I understand, that his Majesty, whose love for the fine arts has not been exceeded by any sovereign in Europe, with the utmost liberality and condescension, has allowed, for the more easy access of artists in general, to be placed, for a certain period, in a public exhibition." "The King," replied LOGIC, "I have also heard it said, possesses so excellent a knowledge of the old masters, that no picture-dealers have had the temerity to attempt to impose upon his judgment."

The DINING-ROOM has a most magnificent appearance. The west end of it opens, by three pair of folding doors, into the Conservatory, the piers of which are looking-glasses. The ends of the room have Ionic columns, in imitation of porphyry. It has looking-glasses placed in all the advantageous parts of the room. The ornaments throughout this splendid apartment are also extremely numerous. The window-curtains are of scarlet silk, and the chairs to correspond are also richly carved and gilt. Five folding French windows, next the garden, increase the effect of this beautiful room, which also abounds with cabinet pictures:—Four different Views of a Calm, by *Van de Velde.* The *Billet-Doux,* by *Gerard Terburg.* An Interior, by *John Steen.* A Music-Party, by

Godfrey Halken. An Interior, by *the same.* An Interior, by *Ostade.* An approaching Gale, by *Van de Velde;* and a Merry-Making, by *John Steen*, close this invaluable collection of paintings.

The CONSERVATORY, which is entered from the Dining-Room by three pair of folding sash-doors of plate glass, operates so interestingly upon the feelings of the spectator, that it can scarcely be described. The perspective of the CONSERVATORY is delightful. It resembles the interior of a small cathedral, and is formed after what is termed the Gothic style of architecture. In some parts of the ceiling are panes of glass, which increase the light and add to the effect. The windows of painted glass contain the arms of all the sovereigns of England, from William I. to George III. On the south side are also the armorial bearings of the kings of England, from William I. to the late reign, to correspond. Tabernacle work and appropriate figures give a delicate finish to the west end of the building; among which is a most exquisitely finished piece of sculpture of *Venus* asleep, lolling on her couch, in white marble, by CANOVA, with a light gauze veil thrown over it: it is a master-piece of the art. Candelabras support lamps of six burners each; and also from the arches are suspended Gothic lanterns, decorated with figures in stained glass. The pavement is composed of Portland stone.

The ARMORY, consisting of three apartments, is a treat indeed, and said to be the first in the world. It is on the attic story of the eastern wing, in a gallery which leads to the upper vestibule, but is not generally shown. Among innumerable curiosities, is a collection of boots and spurs, from the time of Charles I., particularly a pair of Marshal Biron's, musket proof; also the boots worn by George II. Caps, turbans, shields, bows, dresses, &c., of the inhabitants of the southern hemisphere. Different implements of war belonging to Austrian, Persian, Prussian, and English manufacture. Also of the Chinese and Eastern nations. Two models of horses as large as life; one of which is caparisoned with the ornaments which belonged to Murat Bey: the other with the armour and costume of the late Tippoo Saib. The saddle and bridle of the late Hetman Platoff. A coat of mail which belonged to Elphi Bey. A

Persian war-dress. The war-dress of a Chinese Tartar. The dagger of Zingis Khan. A magnificent palanquin of Tippoo Saib's, of ivory and gold; with such a variety of sabres, swords, daggers, &c., as to render this collection unrivalled.

On the "gay party" quitting CARLTON PALACE, TOM exclaimed, "This is a high treat: I have seen all the grand rooms in the Metropolis; but the suite of apartments in this Palace exceeds them all." "It is indeed a high treat," replied KATE; "I am quite delighted! There is such a superior something about these rooms, that they impressively remind one of the interesting fictions we read in the *Arabian Nights'Entertainments;* and seem to partake more of the *magical touch* of the TALISMAN than beholding the reality of works, which, in so eminent a point of view, tend to display the ingenuity and talents of the artists of this country. In short, my dear TOM, I feel much at a loss for adequate expressions to convey my opinion to you of the taste, elegance, dignity, grandeur, richness, beauty, originality, and interest, of this most imposing scene; and without any doubt, in my humble opinion, it must be admitted, by the most fastidious critic, to be the 'NE PLUS ULTRA of LIFE IN LONDON!'" In short, the numerous highly finished cabinet pictures, by the old masters; portraits of all the Royal Family; chandeliers; library; draperies; time-pieces: furniture, &c. &c., form such a combination of talent, that TOM observed, "no person could quit CARLTON PALACE without the most sincere regret that he had not had three or four days allowed him to wander amidst its unrivalled attractions, instead of being hurried through the rooms in the short space of one hour and a half."

CHAPTER XII.

A short Digression in the Shape of an Apology, but not intended by way of an Excuse, for Persons witnessing "Life in London." Peep-o'-Day-Boys. A Street-Row. The Author losing his "Reader."[215] *Tom and Jerry "showing Fight," and Logic floored. Honour among Thieves. The Pocket Book—a rich Anecdote. The Trio visit the Condemned Yard in Newgate. Symptoms of the "Finish of some sorts of Life" in London. A Glance at the Royal Exchange. Tom, Jerry, and Logic entering into the Spirit of the Lark, at ALLMAX, in the East. Invocation to Politeness—a Touch of the Sublime! The Contrast. Climax of "Life in London" in the West. Tom and Jerry on their P's and Q's at ALMACK'S; or, a Fat Sorrow better than a Lean One.*

IF "*MISFORTUNES*," as the old saying has it, "attend the righteous," the wicked, as a matter of course, cannot expect to go *unpunished:* although a man might have the "Old One's[216] *luck* and his own too!" "If," said Logic to Jerry (after the latter hero had been complaining to him on getting up rather late one morning after a night's *spree*, that he thought his *constitution* had got a little *scratch* since he had left HAWTHORN-HALL), "people who are fond of a *lark;* enjoy a *row;* love a *bit of fun;* take a peep at a *fair;* join in a *hop;* go to a *mill;* play at *rouge*

---
215   *Pocket-book:* this loss, at the time it occurred, was severely felt by the Author; but to have lost a single reader of Life in London would have proved much more mortifying to his feelings. He cannot spare *one* of them, even numerous as they are.
216   A *genteel* name for the Devil.

et noir; parade the *lobby;* stroll through the *back-slums;*[217] visit the cock and dog pits; spend a few *interesting* moments at *gaffing;*[218] *blow a cloud* at a free and easy; meet with Mr *Lushington;* drop in on the sly at a *case; floor* the *charleys,* and, after all, *nothing* be the *matter,* why then it is a prime circumstance in the career of a man indeed. But it is five hundred to one, that ALL the above *events* do not *come off-right,* with the most experienced and skilful sportsman: that is to say, my dear friend, if you do not get *punished* in your person, yet you may be most preciously *physicked* in your *clie;* and, if you have even the good fortune to keep your *peepers* from being measured for a *suit of mourning;* your *canister* from being *cracked;* and your face from being *spoiled* among the low *coveys* of *St Kilt's;* you are, perhaps, even in more real danger among the refined heroes of the creation, from paying too much *'attention'*[219] where *politeness* is measured out to the extreme nicety of splitting a hair at the *West End* assemblies.

The Author is most feelingly compelled to acquiesce in the justness of the preceding remarks, made use of by his friend LOGIC, respecting "LIFE IN LONDON," from the great danger he once unexpectedly experienced in only mixing with a private party at the Albany, which originated in a *genteel* suit, although the *finish* of it assumed rather a different complexion. And, like a drowning man who will catch at a straw, the Author, to avoid being totally *shipwrecked* with the public, is induced, as an *illustration* of the arguments made use of by the *Oxonian,* to give the following case in point:—

---

217   Low, unfrequented parts of the town.
218   Termed *low* gambling: yet resorted to by many persons, instead of the old mode of *"tossing up"* Three halfpence are put into a hat, which is then turned down upon a table; and if the crier call heads, and the halfpence are all so, then he wins. It is rather a tedious mode of play, as considerable time is frequently lost before the halfpence come off right either way. However, thousands of pounds have changed masters in this manner, in London, in the course of a short night.
219   Paying too much *"attention"* to the ladies has occasioned more than some JOHN BULL sort of *ill-natured unaccommodating* husbands to give such very polite gallants a dose of *leaden* powder, that has *cooled* their courage, or, at least, *checked* their importunities.

TO THE SUBSCRIBERS TO "LIFE IN LONDON."
THE AUTHOR IN DISTRESS! [220]
He jests at a 'LARK" that never felt a SCRATCH!

My numerous and dearest Friends,

Of necessity, I am compelled to state to you, that, having accepted an invitation from BOB LOGIC, about three weeks since, to spend an evening with him and a few of his *Swell Pals*, at the *Albany*, I pleaded business, and that the "First of the Month" must come. "I know it," replied BOB, "but it shall be a *sober* set-out: PIERCE, you shall *tipple* as you like." In consequence of BOB's *plausibility*, I was *gammoned* to be one of the *squad*. Mixed liquors and *steamers* were the order of the *darkey*. But he praised so highly a cargo of *Daffy*, which he had just received from the NONPAREIL, that *Daffy* and *water* was the preferred *suit*. After a glass or two had been *sluiced* over the *ivories* of the party, which made some of them begin loudly to *chaff,* BOB gave the *wink* to his *slavey,* observing that more hot water was wanted. A large kettle, boiling at the spout, was speedily introduced, but instead of *water,* read *boiling Daffy.* The assumed gravity of BOB's *mug* upon playing off this *trick* was quite a treat; but I am happy to say *Crooky booked* it. "Come, gents," said BOB, "please yourselves, here is plenty of water, now mix away." It had the desired effect. The glass was pushed about so quickly, that the "First of the Month" was soon *forgotten,* and we kept it up till very long after the REGULARS had been *tucked* up in their *dabs,* and. only the *Roosters* and the *"Peep-o'-Day-Boys"* were out on the prowl for a *spree.* At length a *move* was made, but not a *rattler* was to be had. BOB and the party, *chaffing,* proposed to see the *Author* safe to his *sky-parlour.* The boys were *primed* for anything. Upon turning the corner of *Sydney's Alley,* into Leicester-Fields, we were assailed by some *troublesome customers,* and a *turn-up* was the result (as the Plate most accurately represents). BOB got a *stinker,* and poor I received a *chancery-suit* upon the *nob.* How I reached the *upper-story,* I know not; but, on waking, late in the day, I found my pocket-book was absent—without leave. I was in great grief at this loss, not on account of the *blunt* it contained,—much worse—the *notes* in it were dearer than gold to me. The account of JERRY's introduction to the Marchioness of Diamonds, the Duchess of Hearts, Lady Wanton, Dick Trifle, Bill Dash, &c. &c., on his first appearance in Rotten Row with the CORINTHIAN, *booked* on the spot. I was in a complete *funk.* I immediately went to *sartain persons,* and communicated my loss; *how, where,* and *when;* and I was consoled, that, if it were safe, PIERCE EGAN should have it. Day after day passed, and no account of it;—I gave it up for lost, and scratched my *moppery,* again and *again,* but could not recollect, *accurately,* the substance of my notes. I was sorry for myself;—I was sorry for the public. However, on Friday morning last, taking a *turn* into

---

220   Not out of *wind*, nor beat to a *stand-still;* but sorry that I am compelled to *forfeit* on the 1st of January, 1821, being out of *condition* to appear *bang-up* at the *scratch*.

Paternoster Row, my friend Jones, smiling, said he had got the Book:—as he is fond of a bit of *gig*, I thought he was in *fun*,—but, on handing it over to me, with the following letter, my *peepers* twinkled again with delight.

   To the care of Mr Jones, for P. EGAN.

  Sir,—You see as how I have sent that are *Litter*[221] Pocket-Book,. which so much *row* has been *kicked* up about amongst us. Vy it an't vorth a single *tonic*. [222] *Who*'s to understand it? vy it's full of pot-hooks and hangers[223] and not a *screen*[224] in it. You are determined nobody shall *nose* your *idears*. If your name had not been *chaunted* in it, it would have been *dinned* into the *dunagan*. But remember, no *conking*.
             From yours, &c.
 Dec, 29, 1820.   TIM HUSTLE.

The joy I felt on recovering my Pocket-Book I cannot communicate. But that is not all. In my exertions to find it, I picked up a rich anecdote, concerning "*another* POCKET- BOOK," which amply compensates for the unpleasant feelings I have experienced on the above occasion, and which is now given to the public.[225] But in all

---

221 Literary.
222 A half-penny.
223 Short-hand.
224 One pound note. An author, indeed, with money in his pocket-book, would be a novelty in Life in London. But, in the North, they are not quite so SCOTT free in his respect. Merit is, at all times, worthy of reward.
225 A well known dashing PRIG, whose HEAD was considered to have been s*crewed* on the right way, of the name of———. No, No, No! no *nosing;* this hero, with every finger on his hands like a fish-hook, in his way to his lodgings one evening, up Market Lane, the back part of the Opera House, on an Opera night, crossed Lord——— as he was making towards his carriage, and with great dexterity *drawed* the Peer of his Pocket Book. ——— immediately put the best leg foremost, and arrived out of breath at his *panny,* "almost before you could say Jack Robinson." But, on examining the Book, to his great disappointment, it only contained a few trifling memorandums. It was, however, such a beautiful piece of workmanship, that instead of destroying it (his usual precaution), he threw the Pocket Book over to his *hen,* saying, "Poll, my dear, it is a pretty article, and you may keep it for your own use. I feel rather *tired.* I shall, therefore, do no more *work* to night, but go to bed." The Book for a short time was thrown aside, but Poll's *curiosity,* woman-like, induced her again to examine it, when, to her great joy and surprise, she found *a secret pocket* containing £800 in new Bank Notes. Poll, in her eagerness to communicate this good luck to her *flash man,* who was now asleep on the *dab,* almost fell over the chairs; exclaiming, and giving him a shake at the same time, "*You are a pretty* Cove, ———*, an't you?* To nap *a prime* stake *and then to* ding *it.* Here's £800 *for you* (flinging the notes *at him),* and which must convince you,

probability, had it not been for the above *loss*, this *anecdote* would have remained in oblivion; and, therefore, it is, most certainly, an *"an ill wind that blows no one any good"* The return of my Book, however, arrived too late to prevent the following

APOLOGY:

In consequence of BOB LOGIC's *Daffy*, only one sheet of Letter Press accompanies the Plates of No. 5; but to make up for this unavoidable deficiency, THREE SHEETS of Letter Press will be given in No. 6.

I therefore trust, under all the circumstances of the case, a liberal allowance will be made, when it is recollected that such RAMBLES and SPREES FIRST gave the Author an idea of detailing some of the *"rich scenes"* which are only to be found in

"LIFE IN LONDON."

Wishing health and happiness, united with the compliments of the season, to all my numerous Subscribers,

I remain,
Your much obliged and humble servant,
P. EGAN.

Sky-Parlour,
January 1, 1821.

————, that your *MOT* is a *trump!*"

———— scratching his *nob* with joy (something like a criminal receiving *a reprieve from execution), and his ogles sparkling with rapture, burst out with ecstasy,* "My eyes, *Poll*, you are a *trump* indeed! Give me a *buss*. No more naughty tricks now. Our fortunes are made; you shall be a lady, and I will be a gentleman. I know of a prime public-house to let. To-morrow morning I'll take it, and leave a deposit of £10, when the remainder of our lives will then be rendered as pleasant and as smooth as glass." ———— *Had* so much an eye to business, that the *darkey* appeared tremendously long to him. He tossed about quite restless, could scarcely get a few *winks,* and wished for day-light with as great anxiety and eagerness as was displayed by Richard III. in the tent scene.

By heavens! my stern impatience chides this tardy gaited night,
Who like a foul and ugly witch so *tediously* doth limp away!

Day-light had scarcely *peeped* when he jumped from his *dab—bussed* his staunch Poll, and *togged* himself ready to start. This uneasiness is easily accounted for; the doors of the Bank of England had not been opened a minute, before ————, with a trusty *Pal,* had made all the large notes right. He then called and left a deposit of £40 for the house before alluded to; and returned to communicate to Poll what he had done.

————, going out to spend the evening among a few of his associates, *gaffing* was unfortunately for him introduced; and long before the *darkey* had vanished, a run of ill-luck had so far prevailed, that poor ———— was completely *cleaned out:* he had not a feather left to fly with; and was compelled to borrow a *bull* to pay for a *rattler* to carry his unfortunate body home. The *Forty Pounds* were also forfeited.

————, however, soon recovered the shock; and giving Poll a *buss*, exclaimed with great *naïveté*, "*I have only, my Girl, to go to* WORK *for more!*"

Chapter XII.

LIFE IN LONDON.— PEEP O' DAY BOYS, A STREET ROW, THE AUTHOR LOSING HIS "READER", TOM & JERRY "SHOWING FIGHT" & LOGIC FLOORED.

An opportunity presented itself to our TRIO to visit the Condemned Yard in NEWGATE. "It was a mournful sight," LOGIC observed to the CORINTHIAN; "but as it was the intention of JERRY not to neglect visiting any place that might afford him information during his stay in London, he had been induced to make the proposition to HAWTHORN; yet, he was free to confess, it was more especially on his own account, as he was compelled to attend, and companions would, therefore, prove very agreeable to his feelings upon such a melancholy occasion." "We will accompany you, BOB," replied Tom and JERRY.

The Plate represents the Morning of Execution, and the malefactors having their irons knocked off previous to their ascending the fatal platform that launches them into eternity. The Yeoman of the Halter is in waiting to put the ropes about them. The Clergyman is also seen administering consolation to these unfortunate persons in such an awful moment; and the Sheriffs are likewise in attendance to conduct the culprits to the place of execution, to perform the most painful part of their duty, in witnessing the offended laws of their country put in force. It is a truly afflicting scene; and neither the PEN nor the PENCIL, however directed by talent, can do it adequate justice, or convey a description of the "*harrowed feelings*" of the few spectators that are admitted into the Condemned Yard upon such an occasion. The tolling of the bell, too, which breaks in upon the very soul of the already agonized malefactor, announcing to him that he has but a few minutes to live, adds a terrific solemnity to the proceedings:—

> Hear it not, Duncan, for'tis a knell
> That summons thee to heav'n or to hell.

The Condemned Yard is long, but narrow, and contains a great number of cells, one above another, forming three stories in height. Each cell measures nine feet in length, and six in width. Every indulgence is allowed to those prisoners immediately the "*death-warrant*" arrives at Newgate, ordering them to prepare for execution.

Chapter xii.

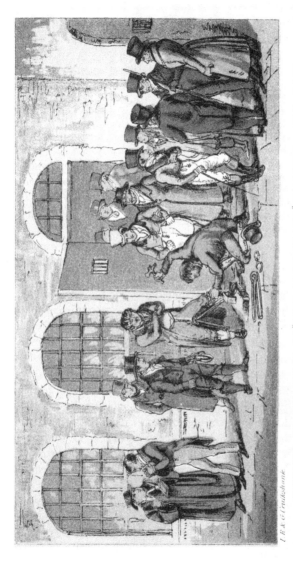

SYMPTOMS OF THE FINISH OF "SOME SORTS OF LIFE" IN LONDON.— TOM, JERRY, AND LOGIC, IN THE PRESS YARD, AT NEWGATE.

They are then allowed to remain in the Large Room (which the Plate represents), in order that the Clergyman may attend upon them as often as they desire it, and who, generally, previous to the morning on which they are to *suffer*, sits up *praying* with them the whole of the night. It is really astonishing, upon most of these occasions, to witness the resignation and fortitude with which these unhappy men conduct themselves: many of the most hardened and desperate offenders, from the kindness, attention, and soothing conduct of the Rev. Mr COTTON, who is indefatigable in administering consolation to their troubled minds, have become the most sincere penitents; nay more, several prisoners, who have received a *free pardon* after having been ordered for execution, have since publicly declared that they should never again be in such a fit state to meet eternity. The criminal on the left side of the Plate, lifting up his hands in the attitude of prayer with the Clergyman, was once a character of considerable note at the West End of the Town, and from his vivacity, then designated "Lively Jem!" He soon ran through a fine fortune; and, to keep up his extravagances, he plunged into those destructive habits which ultimately brought him into this ignominious situation. Lively Jem, like most others, saw his error too late to repair it. He had not strength of mind sufficient to bear with the reverses of fortune; to fall from splendour to poverty was too much for his feelings; and, to avoid the jests and sneers of his once dashing acquaintance, under the appellation of "*poor fellow!*" and being excluded from their company, he thus violently terminated his thoughtless career. Jem had been at college with the *Oxonian*, and as his last request, he had sent a message to LOGIC to attend upon him on this mournful occasion, in order to he the bearer of some important circumstances respecting himself to a female, to whom he had been very much attached, and who had also never been absent from him except this fatal morning. LOGIC was too much of a man to neglect another in the hour of misfortune; and it was to fulfil the request of a dying unfortunate acquaintance, that he came, accompanied by CORINTHIAN TOM and JERRY, to the condemned Yard of Newgate.

Chapter XII.

I.R.& G. Cruikshank.

THE ROYAL EXCHANGE.— TOM POINTING OUT TO JERRY, A FEW OF THE PRIMEST FEATURES OF LIFE IN LONDON.

259

Our heroes were offered a complete view of the prison from the top of it; but this offer was declined, in consequence of Tom's urging the want of time, on account of having some business to transact in the City. The TRIO hastily quitted the gloomy falls of Newgate, once more to join the busy hum and life of society.

On approaching the ROYAL EXCHANGE, TOM observed to JERRY, that they would just look in, and he would point out to him a few of the *primest* features of LIFE IN LONDON. "My dear Coz," said the CORINTHIAN, "you are surrounded by *characters* highly worthy of your observation. Volumes would not contain half their talents; and to their honour be it recorded, the greatest part of them have been the architects of their own fortune. Believe me. JERRY, such a group of Merchants is not to be met with under the canopy of heaven: possessing never-tiring industry, and indefatigable to the end of the chapter, they may challenge all Europe for a comparison, and I will back them two to one; indeed, they have astonished all the world. The name of an English Merchant is a passport in any country. The second gentleman you perceive, dressed in black,[226] from the statue, is a sufficient instance of what may be accomplished by an industrious clever man in England.

The CORINTHIAN proposed to JERRY and LOGIC, in order to *finish* the day, to dine with a friend of his, a sporting man, whose residence was contiguous to the Tower, and from whom he had received numerous pressing invitations; who had also promised to show him a "bit of Life" at the East End of the Town, whenever it might suit his convenience to give his friend a call; and we are sure of a most hearty and welcome reception. "An excellent proposition," exclaimed JERRY, "and I shall *second* it, my Coz." "It has passed, *nem. con.*" said the *Oxonian, cutting* one of JOEY MUNDEN's prime comical mugs, and also endeavouring to imitate KEAN —"To the Tower—to the Tower!" But, rather singular to state, this theatrical flourish had scarcely escaped from the lips of LOGIC, when TOM recognised his friend among the group of merchants. After a hearty shake of the hand, and the intro-

---

226   Mr. ROTHSCHILD.

CHAPTER XII.

duction of Jerry and Logic had been performed, the party soon left the Royal Exchange to partake of an excellent dinner and a glass or two of some fine old wines that would have done credit to the cellar of a duke. The bottle, among these gay fellows, was not suffered to stand still, and the *tastings* of the different highly-flavoured vintages, made the party become a little *talkative* and fit for anything. "You promised me, if you recollect," said Tom to his friend, "that you would show me a bit of fun at this end of the Town; and we cannot have a better opportunity than the present moment." "It shall be so," replied the gentleman, *smiling;* "and as you have your '*Highflyers*' at Almack's, at the West End, we have also some *choice creatures*' at our ALL MAX[227] in the East; where you shall be in less than half an hour to judge for yourself." "Bravo!" said Logic, "a good *pun* and full of *spirit*"Let us be off," urged Hawthorn. "Another bottle, and then—"Tom's friend replied, "All-Max shall be in view."

> Such is the theme that fires my strain,

---

227   Vulgarly called *gin* in the merry days of Sir Jeffery Dunstan, the renowned Mayor of Garratt, but now quite *obsolete* among *genteel* persons; it is, however, still a very palatable subject with most parties. But, as the tender Juliet very properly observes,
> What's in a name? that which we call a rose
> By any other name would smell as sweet:
and so it is with this spirited article. The elegantes, in the vicinity of Regent Street, can take a silver thimbleful of it (only in private), under the pleasing sound of white wine, without a wry twitch spoiling the shape of their pretty indexes, but who might be almost induced to faint or have a lack-a-daisy moment, if asked to take a cordial under the horrid appellation of gin: while Meg of the "back slums" don't care a fig who knows she loves a drap of max; or as how, d'ye see, that she vets t'other eye; as Meg says, it will be all the same one hundred years hence!
> But who's to decide when doctors disagree?

Yet the opinions of such great compounders as Hodges and Deady, united with those busy spinners, Thompson and Lancaster to wit, are completely orthodox, and who hint that the many new reels performed in the most lively manner by novices in the art of dancing, from this moving commodity, and who bar nothing at their cribs, would beat De Hayes and D'Egville to a standstill, with all their superlative knowledge of pirouette motions, either to describe or give such steps a name. Such is the hypocrisy displayed on the one side, and the saucy low independence exhibited on the other, which are to be run against every day in "Life in London!"

> O! may the Muse not toil in vain;
> But all those pastimes now rehearse,
> That well might claim more polish'd verse,
> To which past *fetes* and those to *come,*
> Are little better than a HUM;
> Since *souls of taste* could never choose
> 'Twixt Alexander's famous booze,
> Or Cleopatra's vaunted *fun.*
> When she Mark Anthony had done;
> In short, all these are rows but *windy,*
> Compar'd with a tar's glorious SHINDY:
> For after all is said and done,
> Fighting's to Jack the same as fun;
> His mind on frenzy somewhat borders
> For row, thus under sailing orders;
> While ev'ry messmate, mad as he,
> Sings out for pleasures of a *spree.*
> Anew the theme is here repeated,
> Tars must have grog, and girls be treated;
> Jack, Moll, and Bet, well know the shop,
> The cry, once more, "a hop! a hop!"
> While the elbow-scraper, grown groggy,
> Tunes fiddle up, with senses foggy;
> In fine, do any thing but play,
> *Riot* the order of the day.

All-Max was compared by the sailors, something after the old adage of "any port in a storm." It required no patronage;—a card of admission was not necessary; —no inquiries were made;—and every *cove* that put in his appearance was quite welcome; colour or country considered no obstacle; and *dress* and ADDRESS completely out of the question. *Ceremonies* were not in use, and, therefore, no struggle took place at All-Max for the master of them. The parties *paired off* according to *fancy;* the eye was pleased in the choice, and nothing thought of about birth and distinction. All was *happiness*? [228]— every body free and easy, and freedom of expression allowed

---

228   "It is," said LOGIC to TOM, "I am quite satisfied in my mind, the LOWER ORDERS of society who really ENJOY themselves. They eat with a good appetite, *hunger* being the sauce; they *drink* with a zest, in being *thirsty* from their exertions, and not *nice* in their beverage; and as to *dress,* it is not an object of serious consideration with them. Their minds are daily occupied with work, which they quit with the intention of *enjoying* themselves, and ENJOYMENT is the Result; not like the rich, who are out night after night to *kill* TIME, and, what is worse, dissatisfied with almost everything that crosses their path from the dullness of *repetition.*" "There is too much truth about your argument, I must admit," replied the CORINTHIAN; "and among all the scenes that we have witnessed together, where the LOWER ORDERS have, been taking their *pleasure,* I confess they have appeared ALL HAPPINESS. I am

to the very echo.. The group motley indeed;—Lascars, blacks, jack tars, coal-heavers, dustmen, women of colour, old and young, and a sprinkling of the remnants of once fine girls, &c., were all *jigging* together, provided the *teazer of the catgut* was not *bilked* of his *duce*. *Gloves* might have been laughed at, as dirty hands produced no *squeamishness* on the heroines in the dance, and the scene changed as often as a pantomime, from the continual introduction of new characters. *Heavy wet* was the cooling beverage, but frequently overtaken by *flashes of lightning*. The *covey* was no *scholard*, as. he asserted, and, therefore, he held the pot in one hand and took the *blunt* with the other, to prevent the trouble of *chalking.*, or making mistakes. *Cocker's* arithmetic in his bar was a dead letter, and *the publican's ledger* only waste paper; *book-keeping* did not belong to his *consarn*; yet no one could *read* his customers better than Mr *Mace*.[229] The attention he displayed towards any of his party; when Mr *Lushington* had got the "best of them," showed his judgment; he had a butt of *heavy wet* prepared for the occasion, and also a cask of liquor, which gave considerable proofs of his kindness, that his articles should not be too strong for their already-damaged heads. His motto was "never to give a *chance* away;" and Mr *Mace* had long been christened by the *downies*, the "*dashing covey*." He was "*cut out*" for his company; and he could "*come it well*" upon all points. On the sudden appearance of our "*swell* TRIO," and the CORINTHIAN's friend, among these unsophisticated sons and daughters of Nature, their *ogles* were on the roll, under an apprehension that the *beaks* were out on the *nose*; but it was soon made "all right," by one of the *mollishers* whispering, loud enough to be heard by most of the party, "that she understood *as how)* the *gemmen* had only dropped in for to have a *bit of a spree*, and there was no doubt they *voud* stand a *drap* of *summut* to make them all *cumfurable*, and likewise prove good customers to the crib."

---

sorry I cannot say as much for the higher ranks of society."
229   It is rather a curious coincidence, that the name of the proprietor of ALL-MAX should be *Mace*, which is a slang term for *imposition* or *robbery!*

Life in London

LOWEST "LIFE IN LONDON".—TOM, JERRY & LOGIC, AMONG THE UNSOPHISTICATED SONS & DAUGHTERS OF NATURE AT "ALL MAX" IN THE EAST.

CHAPTER XII.

On the *office* being giving, the *standstill* was instantly removed; and the *kidwys and kiddiesses were* footing the *double shuffle* against each other with as much *gig* as the "*We we-e-e-ps*" exert themselves on the first of May. The CORINTHIAN smiled to himself, as his eyes *glanced* round the room at the *characters*, and observed to LOGIC, in a low tone of voice, "that it was quite a new scene to him, notwithstanding all his previous rambles throughout the Metropolis, but so exceedingly *rich*, that he would not have *missed* it for a hundred pounds." As to JERRY, the GOLDEN ROOM at Carlton Palace, with all its *talismanic* touches, did not appear to have had more effect upon his feelings, when he entered it, than the group of figures, "all alive O!" at ALL-MAX seemed now to operate upon his mind. LOGIC, who was considered an *out and outer,* for continually scouring the *backslums,* both in town and country in search of something new, admitted the scene before him was one of the greatest novelties that he had ever witnessed in low life; and although the *Oxonian* was rather forward on the *bosky* suit, "It is," said he, tapping JERRY on the back "one of the invaluable mines of Nature: her stores are inexhaustible. What a fine subject would a sentimental stroll through London have afforded the pen of a STERNE!" LOGIC's old complaint, the *hiccough,* was creeping fast upon him; and, after tossing off a glass of *max,* making up his comical face, in drinking the health of *Black Moll,*— "JERRY, my boy,

> "Eye NATURE's walks, shoot folly as it flies,
> And catch the *manners* living as they rise:
> VIRTUOUS and *vicious* ev'ry man must be;
> Few in the EXTREME, but all in the *degree:*
> The ROGUE and FOOL by *fits* are fair and wise,
> And e'en the BEST, by *fits,* what they despise.
> Know NATURE's children shall divide her care,
> The *fur* that *warms* a MONARCH *warm'd* a BEAR!"

The orders of the Corinthian had been obeyed like *winking* by the *knowing* Mr *Mace;* and the "fair ones" had, without hesitation, *vetted* both eyes with a *drop* of the right sort, and many of them had, likewise, proved jolly enough to have *tossed off*" a third and a fourth glass. Lots of max were also placed on the table, and the *coveys* were not *shy* or behind-hand in helping themselves. The *spree* and the *fun* were increasing every minute, and the "TRIO" made the most of it, with as much pleasure and satisfaction as the lowest *mud-lark* amongst the group. Logic (as the Plate represents), appeared as happy as a *sand-boy*, who had unexpectedly met with good luck in disposing of his hampers full of the above household commodity in a short time, which had given him a holiday, and was listening to the *jargon* of *Black* SALL, who was seated on his right knee, and very liberally treating the *Oxonian* with repeated *chaste* salutes; whilst *Flashy* NANCE (who had *gammoned* more seamen out of their *vills* and power than the ingenuity or palaver of twenty of the most knowing of the frail sisterhood could effect), was occupying Logic's left knee, with her arm round his neck, laughing at the *chaffing* of the "*lady in black,*" as she termed her, and also trying to engage the *attention* of Logic, who had just desired Hawthorn to behold the *"Fields of Temptation"* by which he was surrounded, and *chanting*, like a second Macheath:

> How happy could I be with either,
> Were t' other dear charmer away;
> But while, you both *mug* me together,
> You'll make me a *spooney* (*Hiccoughing*), I say.

Jerry, whose time had been employed in waiting upon the heroines generally, is seen *ginning the fiddler*, in order that the "*harmony*" might not cease for a single instant; but the black *slavey*, who is entering the room, is singing out, "*Massa*, you ought to be shamed; your fiddle is drunk; you no play at all!" Tom inquired of the *covess* of the *hen* (who, by-the-by, was quite pleased with the Corinthian, from the very liberal manner in which he had dropped his *blunt* at her house), the names of the dancers, of whom he had observed that—

> Sure such a pair were never seen!

"*Vy*, Sir," replied Mrs *Mace*, "that *are* black *vomcm*, who you *sees* dancing with *nasty Bob*, the coal-*vhipper*, is called *African Sall*, because she comes from foreign parts; and the little *mungo* in the corner, holding his arms out, is her child; yet I *doesn't* think *as how*, for all that, Sall has got any husband: but, *la!* sir, it's a poor heart that never rejoices, *an't* it, sir?" Our heroes had kept it up so. gaily in dancing, drinking, &c., that the friend of the CORINTHIAN thought it was time to be *missing;* but, on mustering the TRIO, LOGIC was not to be found. A jack tar, about *three sheets in the wind,* who had been keeping up the *shindy* the whole of the evening with them, laughing, asked if it was the gentleman in the *green barnacles* their honours wanted, as it was very likely he had taken a voyage to *Africa,* in the *Sally,* or else he was out on a cruise with the *Flashy Nance*; but he would have him beware of *squalls,* as they were not very *sound* in their *rigging!* It was considered useless to look after LOGIC, and a *rattler* was immediately ordered to the door; when JERRY, TOM, and his friend, bid adieu to ALL-MAX. Our heroes only stopped to put down the friend of TOM, near the Tower, till they arrived safely at *Corinthian-House.*

The clock had announced *three* before Tom and his Coz. were able to lift their *damaged* heads from the pillow, and meet together, at breakfast, in the *Chaffing Crib;* but no LOGIC had arrived, as heretofore, to pop his comic *mug* in at the door, with his usual friendly salutation of "*How are you, my boys, after the lark?*" Two large cups of tea were necessary to cool and moisten JERRY's *chaffer*, which the MAX had made feel like a piece of *dry wood* in his mouth, before he could articulate to the CORINTHIAN that he was almost afraid he should never have got the use of his tongue again; and, bursting out into a laugh, said, "We had rare fun last night; so much so, that it almost seems to me like a vision. I hope the *Oxonian* is safe!" "We had rare fun, indeed," replied Tom; "but Logic seems determined to *push* his voyage of discovery a point further, at least, than we did. I am sorry Bob is not here, as I recollect it is the night at Almacks, and he would have proved an excellent *finger-post* to you on this occasion: we must, therefore, get ourselves to rights as soon as possible. This will also be a rich treat to you, Jerry; and the contrast will be delightful; more especially, as the time is so short that we shall pass from All-Max in the East to ALMACKS in the West almost like the rapid succession of scenes in a play, which will tend highly to increase the effect, and likewise afford a good opportunity for observation. But I must impress upon you, my dear Coz. that what with the time occupied with dinner, dressing, &c., we have not a minute to lose:—

> "What sounds were those?—O, earth and heaven!
> Heard you the chimes—*half-past eleven?*
> They tell, with iron tongue, your fate,
> Unhappy lingerer, if you're late.
> Such is the rule, which none infringes;
> The door one jot upon its hinges
> Moves not. Once past the fatal hour,
> WILLIS has no dispensing power.
> Spite of persuasion, tears, or force,
> 'The LAW,' he cries, 'must take its course,'
> And men may *swear,* and women *pout,*
> No matter,—they are ALL SHUT OUT."

"I am surprised," said JERRY, "that the lady *patronesses* should be so '*mechanical* in their *movements:* it is positively reducing the importance of a *duchess* to the parallel of a *charwoman,* to keep to '*her time!*' It is quite enough for the manager of a theatre to compel his performers to commence the play at a precise hour; but for the higher classes of society to be *pinned* down to a *second*, it is really too bad;—beings that ought to be as free as air. It must have been a novelty indeed when this revolution was first attempted in the regions of fashion. It surely produced a *row?*" Yes," replied Tom; "it rather created some *feverish* symptoms amongst the *great folks*, such as wounded pride, &c.: but that is not all; that is not the worst of it:—

> "Suppose the PRIZE, by hundreds miss'd,
> Is your's at last.—You're on the list.—
> Your voucher's issued, duly signed;
> But hold,—your *ticket's* left behind.
> What's to be done? there's no admission:
> In vain you flatter, scold, petition,
> Feel your blood mounting like a rocket,
> Fumble in vain in every pocket;
> The rule is strict, I dare not stretch it,'
> Cries WILLIS; 'pray, my Lord, go fetch it.
> 'Friend, I'm the *Ministry*,—give way!'
> Avaunt, Lord Viscount Castlereagh!
> You're doubtless, in the Commons' House

A mighty man, but *here* a *mouse!*
We show no favour, give no quarter,
Here, to your riband or your garter.
Here for a *Congress* no one cares.
Save that alone which sits up stairs.

'Fair Worcester pleads with Wellington:
Valour with beauty. Hence, begone!
Perform elsewhere your destin'd parts,
One conquer kingdoms, t' other hearts.
My Lord, you'll have enough to do;
ALMACKS is not *like* WATERLOO.'
For the first time in vain, his *Grace*
Sits down in form before the place;
Finds, let him shake it to the centre,
ONE fortress that he cannot enter.
Though he should offer on its borders
The *sacrifice* of HALF his orders.

"Thus our fair sovereigns 'rule the ball!'
Thus equal are their laws for all.

Therefore, my dear Coz. I need not impress upon you the necessity of being particular about your ticket. Do not forget to put it in your pocket. WILLIS is a different man altogether from Mr *Mace;* he is not to be *gammoned* with a *slug*. We must also mind our P's and Q's at ALMACKS; more especially as we have been so free and easy lately among the *flash* part of mankind, or otherwise we shall be in danger of letting the blackguard *peep*. It is, believe me, like treading upon *classic ground:* at every step you take, the ARTS[230] not only stare you full in the face, but, on turning round, you are sure to come in contact with the SCIENCES. It is the rallying point of *rank*, wealthy talents, and beauty: it is, likewise, the meridian of fashion, style, elegance, and manners, from the *alpha* to the *omega*.

Oh!—— could you now but creep,
Incog, into the room, and peep.

O that I dared, since hearts of iron
Melt at the strains of MOORE and BYRON-,
Borrow their thoughts and language now

---

230   This appears something like a *pun,* but we do not believe the CORINTHIAN intended it as such: it was the *forte* of Logic; but Tom was more serious in his remarks.

> To *paint* our Almacks' BELLES! for how.
> Unless *their* muse my fancy warms,
> Describe such features and such forms:
> The hair in auburn waves, or flaxen,
> Shading their necks and shoulders waxen;
> The curls that on fair bosoms lie
> In clusters of deep ebony!
> How dare to dwell ('tis so immoral)
> On downy cheeks and lips of coral.
> On eyes of sapphire or of jet,
> Beneath their brows, o'er-arching, set
> (EYES which, no matter what their hue,
> Are sure to *beat* you—black and blue).
> Or *shapes*, as if by SCULPTURE moulded,
> In shining drapery enfolded!
>
> "To give their graceful motions scope,
> Now, *tightly stretched,* the barrier rope
> Hems in quadrillers, nymph and spark,
> Like bounding deer within a park;
> Now *dropped,* transforms the floor again.
> For waltzers, to an open plain.
> Approach, O votary of Hymen!
> Be thou of forward or of *shy* men.
> Approach, and at the luck rejoice
> Which yields such beauty to your choice.

The very air you inhale at ALMACKS is different from the plebeian atmosphere, being scented with the evaporation of the essences and richest perfumes from all quarters of the globe." "A little different, I hope, from the Jacco Maccacco concern," observed Jerry, smiling. "Yes; a *shade* or two," said Tom. "But to obtain a *footing* at this splendid assembly might almost be considered as a *step* towards being presented at court, ROYALTY condescending to become visitors at ALMACK'S. An introduction to this *climax* of Rank is of the utmost consequence to enterprising men, operating as an important PASSPORT to every other place of high breeding in the kingdom; and it also prevents the trouble of a thousand inquiries respecting the *pedigree* of the individual in question, when he boldly makes known the *laconic* but *pithy* expression of—'I have passed *the* SCRUTINY at ALMACK'S!!!'[231] Indeed,

---

231   Something like the *stamp* of goodness (if comparisons are not viewed as a profanation of this high subject), made use of by the jockeys at Newmarket, when they say *"Smolensko won the Derby."* It is a *multum in parvo* touch upon the understanding; and more convincing perhaps than the perusal of volumes.

CHAPTER XII.

if it were possible to call to your aid the waters of Lethe, to cleanse your pericranium of all ideas of 'the *slang*' for a night, upon entering those regions of refinement, or if it were only to obtain a few drops to pour over your tongue, to bury in oblivion all thoughts of vulgarity and coarseness of disposition, it would be highly advantageous towards your attraction. However, it is highly essential to invoke the apotheosis of Chesterfield to hover over you with his polished *scale* of superior politeness; but, above all, do not fail to call to your assistance the shades of Hervey, Addison, and Milton, to ornament your style of conversation with a few of their irresistible touches of the *flowery*, ELEGANT, and SUBLIME, in order to encounter with any degree of success the *imperious* Duchess—the *proud* Marchioness—the *stiff* Countess—the *starched-up* LADY—the *consequential* honourable FAIR ONE— the *upstart* MRS—the *contemptuous* BEAUTY—the *pert* COQUETTE—the *turn-up-nose* DEMURE CREATURE—the *squeamish* Miss, and the *fastidious*[232] PATRONESSES, that parade up and down here, as the arbitresses of fame and fortune. To become a hero in this *looking-glass* sort of life, my dear JERRY, you ought to be as much *made-up* as the measured statue of the *Venus de Medici*. To walk like JOHN KEMBLE in *Coriolanus*—to make a bow after the graceful manner of GEORGE THE FOURTH—to take Moccabaw, and show your diamond ring (so as not to appear to do it), like DR PLEASE'EM. To sport a toe after the agility of a *Vestris*—to lead your partner to join the dance with the confidence of an ELLISTON in the *Honey-Moon*—to

---

232   Excessive refinement; the nicety of splitting a hair into a thousand threads. One of the subscribers, a lady who was rather *dim* in her *sparklers*, also a little touched in her *upper-works*, a complete *hack* at all the places of fashionable amusement, and jaded almost to death with the luxuries of this life, was, one evening, on the sly, taking a *few winks*, when she was suddenly brought to herself, in consequence of a large fly having alighted on her pale and wan *index*. In the confusion of the moment, she demanded to know, in an imperative tone, what rude being had taken such an outrageous liberty with her person? "My dear madam," said an elegant witty female near her, "you are quite mistaken; it was a large *'blue bottle*.'" "Well, *blue bottle* or not," replied the *fastidious* lady, pettishly, "Willis ought to be fined for letting a *blue bottle* in without a ticket. I am sure, the admission of *blue bottles* must have been resisted by the lady patronesses; but, if not, I shall make it a special matter of debate at the next meeting of the Committee."

cock your glass, like any impudent fellow you know, and to stare, stare, and stare again; and to flatter, *congee,* and *hum* these elevated dames, like a quack doctor! Yet, even then, with all this *load* of accomplishments, you will stand in great danger of being *cut-up* into *slices,* and handed round for the *taste* of the company. My dear Coz., as a *stranger,* you must undergo it; I have run the gauntlet; and I am, therefore, preparing you accordingly, as I was almost going to say (laughing), to take 'the *Veil;'* and if you can take the lady with it—such a *divinity* as I will show you—then your visit to ALMACK'S will be, at least, worth a *plum* to you. But I am, perhaps, proceeding too fast, Jerry'? Your old dad, I now recollect, gave me to understand, that, whenever you become *serious* to take a partner for life, he wished the lady to be the lovely MARY ROSEBUD of *Hawthorn Village;* however, be that as it may—

> "Ere you try your fortune, lend
> An ear to good advice, my friend:
> *They* deem no folly half so great
> As LOVE, without a LARGE ESTATE;
> Do what you will, say what you can,
> 'MANORS,' they tell you, 'make the man!'"

"You will mix, my dear Coz., with numerous *great folks,* such as *great* COMMANDERS, *great* STATESMEN, *great* COURTIERS, and also with men possessing GREAT talents; yet you will find but few *characters,*[233] in comparison with the inferior scenes of life; at least, with very few persons who have an opportunity of showing

---

233   "Perish the thought!" *Hear* it not on the *Corinthian Path!**—*Tell* it not at SAM's, that CHARACTERS are not to be found in the GREAT *World!* It may, perhaps, be necessary, in point of explanation of TOM's idea upon this subject, to state, that his allusion went to those persons whose riches afforded them so much time and so many opportunities of becoming correct in their movements; and who had also obtained, in a great measure, the mastery over their passions, by repeatedly asking themselves the following questions, whenever they doubted the propriety of their previous conduct:—What sort of a man am I? Did I behave like a man of honour to the wife of my intimate friend? Have I ever lost sight of the conduct of a gentleman? Is there anything disagreeable in my deportment towards my inferiors? Do I keep my tradesmen too long out of their money? Am I a flatterer? &c. "If," said the CORINTHIAN, "any gentleman can answer these questions satisfactorily, it may operate as some excuse for his being upon *'good terms'* with himself."
*Regent Street

themselves in a prominent point of view at this grand Emporium of GREATNESS. In the higher walks of society, you cannot expect to meet with much *originality* of CHARACTER—the *stimulus* to provoke it is wanting—PROPERTY operates against it—and the *great folks* are principally *trained* from their *cradles* to behave and act like ladies and gentlemen: there is a *scale* for it, but ultimately it becomes a mere matter of *routine*. A decorous deportment is instilled into them from the moment they can lisp; and notions of PROPRIETY are continually enforced upon their memories, by their anxious tutors, till they get out of their leading-strings. If BURKE had possessed a long purse, in all probability the *'Sublime and Beautiful'* might never have made its appearance; nor the *Duenna* of SHERIDAN have ever enraptured the public. ALMACK'S is, however, a splendid view of human nature, set-off to the *best* advantage—with the *best* DRESS—*best* ADDRESS, and also *finished* with the *best* BEHAVIOUR. Yet, notwithstanding all this *preparation* of the mind, you will sometimes perceive that RANK is even *rankling* to RANK, although it is *stifled* by *politeness*. The 'COUNTESS' can show her *precedency* for place, with the highest marks of *hauteur*, over the 'LADY and the 'DUCHESS,' with a toss of the head, can give the *hint* to the 'MARCHIONESS' that she takes the lead of her. But far be it from me, JERRY, wantonly to *satirise* any of the classes of society, from the highest to the lowest of mankind; as I am perfectly convinced, in too many instances, that both of them have been traduced and libelled, by numerous persons, who have had no opportunity of judging of either of them but at the distance of *extreme* PERSPECTIVE. Upon a more intimate acquaintance with the RICH, in spite of their follies and extravagances, you will perceive that a vast majority of them possess very superior traits of mind, and whose conduct *alone* adorn and elevate the human breast; while a real knowledge of the *movements* of thousands of the middling classes of mankind, in their feelings and dispositions towards alleviating the distresses of their poorer fellow creatures, would make a most interesting volume to those persons ignorant of 'LIFE IN LONDON.'"

Our heroes were now dressed for the assembly; and the

elegance of Tom, and the fine manly frame of Jerry, almost bid defiance to the *grin*[234] which they otherwise might have encountered on making their bows at a place of such classic nicety. "By Jove," said the Corinthian, "we are nearly too late;" and, in consequence, he ordered his coachman to make great haste for ALMACK'S. The whip of Tom's coachman soon brought his master's chariot into the string of carriages, which were so exceedingly numerous, that the Corinthian again expressed his fears to: Jerry they should be too late to gain admission.

"I must once more remind you, my dear Coz," said Tom, "that we must be on our P's and Q's; and, if you should find me *tripping*, as I by no means consider myself infallible, you will gently bring me back to my recollection by merely saying 'Lethe;' and, in turn, if necessary, I will perform the same kind office towards you." "I shall bear it in mind," replied Hawthorn.

The grand object was at length accomplished, the clock wanting five minutes of half-past eleven when Tom and his Coz entered the Ball-Room at ALMACK'S: but, from the splendid character of the company, which the Corinthian had previously given to Jerry, the latter felt more than a little embarrassment on finding himself so suddenly in the company of Royalty: also, mixing with Princes, Ministers of State, and foreigners of distinction—coming hastily in contact with Dukes and Duchesses—running against Marquises and their *better halves*—passing Countesses, in rapid succession— meeting with Right Honourable Ladies like flowers in a garden—jostling against lots of rich but *plain* Mistresses, and surrounded by high and mighty Commanders—mobs of Earls and Lords—Generals—Admirals—groups of Colonels and Majors—hosts of Military and a few Naval Captains—batches of Baronets — eminent Counsellors,—numerous Sirs, and myriads of Misters. For a short period, Jerry was at a complete *standstill;* his P's and Q's he now found to be the most difficult letters in

---

234   A low *slang* term made use of in opposition to the *stylish* phrase of Quiz. It is considered rather an unpleasant circumstance to persons entering a splendid ball-room who are not accustomed to it. At all times it should be executed in a graceful manner.

the alphabet to become the master of; and his eyes, penetrating as they were, seemed quite insufficient to survey this brilliant assemblage with any degree of accuracy; in short, HAWTHORN was so *dazzled*, that his hand had nearly reached his head, to scratch it from the act of surprise, when his P's silently reminded him that it would be instantly noticed as *vulgar;* and he was almost lapsing into a *reverie*, from the impression which this conglomeration of GREAT FOLKS had made upon his *feelings*, when his Q's whispered into his ear to assume a confidence, and to recollect, that, although JUPITER had profusely bestowed his showers of gold on this assemblage of heroes and heroines, that they were nothing more than—MEN and WOMEN. This "mind's eye" electrifying touch quickly restored animation, and Jerry once more recollected that he was at ALMACK'S. The old acquaintances of TOM soon came around him, glad to welcome the Corinthian again amongst them; and Jerry had also the honour of being recognised, with the most friendly nods, by several ladies and gentlemen, to whom he had been previously introduced by his Coz. This ray of *sunshine*[235] operated like a reviving cordial to Jerry, and his confidence was so much increasing, that he ventured to observe, but in a very low tone of voice, that, "certainly, there was almost an immeasurable distance, 'Ossa to a wart,' between the appearance of the rooms, the music, and the *women,* at ALL-MAX, and" "Hush! h-u-s-h!" from the CORINTHIAN, with a significant look, accompanied with, "LETHE!" JERRY, finding that his sentinels the P's and Q's were absent from their posts, became *dumb* again in an instant.

On joining the promenade and *conversazione* of so brilliant an assemblage of nearly five hundred persons, it was impossible for JERRY to remain long silent, in spite of the CORINTHIAN's well applied signal of "LETHE!" "The exquisite *beauty* of some of the female faces— the *interesting* features of others— the *diamond* eyes of many—the numerous lovely *busts—complexions* so sweet

---

235   The *nod* from a great man, to many individuals, operates like new life, and emboldens them to do many things they would otherwise *shrink* from; while, on the contrary, the "*cut direct*" comes with the *severity* of a paralytic stroke on the feelings of the poor *cuttee!*

as almost to defy competition—*pearly white teeth*, which rival the finest ivory—and the dresses altogether so costly and elegant," exclaimed JERRY, "that I must be a *dummy* indeed, if I could pass such sweet creatures without being in raptures with them. But can you inform me, my dear Coz, who that fine tall lady is, something about the size of Mrs *Mace,* and who is in conversation with a lovely girl near the orchestra?" "Make no *such* comparisons *here*— LETHE!" whispered the CORINTHIAN. "A palpable hit, I now readily admit," replied HAWTHORN; "but, nevertheless, I am rather anxious to learn her history, as the *Oxonian* informed me, when we once passed her in the Park, that she was a most interesting *character.*

"That lady," said TOM, "is a MINE of wealth; not merely from the immense fortune she has at her command, but from the invaluable qualifications she possesses as a wife and a parent. She is one of those prominent females, in the direction of her estates and household, that you never hear of the husband, except when he is called to dinner, or orders his servant to light him to bed: yet he is no JERRY SNEAK either; but, on the contrary, his *rib* married him for love, bestowed her great fortune on him as the object of her choice, honours his character, and she is particularly fond of his company. A fine family has been the issue of this marriage; and the *divinity,* I told you of, is one of her daughters, who stands close to her. The Lady of——— does not, as it is vulgarly termed, absolutely *'wear the breeches,'* although she *'rules the roast;'* yet she has no tyranny attached to her disposition. She is a noble mistress to her servants, a perfect lady to her tradespeople and dependants, an honourable acquaintance with an enlarged mind, and her mansion, near the Regent's Park, to all her visitors, is a complete picture of magnificence, heightened by hospitality. I have not the honour of knowing her personally; but she is a most amiable and clever woman: and her notions of propriety, particularly what concerns her own family, are of so excellent a description, that they might be quoted as an example to others. The Lady, of———is not *precise* either; nor does it arise from rigid formality, or the superficial kind of *punctiliousness* of a Chesterfield. No; *her* ambition is of a higher cast than to leave, for the *improvement* of society, a posthumous work on behaviour. The Lady of ——— has travelled through the regions of fashion with her eyes open; she has not been blinded by the *follies* of the *great*, and she has also dared to think and act for herself. Her whole family have felt the advantages of her *perception*, their happiness has been enlarged from it, and it is not disgraced by anything puritanical or hypocritical. It is, as it appears to be, a *great one;* and it is entirely owing to the exertions of the Lady of————, who has obtained for it—this CHARACTER. These are her grand points. She is well aware that *'young men'* will be young men; and that, after arriving at a certain age, anything like *control* or *remonstrances* made to them from a parent on account of improper connexions, loose conduct, and late hours, occasion domestic broils and quarrels; and the family to which they belong is not only thrown into confusion, but too frequently rendered unhappy. Therefore, in order to avoid these disgusting scenes occurring in her mansion, but more especially to prevent her daughters from having any bad examples set before them in the persons of their relatives, she has for her eldest son, who is an M.P. a little more than of *age,* not only provided a separate establishment, but allows him £4000 per annum. To a second son, nearly twenty years old, she allows £2000 per annum, on the same liberal principles. By which means, the brothers and sisters meet under her roof like ladies and gentlemen. One more singularity the Lady of ———, possesses, is, that she never takes more than one daughter with her at a time to assemblies, &c. You therefore perceive," my dear Coz, "that she is armed at all points. Her daughters are not only thought to be lovely in person, but amiable in disposition; and those individuals who may become their husbands will find that, independent of all their other accomplishments, they may, at least, be valued as *sugar* PLUMS. Gentlemen of moderate fortunes have no *chance* whatever of obtaining the title of son-in-law to the Lady of ———; the vast splendour of her style of living soon gives the *hint* to any aspiring hero, that he must have parks of golden artillery before he can ensure a conquest. The respectability of her house she is determined to keep up. Her fortune, when she became the Lady of————, at an early age, was £60,000 per annum: and from her own attention to it, she has increased its value considerably, by not suffering herself to be made the dupe of stewards, or kept in the dark by her solicitors. She is indefatigable in daily looking into her accounts upon the subject, and answering all letters of importance herself. In a word, JERRY, the Lady of ——— must be viewed as a phenomenon in the Fashionable World."

"I am sorry LOGIC is not with us," said JERRY. "I am equally so," replied the CORINTHIAN; "more particularly on your account, as BOB would have furnished you with plenty of ANECDOTES of several of the GREAT FOLKS present that I am not acquainted with. But the *Oxonian* does not like *etiquette*. He is too fond of *fun:* he could not have carried on any *lark* here; and, in all probability, he would have declined accompanying us. You must have observed with what glee he enjoyed the lively jig between the *Coal-Whipper* and the *African Lady*, at ALL-MAX; besides"——— "LETHE! LETHE! LETHE!" cried JERRY, hastily. "I bow with submission," said TOM; "and you must now perceive the value of a monitor at your elbow, my COZ." "I do, indeed," replied HAWTHORN, "and I sincerely acknowledge how deeply I am indebted to your kindness for the pains and trouble you have taken with me, since my arrival in the Metropolis, to obtain a complete view of 'LIFE IN LONDON.'"

The more Hawthorn mixed with the splendid groups of promenaders, the more he attended to their *conversation*, although at times it appeared to him as if they did not hesitate to *bespatter* a few of their most intimate acquaintance with some little *satiric* touches on the defects of each other; not altogether unlike the *vein* of irony displayed in the "*School for Scandal*" in cutting a public beauty *piece*-meal, till, in idea, she becomes completely deformed and ugly: also, in witnessing the *sang froid* displayed by the heroes in losing their money at the card-tables, out of compliment, as it were, to their *fair* antagonists; and in eagerly swallowing the *bonnes bouches* and *piquant sauce*, served up in rich style by the *ladies of quality*, to enliven the play, as well as *garnishing* the table with

CHAPTER XII.

some highly interesting anecdotes[236] of the GREAT WORLD.

The *taste* and elegance, in general, displayed by the dancers, likewise, claimed the peculiar attention of JERRY: so much so, indeed, that he observed to his COZ, "he felt forcibly convinced of the advantages that must result to a person possessing anything like a MIND in being admitted to the company of *well-bred* persons." "Yes, my dear friend," replied the CORINTHIAN, "your observations are perfectly correct, if a person can select the WHEAT from the *chaff!* But the immediate pursuits of too many young men, I am sorry to say, are only to *mix* with GAIETY — *hunt* continually after PLEASURE — *aim* at the STYLE — follow the FASHION — *copy* the FOLLIES — and *launch* into the extravagances attendant upon HIGH LIFE.[237] IMPROVEMENT is not their

---

236 The following circumstance is a fine specimen of the "high mind" possessed by a *Lady of Quality*, notwithstanding her great *penchant* for gambling. The beautiful Mrs C. a few years since, at one sitting, won, of a Sporting Baronet, £5000; but, previous to the latter gentleman quitting England, which he was compelled to leave rather unexpectedly, meeting with the most distinguished Political Orator of his day, he begged it as a favour, that he would convey the above sum to Mrs C. It was, however, unfortunately lost the same evening at a gambling-house. In little more than a twelvemonth afterwards, the Baronet returned to England; and having accidentally met with Mrs C. in a fashionable party, she politely gave him a *hint*, that there was a *small sum* between them.

"Oh," said the Baronet, "I paid it for you to———."   Mrs C., with a smile, and generosity of disposition unequalled, replied, "Yes, yes, Sir———, I now recollect it; but amongst my numerous engagements it had slipped my memory, and I am sorry I mentioned it." The great character alluded to, was, by this high-spirited female, thus saved from reproach; and it is said, that that great orator had, in the course of his life, won and lost nearly a MILLION of money!

237 A most melancholy instance offers itself, and more might be quoted, to depict the consequences resulting from too great an attachment to *high company*, on the entrance of a young man into LIFE IN LONDON. A more afflicting case never excited pity than the late unfortunate HENRY WESTON, which occurred a few years since. He was a young man of great acquirements and elegant person; to which might be added, an amiable and generous disposition, that had endeared him to a most numerous and elegant circle of friends, with a sincerity rarely to be met with. At an early period of his life, young WESTON was introduced to the Bank Directors of England, under the most flattering recommendations, and a situation of unbounded trust was committed to his care, with the allowance of a great salary. But he commenced a *gentleman* too soon; and one species of dissipation brought on another, that no great length of time elapsed before the gambling-houses at the west end of the town became the principal scene of his operations. It is true that

object—it never entered their heads. To *seek* after the virtues, the talents, the fine and real notions of honour, which are prominently to be witnessed among the upper circles of society, if traced in their proper sources, for the sake of EXAMPLE, would be *scouted* as a downright *bore;* laughed at as a *waste of time;* and the person so employing himself, *satirised* as one of the *crying philosophers.* My dear Coz, I abominably hate *cant;* I despise *hypocrisy;* I detest *imposition* in any shape; and I really am *fond* of Life in London. I make no hesitation in avowing it. But it is only in ball-rooms that many persons think they possess an *existence;* have *animation* at an opera; *spirits* in a theatre; and enjoy life only at a rout. IMITATION is too much the order of the day; and the greatest anxiety with most individuals (the *lovers* and *devotees* to fashion), is to appear what they are not; to copy some stylish hero for their *model,*

---

he began with trifling bets, but he rapidly increased them to such enormous sums as to *astonish* the most affluent and spirited adepts! His connexion with the Bank was no secret, and his importance at the tables so high, that it became a common phrase at the west end of the town, "ABRAHAM NEWLAND *against the field!*" His *word* was *good* to any amount, and he soon proved to the frequenters of the tables a *rich customer* indeed. It can be a matter of no surprise to assert that young WESTON was a great loser. Loss succeeding loss, his *real* situation at length discovered itself to him; but *disguise* was at an end; and he had gone too far, before he was completely convinced of his error. It was then too late: it was irretrievable. Defalcations to the most alarming amount appeared against him; and a prosecution was commenced by the Bank. He was suddenly hurried from the hot-bed of luxury and dissipation, to contemplate the horrors that awaited him. The dreadful clanking of the chains of criminals like himself now only saluted his ear, encompassed, also, by the dreary walls of a prison; and, far more terrible than all the rest, the workings of a self-upbraiding conscience! The transition was so awful that it shook him to his very soul. It was almost like a vision. His time, too, embittered by a doubtful suspense, till he was pronounced GUILTY, at the bar of the Old Bailey, and sentenced to death. His contrition was manly, and he endeavoured to make all the restitution possible. His unhappy fate was deplored by his prosecutors, and a powerful intercession was made by his respectable relatives; but all attempts to save his life proved fruitless — stern JUSTICE demanded her victim, and, in the presence of thousands of persons, he expiated his offence on the public scaffold. He thus suffered in the prime of his youth: the hopes of his family were crushed, and the once interesting HARRY WESTOX, the pride of his acquaintance, was. *only* remembered to be disgraced! So great were the sums of money squandered and lost by this unthinking young man (considerably above £100,000!) that an application was made to the Lord Chief-Justice Kenyon, as to the legality whereby they might be recovered, on pointing out the houses in which they were lost.

but whose *dress* at most they merely *imitate,* and which generally fits them after the manner of a *'a pursers shirt upon a handspike!'* " "Lethe! dear Tom," said Hawthorn, laughing at this vulgar, but characteristic *pointed* simile. "Another hit, I confess, my Coz," replied the Corinthian; perhaps the 'ass in the lion's skin' might have been better; but I mean that such *soi-disant* floods only swim upon the *surface;* and after all their DAY and night *experience,* can only be pronounced—SMATTERERS. And"—— The remarks of Tom were rather abruptly terminated by the Hon. Dick Trifle, who came skipping up on his toes to the Corinthian, offering his hand, saying, "My dear f-a-e-l-l-o-w, you must excuse me, but what can you have been *preaching* about so long to your friend from the country? The Marchioness of Diamonds and myself have been *nodding* to you several times, and have felt surprised that we should not have attracted your notice. You positively have both appeared as if in *reveries* for the last five minutes, and that you were lost to this enchanting scene. Oh, it is positively shocking to *sermonise,* my dear f-a-e-l-l-o-w, at ALMACK'S. If you continue to remain so *grave,* I must really order you a *pulpit.* You must come and join us—we cannot do without you any longer. See, the Marchioness beckons us!—How's Bob?" "Be kind enough to inform the Marchioness we shall do ourselves the honour to attend upon her commands without delay," answered Tom. Trifle skipped off, in the same frivolous manner as he came to them, to join the company of the Marchioness. On his departure, Jerry (*laughing* with a sort of contempt), said, "He is the completest *Dandy* I ever saw; I think LOGIC called him an EXQUISITE. He appears to me to he neither a man nor a woman. Such a thing would be of no *use* in Somersetshire; and I imagine of none either in the GREAT or *little* world in the Metropolis, except as a mark for RIDICULE to *shoot* at!" "Stop," my dear JERRY, said TOM, with a suppressed laugh; "remember LETHE!"

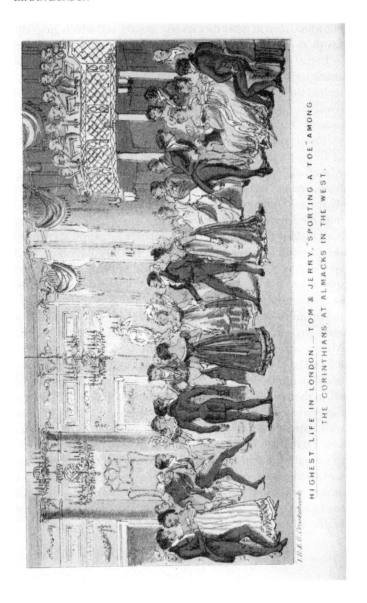

HIGHEST LIFE IN LONDON.—TOM & JERRY "SPORTING A TOE" AMONG THE CORINTHIANS, AT ALMACKS IN THE WEST.

CHAPTER XII.

The CORINTHIAN and JERRY were soon in the presence of the MARCHIONESS, who received them in the most welcome manner, and also congratulated HAWTHORN upon seeing him at ALMACK'S; at the same time introducing our heroes to the two Misses TRIFLE, the cousins of the EXQUISITE. "We can make up a party for a Quadrille," said the MARCHIONESS to the CORINTHIAN, with a most gracious smile. "Certainly, Madam," replied TOM; "and if you will permit me to offer my hand to the eldest Miss TRIFLE, and to recommend my Coz as a partner for her sister, I shall consider it as a high honour conferred upon us." It was immediately agreed to; and our heroes were enabled to join the dance without the assistance of the *explanatory* card. The appearance of the MARCHIONESS was so brilliant, from her display of *diamonds*, that JERRY was nearly in want of the word "LETHE," to call off his attracted eyes to his lovely partner that stood before him. The Hon. DICK TRIFLE formed one of the Quadrille (as the Plate represents), but his female cousins had nothing *trifling* attached to them, excepting their *name*. Indeed, on the contrary, they were superior girls, handsome in their persons and interesting in their manners; and JERRY felt quite pleased that he had been so fortunate as to procure such an agreeable lady for his partner. But the dance had scarcely commenced, when HAWTHORN perceived, among the promenaders, his "fair incognita" at the Masquerade, LADY WANTON. The hitherto attractions of his partner were all forgotten in an instant. He was on the *fret*, and almost determined to pursue her; so strongly did he feel the impulse of the moment. But his- P's and Q?s had now returned to their duty, and whispered to him, it would be highly improper to do so. Good-breeding forbade it; and the respect and attention which were due to his partner, required him to keep his station, if he wished to support the character of a *gentleman*. Poor JERRY now, indeed, felt the want of the *card* to point out to him the figure of the dance; as his eyes, instead of being fixed on his partner, were directed to the spot where Lady WANTON was walking. The face of the latter heroine, on suddenly encountering our hero, was of a crimson hue, and, instantly, in a confused state, she obscured herself in the thickest part of the promenaders, and was soon lost sight of by HAWTHORN. Upon the conclusion of the dance, our hero, by way of an excuse, complained of a slight sprain which he had met with in his ankle, and, in consequence, excused himself from, *waltzing* with Miss TRIFLE, being the best apology he could, under such, circumstances, make to his lovely and engaging partner. To prevent *detection*, JERRY was compelled to sit down, though he would have taken to his heels, if he could have done so without observation; and his eyes were wandering over the assembly, in hopes of obtaining another glimpse of the lady in question; but the bird had flown; he had not *marked* it down as heretofore; and although as keen a sportsman as ever entered a field, he was *here* completely at fault. ALMACK'S had now lost its charms, owing to this disappointment: it was a mere desert to him: HAWTHORN was intent upon another subject; and many great personages, who were well worthy of his attention, were passed over with the utmost indifference. The CORINTHIAN was equally in the dark as to the truth of the sprain; and the only pleasure now felt by JERRY was in taking his leave of the MARCHIONESS and the Misses TRIFLE, to accompany TOM once more to Corinthian House.

CHAPTER XIII.

Logic's Descriptive crambo Chaunt of the Traits of the Trio. Tempus Fugit in the Metropolis. Varieties of Life in London. Tom, Jerry, and Logic sporting their Blunt at the Royal Cockpit. What is termed, "A friendly Game of Whist." The Trio "larking" at the Grand Carnival. A Peep *en passant* at the Green-Room at Drury Lane Theatre. A Stroll to the London Docks. The Effects of tasting Wine in the Wood. The Italian Opera.

The Oxonian, on his safe arrival at the *Albany*, after his cruise at All-Max, only stopped at his chambers to change his apparel, which was rather out of order, and then made the best of his way to inquire after his *pals* at *Corinthian House*. It was the custom of Logic never to permit the *Rainbow*[238] to announce him, being an enemy to formality: he, therefore, *sans ceremonie*, while Tom and Jerry were descanting upon some of the splendid characters that had crossed their path on the preceding evening, suddenly opened the door, just wide enough to present his well-known comical phiz to their view, singing:—

> Life in London, my boys, is a round of delight;
> In frolics, I keep up, both the day and the night,
> With my Tom and my Jerry, I try to "*get best*"
> Of the Coves in the *East*—and the Swells at the *West!*
> Such *pals* in a *lark*, we the *town* can defy, O!
> Then join me in *chaunting* our *precious* TRIO.
>   WHO,

---

238   A knight of the rainbow; a cant phrase for a footman in livery, in allusion to the various colours of his jacket.

Life in London

For drinking and dancing,
Milling *and* chancing,[239]
And in sporting the *blunt;*
For *prime fun,* on the hunt;
In "Fields of Temptation,"
In high or low station:
With a DUCHESS so grand.
Or a *nymph* of the Strand;
View the MOTS in the *Lobby,*
Twig TOM, JERRY, and BOBBY;
Who, on quitting the SPELLS,
Swallow *Ruin*[240] with *Belles,*
Yet are up to their *slum;*
But a fig for each Bum:[241]
When in want of the *Swag,*
Then *gammon* the BRAG;[242]
In the Coffee-Shops peep,
Twankey *take with a* Sweep,
And there hold a parley,
To "GET THE BEST OF A CHARLEY!"
Or, in a street row,
Cut away like a plough,
And *floor* all the *Chaps,*
But be shy of the TRAPS:
With the "Peep o' day boys,"
Hunting up *dirty Toys.*[243]
At ALL-MAX in the *East,*
Toss off *Gin* like a feast;
At ALMACK's in the *West,*
True politeness the zest;
To Waltz *or* Quadrille,
LOTS OF PLEASURE—our fill;
The "double shuffle *or* cut;"
At "ALL-FOURS" or to PUT.
Then a hand take at WHIST,
With the best on the list:

---

239 *"I'll chance it."* A common expression among sporting men, when the object in view is doubtful of accomplishment.

240 *Blue.* But *ruin* is to be met with of all manner of *colours.*

241 A Bailiff. By the most intimate acquaintance of LOGIC, who were well aware of the game he had been playing for some years, this *flourish* might be viewed as rather *bouncing* a little; but the CORINTHIAN was too Well-bred to *query* the circumstances of any friend.

242 *Money-lenders.* LOGIC termed those persons *Brags,* in consequence of their repeatedly advertising to render embarrassed individuals assistance, yet making them *pay* well for it; something after the old adage, that "BRAG's a good dog; but *Holdfast* is a better!"

243 LOGIC's *phrase* for the unfortunate peep o' day women of the town, who wander about from one coffee-shop to another, till day-light breaks in upon them, and whose pockets are "full of emptiness." Also, when the *dab* is not to be had upon *tick.*

Chapter XIII.

Rouge-et-noir and Hazard—
With each *knowing mazzard*;[244]
Yet you always must win,
At E. O. and Berlin:
At strong "knock'em down,"
Do your best for a Crown;
And give the *Flats* rue,
At "Crib,"*or* "Lant Loo."
With low flash *and* rich style,
The dull hours to beguile:
When your spirits do *flag*,
Throw yourself in a *drag;*
    Then,
Let us ask who can beat, O!
The trio—the trio—the trio?

LOGIC would not be interrupted till he had finished his crambo chaunt, when he was received with that kind of hearty welcome by our heroes, which recognises the return of an old acquaintance to a company, whose lively talents never fail to set the table .in a roar. Both the Corinthian and Hawthorn held out their hands to him; when the former, laughing, observed, "My dear Bob, I am very glad to perceive you have returned safely into port, as the last advices we received were that the *Oxonian* had been *cast away* on the Coast of Africa." "Another report," said Jerry, "was, that you had been capsized by the *Flashy Nance."* "These *innuendoes* won't do, my friends," replied Logic. "It is true, I have been under an *embargo* for a short period; but I would also have you to understand, that my *despatches* are sealed: and I have not as yet arrived at the proper destination where they are to be broken open; therefore, a truce, if you please, at present, to any further inquiries on that head. Take it for granted; that I am returned safe and sound, both wind and limb; and am quite ready to start upon another scent. But come, let us be *jogging. Tempus fugit*, my boys, I am going to the Royal Cockpit, in Tufton Street, Westminster; and you and the Corinthian promised to accompany me the first good day's Play of Cocks that was announced." "Indeed, you are right," urged Hawthorn; "I really think Time has wings in London; at least, I have found it so. It is true I have gone to rest,

---

244   One of the numerous slang phrases for the head.

but I have scarcely had *forty winks* before it is one or two o'clock in the day; and half a dozen glasses of wine after dinner have not passed my ivory, when night has arrived. I have," continued JERRY, smiling, "properly reversed the order of things, since I have made my appearance in the Metropolis: and I also find, by experience, that JERRY in the country was quite a different personage to Mr HAWTHORN in town."

The *Oxonian* was as gay as a lark; and he did not appear to have quite recovered from the effects of his recent cruise. In answer to JERRY, he again burst forth, *chaunting*—

> Who dares talk of hours? Seize the bell of that clock;
> Seize the hammer, and cut off his hands;
> To the *bottle*, dear *bottle*! I'll stick like a rock,
> And obey only PLEASURE'S commands.
>
> Let him strike the short hours, and hint at a bed;—
> Waiter, bring us more wine,—what a whim!
> Say that TIME, his old master, for TOPERS was made,
> And not *jolly* TOPERS for *him*.

The lively TRIO, once more complete, again started off in high spirits to pursue the *game* in view; but they had not proceeded far on their route, before the *Oxonian* burst out into a laugh, and, touching JERRY on the shoulder, said, "My dear boy, they have found you out at last. Only turn round, and you will have a very fine view[245] of LIFE IN LONDON of your own *making*. You will also perceive the *man with the gold-laced hat and coat*[246] waiting to pay his respects to you.'

---

245   The *Oxonian*, most likely, borrowed this idea from the old saying of the three finest sights in the world:—a pregnant female, a ship in full sail, and a field of ripe corn.
246   The Beadle of the Parish. This hero of the staff generally being sent to take up those persons who are humorously termed "the *Face-Makers!*"

Chapter XIII.

TOM, JERRY & LOGIC, BACKING TOMMY, THE 'SWEEP, AT THE ROYAL COCKPIT.

"I must admit," replied the CORINTHIAN, smiling, "it is a *fertile* prospect; but it is one of those *prominent features* of LIFE which rather belongs to the country, and is more frequently witnessed in villages than in large towns, an't it, Coz? Indeed, JERRY, your *experience* in those matters entitles you to decide the question, in preference to us Metropolitans. Is it not so, BOB?" "Most certainly," said LOGIC; "but I have no doubt the countryman will be able to *hedge* off from the subject, as we know he is a good sportsman." "Well done, my friends," exclaimed HAWTHORN; "so in order to preserve the reputation of the London females, I am to libel the unsuspecting, innocent, harmless country damsels at the expense of their general characters. No, my dear fellows, I love the sex too well to utter one word of reproach against them, either in town or country, for being—*kind;* and if anything should be the matter, I hope I shall never so far forget myself as to want (as you term him, BOB), the man with the gold-laced hat and coat,' not merely to compel me to do my duty, but to perform the highest act of a man's life—that of protecting a female in distress!" "Bravo," said LOGIC; "very nobly expressed. You are *game* to the back-bone, JERRY; and I see, with pleasure, we shall be able to make something important of you before your return to *Hawthorn Hall;* and that. LIFE IN LONDON will not be thrown away upon your mind. After you have sown your *wild oats,* as the old women have it, you may become an excellent, liberal kind of *beak*, and I hope I shall live to witness your name in the commission of the peace for Somersetshire." "I hope so too," answered the CORINTHIAN; "but I am afraid the *poachers* would stand but a queer chance, if any of them were brought before Justice HAWTHORN!"

On their way to the Cockpit, JERRY advised the CORINTHIAN and LOGIC to *back* the *Countryman,* designated TOMMY *the Sweep.* "That won't do," replied the *Oxonian;* "the *Yokels* have always been beat in London!" "Nevermind," answered HAWTHORN, "I'll give you that in; but *Tommy* will take the *shine* out of *the Cockneys* this time. He is a capital feeder, and an excellent judge of cocks; he is, I understand, familiar with all the various breeds, and well acquainted with the properties of the right *shitten* winged colour, the Shropshire reds, the Staffordshire jet blacks, &c." "I think we may as well, BOB," said the CORINTHIAN, "yield to JERRY's *judgment* upon this occasion." "It shall be so, then," said LOGIC." HAWTHORN was no *novice* at cocking; and the interior of the Pit afforded him but little variety for observation: the confusion of voices; the bettings of 2 to 1, 5 to 4, &c.; the poundage; the anxiety displayed by the backers, on the telling out of the cocks, were exactly the same as JERRY had previously witnessed in the country: but the singularity of the remarks, and the knowing looks of the visitors, both high and low, did not fail in making an impression on his mind. It is rather singular to remark, it was the first time that a *London Feeder* was beaten on his own ground; and TOM and LOGIC "won their *blunt*" in consequence of *backing* the opinion of HAWTHORN. The group of persons assembled in the Pit, as represented in the Plate, is accurate to a point.

The *swell* BROAD[247] coves who had lost their money in the Pit with TOM and JERRY were determined, if possible, to get it soon back again; and, therefore, in the most polite manner, invited, nay pressed, our heroes to take dinner with them at their house, near St James's Park. LOGIC excused himself on account of some prior engagement; but the CORINTHIAN and JERRY, supposing it nothing more than a *gentlemanly* sort of invitation, accepted it without the least hesitation. Indeed, upon this *suit* some of the *best judges* in the kingdom have been "*had.*" Inviting a man to a *swell* dinner, and making him pay *five guineas* a mouthful for it afterwards, is no new feature in LIFE IN LONDON. It is THREE playing ONE; and JERRY stood the *nonsense* in prime style. *Blacky*, although in the character of a servant, was *in it*—and did not want the *hint* to ply the wine often enough to Hawthorn. Tom was also a brother sufferer. The *blade* who throws his eyes over his cards to receive the *office* from his *pal*, who is getting a sight of Jerry's cards from the glass, is well delineated in the Plate; indeed, the whole group is well worthy of observation. How are we *ruined* in London?

---

247 Elegantly dressed card-players; also possessing a good address, with other requisites befitting them to keep company with gentlemen.

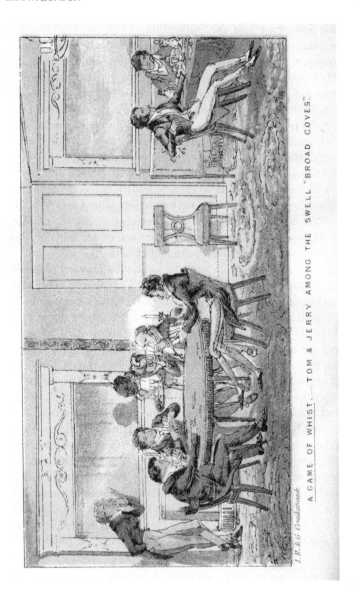

A GAME OF WHIST.—TOM & JERRY AMONG THE SWELL "BROAD COVES".

CHAPTER XIII.

But then it is only taking a *friendly* game at whist. When Logic heard of the above circumstance, on giving our heroes a call, the next morning, he laughed heartily at their being *maced:* observing, "That he ought to think himself very lucky he had escaped such a *friendly* invitation. But never mind, my boys," said he, "every one must pay for his *learning;* and it would be unhandsome to *bilk* the schoolmaster—wouldn't it, JERRY? Yet I think it would have been as well for both of you *(in an ironical manner),* if your *despatches* had been *sealed* upon this voyage. But a truce to complaint. Here is more fun in store for us, and I have purchased tickets for the Grand Carnival at the English Opera House this evening. The advertisement sets forth, that it is an attempt to render Masquerades a popular species of amusement in the Metropolis." "I must confess, Bob," answered the Corinthian, "you are a *prime* caterer for the trio." "I am also much indebted to my friend Logic for his exertions," said Jerry, "to give me a sight of everything interesting in London; and, also, for his excellent company on most of the occasions. I am no flatterer, Bob; and, believe me, I was not a little vexed on account of your absence the other evening at ALMACK'S." "But I was with you at ALL-MAX," answered Logic, making up his comic face laughingly irresistible; "and I'll bet you seven to four, for a bit of good truth, the lively *jig* of *African Sall* in the East against the quadrilles and waltzing of the *diamond squad* in the West, for *gig fun, life, and character.*" "Lethe," replied Jerry. "I am not up to that phrase; it is *new,* I suppose," said the *Oxonian,* "and you want to *quiz* me," "No, no, BOB," urged HAWTHORN, "I must give you '*best*' in that respect; but it was the *cue,* or byword, which I was to take from my Coz, whenever he thought I was getting out of the line." "And not a bad idea[248] neither," replied LOGIC; "but you will have no occasion to sing out

---

[248] It is not unlikely that CORINTHIAN TOM took this hint from the *Duke of Argyle* (in the Heart of Mid-Lothian, as performed at-the Surrey Theatre), who advises *Jeanie Deans,* previous to her interview with the Queen, to observe his motions, in order that she may behave correctly when telling her story in the Royal Presence. "For instance," says the Duke, "when you observe me touch my cravat, proceed no further upon that subject."

'LETHE' to-night at the CARNIVAL, I'll answer for it. However, let us make up our minds as to the *Characters* we intend to assume. I shall go as Dr *Pangloss*." "And I as *Rover,*" said the CORINTHIAN. "Not much *assumption* in that, I believe," cried the *Oxonian;* "but you must excuse me, my dear TOM." "I intend to personify *Hodge,*" observed JERRY; "and then, perhaps. as a *countryman*, I shall not be so likely to commit myself." This point being settled, the time soon arrived for the TRIO to enter into the *lark* at the GRAND CARNIVAL. The *experience* HAWTHORN had now had made him rather bold: he trod the boards like an old *stager,* and entered the *Masquerade* loudly singing,—

> "I'm a poor country booby, and have lost my way,
> And com'd here to look *after a* zarvice;
> But, my sweet ladies, don't lead I astray,
> As I have no cash to call for a *Jarvis.*"[249]

The CORINTHIAN was so complete a *Rover* with all the *fair ones* present, that he was pronounced by them a *real character;* and, most certainly, stood in no need of a *mask* to conceal his designs. LOGIC likewise entered so much into the spirit of the scene, in quizzing several Masquers with his LL.D. and A.S.S., that his *kicks* were much oftener *felt* than *relished.* Upon "*Puss in Boots*" presenting his card to the *Oxonian*, the latter, who was aware of his person although disguised in this character, "by way of a *pun*, said to him, "Mr Puss, I do not observe any *Peake* to your boots?" "Never mind," answered the CORINTHIAN, "although *Puss* is no *translator*, yet his works do not want for *point* neither!" "Pugh!" said Jerry, laughing, "with all your pretended knowledge of Mr *Puss,* you are both out, as he has got a better *seat of work* than *translating*, I assure you,—he belongs to the *Treasury.*"[250]

---

[249] This *expression* was rather too *flash* for a countryman; but a man does not always study his *character.*

[250] Mr R. B. Peake, jun. treasurer of the English Opera House; a gentleman of considerable talents, not only as an artist, but as a lively, witty, dramatic author. His "Costume of a Journey to Paris"—"Actor and Amateurs"—"Walk for a Wager," &c., and also a portion of the last two pieces of Mr Matthews's "At Home," sufficiently speak for themselves.

Chapter XIII.

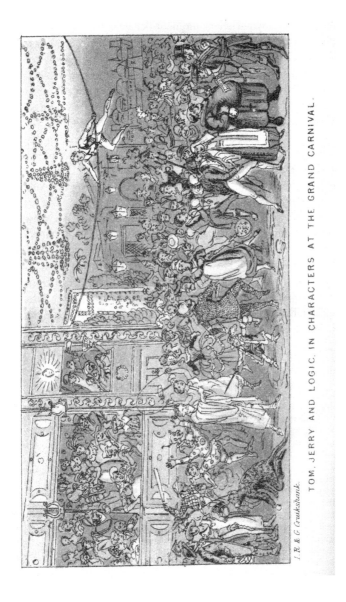

TOM, JERRY AND LOGIC, IN CHARACTERS AT THE GRAND CARNIVAL.

Nothing of any particular moment occurred to our trio; indeed, it might be said to be the same thing over again to Jerry, with the difference only of greater talents having been displayed by some of the *characters:* but no one of the masquers present created more *fun,* showed more *lark,* or entered more into the *spirit* of the scene,[251] than did Tom, Jerry, and Logic, and they returned to *Corinthian House* quite fatigued from their exertions.

Our heroes did not rise till late the next morning, but breakfast was scarcely over, when the order of the day was gone into, and, as usual, "Where shall we go this evening?" said HAWTHORN to his Coz. *"Apropos,"* replied the CORINTHIAN, "I have the offer of an introduction to the performers in the Green-Room of Drury Lane Theatre." "Excellent," exclaimed JERRY; "it is DON GIOVANNI tonight, and the numerous characters that piece contains will afford us plenty of fun! Besides, if it were nothing else but the introduction of one DON to another." TOM smiled at this compliment, but made no answer to it. After some observations on the *mechanism*[252] or *acting* of plays, upon their entrance into the Green-Room, the CORINTHIAN said to his Coz, "You perceive, JERRY, as a proof of my argument, that, when the *call-boy* informs

---

251 Most of the *Characters* who were at the GRAND CARNIVAL may trace themselves by a close inspection of the Plate. The Man in Armour, Puss in Boots, the Maid who attacks her Lovers with a Warming-Pan, the Girl with the Skipping-Rope, the NONPAREIL sparring, the Juggler with the Cups and Balls, the Slack Rope Vaulter, Moll Flagon, the fine Lady of the last Century, the fat Friar, the Undertaker, &c., &c., are all sufficiently prominent to speak for themselves. The Plate is a very accurate representation of that grand scene. The view of Venice in the back-ground; the Swiss Cottages; and the Masquers in the Boxes, render the *tout ensemble* highly interesting.

252 It is curious to observe on the performance of a new play, got up in haste, where the actors in general have scarcely had an opportunity of knowing anything more about the piece than their own *individual characters,* written out for them by the prompter, and which may be placed in the middle, or near the end of the performance, how they fall in, acting with that sort of animation and feeling, which tend to impress upon the minds of the audience, that their energies are actuated by the whole story of the play, either in eliciting tears or producing roars of laughter. Nay, more, some of the actors in the piece, who are not wanted till a certain period, may be enjoying themselves at the distance of Barnet from the theatre when the play commenced, and yet arrive in due time to do their duty in their *precise* situation. This, however, looks something like *mechanism,* as TOM remarked.

the actors they are wanted upon the stage, they immediately place themselves in their situations, like joints put together belonging to a piece of furniture." "You have a very pleasant life of it, indeed," HAWTHORN remarked to one of the performers who stood near to him, "and you must be the most cheerful beings upon the earth; as you appear to be always merry, singing, and dancing." "Yes, sir," replied the hero of the lamp, "we certainly do appear so before the curtain; and I verily believe the audience in general entertain that opinion; but, if you will permit me to change the scene, I will show you that it is far more difficult to *please* the *company behind* GREENY, [253] I beg pardon, sir, I should have said, than the audience *before* the *curtain*. To be candid, it is one of the most envious professions in existence—*praise,* to others is like death to us; and, behind the scenes, merit is rarely acknowledged or meets with any thing like fair play. If an actor succeed, and bring *money* (for money is the touchstone of excellence, more than any other quality, in the Treasury), then I admit he is everything; as well as almost being surfeited with praises and offers of kindness; and objections to his size, voice, and other imperfections which might have been made against him when applying for an engagement, are all forgotten in an instant. The greatest tragedians and comic actors who have been established with the public for years, some of whom are nearly upon the verge of visiting '*that bourn from whence no traveller returns,*' would almost sooner part with their lives than lose a *hand,*—I beg pardon, sir, than a single *grain* of applause. The dismissal of an underling actor would undoubtedly follow, if he dared to commence his speech before a great comic performer had done 'CUTTING OF MUGS;' [254] or, have *swallowed* his three rounds of applause. I beg pardon, sir, for being so technical; I mean making wry faces: and you must also wait, if it be till Doomsday, before you attempt to quit your position, if a distinguished tragedian has not electrified the audience with his grand *start!* Several performers of note, too, have thought it beneath their dignity to give an infe-

---

253   "One man in his time plays many parts:" and actors, like most other professions, have a *slang,* or *cant,* of their own.
254   This was rather a *sharp* cut; if not a KEAN hit.

rior actor his *cue,* when he has been at a loss, and have preferred seeing the latter appear ridiculous, thinking it tended to raise their importance with the audience, respecting their being *perfect.*" "I have witnessed that circumstance several times in the country, I must confess," answered Jerry. "Before you are up," resumed the actor,—"but I hope you will excuse me, sir, I mean to say, that when a person first enters the *profession,* and during the time he is going round the country for practice, he has so many parts to learn that he has scarcely any time for sleep: and, after having been for years in this uncertain pursuit, should he have the offer of a *trial* night, [255] at London, he is more frequently *damned* than otherwise, which so reduces the actor in the estimation of his hitherto judges in the provincial towns, where he has been once a great favourite, that it operates like an *extinguisher* to him as a performer. The *engagements,* too, should a country actor be lucky enough to make one, are now made upon such precarious terms, that he is liable to be *brushed off* at the end of the first season. An actor likewise ought never to be *ill,* as the public too often think it is merely an excuse: besides, a performer is often compelled to play with a heart full of grief, and perhaps, at the same time, overwhelmed with misfortunes, yet he must appear as gay as a lark, and as if he was one of the happiest beings in the world. It is a most arduous profession. A performer ought also to possess the incalculable advantages of education, a free intercourse with polished society, and a general knowledge of countries and history; be completely master of the various traits of human nature, the passions necessarily subservient to his will, and, as *a pendulum* to the whole, the acquirements of a *gentleman.* But, notwithstanding all the above *unities* towards perfection, without the possession of a vigorous mind, *eminence* will not await his efforts. The *fame* of an actor is likewise composed of the most perishable materials; and his *talents* are entirely left to the *recollection* of his audience to be preserved from oblivion.

---

255   SIXTEEN, it is said (if not more), *Dennis Brulgrudderys* have made their appearance at Covent-Garden Theatre, since Mr *Johnstone* left that house, and not *one* of them has been able to establish himself in that character.

Chapter XIII.

THE GREEN ROOM AT DRURY LANE THEATRE.—TOM & JERRY INTRODUCED TO THE CHARACTERS IN DON GIOVANNI.

The works of the painter may be condemned and the subject removed; but he can paint, paint, and paint again, till success crown his efforts. Should the labours of the poet prove displeasing, a new production may place him in a more eligible point of view; and the *persons* of the painter and the poet are never put in competition with their talents. But to the player, *figure* is of the utmost importance, as a prepossessing appearance is half-way towards success:—

> "The critic's sight'tis only grace can please;
> No *figure* charms us if it has not ease."

The mere circumstance of changing the name of any favourite actress from Miss to Mrs is a dangerous, experiment, and the hitherto attraction, in spite of superior talents, generally subsides, and a new *single* performer must be obtained to feed the inexhaustible demands of *novelty*, Added to all these circumstances, sir, the poor performer has also to withstand the *torrent* of newspaper criticism, and placidly to bear being *cut all* to pieces." "I think," said Tom, interrupting the complaints of the former, "not only the actors but the proprietors of the theatres are much indebted to the exertions of the press in their liberal recommendation of the performances to the public: but," continued the Corinthian, *smiling*, "it must be rather a difficult matter for those theatrical 'writers to *split* their *candour*, who are in the habit of cutting up a performer's beef, to turn round and cut up his person afterwards; indeed, it is but fair, under such circumstances, that the *critic* should give the *balance* in favour of his friend. It might be better, perhaps, on the score of *impartiality*, or to prevent any imputation of favouritism, that the newspapers should not receive free admissions; but it operates, in my opinion, very little against giving their opinions independently." "Well, sir, I will not dispute that circumstance with you," replied the actor; "but the tyranny and caprice of the managers are" "Sir," said JERRY, in order to *cut* the subject, "you must excuse us, as we have an engagement to fulfil, and are *tied* to time." Our heroes now took their departure; but HAWTHORN observed to his Coz, "that he was not an advocate for the *Don* being performed by a woman; and he did not like, without disparagement to the ladies, to witness this *transposition* of *characters*. I cannot make up my mind," continued JERRY, "that the females who are engaged in the same piece can act their parts with such spirit and feeling as when a man is their hero." TOM and JERRY took a *saunter* through the house, a *strut* up and down the saloon and lobby, and a *peep* into a *sluicery* or two, to see if any thing "new" was stirring; but, as nothing "*turned-up?*" to excite the peculiar attention of our heroes, they made rather an early night of it, and reached *Corinthian House* in decent time, where a light supper, a pleasant bit of chat on the occurrences of the day, and a social glass of wine, beguiled an hour or two, till the *dustman* made his appearance, and gave the *hint* to TOM and JERRY that it was time to visit their beds.

Our heroes mustered somewhat earlier than usual the next morning, and a stroll to the London Docks was the pursuit in view. "Suppose," said LOGIC, "on our road, we stop and take a bird's-eye view of Newgate, from the top of the prison, which we neglected at our last visit." "With all my heart," exclaimed JERRY. On ascending to the top of Newgate, the TRIO expressed themselves much pleased, on looking down into the different yards, and witnessing the excellent mode of discipline practised in that prison, of sorting the criminals into classes, according to their distinction of crimes. "It appears to me," said TOM, "impossible for any prisoner to make an escape." "I agree with you," replied LOGIC; "look there! (pointing to the watch-box), both day and night a man is always on duty, who is relieved at certain hours."

On the approach of our heroes towards the London Docks, the *Oxonian*, with a smile, asked his companions, "if they had a mind, as they were so near, for another night at All-Max?" "Not yet awhile," replied Hawthorn. Upon traversing the Docks, the Corinthian met with his wine-merchant, who politely pressed the trio to descend into a vault, to taste some capital wines which he had recently purchased in the wood. Logic, with a grin, said to Jerry, "it was not only a good *move*, but there was a great deal of *taste* about it.

Life in London

TOM, JERRY & LOGIC. "TASTING" WINE IN THE WOOD, AT THE LONDON DOCKS.

CHAPTER XIII.

The Corinthian and Hawthorn were both upon their guard, but Logic, who was a dear lover of wine, *tasted, tasted,* and *tasted*[256] so often, that he ultimately became *non compos mentis,* and required the assistance of a *drag* to convey him home to the *Albany.*

"I am sorry this '*tasting*' circumstance occurred," said TOM to his Coz, when taking their wine after dinner, "as I very much wished for BOB to have gone with us this evening to the Opera. But we must do without him."

The spacious appearance of the Italian Opera House, the brilliancy of the audience (particularly the display of full-dressed persons in the pit), and the comforts of the CORINTHIAN's box, afforded JERRY much delight and satisfaction. "But," said HAWTHORN, "it appears to me that the company, generally, value this theatre more for a lounging fashionable place of meeting with each other than to listen to the performances; and the great mass of the spectators, I believe, are also in the dark as to a *conversant* knowledge of the dialogue. To *look* and to be *looked at,* to be superbly attired, as leaders, on the one side, as well as numerous persons on the other to follow the fashions, are features of a more prominent description. However, it is most certainly a brilliant spectacle, and I have no doubt but many persons of superior *taste* visit the Opera House for no other purpose but the gratification they feel at the talents displayed by the performers. The dancing, I confess, is so truly elegant that I want words to express my admiration of it. But, my dear Coz," said JERRY, laughing, "to have one's box at the Opera, you know, is quite the *ton!*" "I have no fault to find with your portrait of this fashionable *picture* of LIFE IN LONDON," replied TOM; "at least, the outline is good; and, instead of any prejudice being exhibited against the Italian Opera, I think it ought to be viewed as a stimulus towards the improvement of our male and female singers; and, without any disparagement or illiberality, I consider the English performers now as powerful rivals." On our heroes descending into the pit,

---

256 Some excuse might be offered for LOGIC in this particular instance; as many persons have been *overcome* before they were aware of it, from being *gammoned* to *taste* wine in a vault. It is fine fun for the cellarmen, but nothing *new* to them.

by way of a look to see who was there, the Hon. Dick Trifle immediately caught the attention of the Corinthian, with "My dear Tom, I am glad to see you; won't you pay your respects to the Marchioness? her Ladyship is here, accompanied by my cousins. Come, Mr Hawthorn, let me conduct you to the box of the Marchioness." Our heroes were in the presence of this dashing heroine and the Misses Trifle without delay. Jerry's sprain was inquired after, with much politeness by the ladies, and the remainder of the evening was *chatted* away in the most *agreeable* manner, but a little at the expense of some of the *intimate* friends of the Marchioness, who were good-naturedly ridiculed for their peculiarities of taste, look, and dress; indeed, so much were they all engaged with the elegant satire and anecdotes with which Trifle so amply furnished them, that scarcely any of the party had an opportunity of bestowing a single glance at the performances. "Trifle," said the Marchioness, "who was that *rotunda* kind of a female in company with the person I saw you in conversation with when I entered the house?" "She is the wife of a great contractor for hides and tallow," replied Trifle. "Her husband, I am told, was originally a charity-boy: but I have no connexion with him, I assure your Ladyship, having merely met him on the 'Change one morning when I was in company with a friend of mine. The contractor recognised me first, or else you may depend I should not have noticed the f-a-e-l-l-o-w; but, nevertheless, he is now immensely rich, and looks upon himself as good as a Mar———." "Stop, stop, Trifle," said the Marchioness, interrupting him, with a toss of her head; "do not *soil* the title with such a *greasy* subject. Good heavens! what can such people mean by showing themselves at the Opera; are there not the theatres and other minor places of amusement for *folks* of that description?" "*Vary* true; perfectly correct, Madam; I am at a loss to know what sort of feelings they possess," replied Trifle, taking a pinch of snuff. On the dropping of the curtain, the Corinthian and his Coz begged the honour of conducting the ladies to their carriage, which the annexed Plate so characteristically delineates; and also the bustling scene, which did not escape the observation of Jerry.

Chapter XIII.

OUTSIDE OF THE OPERA HOUSE AT NIGHT.—GALLANTRY OF TOM & JERRY.

The vociferations of "The M%%ARCHIONESS%% %%OF%% D%%IAMOND%%'s carriage stops the way." The loud cries of "Coach unhired," from the link-boys; and, "Does your honour vant a coach? This way, your honour," &c. The numerous livery servants in attendance; and the frequent rows between the police officers and the *gay* young coachmen endeavouring to get up first to the door, almost at the hazard of their own lives, injuring their horses, and having their carriages shattered to pieces in breaking through the line, merely to gratify the wishes of some of their high-spirited mistresses, who think broken panels a trifle in comparison to their being kept *waiting;* or, with a smile, pardon the *gallantry* of their coachmen for running down a *Jarvy in his crazy hack* and *load* of company, who had dared to have the presumption of taking *precedence* of persons of Q%%UALITY%%.

CHAPTER XIV.

The Trio making the most of an Evening at Vauxhall. Tom and Jerry visiting the Exhibition of Pictures at the Royal Academy. Hawthorn, Tom, and Logic "Masquerading it" among the Cadgers in the "Back Slums" in the Holy Land. The Corinthian and his Coz taking the Hint at Logic's being' "Blown up" at Point Non-Plus, or long wanted by John Doe and Richard Roe, and must come. Symptoms of Jerry being rather out of Condition.

LOGIC SHOWED HIS merry face earlier than usual at Corinthian House, and in consequence the trio was complete at breakfast; but by way of an apology, or rather to prevent any criticism upon his conduct at the Docks, he punningly observed, "that he felt confident, a Man of Taste was always a welcome guest to his elegant friends at any hour." This had the desired effect; and some other novelty was immediately sought after to keep our heroes in motion. "I perceive," said Tom, "on perusing the newspaper, Vauxhall Gardens are open, and therefore, Jerry, to-night we will pay them a visit." "It is an extraordinary place, indeed," replied Hawthorn, "if my Old Dad and Mam have not exaggerated its grandeur; but, as the old people have not been much used to sights, it may account for their astonishment and rapture in speaking about them." "I am not surprised at that," answered Tom, smiling; in my humble opinion, it has not its equal in the world. There is nothing like it in Paris. PLEASURE holds her court at *Vauxhall*. In those gay regions, you are liable to jostle against the *gods* and *goddesses*—

Bacchus you will find frequently at your elbow—Venus and the *Graces* passing and repassing, yet condescendingly *smiling* upon you—Momus surrounded by fun and laughter—Terpsichore attending upon your *steps*—and Apollo winding up the whole with the most pleasing harmony." "No Lethe, then is necessary at Vauxhall, I suppose," said Jerry, ironically, interrupting Tom. "Yes, my dear Coz," answered the Corinthian. "It might be inferred that nearly, if not all the visitors, upon entering Vauxhall Gardens, had drank of the waters of Lethe, for everything else seems to be *forgotten* on joining this enchanting scene: however, I can speak for myself in this respect." "Excellently well defined, Tom," replied Logic. "To me, Vauxhall is the festival of Love and Harmony, and produces a most happy mixture of society. There is no *precision* about it, and every person can be *accommodated*, however *substantial*, or *light* and *airy* their *palates*. If *eating*, my dear Jerry, is the object in view, you will perceive tables laid out in every box, and the order is only wanted by the waiter instantly to gratify the appetite. If *drinking*, the *punch* is so prime, and immediately follows the call, that it will soon make you as lively as a harlequin. If inclined to *waltz or* to *reel*, partners can be procured without the formality of a master of the ceremonies. If you are fond of *singing*, the notes of that ever-green, Mrs Bland, never fail to touch the heart. If attached to *music*, the able performers in the orchestra, the Pandean minstrels, and regimental bands, in various parts of the gardens, prove quite a treat. If *promenading* is your forte, you will find illuminated walks of the most interesting and animated description. Numerous persons of the highest quality: myriads of lovely females, with gaiety beaming upon every countenance; and the pleasure of meeting with old friends and acquaintances, render the *tout ensemble* impressively elegant and fascinating. Even the *connoisseur* in paintings may find subjects at Vauxhall too rich to be passed over in haste. In short, there is such an endless variety of amusements, in rapid succession, from the song to the dance—from refreshment to the glass—from the cascade to the fireworks, that time positively flies in these Gardens. *Reflection* is not admitted; and the *senses* are all upon the alert.

CHAPTER XIV.

You may be as *extravagant* as you please, or you need not spend a single *farthing*, if economy is your object, and not be found fault with neither. If you like it so best," continued the *Oxonian*, smiling, "you may be as gay as a dancing-master, and enter into all the fun and frolic by which you are surrounded; or you can be as *decorous* as a parson in his pulpit, and be nothing more than a common observer. But if *enjoyment* is your *motto*, you may make the most of an evening in these Gardens more than at any other place in the Metropolis. It is all free and easy—stay as long as you like, and depart when you think proper." "Your description is so flattering," replied Jerry, "that I do not care how soon the time arrives for us to start." Logic proposed a "bit of a stroll," in order to get rid of an hour or two, which was immediately accepted by Tom and Jerry. A *turn* or two in Bond Street— a *stroll* through Piccadilly—a *"look in"* at Tattersall's—a *ramble* through Pall-Mall—and a *strut* on the *Corinthian Path*, fully occupied the time of our heroes till the hour for dinner arrived, when a few glasses of Tom's rich wines soon put them on the *qui vive;* Vauxhall was then the object in view, and the trio started, bent upon enjoying all the pleasures which this place so amply affords to its visitors.

"It is really delightful," exclaimed JERRY, on his entering the Gardens, during the first act of the concert; "I was, on my first visit, enraptured with Sydney Gardens, at Bath; but, I must confess, that the brilliancy of this scene is so superior that it appears to me like a NEW WORLD, and you have not, my friends, *overrated* it."

Hawthorn, under the guidance of his *pals*, was not long in exploring the illuminated walks, the rotunda, and everything belonging to this fashionable place of resort. Our hero was in high spirits; Logic was also *ripe* for a *spree:* and the Corinthian so agreeable in disposition, that he made known to his two friends he was ready to *accommodate* them in any proposition they might feel inclined to make. Jerry expressed himself much pleased with the arrangement and performance of the concert; and he likewise observed, the music of the songs reflected considerable credit on the talents of the composer.[257] On passing through the rooms attached to the rotunda, in which the paintings of *Hogarth* and *Hayman* are exhibited, and also the portraits of the late King and Queen, on their coming to the throne, Jerry, with a smile, retorted upon Logic, "that those paintings certainly could not be passed over in haste, and if the proprietors of the *Gardens* thought *catalogues* were not necessary, it would, however, prove much more pleasing to the visitors if a few lines were painted under them, by way of *explanation."* "I must agree with your remarks," replied Logic; "no visitor ought to be suffered to remain in the *dark* on any subject amidst such a blaze of illumination. Never mind criticising any more about these pictures; let us retire to a nice little box, for I assure you my *ogles* have feasted long enough, and I stand in need of much more substantial refreshment. Some burnt-wine, *ham-shavings,*[258] chickens, sherry, and a lively drop of arrack-punch, my boys, will enable us to finish the evening like *trumps."* "A good proposition," cried TOM. "It is," said JERRY; and I second it." The TRIO immediately left the *gay* scene, for a short period, to partake of all the *choice* articles which the larder could produce to please their palates. The *bottle* was not suffered to stand still by our heroes, and the *punch* also moved off with great facility, till the lively "military band invited them once more to join the merry dance, when Logic, full of fun and laughter, said, "he was now able to *reel* with any lady or gentleman in the Gardens." "Yes," replied TOM, laughing heartily, "I'll back you on that score, Bob; but not to *dance."* The elegant appearance and address of the Corinthian soon procured him lots of dashing partners: Jerry was

---

257   Mr PARRY, the celebrated composer of-the Welsh Melodies and several other popular pieces of music; a gentleman well known in the musical world, and who has risen to the well-merited eminence he now enjoys entirely from the possession of superior talents. Mr PARRY was originally the master of the Derbyshire band, and the fife was the first instrument he excelled upon, when quite a boy; but his performances on the flageolet arc exquisitely fine, and the admiration of all those persons who have heard him.
258   In allusion to the *thinness,* and artist-like, manner in which the *ham* was brought to table. Logic offered a bet to Jerry "that it was not *cut* with a *knife,* but *shaved* off with *a plane;* and, if necessary, from its transparent quality, conceived it might answer the purpose of a *sky-light!"*

not behind his Coz in that respect; and the agility both our heroes displayed on the "light fantastic toe" attracted numerous *gazers,* as the Plate represents. Logic, who was for "pushing along, keep moving," as he termed it, was interrupted in his pursuit by a *jack-o' dandy* hero, and who also quizzed the *Oxonian* with the appellation of "*Old Barnacles.*" Some sharp words passed in reply from Logic, when the *dandy*, who was rather, *snuffy,* as well as impudent, put himself into a posture of defence, crying out, "Come on, my fine *faelow*, I'll soon spoil your daylights." The *Oxonian* immediately gave the *dandy* so severe a blow on his head that he measured his length on the ground like a log of wood: and, on Logic's perceiving the fallen *dandy* quite terrified, he assumed to be in a most violent rage, and addressed two of the sisterhood near him, with "My dears, if you do not hold my arms, I am so tremendous a fellow, I shall certainly do him a mischief." This piece of bombast had the desired effect; and the *dandy*, amidst roars of laughter, endeavoured to get up and run away; but Logic held him, and said, "That was the way he took to *correct* fellows who addressed him improperly; and, to prevent mistakes in future, he advised him to remember Mr *Green Specs*." The *Oxonian*, anxious to keep up the fun, pretended, all of a sudden, to be in great agony, and, putting up his hand to, his head, exclaimed, in a piteous tone, "I have got the worst of it after all; I have lost an eye." "I hope not," said a lady, a little advanced in years, who was an observer of the scene, apparently much grieved at his misfortune. "Never mind, my love," replied Logic; "it is only a *green* one; I can get another," showing his spectacles, with one of his glasses out. Bob now *reeled* off, receiving the applause of the spectators as a very funny fellow. On the conclusion of the dance, Tom and Jerry traversed the Gardens, and enjoyed themselves to the utmost extent in all the variety they afforded, till day-light had long given them the hint it was time to think of home. Logic, as upon former occasions, was not to be found; and the Corinthian and his Coz were compelled to leave Vauxhall without him.

It was late in the day before our heroes took their breakfast at *Corinthian House;* and the dinner was equally behind the usual time, in proportion; but, before half of the first bottle of wine had been drank, LOGIC popped in with his "How do you do?" "I am glad to see you, my dear BOB," said TOM, smiling; "but you *bolted* from us last night: I hope you did not lose your way in the *dark walks*, as I know it is rather a dangerous passage, particularly for *blinkers:* however, you are safe now, and I shall not ask any further questions upon that head; but, as my Coz and I intend to have a *lounge* tomorrow at the Exhibition of Pictures, at Somerset House, if you will accompany us we shall esteem it as a favour." "I am sorry that a previous engagement of some importance prevents my accepting your offer, as it is a *bob*[259] well laid out," answered the *Oxonian*. "I agree with you, LOGIC," replied TOM; "it is, I think, not only one of the cheapest but the best shilling's worth in London; and it is so truly rational and interesting, that you reflect upon it, at any period, with the greatest satisfaction and pleasure to your feelings." "A *nod* is as good as a *wink* to a *blind* horse," cried LOGIC, making up one of his funny faces. "It is true, there is no fear of *dark walks* at the Exhibition, although you are sure to meet with a number of *dark* subjects: but I know of no person more competent to explain to JERRY the advantages of *light* and *shade* than CORINTHIAN TOM." "Upon my honour," observed the latter, "I meant no allusion to"—— "No apology is requisite," said LOGIC, "and I beg you will proceed without further interruption." The CORINTHIAN, in continuation, observed, "That, to a person who is not a *connoisseur* in paintings, a visit to the Exhibition is a treat; but, to the real lover and promoter of the fine arts, in order to witness the improvement of the *experienced* artists, and the rising talents of the young painter since the last season, is an inexpressible pleasure. However, *one* visit will not do, JERRY; the *first* must only be considered as a mere *glance* at the pictures, and to *mark* your *catalogue* with any subjects that may have made an impression on your mind in your hurry and bustle through the rooms, not only to save your time, but that it may be profitably occupied on a *second* visit.

---

259   *Bob*, a shilling.—*Cant.*

CHAPTER XIV.

TOM JERRY AND LOGIC, MAKING THE MOST OF AN EVENING AT VAUXHALL.

A *third* attendance at the Exhibition will tend, in a great degree, to make you familiar with the paintings you have previously selected for your observation; and a *fourth* visit, in all probability, may enable you to decide satisfactorily to yourself on the merits of those subjects which had claimed your attention. Indeed," continued the CORINTHIAN, "the portraits are so numerous that to dwell upon those *likenesses* with whom we are not acquainted, might almost be considered little more than a loss of time. The statesman, the, general, the judge, the divine, the physician, the author, the actor, and the sculptor, or any individual who has raised himself above the crowd from the possession of superior talents, cannot be passed over with indifference and haste. It is natural," urged Tom, rather animatedly, "that we feel anxious to gain a sight of that man, in any walk of life, in whom the public have an interest; and if the *original* is not familiar to the eyes of the world, then his *portrait:* becomes interesting, and is fastened upon with the most marked attention. The *beauty*," said Tom, "who. is a reigning toast, however unknown, I must admit, Jerry, would betray a want of *gallantry* to pass over her picture with *coldness;* but to *gaze* on the portrait of a duke, who, perhaps, may have no other *recommendation,* to society than his. being born to fill so high a situation in life, however flattered by the great talents of the artist to render it attractive, I must confess, is nothing more to me than a pretty painting, and without interest; yet, in tracing the features of the *philanthropist*, the *scholar*, and the *hero*, such portraits, in themselves, become perfect studies, in order to view the *feeling* that adorns the *face*, the *intelligence* which decorates the *mind*, and the loftiness of character that depicts a nobleness of disposition and greatness of soul, cannot fail to be a source of infinite pleasure and delight." The TRIO spent a pleasant evening together, and TOM and JERRY expressed much regret, on the departure of LOGIC, that he could not accompany them to the Exhibition; but the *Oxonian* promised to visit them early the next evening.

Jerry felt rather anxious for the time to arrive to enjoy the lounge at the Exhibition, more especially from the lively description given of it by his Coz, and, on the removal of the breakfast things, he solicited the CORINTHIAN to be off without delay. On viewing the rooms, Hawthorn observed to Tom, "It was not only a most interesting sight, but he thought a valuable one, as it afforded a fine opportunity for a stranger to witness the talents of most of the artists of the Metropolis in so short a time, owing to their being placed in competition with each other. It also appears to me, that we are surrounded with a host of critics; as I have heard no other remarks, but 'What a shocking daub!— a most miserable likeness indeed!—it is as coarse as signpainting,' accompanied with grimaces and shrugs of the shoulders;—contrasted with 'The execution is fine!—full of character! — it is positively life itself! — what exquisite touches!—the colouring is delicious!—the drapery is delightful!—but, my dear Madam, only look at the beauty of the frames!'" "Not *'Critics,* my Coz," answered Tom, with much severity of manner; "I had rather you had called them flippant *soi-disant* judges." Our heroes were now agreeably relieved by the appearance of the Misses TRIFLE, who joined them in the most friendly and polite manner, and also amused them with their trite and elegant remarks on the paintings and various characters they accidentally mixed with in their walk through the Exhibition, which the Plate represents. TOM and JERRY again had the honour of conducting the ladies to their carriage, and returned to *Corinthian House* to dinner, more than usually pleased with their morning's excursion.

"We have witnessed a great many *rich scenes,*" said the CORINTHIAN to JERRY, as they were chatting over a glass of wine, upon the removal of the tablecloth, "since your arrival in London; but I have one in store for you, which I think will *equal* any of them, if not EXCEED them all." "Indeed," answered JERRY; "what can that be?" "It is a meeting of the *Cadgers,* to spend the evening, after the *fatigues* of the day are over: but," said TOM, "it will be of no use, my dear Coz, if you do not go in *character.* You will then find the *Grand Carnival,* or the *Masquerade* at the Opera House, nothing to it, by comparison. *Disguise,* on our parts, is absolutely necessary; for, if we were detected, I would not answer for the consequences; therefore, we must at least assume the outward appearance of

Beggars." "But how is that to be done?" said JERRY, smiling. "There is not the least difficulty," replied the CORINTHIAN, "as I have the dresses by me, worn when I accompanied LOGIC to witness this extraordinary scene; and, as we shall not leave the house till after dark, it will be to me little more than routine, and we shall join the Beggars with as much ease as we entered the merry party at ALL-MAX. But, you know, we expect LOGIC every moment, and we will place ourselves under his *management.* Indeed, you ought not, JERRY, to return to *Hawthorn Hall* without taking a *peep* at the *Cadgers,* at the *Noah's Ark,* to use the slang of the *Oxonian* in the *back slums,* in the *Holy Land.* It is a *rich* view of Human Nature; and a fine page in the Book of Life; but it almost staggers *belief* that mankind can be so debased; that *hypocrisy* should be so successful; and that the fine feelings of the heart should become so *blunted* as to laugh at the charitable and humane persons who have been imposed upon to relieve their assumed wants, and to fatten on their daily crimes, without showing the least remorse. But the Metropolis is so extensive, the population so immense, and the opportunities occur so frequently to impose upon the credulity of the passenger in his hasty walks through the streets of London, who has scarcely time to read as he runs,' account, in a great degree, for the *Beggars* escaping without detection. In order to prepare your mind for the scene you are about to experience, be not surprised, my dear JERRY, in observing the *Beggar* who has been writhing to and fro all the day in the public streets in terrific agony, to excite your charity and torture your feelings, here meet his fellows to laugh at the *flats,* count over his gains, and sit down to a rich supper. The wretch who has also pretended to be *blind,* and could not move an inch without being led by his dog, can here see and enjoy all the good things of this life, without even *winking.* The poor married woman with twins, who you are led to imagine, from her piteous tale, has been left in distress, in consequence of her husband having been sent to sea, you will find is a single woman, and has only *hired* the children from poor people, who lends them out for the purpose, joins the party, at

CHAPTER XIV.

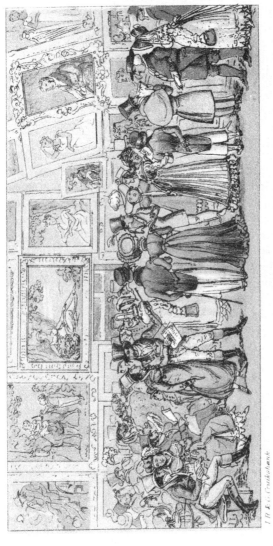

A SHILLING WELL LAID OUT. TOM & JERRY AT THE EXHIBITION OF PICTURES AT THE ROYAL ACADEMY.

the *Noah's Ark,* to laugh at the fools who may have relieved her pretended wants in the course of the day. You will, JERRY, likewise witness the *chap* who has been begging upon *crutches* through the streets, the first to propose a dance, after he has carefully deposited his stilts, and to join in a *reel.* The *starved* fellow, who calls his God to witness, as the passengers pass by him, 'that he has not tasted a bit of bread for two days;' and although he has a bag full of broken victuals given to him by the humane and charitable cooks, he would not put a bit in his mouth, his *appetite* being so *nice,* may be seen among this diabolical set of impostors blowing up the cook for sending in his rump-steaks without the garnish of pickles and horse-radish, and selling his bag of *grub* to some really poor and industrious persons. The hypocrite who has been singing hymns, in hopes to excite the pity of the passenger on account of his religious conduct, now empties himself by swearing a lot of oaths, and uttering other horrid imprecations on account of the bad day's work that he has made. The *pregnant* female is here delivered without the help of an *accoucheur;* while roars of laughter resound from one end of the room to the other, in witnessing her remove the *pillow* from under her stays, drinking success to begging, and singing—

> "There's a difference between a beggar and a queen,
> And the reason I'll tell you why:
> A queen cannot swagger, nor get drunk like a beggar,
> Nor be half so happy as I, as I."

The *Sweeper of the Crossings*[260] near some of the squares, whose

---

260   One of these *genteel* impostors, in the summer of 1820, was taken up as a vagabond, and committed to the House of Correction, in Cold Bath Fields, for a month, for his saucy behaviour to a lady who had refused to relieve his importunities. On his examination before the Magistrate, it turned out that he was a journeyman tin-man by trade; and, on his being searched, twenty-five shillings were found in his pockets. For the first two days of his confinement he was *sulky* and refused to eat such wretched refreshment, as he termed the allowance of the House; but, on recovering his temper, he laughed at the *flats,* and asked, "Who would *work hard* for a few shillings per day, when, with only a *broom* in his hand, a *polite bow,* and a *genteel appearance,* at the corner of any of the Squares, the *ladies* could be *gammoned* out of pounds per week; and it was a bad day indeed, that did not produce him from

genteel appearance excites the compassion of the ladies, who are often heard to exclaim, 'What a pity it is that such a genteel man can get no employment!" also joins in the laugh, among the begging fraternity, at the credulity of mankind; and is enabled, from his deception, to indulge himself with brandy and water, and much better living than thousands of hard-working journeymen in the Metropolis. In short, my dear Coz, a volume would not contain one half of the impositions that are daily practised upon the public by the beggars of the Metropolis; notwithstanding the exertions and *exposé* of the Parish Officers, the Police, and the Mendicity Society; or, as our friend BOB emphatically observes, 'every hair of your head will be as thick as a broomstick' on entering this assemblage of *rascality, wickedness*, and *deceit.*" "I am quite impatient for the time to arrive," said JERRY, "and pray let our disguises be got ready."

To the great gratification of JERRY, LOGIC now joined our heroes; and the TRIO started as soon as the darkness of the evening answered their purpose; when it was not long before they entered the *back slums*, and found themselves in the midst of the *Cadgers;* but, previous to which, the *Oxonian* observed to HAWTHORN, that, if it was not necessary to cry out "LETHE" among the *Cadgers,* it was essentially requisite for him to mind his P's and Q's, that no detection might take place. The scene was so *rich*, that JERRY whispered to LOGIC, "of all that I have witnessed, this must be pronounced as the *climax*"P," answered the *Oxonian;* "no more *magging.* Observe and be *silent."* Although Tom was disguised as a *beggar*, yet he did not lose the traces of a *gentleman;* according to the old adage, that a gentleman in rags does not forget his real character. JERRY did not make his look *beggarly* enough; but LOGIC *gammoned* to be the *cadger* in fine style, with his *crutch* and *specs;* indeed, if it had not been for the fun, flash, and confidence of the *Oxonian*, they must have completely failed in this expedition. *Peg,* the ballad-singer, all in tatters, and covered with various-coloured rags, yet her pretty face did not escape the roving

---

sixteen shillings to a pound."

eye of Tom, upon her winking and leering her ogles at him, and chaunting the ballad, "Poverty's no sin," in hopes to procure a *new fancy-man*. Massa Piebald, as they termed him, on account of his *black* mug and white *mop*, was *chaffing* the little *cove*, that, as he had no *pins* to stand upon, he must have a *perch;* and, as he was no *starter*, he proposed him for their chairman. The *no-pinn'd* hero, on being elevated, gave, as a toast, success to FLAT-*catching*," which produced roars of laughter and shouts of approbation. The fellow sitting near the stove, whose face seems on the *grin*, from the pleasure he feels on *scratching* himself, offers to lay a quart of *heavy* that he has not *cut his nails* for the last twelve months, he has had such active employment for them. Quarrelsome old *Suke,* who has been *hobbling* all the day on her *crutches* through the streets, now descends the ladder quickly to join the party, and is *blowing-up* her *ould man* for not taking hold of her crutches, "as he knows she doesn't vant'em now." Behind the stove, the row has become so great, from the copious draughts of liquor and jollity of the *Cadgers*, that the gin measure and glasses are thrown at each other; and their crutches and wooden legs are brought in contact to finish the *turn-up*, till they are again wanted to *cadge* with the next day. The black one-legged fiddler is *strumming* away to enliven the party; and the *peck* and *booze* is lying about in such lots, that it would supply numerous poor families, if they had had the *office* given to them where to apply for it. The whole Plate is equal to any thing in Hogarth's collection; it may be examined again and again with delight: and the author thinks, that his readers will agree with him, that he has not travelled out of his way to thank the artist for the powerful talents he has displayed in portraying such a scene of LIFE IN LONDON. Our heroes made their *lucky* as soon as they conveniently could, when LOGIC gave the *hint* to be off; and the TRIO congratulated themselves upon their safe arrival at *Corinthian House*, and also upon the enjoyment of such a portraiture of the versatility of the human character.

Chapter XIV.

TOM & JERRY "MASQUERADING IT" AMONG THE CADGERS IN THE "BACK SLUMS," IN THE HOLY LAND.

LIFE IN LONDON

TOM & JERRY TAKING THE HINT AT LOGIC'S BEING BLOWN UP AT "POINT NONPLUS" OR, LONG "WANTED" BY JOHN DOE AND RICHARD ROE AND MUST "COME".

Chapter XIV.

In consequence of three days having elapsed, and the *Oxonian* not paying our heroes his usual morning-visit, "I am afraid all is not exactly right with Bob; suppose we give him a call at the *Albany*," said Tom. "With all my heart," replied Hawthorn: but our heroes, on entering the chambers of the *Oxonian*, found him "*in trouble.*"

The secret of Logic's circumstances could, therefore, no longer be hid from his two staunch friends: in fact, the *game* was played out; but, to use his own words, he "*was blown up at Point Non-Plus,*" and the officer now put the climax to the sentence, that he had been "*long wanted by* John Doe *and* Richard Roe, *and, therefore, must* COME!" The dashing career of the *Oxonian* was, in consequence, stopped; and the officer, for his own safety, was compelled to put him under the *screw*. This *hint* was quite sufficient to the Corinthian and his Coz.

"My dear Bob," said Tom, smiling, on wishing Logic good-bye, we shall be sure now always to find you '*at home;*' something like a great actor; but no '*Trip to Paris.*' Bob, alter your card to—'at home,' and you will yet be able to *gammon the flats*. I shall call and see you soon." Jerry expressed himself much pleased at the quiet, handsome, and gentlemanly manner in which this *caption* had been made. "No noise," said he, "and done with so much *secrecy* and *respect* towards character." "Sir," replied the officer, "when gentlemen act like gentlemen, the officer, who is compelled to do his duty, never forgets to pay that sort of respect and attention to those persons who conduct themselves accordingly; nay, more, he feels a pleasure to grant all proper indulgence to every individual without distinction." "Here is your good health," said Jerry; "and I thank you for your politeness towards my friend; but I understand it is your general character to all persons who wish to do what is right." Our heroes now took their departure from the *Albany*, observing to Logic, "that, upon receiving his card, '*at home,*' they should immediately do honour to it by an early visit."

The Corinthian and his Coz were sincerely sorry for Logic's change of circumstances; and, although they appeared to treat the matter lightly in his presence, yet it was done in order to keep up the spirits of the *Oxonian*. On the return of our heroes to *Corinthian House*, they appeared very *flat*, in consequence of the *separation* of the TRIO; indeed, JERRY had slightly complained, within the last few days to LOGIC, that he did not feel himself quite right; he could not *peck* as he wished, and that his *strength* was on the decline; but yet he found it impossible to refrain from joining his *pals* in any *lark* that might be proposed to him; and HAWTHORN smilingly observed to his COZ, "That he was too *game* to give in till he was *dead beat*, and he would only desert the CORINTHIAN when he could not come to *time*." "Yes, yes," replied TOM, "I do not doubt your *pluck;* but hard work will overcome the strongest men, and Nature must have rest."

CHAPTER XV.

The Oxonian's CARD. TOM and JERRY visiting LOGIC on "board the Fleet!" The Humours of a Whistling-Shop. LOGIC's Horse. JERRY "beat to a standstill!" Dr PLEASE'EM's Prescription. The Oxonian and TOM's Condolence. A Man cannot have his Cake and eat it. PLEASURE versus PAIN. The MANUSCRIPT. White Horse Cellar, Piccadilly. TOM and LOGIC bidding JERRY "good-bye" on his Return to HAWTHORN HALL.

O<small>N THE</small> C<small>ORINTHIAN</small> and Hawthorn meeting in the *Chaffing Crib* to breakfast, they found the following card placed on the table, which prevented anything like *study* in what manner they should spend the day:—

AT HOME.

"B<small>OB</small> L<small>OGIC</small> presents his compliments to C<small>ORINTHIAN</small> T<small>OM</small> and J<small>ERRY</small> H<small>AWTHORN</small>, E<small>SQ</small>., and will be happy to see them in *Freshwater Bay,* on board the *Never-wag* man-of-war, on the homeward-bound station. He has also to inform them that he has a new ship, the *Albany* having recently *blowm up at Point Non-Plus*, owing, it is supposed, to its having remained too long in the *River Tick,* and cruising off the dangerous point of *South. Jeopardy.* B<small>OB</small>, however, has no fear, at present, of going *abroad,* not being under *sailing orders;* but, nevertheless, if his old P<small>ALS</small> are not afraid of sea-sickness, he can give them a small trip to the *Isles of Bishop and Flip.* On inquiring for B<small>OB</small> L<small>OGIC</small>, at the *hatchways,* any of the *screws* will direct you to my *berth* in the *New Settlements.*

"ONE OF THE FLEET."

"Still punning," said T<small>OM</small>, "as full of *flash* and Oxford *slang* as ever, and laughing at his misfortunes. Indeed, LOGIC is a happy, lively fellow, and quite a philosopher. We must not neglect him." "So say I," replied HAWTHORN: "let us, therefore, lose no time, my Coz, as I am very anxious to see how the *Oxonian* bears confinement." Upon the arrival of our heroes at the *Fleet*, the apartment of LOGIC was found without any difficulty. BOB had scarcely caught a glimpse of the CORINTHIAN and JERRY, when he instantly put out his hands to them, with as much glee as if he had been at the *Albany*, singing the old *chaunt* of—

> Welcome, welcome, brother debtor,
> To this poor but merry place,
> *Where neither* bailiff, dun, *nor* setter,
> Dares to show his *measly* face.

"My boys," said LOGIC, "I am glad to see you, and I call this visit manly and very kind." "I am sorry," answered the CORINTHIAN, "that things were not managed better, so as to have prevented"—— "Do not mention it, my dear TOM," replied BOB: "on the contrary, I feel indebted to my friends for their attention towards me: they have, it seems, thought my *larning* was not complete, and have again sent me to *College*, to *finish* my *education!*" "Do not treat it so lightly, LOGIC," urged the CORINTHIAN. "A sea full of tears, or volumes of *grief,* cannot alter what has happened," said the *Oxonian;* "and I have no doubt it is all for the best, as, in future, it is my intention to '*look into*' my affairs, instead of '*looking over*' them. I am also convinced, that, with a little care and *management*, my circumstances will soon be in such, a train that I shall ultimately recover myself, and profit from my experience; therefore, a truce to complaint. Let us spend the day comfortably; and, in the evening, I will introduce you both to my friend, the *Haberdasher.* He is a good *whistler;* and his shop always abounds with some *prime* articles that you will like to look at." The TRIO was again complete; and a fine dinner, which the CORINTHIAN had previously ordered from a coffee-house, improved their feelings; a glass or two of wine made them as gay as larks; and a *hint* from JERRY to LOGIC, about the *Whistler,* brought them into the shop of the latter in a *twinkling*. HAWTHORN, with great surprise, said, "Where are we? this is no *haberdashers*. It is a" —— "No *nosing*, Jerry," replied Logic, with a grin. "You are wrong. The man is a dealer in *tape;*" and then whispered something into Hawthorn's ear, observing to him, at the same time, "to *cheese*[261] it! This is a fine picture resulting from Life in London," continued the *Oxonian;* "and it is here that you are compelled to mix with the *remnants of* all classes of it, from the ruined HERO, descending, step by step, down to the very *dregs* of mankind. *Disguise* is not necessary within these walls; one man is as *good* as another: indeed, they are all of so *valuable* a description," said Logic, with a smile, "as to be put under the restraint of *lock and key*, in order to prevent the *loss* of a single individual. We look upon each other as brothers in distress—fellow *collegians,* and, from a kind of *sympathy,* unite to serve one another. The *cleaned-out* GAMBLER—the *dissipated* SPENDTHRIFT—the DEBAUCHEE—the *extravagant, dishonest, fashionable,* TRADESMAN—the *pretended* MERCHANT—the *pettifogging* LAWYER—the *fraudulent* BANKRUPT—the *bold* SMUGGLER—the *broken-down* CAPTAIN —the *roguish*—the *foolish*—the *schemer*—the *swindler*—the *hypocrite*—and the *plausible,*—the *poor gentleman*—and the really well-meaning, but *unfortunate fellow,* all meet over a glass of grog here, 'hail fellow, well met.' It might, my dear JERRY, without offending propriety, be denominated a small *map* of London; or a peep behind the curtain into the artifices, trick, fraud, deception, ingenuity, and low cunning exercised by the DEBTORS of the Metropolis, who have had the 'best' of their *creditors* out of doors, and who now assemble to *finish* the business, to make them have the 'worst of it;' or, in other words, ultimately *saddling* their creditors with the whole of the law-expenses. But this is not all: at the expiration of a short time, they are once more enabled, with the utmost *nonchalance*, to meet an *old* creditor with a *new* face, as if nothing had transpired between them;—such are the *purifying* effects of being WHITE-WASHED!

---

261   *Cut it,* take no notice of it.—*Slang.*

A WHISTLING SHOP. — TOM & JERRY VISITING LOGIC, "ON BOARD THE FLEET".

And should the creditor appear angry at this circumstance, or give vent to his feelings, the debtor has only to cry out "LETHE." JERRY smiled at this allusion. "It is almost as impossible to frame an act of parliament accurate enough to draw that nice distinction required between the honest and the fraudulent debtor, as it is to make a law that cannot be evaded. It is true," observed LOGIC, "a great many *flats* are brought in here; but, such is the *harmony* of the place, that, in the course of three months, they all go out as *sharps*. It is a complete school, and all the *heads* of the *Whistling-Shops* are put together to decide upon any knotty case, and also to give advice, if necessary, to the individual seeking it. If not, HAWTHORN, where is the utility of going to College? Invention is continually on the rack, and the principal study of each individual here is *how* to get out." The annexed Plate is a most spirited accurate sketch of the visitors at the *Whistling-Shop*, when TOM and JERRY called in with LOGIC. The TRIO speak for themselves, where the *Oxonian* is entertaining his *Pals* with anecdotes of his fellow collegians. The *bold* SMUGGLER, who has often set wind and weather at defiance, is *blowing a cloud,* and making himself happy over some *tape,* in spite of the heavy sentence of the law. The GAMBLERS, in lieu of *Hazard* and *Rouge-et-Noir*, fill up their time with as much energy at "*Put,*" so that they can but keep the "game alive." The *Haberdasher* is busily employed in measuring out *tape* for his customers. The poor, honest, but almost brokenhearted, TRADESMAN near the door, upon whose face misery is so strongly depicted, surrounded by his unhappy but faithful wife and two children, is listening to the affecting information that she has *pledged* the last article she had left (his waistcoat) for only eighteen-pence, in order to purchase her a loaf. This is a rich little bit, and also equal to anything of *Hogarth's* for its fidelity of nature and truth. The RACKET-PLAYERS have just called in for a *whet* and off again. The *poor* AUTHOR, who is in the act of study, leaning his head upon his hand on the mantelpiece, is another fine touch of the artist. The *face* of the AUTHOR bespeaks a heart full sore; "and his belly," said LOGIC, "has long been at variance with his head, notwithstanding his vast portion of *brains,* in not providing for it better. He is not a bad poet either; and, poor fellow, he has just sent an article to one of the Editors of the Magazines, in hopes that it will produce him the *needful;* [262] and he is now between hopes and fears upon the subject, waiting the return of his messenger. He has presented me with one of his pieces against *gambling*, which, by the by, is rather satirical upon us lads at the west end of the town; but you shall judge for yourself, JERRY, as I have it in my pocket; and here it is:"—

THE GAMBLER.

The lamps refract the gleam of parting day,
The weary vulgar hail the friendly night,
The gamester hies him to his darling play,
And leads the way to deeds that shun the light.

Now reigns a dreary stillness in each street.
And mortal feuds are hush'd in breathless calm,
Save where the votaries of Hodges meet,
And springing rattles sound the shrill alarm.

Save that from yonder lantern-lighted walk,
The drowsy watchman bawls with clam'rous din,
At such as stopping in the streets to talk,
Omit the tribute of a glass of gin.

Beneath that roof, that ruin-fraught retreat.
Where beams the fanlight o'er the guarded door,
Each wedg'd by numbers in his narrow seat.
The faithless gamblers chink their current ore.

The trist entreaties of impassion'd grief,
The piteous tale of family distress'd,
The stranger's ruin, or the. friend's relief,
No more shall raise compassion in their breast.

For them no more the midnight rush shall burn,
Or wearied menial be detain'd from bed:
No, wives expectant watch for their return,
Or anxious listen to each passing tread.

Oft do the purses of the victims fail,
Their fury oft on box and dice they wreak,
How jocund look they, if their luck prevail!
How grand their manner when they deign to speak!

Let not the legislator deem it harm,

---

262   One of the numerous *cant* phrases for *money.*

That *others* trifle with the laws *he* breaks;
Nor rich knaves hear, with counterfeit alarm,
That men distress'd will often *make mistakes*.

The boast of honesty, the lady's dread power,
And all that pride of feeling can achieve.
Await alike th' inevitable hour,—
The rage for gaming leads us all to thieve.

Nor scorn, ye rulers of the state's finance,
The prompt expedients of these pilf'ring scenes,
Where, thro' the aid of rapine, they enhance
The scanty budget of their ways and means.

Can stories sad, or supplicative grief,
Back to the owner bring his valued dross?
Can blunt rebuffs administer relief,
Or aidless pity compensate his loss?

Perhaps amidst that motley group there stand
Some who once graced far other scenes of life,
Dupes that have mortgaged the last rood of land,
Or lost the fortune of some hapless wife.

But rife examples, which bid wisdom think,
Their frantic folly never can appal,
Blind Av'rice leads them to the ruin's brink,
And dark despair accelerates their fall.

Full many a trinket, pledged for half the cost,
Hath raised the means of venturing *once* more:
Full many a watch is destined to be lost,
And run its time out in some broker's store.

Some fancy shirt-pin, that hath deck'd the breast,
On plaited cambric, starch'd in spruce array;
Some ring, memento of a friend at rest;
Some seal or snuff-box of a better day.

The servile tongues of borrowers to command,
The tributary dues of boxes to evade,
To spread the paper'd plunder in the hand,
And read their consequence in homage paid;

Their luck forbids; nor circumscribes alone
To them its evils, but its range extends;
Forbids the needful purchases at home,
And shuts the door of welcome on their friends;

The petty processes of law to stop,
To prove how groundless are the landlord's fears,
Or gain fresh credit at the chandler's shop,
By paying off the grocery arrears.

Far from all dreams of splendid opulence,
Their wish is answer'd if their way they clear;
Well can they dine for twelve or thirteen pence,
Including waiter and a pint of beer.

Yet e'en their painful efforts to exist,
Some knaves in heart, *as* yet unskilled *to cheat,*
With, secret whisper, when a piece is miss'd,
Will strive from pique or envy to defeat.

Their *names,* their *means,* on which at large they dwell,
Invade at intervals the startled ear,
And many an anecdote in point they tell.
That teaches gaping novices to fear.

For who, to damn'd fatality a prey,
Gives his last piece without concern or pain,
Leaves the warm circle of the crowded play,
Nor asks the table if a chance remain?

To some stanch friend is the decision left,
Some sturdy swearing the event requires;
E'en the chous'd fools are conscious of the theft,
E'en on their oaths would not believe such liars.

For thee, who, absent from the wonted game,
Dost think these lines some pointed truths relate?
If when is heard the mention of thy name,
Some fellow-sufferer shall ask thy fate;

Haply some wight loquacious may reply,
"Oft times we met him at approach of night,
Brushing with haste along the streets hard by,
As if all matters were not going right.

"There, in some house, where charges are not high.. And penny candles shed a glimm'ring light,
He'd give the maid some cheap-bought scrap to fry,
Of which he'd eat with ravenous delight.

"There, in some corner, shunning to be seen,
He'd draw his hat down o'er his prying eyes,
Or with a handkerchief his visage screen,
Like one who fear'd a caption by surprise.

"One night we miss'd him in his usual seat;
We search'd both kitchen and the scullery;
We search'd again, nor in his old retreat,
Nor at the Tun, nor at the Bell was he.

"At length a letter to discovery led,
With sep'rate notice serv'd at each friend's door,
Reminding his 'creditors he was not dead,
But meant to *live* to owe them something more.'

CHAPTER XV.

LETTER.

> Here rots in jail, with scarce one hope on earth,
> A wretch that's sacrificed to love of play;
> Success *at first* to golden dreams gave birth,
> And fortune flatter'd only to betray.
> Large were his losses, yet no loss deterr'd;
> Those mischiefs follow'd, such as seldom fail;
> He gave his friends (*'t was all he'd left*) his *word;*
> He gain'd by *Hazard (as most do)* a *Jail.*
> Seek not his future prospects to reveal,
> Nor draw conclusions to prejudge the fact;
> In anxious dread (which *most of you* must feel),
> He waits the *benefit* of the INSOLVENT ACT.

TOM and JERRY did not quit the company of LOGIC till the last bell was rung, and the cry of "strangers all out" rendered it necessary: but, previous to which, LOGIC said, "I will very soon give you a call. I have often been upon *good* TERMS with myself: but now I am obliged to be upon *terms* with others." "Always *punning,* BOB," answered the CORINTHIAN. "Well, well, but without *joking,* if it was not so late, I would show you my horse,"[263] replied LOGIC. "You cannot keep a horse here! Come, that won't do, BOB." "I can't say so much, perhaps, for a *filly*" urged HAWTHORN, smiling. "THERE NEVER WAS SUCH TIMES AS THESE," said the *Oxonian,* making up one of his funny faces; "and I'll bet you 'a rump and a dozen' that I not only keep a horse, but, what makes it the more extraordinary, he is never *hungry* nor *dry,* nor does he put me to the expense of a *stable,* he is of so *accommodating* a disposition: and next time you see me at *Corinthian House* I will show him to you." LOGIC accompanied his friends to the gate, when the lock and key separated the TRIO; but TOM and JERRY promised a second visit in the course of a day or two.

On quitting the *Fleet,* the rain came down in torrents, and our heroes were nearly wet through before they met with a *rattler* to convey them to TOM's residence. Upon their arrival at *Corinthian House,* HAWTHORN complained of chilliness and other unpleasant

---

263   A *cant* phrase for "*a day's rule,"* during TERM time; an indulgence allowed by Act of Parliament to debtors, in order that they may not only visit their friends and creditors, but be enabled to transact business with more facility respecting their emancipation.

symptoms; and the next morning he was so unwell that he could not meet his Coz at breakfast. JERRY did not like, but he was compelled, to send an *excuse* for his absence; he, however, promised to be down to dinner, observing to the *slavey* that he was only in want of a few hours' rest to compose himself, in order to remove a slight cold. But a *screw* was *loose;* and two or three days passed over without his being able to quit his room. Indeed, JERRY "kept it up," in *prime* style, to the last; and, although he was a little *queer* in his health, he was too *proud* to notice it; yet he now positively began to droop—his spirits were getting very low—he was "out of *wind*"—"all to pieces"—the *day* and *night-work* had been too much for him, and, all of a sudden, he was completely 'beat to a *standstill*." Like most strong young men, he had previously flattered himself that his *constitution* was able to stand anything; indeed, HAWTHORN had been so actively engaged since his arrival in the Metropolis, that he could not spare the time to give his *constitution* an audience for only a few minutes, but, like a creditor who has been put off from time to time, at length gains a *hearing*, when the evil day can no longer be resisted. It spoke to him so feelingly, that JERRY consented to receive a visit from the CORINTHIAN'S physician, Dr PLEASE'EM.

TOM, knowing the *Oxonian's* taste, immediately sent the following *flash* note to him:—

> Dear BOB,
> No more *whistling* for us on *board* the *Fleet* yet awhile. Poor JERRY *is floored!* A *cold* has got the best of him; and he cannot quit his *roost*. HAWTHORN is as *flat* as a *pancake;* therefore, mount your *prad* and come to him without delay. Never mind your *spurs;* but bring *lots* of *spirits* with you, as JERRY is quite *out* of that *commodity:* but Dr. PLEASE'EM has him in *tow*!
>
> TOM.

The *Oxonian's* answer, which the messenger returned to the CORINTHIAN, was short, but comprehensive:—

> Dear TOM,
>   I'll come to you like a *shot*.
>
> BOB.

Chapter XV.

JERRY "BEAT TO A STAND STILL" Dr PLEASE'EMS PRESCRIPTION, TOM AND LOGIC'S CONDOLENCE; AND THE "SLAVEYS" ON THE ALERT.

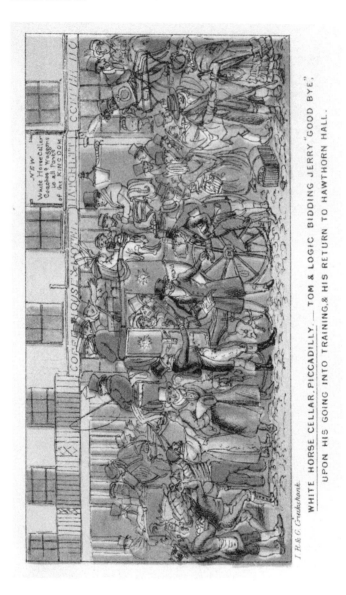

WHITE HORSE CELLAR, PICCADILLY. — TOM & LOGIC BIDDING JERRY "GOOD BYE", UPON HIS GOING INTO TRAINING, & HIS RETURN TO HAWTHORN HALL.

CHAPTER XV.

Dr PLEASE'EM and LOGIC met together at *Corinthian House*, and soon made their appearance in JERRY's apartment. This celebrated doctor's acquaintance with men and manners rendered him so pleasant and jocular upon all occasions, that he talked to his *patients* in their own way, and smiling in poor JERRY's face, on feeling his pulse, observed, "My dear sir, you have been *trotting* too hard. As a good sportsman you should have had more respect for your cattle. Your *nag* has got the worst of it. You should have pulled up rather sooner; but I am in hopes that a small *taste* more of physic,[264] and a little *training* in the vicinity of *Hawthorn Hall* will put you all to rights again."

JERRY, although somewhat different in *character* from

> Patience sitting on a monument
> Smiling at grief,

plucked up a little at the Doctor's cheering remedy; but LOGIC's first satiric salute tended rather to depress HAWTHORN's feelings, on observing, "My dear boy, this is indeed meeting an OLD FRIEND with a *new face*. What has become of that athletic broad *back* which so *tickled* Mr PRIMEFIT, when he first took *measure* of your person? Where are those lusty shoulders, that fine ruddy huntsman's *countenance*, which so much attracted LADY WANTON in the Park? those round *pins* that enabled you to vault over a five-barred gate, or to run a mile in five minutes when at *Hawthorn Hall?*" Poor JERRY shook his head and attempted to smile; but he was too ill to relish these *jokes*. "Come, JERRY, never mind, give us the *view halloo,*" continued LOGIC, smiling; "you are not beat yet, only a little *touched* in the *wind*. Two birds out of the TRIO have been caught—you are *winged,* JERRY, and poor BOB's *caged.*" Here JERRY laughed in spite of himself at these allusions. "But where were your P's and Q's upon this occasion? Had you no friend near you (smiling and nodding at the CORINTHIAN) to whisper into your ear 'LETHE?' My dear friend, do not complain;

264　LOGIC whispered to TOM, with a grin, "That the number of bottles on the mantelpiece (as represented in the Plate) did not exactly agree with the Doctor's idea of a 'SMALL taste of physic!'"

a man cannot eat his cake and have it. It is all the fortune of war: the *pain* you feel is but little in comparison with the *lots* of *pleasure* you have enjoyed; indeed, the *balance* is considerably in your favour. It is true, that my friend TOM has observed, LIFE IN LONDON *is* DEATH; but, JERRY, that is not your case at present. You will be as *alive* and *leaping* as ever on your return to the country, if you call to your RECOLLECTION the variety of rich scenes you have witnessed during your short stay in the Metropolis; and go over in your mind the introduction to Mr PRIMEFIT, and the *gay show* in HYDE PARK; the *anecdotes* and *stroll* in the SALOON; taking *Blue Ruin* in the SLUICERIES; the *lark* at the COFFEE-SHOP; the *spree* and *gammon* before OLD SNOOZY; the feeling JARVIS, the good BEAK, and the unfortunate *Cyprian* at Bow STREET; the *Art of Self-Defence* at Mr JACKSON's Rooms; drinking Punch out of the *Champion of England's Cup;* winning your Money on JACCO MACCACO; getting the best of a *Charley; a look in* at TATTERSALL'S; the *gay Moments* with CORINTHIAN KATE and the *lovely* SUE; the *Assault* at O'SHAUNESSY'S; the Old FORTUNE-TELLER; the grandeur and imposing appearance of CARLTON PALACE; the *Row* in LEICESTER FIELDS with the *Peep o'Day Boys;* the Morning of Execution—*Finish* of some' sort of LIFE IN LONDON; the interesting groups of Merchants at the ROYAL EXCHANGE; —principally the *Architects* of their own Fortunes; the rich Contrast of Characters at ALL-MAX and ALMACK'S; the ROYAL COCK-PIT; the *gammon* and *trying it on* qualities of the *Swell Broad Coves;* the *Humour* and *Fun* at the GRAND CARNIVAL; DON GIOVANNI and the GREEN-ROOM; *tasting* WINE in the *Wood;* the OPERA HOUSE; making the most of a Night at VAUXHALL; a shilling well laid out at the ROYAL ACADEMY; masquerading it among the *Cadgers; poor* BOB blown up at *Point Non-Plus;* the chequered Scene of Mankind at a WHISTLING-SHOP; and, by way of a CLIMAX, my dear JERRY, think of yourself 'BEAT TO A STAND-STILL,' and the emphatic words of the POET:—

> *Ah, me!* sic transit gloria mundi—
> Such things will BE till morn and sundie,
> And earth our ashes, our pale embers cover:

> And really, when we SUM UP ALL,
> What's LIFE?—a BLAST— a *little* squall.—
> Death's calm must come at last, and all *is* OVER—
> All in our tomb's in peace—not ONE
> To read 'Hic JACET,' on the *stone.*"

The CORINTHIAN endeavoured to support the arguments of LOGIC, and said, "his COZ was worth a hundred *dead ones;* and if HAWTHORN paid attention to himself for a few days, in all probability he would be able very soon to set out for *Hawthorn Hall.*" "I sincerely hope so," echoed LOGIC, "and if he does not return to the country, exactly in such sound health as when he left it, how much better, may I ask, does JERRY return both in *experience* and in MIND. His constitution may be *renovated* on his arrival at *home,* where his *intellects* might have no *chance* of improvement. His view of Society, since his intercourse with the Metropolis, is more enlarged; he has mixed with the *good* and *bad* of all sorts; he has seen the most *virtuous* and the most *depraved* of mankind, in their true colours. The advantages resulting from the *connexions* with the one, and the evils arising from *associating* with the other, have been clearly pointed out to him, with the most beneficial effects. He has been an apt scholar; and, making some allowance for the effervescence of youth, I most candidly pronounce him a materially improved young man from his *en passant* review of LIFE IN LONDON."

The *Oxonian,* previously to taking leave of Jerry, observed to the *slavey,* with a grin upon his mug, who was warming the bed, to "tuck up her young master comfortably, and not to let him want for anything, as he was sure the young Squire would requite her services liberally." Then, turning to Jerry, in order to keep up his spirits, Logic commenced the following lively air:—

> Oh! there's nothing in life can sadden us,
> While we have wine and good-humour in store,
> With this and a little of love to madden us,
> Show me the fool that can labour for more.
> Come, then, bid GANYMEDE fill ev'ry bowl for you,
> Fill them up brimmers, and drink as I call;
> I'm going to toast every nymph of my soul for you,
> Ay, in my soul, I'm in love with them all.
> *Dear Creatures!* we can't live without them,;

> They're all that is sweet and seducing to man,
> Looking, sighing, about and about them;
> We DOAT on them, DIE for them, all that we can.

"My dear Coz," said JERRY, "do not forget to let me have a part of the Manuscript you promised me (the *Programme* of your Ballot of Action), as it will tend to pass away many dull hours during my illness." "I will look for it in the Library, and send it you instantly," replied TOM. The *Oxonian* and TOM took their departure, begging JERRY to have a little *patience*, and to keep up his spirits. HAWTHORN was soon put in possession of the following Manuscript, which he began to peruse rather eagerly:—

THE HERO OF THE CAVERN.

THE family of CIPRIANI was one of the most renowned in Italy, and nearly related to the Doge of Venice: throughout its long line of ancestry, its uniform character had been brave in war, generous in disposition, and virtuous in principle. The MARQUIS felt all the energies of his great progenitors, and in himself was looked up to as the pride of the nobility; his manners, though extremely conciliating, were nevertheless dignified,—and his vast affluence, united with a liberality of mind, made his palace the epitome of elegance and grandeur.

The MARCHIONESS was extremely beautiful in person, and could also boast of a genealogy equal to the MARQUIS; and while her affability and condescension were the universal theme, her cultivated mind was the admiration of those circles in which she moved. A unity of sentiment pervaded the breasts of the MARQUIS and MARCHIONESS:—love had taken sovereign possession of their hearts; and the sordid idea of adding to their coat of arms, or extending their estates, never made its way into the contract. They saw and were enamoured with each other; and no obstacles operating against their union, the MARQUIS led the lovely ISABELLA, at the age of seventeen, to the altar of Hymen, to cement that attachment which had previously been the immediate object of their souls.

The MARQUIS and MARCHIONESS were the pattern's of

-connubial felicity, and their wishes were crowned with a son and daughter. Rosalvi was under the superintendence of the Marquis, whose constant study was to instil into his youthful mind correct principles and true notions of honour, as the only basis on which great characters can be formed; while the Marchioness, equally attentive to the gentle Isabella, enriched her youthful ideas in the paths of virtue, which so dignify and elevate the female sex. Their assiduities were repaid; and the Marquis and Marchioness congratulated each other on the improvement of their offspring. Time imperceptibly stole away:— Rosalvi was fast approaching to manhood, and Isabella was assuming that appearance which "awakens the soul to love!" Their parents saw it with secret gratification; and the Marquis, in the fulness of his joy, was determined to celebrate the return of his marriage-day with uncommon pomp and magnificence, in order that his son and daughter might be introduced to the world, in the true style of splendour becoming the ancient house of Cipriani. Invitations were given to the nobles around, and it was a scene of true hospitality and festivity.

The Palace of Cipriani was the seat of happiness; and it was so strongly protected by mutual confidence, that jealousy had never even assailed the outworks: to gain an entrance seemed impracticable.

Thus were the noble family of Cipriani situated, when Count Louis, from Paris, made his appearance amongst them. His figure, by its fine symmetry, was truly commanding; his lively air and graceful manners were equally fascinating; and the elegance of his apparel was *studiously* calculated to improve and give effect to his person. The Count could not fail in proving attractive: he had been reared without control, and travelled to improve his taste, but not to cultivate his mind. His ideas were vitiated ere they began to expand; and his early intercourse with the depraved part of society had, so corrupted his morals, that sensuality was the extent of his pursuit. His language had all the glare and pomp of sentiment, while his feelings were cold and deliberate. He completely deceived the unwary, while the best-informed were deluded by his specious candour. The COUNT was the model of art—NATURE was exiled from his composition—and he possessed the exterior of a man, without those requisites which constitute the human being. Those little sensibilities that operate so powerfully upon the constitution, in giving the courage of a lion, or the subduing meekness of the lamb, were usurped by the callous: in short, he was a complete master of *finesse;* and in raising a passion in another's bosom, without feeling the same emotion, he might be termed a proficient. The plans of the COUNT were so artfully concealed, that they were seldom frustrated; and his plausibility of demeanour defied all suspicion. Wherever he meditated an overthrow he was but too successful; and when happiness seemed conspicuous, nothing short of destruction would satisfy him. His conquests had hitherto been so easily obtained, that he was satiated with his own achievements; as his routine of company had been marked more by the loose and gay votaries of pleasure, than with the rational and domestic intercourse of those persons who cherish *amusements* as the pleasing medium of relaxing and invigorating their understandings. The proud situation of the MARCHIONESS, and her distinguished virtue, fired his, lustful ambition. The object was daring, but his pride was insurmountable. The COUNT had never yet retreated. The greater the obstacles to which he was opposed, the more ardour he evinced; and so determined was he in his mind, that sooner than appear insignificant in his own eyes, he would obtain victory even if it cost him his existence. He was the bane of society in those circles in which he moved: and *such* was the character that had found its way into the Palace of CIPRIANI!

His letters of recommendation (from a warm and long-attached friend of the MARQUIS, and who had been completely duped as to the real character of the COUNT) gained him the respect of the whole family. His insinuating address, his elegant conversation, and lively sallies of wit, rendered him the life of the company; and with his talent for dissimulation, he so soon ingratiated himself into their confidence and good wishes, that he was entreated to make the palace his residence till necessity compelled him to depart.

Chapter XV.

When he first saw the Marchioness he was struck motionless with her beautiful and interesting appearance! His hitherto frigid heart, for the first time, felt something like a tumult! It was about to experience a change. The *deliberate* conqueror was lost in the restless captive! and he trembled at losing his power! The Count scarcely recovered from the shock, when he planned the destruction of the Marchioness. His invention was on the rack, as the execution of his scheme required the most delicate mode of assault. The Marchioness was not to be won by the common forms of gallantry; and the Count was too great an adept not to be aware that it would require some study to discover the vulnerable points on which he might commence his plans without the danger of being defeated!

From displaying the greatest vivacity, of a sudden he became pensive, much dejected, and preferred solitude to company. It was noticed by the whole family with regret. Some days elapsed in the continuation of this conduct, when one evening, as the Marchioness was taking the air alone in the garden, turning down one of the walks, she heard a sigh! and, on looking up, beheld the unhappy attitude of the Count. He appeared as if lost in a reverie! The Marchioness beheld his altered form with astonishment!—his countenance betrayed the workings of inward grief!— and so sudden a change could not but arrest her attention! The Marchioness approached the Count, and, with that tender solicitude which adorned her character, anxiously inquired the cause of his wretchedness? The Count paused—looking wildly round him: at length, in trembling accents, he thus addressed her:—

"Beautiful Marchioness!—Behold a wretch doomed to perpetual misery! In vain have I endeavoured to suppress a fruitless passion, which has nearly consumed me; but you have commanded and I must obey. O lovely fair one! *your beauty and accomplishments have ruined my peace of mind!"*

The Marchioness started with surprise and indignation, but, instantly recovering herself, threatened to make the Marquis immediately acquainted with the daring insult. The Count fell on his knees, shed a torrent of tears, and in the most supplicating tone solicited pardon:— *"Amiable* MARCHIONESS! *Forgive that unhappy man whose* ONLY *crime is in loving one whose powerful attractions have broken down all his resolves. Pity rather than condemn! I will instantly quit the palace; and seek some obscure corner of the world: death to me will prove a friendly boon, and my last words shall invoke a blessing on thee I"* The tenderness of the sex prevailed; believing his manner sincere, his pardon was granted, and the MARCHIONESS hastily withdrew from so dangerous a situation.

The COUNT's eyes flashed with fire, and he congratulated himself that he had made *some* impression. The MARCHIONESS returned to the Palace agitated; but, fearful of the consequences, she did not communicate the fatal disclosure to the MARQUIS. The MARCHIONESS had loved her husband with a conjugal affection which could not be surpassed; and never till that moment did her bosom feel the slightest alarm. She examined her heart, and found it true to its lord and master: she meditated no dereliction; and thought herself *too* confident in her position. The crime of the COUNT was—LOVE! and *was* it a crime to avow what all Venice loudly declared the MARCHIONESS to be, "the most beautiful of her sex!" FLATTERY became his apologist—self-vanity pitied his youthful admiration; and this dangerous palliation of an offence, in the first instance, ultimately proved the dreadful overthrow of the MARCHIONESS.

The COUNT's pretended wretched state of mind, *on her account,* agitated the feelings of the MARCHIONESS: his stay was protracted; and he was too great an adept in artifice to be dismayed at *one* denial! The COUNT, therefore, ventured to repeat his unlawful passion; and he flattered himself that he had not met with so severe a rebuke. His poison, he perceived, had taken a small effect; and. contamination, he hoped, would soon follow. He was but too successful. The slightest look of the MARCHIONESS was now magnified by the COUNT into cruelty and indifference; and he had the boldness to remark that the most trifling negligence was coldness and disdain. The MARCHIONESS's nights were restless, and her days irksome. Her serenity of mind was gone. The COUNT' observed it with horrible exultation; and no sophistry was left untried to facilitate his guilty purpose. Every day the MARCHIONESS's resolution became more warped; till at length the artifices of the COUNT prevailed, and she became the innocent victim of his treachery, In one dreadful moment—her honour, virtue, and spotless fame were dethroned! The sight of her injured lord was worse to her than death; and, to avoid that meeting, she closed her wretchedness by flight.

The absence of the MARCHIONESS, together with the abrupt departure of the COUNT, too soon developed the horrid circumstance to the MARQUIS. The shock was too much for him: he lost his manhood, his faculties were convulsed, and he was the most miserable of men! The reflection was terrific. The companion of his youth; the mother of his lovely children; and the pride of his heart;—all, in one moment, lost to him for ever! Dreadful reverse, thus to be plunged from, the summit of happiness to the abyss of misery!

ROSALVI underwent a thousand afflicting sensations. The circumstance of his beloved mother having become so abandoned, shook him to the centre. The tender affectionate ISABELLA was inconsolable. The chasm occasioned by the flight of her wretched parent was awful. They could not look upon each other without emotion. They were the sad mirrors of grief and distraction! The MARQUIS embraced his son and daughter, while the involuntary tear stole down his noble countenance; his sensibilities had nearly exhausted his heart, but his injuries gave him animation to seek redress, and in a paroxysm of rage he drew his sword. ROSALVI followed the example of his father; but the MARQUIS enjoined him to remain, and pointed to ISABELLA for his protection. He then wildly sallied forth.

The COUNT was aware that, during the existence of the MARQUIS, there might be a possibility of his losing the MARCHIONESS. She might also repent and wish to return to; her injured family; or the power of the MARQUIS might take her from him, and place her in a convent. His diabolical pride caught the alarm, and only in the death of the MARQUIS he thought his object would be gained—the *security* of the MARCHIONESS. No time, therefore, was to be lost. Bravoes were hired to watch and assassinate him; but so eager was the COUNT for the execution of his plan that he arrived at the spot before the assassins, and the MARQUIS must have escaped their vengeance had not the COUNT attacked him suddenly and mortally wounded him, then making his escape unnoticed. Some passengers, shortly afterwards, discovered the MARQUIS weltering in his blood, and conveyed him to his palace.

The Count hastened back to the Marchioness, and with cold and deliberate exultation related his murderous achievement. With insulting mockery, he wished her to visit and console the feelings of the dying Marquis! But for this mark of his *liberality*, it must be understood that she must return immediately, on pain of his vengeance. The Count congratulated himself, with a sneer, that she was *now* riveted to him, and could not look for shelter anywhere but in the arms of her seducer and the murderer of her lord. Affection was not yet extinct in the Marchioness's bosom. For the moment, she lost sight of her crime, and impatiently flew to the presence of her expiring husband. The Count observed her *anxiety* with indignation. It rankled in his proud heart, on perceiving that every spark of *remembrance* was not yet eradicated from the breast of the Marchioness, and that *he* alone was not the only attraction.

The meeting of the MARQUIS and MARCHIONESS was so truly afflicting that description fails in attempting to repeat it. The MARCHIONESS gained the palace, and rushed into the chamber with the wildness of a maniac. She beheld the once happy partner of her life in the struggles of death, and the unfortunate ISABELLA consoling the last moments of her beloved father, and weeping over him. The sudden appearance of the MARCHIONESS flashed across his disordered brain like a phantom; and, from the dreadful agony with which his mind was torn, the MARQUIS fainted. The MARCHIONESS gave way to despair. The scene before her awfully pointed out to her the nature of her offence,—the honour of the MARQUIS sullied; his family disgraced; and, to close the horrid catastrophe, deprived of his life; and all these dreadful circumstances occasioned by his depraved wife. Terrible reflection! Her nerves were too weak to bear up against the contending passions that raged within her bosom: her heart nearly burst with agony: her senses seemed bewildered; and her violent screams of frantic horror once more restored the MARQUIS to his faculties. The remorse of the MARCHIONESS sensibly affected him, and his noble soul pitied her wretchedness. Love was not yet extinct in the heart of the MARQUIS; but it was too late to expostulate with her on her conduct. The icy hand of Death had seized on his nearly exhausted frame; and the MARQUIS had scarcely time to articulate, "*Instantly quit your seducer for ever! Retire from Venice with your daughter! Teach her the ways of virtue; and pray for forgiveness.*" The MARQUIS gasped for breath, and the MARCHIONESS, suffering under the most excruciating misery, exclaimed, "I WILL!" The MARQUIS joined the hand of ISABELLA in her mother's, and, pointing to heaven, uttered *"Swear!"* The MARCHIONESS, in the fervour of the moment, dreadfully impressed with the horror of her crime, "*swore to leave her seducer, and bring up* ISABELLA *in the paths of virtue!*" The MARQUIS felt composed, and with a placid smile and resignation at this step towards atonement, pronounced her pardon and expired! It was an awful moment, and every apartment of the palace seemed to upbraid her with her infamy. The dying groans of the MARQUIS still echoed through her brain; and it was not until the arrival of a servant from the COUNT, who had made his way into the palace in disguise, that her distracted attention was called to *depart!* The MARQUIS was no more; and the note from the COUNT threatened her life if she refused to obey his orders. In a moment of terror she returned to the society of one for whom she had sacrificed every other consideration. Her guilty passion prevailed. *Reflection* was madness! *Propriety* had long been banished from her conduct! and the terrible effects of her OATH were, for a short time, lost sight of in the corrupt embraces of her infernal and malignant seducer.

ROSALVI, after seeing the remains of his illustrious father deposited in the tomb of his ancestors, departed from the palace in the dead of the night, unknown to any of his domestics; and when the sun rose he shunned the face of every human being.

He thought the finger of scorn was held up to him as he passed along; and, casting a farewell look on the proud dome of the Palace of Cipriani, he exclaimed, *"Never will I return till my honour is revenged!"* His noble heart was nearly rent asunder when he reflected on the high repute in which his family had stood for centuries; both his father and mother models for imitation; and his own entrance into life marked by disgrace and infamy. His noble nature recoiled at the bare idea of these dreadful circumstances, and produced paroxysms of rage and melancholy which rendered him insensible to his future welfare! He travelled he knew not whither, until, overcome by fatigue and wretchedness, he threw himself prostrate on the earth! It was in this state he was found by a daring banditti, who had long infested that part of the country. They viewed ROSALVI with surprise, and instantly demanded his purse and sword. He resisted their demand with such dauntless intrepidity, that several of them felt the imprudence of their attack; and he did not resign the contest till the superiority of numbers compelled him, by depriving him of his weapon. His life was burden to him: he solicited the banditti to put an end to his existence; and, without fear, presented his breast to their swords! They were astonished at his courage; and his manly and dignified appearance awed them into respect. The captain of the banditti had recently fallen, and, without hesitation, they wished him to be their leader, and promised him obedience. ROSALVI, who had forsworn the world, embraced their proposal without a second thought, and instantly marched off with them to their cavern.

ISABELLA's cup of misery was full indeed. Her father killed—abandoned by her mother—and her brother fled from her presence, the Palace of Cipriani, once the delight of her youth, when animated by her relatives, was now rendered odious to her sight. Her situation was truly lamentable: a wretched helpless female, having no one to look up to for succour, and surrounded by strangers. Her residence, therefore, filled her with the most poignant distress; and, to dissipate her grief, she felt the enthusiastic notion of going, disguised as a cavalier (to make her plan more successful), supported by some of her trusty domestics, in search of her faithless mother, to reclaim her, if possible, and also to place her in a convent for the remainder of her life; in order that she might make some atonement for her offences. Leaving the palace under the care of proper persons, Isabella set out on her journey, animated with the arduous enterprise in which she had engaged.

Rosalvi, when alone, was dejected, and deeply felt his dreadful change, in respect to the situation he was intended to occupy in society. From being the first noble in the state, he was now reduced to the acknowledged leader of a band of robbers;—alarming degradation! An outlaw! But to whom was he indebted for this change? His mother! His blood would freeze with horror at the remembrance, and he welcomed death as his only friend. The banditti observed it; but he assured them they were griefs of a private nature that thus harassed him. The banditti were satisfied, and pitied his sorrows. His honour was so conspicuous, that his orders never occasioned the slightest murmur; and his peremptory charge to them, *"never to lose sight of humanity!"* was obeyed. He was literally adored by the gang, and they had never been so invulnerable until he had become their leader!

The Count and Marchioness lived in a continual state of alarm, for fear of discovery. Misery was their principal guest: sleep was banished from their adulterous couch, and terrifying dreams haunted their imaginations. They also looked upon each other with disdain. The Count, *tired* of his conquest, would have discarded the Marchioness, but the terror for his own preservation compelled him to remain in her presence. Fascination was no longer in their possession, and the Marchioness now viewed her seducer with *disgust,*—the MURDERER of her lord, with *horror,*—and the *wretch* who had caused her to break her OATH, in the shape of an infernal! But *their* crimes were so interwoven, that *separation* must create alarm: and thus they lived together, the object of each other's detestation. Continually changing their place of residence, they travelled all the by-ways of the country, to avoid being pursued, and were attended by only one servant. In one of those excursions they were surprised by the banditti; the COUNT fought desperately, but was, at length, overpowered, and they were both conducted to the cavern. ISABELLA and her little party were also taken by another detachment of the gang, and soon found themselves the inmates of the same prison!

ROSALVI, in viewing the captives, soon recognised his faithless parent and the murderer of his father. Struck with horror at such an unexpected meeting, he rushed upon the COUNT with a terrible impetuosity, exclaiming, "*Monster of iniquity! thank Heaven I have found thee at last! thou shalt not escape my vengeance! draw, and defend thyself!*" Disdaining unmanly revenge, and with a generosity bespeaking his noble heart, he commanded the banditti not to interfere! A desperate fight ensued, and the COUNT fell dead at his feet. He viewed the body with a wild and terrific satisfaction; but, in turning to his mother, his reason forsook him, and at the instant he was about to plunge his sword, reeking with the blood of the COUNT, into her bosom, ISABELLA rushed between them, pitifully uttering, "Oh, spare my mother!" ROSALVI's feelings returned. His sword dropped from his hand, and he embraced his sister. The MARCHIONESS fainted on witnessing this dreadful catastrophe and heart-breaking interview; but on her recovery she solicited her children to be sent to a convent, that she might pass the remainder of her days in penitence, ROSALVI immediately quitted the banditti, after admonishing them to return to a virtuous course of life; placed his mother in a religious house; and, with ISABELLA, threw himself at the feet of the Doge, who granted him a free pardon; and ROSALVI and the lovely ISABELLA once more were reinstated in the palace of their ancestors.

In the course of a short time, from the unremitted attention and skill of Dr. PLEASE'EM; the care and anxiety of the prime OLD NURSE to get her master's cousin again on his legs, and the industrious good-natured young Slavey to fetch and carry everything for him like a fond Spaniel; the constant visits from the Corinthian to cheer him up; and the enlivening calls of the Oxonian to laugh him out of his complaint; Jerry was so far recovered as to make the necessary preparations for his return to *Hawthorn Hall;* and Logic, in order to take his farewell of Jerry, was obliged once more to employ his *White Pony*. It was not long before the morning arrived that was to separate the trio: "But let us hope not for ever," said the *Oxonian* to Jerry, giving him a hearty shake of the hand; "and believe me, Hawthorn, I wish you as well as one man can wish another: and the only favour in return which I ask of you, Jerry, in your retirement is, that whenever you peruse any shipping intelligence, think of Poor Bob on 'board the Fleet.'" "If," replied Jerry, "you should ever find me to have forgotten the kindness, the attention, and the valuable information which I have so repeatedly received from the honest-hearted, merry Bob Logic, then think that Hawthorn ceases to have an existence, and that he is not worthy of being enrolled in the circle of your friends. But, Bob, if you believe there is anything like Life OUT OF London, and you can quit the Metropolis to spend a month or two with me at *Hawthorn Hall*, rest assured that I shall feel it a duty incumbent on me to render your time agreeable and happy." "Stop, stop, my dear Jerry," replied Logic; "recollect that my *horse* will not carry me quite so far at present. It is true he is *accommodating* enough in London; but I am not on such good *terms* with him, as to travel upwards of one hundred and twenty miles with *safety*."[265]

The White Horse Cellar, Piccadilly, was now the parting-scene, and the hand of the clock pointed very near to the time for the departure of the coach. The bustle of this place prevented the TRIO from much conversation; but the *separation* of such *stanch pals* was rather a trying moment to the *feelings* of poor JERRY: and though he was above *blubbering* like a *Johnny Raw*, yet his HEART was rather *touched*, and his *ogles* underwent some *queer* sensations, which he endeavoured to suppress, when *Coachy* asked "if all was right," and began to smack his whip.

The hearty grasps of the hand, and the *good-byes* were over between HAWTHORN and his *pals*, and TOM and LOGIC were only waiting to see the coach start, when JERRY, with much eagerness of expression, as if he had forgotten to mention the circumstance previously, said, "My dear Coz"—but the coach was now fast

---

265 It has been asserted that the Rules of the Fleet have extended to the East Indies; but LOGIC thought if there was a *precedent* for such extension, it was a *bad one*, and he did not mean to risk it.

rattling over the stones, and the last broken sentence which the ear of the CORINTHIAN caught was, "Mention me in the kindest manner to the lovely SUE; tell her I am only gone into *training*, and in the course of a few weeks I shall most certainly return to London to enjoy a few more *Sprees* (which I have so unexpectedly been deprived of), and also to have with her the pleasure of another game at"————

THE END.

Printed in Dunstable, United Kingdom